Enoch Arnold Bennett, the son of a solicitc
Staffordshire. At twenty-one, he moved to
solicitor's clerk, but he soon turned to wr
editing a women's magazine. After the publication
From the North in 1898, he became a professional writer. He moved to Paris and became a man of cosmopolitan and discerning tastes.

Bennett's great reputation is built upon the success of his novels and short stories set in the Potteries, an area of north Staffordshire that he recreated as the 'Five Towns'. *Anna of the Five Towns* and *The Old Wives' Tale* show the influence of Flaubert, Maupassant and Balzac as Bennett describes provincial life in great detail. Arnold Bennett is an important link between the English novel and European realism.

He wrote several plays and lighter works such as *The Grand Babylon Hotel* and *The Card*.

Arnold Bennett died in 1931.

BY THE SAME AUTHOR
ALL PUBLISHED BY HOUSE OF STRATUS

The Clayhanger Series

Clayhanger
Hilda Lessways
These Twain
The Roll Call

Five Towns Series

A Man from the North
Anna of the Five Towns
The Card
The Old Wives' Tale
The Regent
Tales of the Five Towns

Fantasias

The City of Pleasure
The Ghost

Novels

Accident
Buried Alive
The Glimpse
The Grand Babylon Hotel
The Pretty Lady
Riceyman Steps
Teresa of Watling Street

Non-fiction

How to Live on 24 Hours a Day

ARNOLD BENNETT

LORD RAINGO

First published in 1911

This edition published by House of Stratus, an imprint of Stratus Books Ltd, 21 Beeching Park, Kelly Bray, Cornwall, PL17 8QS, UK.

www.houseofstratus.com

Typeset, printed and bound by House of Stratus.

A catalogue record for this book is available from the British Library and the Library of Congress.

ISBN 07551-159-5-3
EAN 97807551-159-5-2

Part One

1

Examination

Fifty-five. Tallish – but stoutish. Dressed like the country gentleman which he was not and never would be. Not by taking any amount of thought can you become a country gentleman. From the lower part of his krge and somewhat neglected gardens he looked down Moze slope and over Mozewater. Six miles off Eelpie Sand gleamed dangerously in the March afternoon sun. The tide was rising, creeping with stealth into all the inlets that bordered the Spanish Main of Mozewater. The explosives factory in the middle distance stood now on a tongue of land; in two hours it would be a solitary chimney sticking up forlorn out of the Spanish Main. The tide was never still. Four times a day it punctually changed the face of sixty square miles of earth, omnipotently heedless of air-raids, gun-fire, rumours of invasion. You might go to bed with the moon pouring silver on to an ocean, and get up to see the sun enlighten a sinister marsh intersected by creeks and rivulets. Every aspect of Mozewater enchanted Mr Raingo, drew him out of his own melancholy and futility into a melancholy and futility greater, grander, and far more beautiful. There was a speechless poet hidden somewhere in Mr Raingo, that died often and came back to life, and was authentic.

He opened the wicket and strolled slowly down Moze slope, and in half an hour was level with the vast, semicircular dyke.

Two Thames barges, each manned by two men and a dog, were manoeuvring gingerly up the shallow channels towards the ancient quays and wharves of Flittering – last outpost of solidity against the North Sea. He walked through the village, nodding benevolently here and there to humble persons who saluted him with deference as the richest man in the peninsula and perhaps in the county. As he reached Miss Osyth Drine's cottage – last outpost of the last outpost – and the road dwindled into a green track, a man rather like himself in age and build emerged from the cottage, jumped with enviable agility on to a bicycle and, having perceived Mr Raingo, at once jumped off again.

"Mr Raingo?" said the cyclist. "I thought I couldn't be mistaken. I wonder if you'd be so very kind as to give a message to Mrs Raingo from my wife, and say how sorry she was not to be in when Mrs Raingo called"

"I certainly will," answered Raingo, urgently asking his memory to identify this slightly too deferential khaki gentleman with the stars of a captain on his tunic.

"I'm Heddle," said the cyclist.

"Of course you are, "Raingo agreed with quick urbanity, offering his hand. It was the doctor who had come newly to Hoe village two years earlier and had almost immediately afterwards joined the Royal Army Medical Corps and vanished into distant fields of war. "You've been in Palestine, I think?"

"Yes. Invalided home. I may get charge of a hospital, and in the meantime I'm doing a bit to my own practice." A short, dry laugh.

They walked along together, the bicycle between them.

"Too eager to know me," thought Raingo, with all the suspiciousness natural to his wealth. "Too much kowtow. Too pleased to be talking to me. Not a snob. Only simple. Roughing it and God knows what in Palestine. It would have killed me. And now he's an invalid dashing about on a bike. And my age if he's a day!"

And Raingo, in his secret humiliation, admired the fellow, and had a wild, absurd desire to justify his own inactivity to the simpleton. And Mrs Raingo had neglected to pay her formal call for two years or more, and even now had probably only called because the husband was at home again. Disgusting. Intolerable. He considered that if a woman believed in the propriety of the astounding country ritual of calls, she ought at least to perform it conscientiously and not insult her neighbours by negligence. Two years! And more! Raingo mentioned the war news.

"Yes. Serious!" said Captain Heddle. It was his sole and sufficient comment on the great German push. "I think we shall hold them," said Raingo. "You do?" "I do."

"Well, I'm immensely relieved to hear you say so," said Captain Heddle, with obvious sincerity. He was immensely relieved, because Mr Raingo, being a millionaire, must have information, and must possess judgment, denied to simple soldiers. "I know nothing – nothing," said Raingo. But Captain Heddle refused to credit that; he put it down to the modesty of the great, and remained firmly in a state of immense relief.

"I should like to consult you," Raingo burst out surprisingly. Captain Heddle was raised into bliss. "One of these days," said Raingo.

"Any time. Now. I'm at your service. An honour, I assure you." (Why did people always go on in this style?) "I could call round to-morrow, if that would suit you."

"I won't trouble you to call. I'll come to you. Later this afternoon, say."

Raingo was very urbane, winning, determined if possible to cure the simpleton of his subservience. They walked side by side slowly up the acclivity to Hoe, the inland metropolis of the peninsula, noting camouflaged block-houses, barbed wire, and other preparations to resist invasion. Captain Heddle said that in any case he should not have ridden up the hill. "I have to keep an eye on my heart," he said.

"Heart!" said Raingo. "That's my trouble, that's just what I wanted to see you about."

They were immediately brothers.

The front door and the garden door of the doctor's house behind Hoe church were both open, and the wind blew through the sunlight-flecked house. The doctor led his august patient into the drawing-room. A poor little room, yet it had the same essentials as the drawing-room at Moze Hall: piano, flowers, photographs. What more could you want?

"My wife isn't in apparently," said Captain Heddle, disappointed; he had clearly taken Mr Raingo to the drawing-room in order to display the captive to Mrs Heddle. They passed through a corner of the unkempt garden into the "surgery," which was very small and very shabby, and Raingo began to feel a thrill of expectation. But the doctor was talking about gardens, the Jordan valley, troopships, the popular press, universities.

"That's it," thought Raingo. "He can't concentrate. That's why he's where he is, at his age. Every chance – education, connections, strong, cheerful, and he's a. village doctor! When the deuce does he intend to start?"

Then, still chatting, the doctor found a stethoscope, and said: "Now shall we examine the unruly member?" Raingo lay down on a high and singularly lumpy sofa, and unbuttoned everything over his chest, and yielded himself like a child to his brother in age bending above him. And for Raingo the grey-haired simpleton was instantly transformed into a medicineman, a magician, an arch-priest endowed with recondite knowledge and unquestionable judgment. Raingo had consulted nearly all the greatest specialists in London and had got no help, no encouragement. His wife had accused him of a mania for doctors; and it was her attitude that had made him see this doctor in his surgery instead of asking him up to the Hall. Fifty times he had lost faith in doctors, but at every fresh doctor he mysteriously found faith again. Heddle was a simpleton, but simpletons had a knack on occasion of being deeply wise, of being seers. He could not concentrate – but he was concentrating now. And might not the state of his own heart have given him a special interest in hearts and therefore a special perception? Did not genius sometimes hide unappreciated in villages?

"The hour of my salvation may be at hand. This simpleton may be my deliverer," thought Raingo. And if it was to be so, the Germans might take Bailleul and drive the Allies into the Channel – he would have such a basis of happiness as no misfortune exterior to himself could shake. He knew then, and admitted, what really mattered to him and what didn't.

The doctor sounded him with an almost exasperating thoroughness. Then the patient had to sit up, and his back also was listened to and overheard.

"Well, this is a long-standing affair," said the doctor at last, gently.

"Yes, yes." Raingo grew garrulous, and related all that all sorts of doctors had told him. The doctor said nothing.

"How long do you give me?" Raingo demanded wistfully, like a defenceless victim. For twelve months past no doctor had given him more than five years – he wanted ten; he longed for ten; he would be content with ten.

"Pooh!" exclaimed the doctor breezily. "You might live any time. Five, ten, twenty years. I knew a case, not exactly the same as yours, but very similar – it was a dozen years ago, and I do believe the cove is still alive."

"Really!"

"Of course you must take care, as I do myself. You don't want to go and catch pneumonia, you know. That might be – er – serious."

Raingo's eyes were moist with gratitude. He was a boy, he was nearly a girl. The war was a skirmish without importance.

"What's this? I can't take this, my dear Mr Raingo. I really can't!" said the doctor, staring at a five pound note and two half-crowns which Raingo had laid on the surgery desk.

Picking up his hat, Raingo heartily shook the doctor's hand.

"Try!" said he, with a glance suddenly impish. "Try to take it. Do your best. And if you fail, let me know."

He was permitting himself a rich man's freedom. The doctor laughed awkwardly, but his dignity was reassured by the warm, grateful pressure of the patient's fingers.

2

Moze Hall

Moze Hall was incommensurate with the wealth of Raingo. It stood only about forty yards back from the Harwich road (but was well screened therefrom by trees), and comprised about twenty-five rooms, of which only three were bathrooms. Nevertheless the entrance-hall and the reception-rooms on either side of it were imposing, and there was one large bedroom – his wife's. He had bought the place in 1911 from the executors of his wife's father, and had modernized it, though not thoroughly. However, it sufficed him; and Adela, who had lived in it as a child, loved it – after her fashion of loving. Architecturally it was without style or charm, having been built in 1820. The terraced gardens at the back of the house, with wondrous views over sea and land, were beautiful – except in war time.

Raingo now entered his domain from the road. Weeds had effectively colonized the front garden; the paint was peeling off the gate and off the woodwork of the facade; but these things were excusable and even laudable in the long national ordeal, and they did not offend Raingo. He rang the front-door bell, opened the door, and went in. When he wanted immediate attention on coming home he would ring from outside – it saved time. He drew a chair to the edge of the mat and sat down with his feet on the mat. His intention was to send Skinner, the old butler, for a pair of pumps and to change his very dirty boots on the mat – he had a strong objection to making a mess in the house and an equally strong objection to the labour of cleaning muddy boots on scrapers and mats. His boots Were vile with Essex clay, because, out of regard for Wrenkin, he had paid a visit to the great byre, where a few pedigree cattle were huddled.

Wrenkin, aged forty-seven, was the factotum of the estate. An all-round, efficient, honest, industrious, shabby and disagreeable man! He maintained the radiators and the hot-water supply, manufactured the electric current, kept Raingo's car in order, grew vegetables and fruit, fought rear-guard actions against weeds, the cook, and his mistress, and wangled coal and coke from Harwich. All for two pounds a week. He believed himself to be, and not without some justification, the most remarkable man that ever lived. Everybody hated him except his master. These two understood one another and conversed together on the plane of masculine realism.

No one answered the bell. Raingo opened the door again and rang a second time furiously. There were two telegrams and a circular on the hall table. He opened the telegrams. For his own sake and for the sake of the village he subscribed to the Central News service of war-telegrams. One of the messages read: "Official. Germans broke through West Quentin we retiring good order to prepared positions elsewhere enemy held." The other: "Official. Fighting whole front until late last night we continue hold enemy whose losses exceedingly heavy."

"And what about our losses, you ostriches?" murmured Raingo.

Still no one answered the bell. He took off his boots and padded farther into the main hall, crying: "Skinner! Skinner!" Not a sound in the house! What a house! A nice thing, that with five servants in the place, and him a millionaire, he should be reduced to padding about in his socks! He heard a movement above, went towards the stairs and had a glimpse of a print skirt behind the banisters of the landing.

"Edith!" A scurry, and silence.

"Edith!" he roared, with compelling command in his exasperated voice.

A girl appeared, flushed. Yes, it happened to be Edith, one of the housemaids. She was a disgraceful sight, and knew it. Half-past five and she was still in her morning blue print, dirty apron, cap awry!

"Where's Skinner?"

"He's lying down, sir – not very well."

"Your mistress out?"

"Yes, sir."

"When will she be back?"

"She didn't say, sir."

"Well, if Skinner is unwell somebody else ought to be ready to answer the door. Supposing it had been a visitor." Edith's lower lip fell. "There's no excuse for any disorganization inside the house. Tell the cook from me. And here! Take these boots away and bring me some pumps – bottom of my wardrobe, left hand."

What a house! She was a pretty girl, probably about seventeen, with a grimy, perfectly exquisite complexion. And he had scared all the blood into her head.

"Not her fault!" he reflected. "She thinks she's guilty because she can't think straight. She isn't guilty. It's somebody's business to be looking after her and somebody isn't doing it."

He felt the sinister charm of beauty victimized. When she got back (with her apron turned – he said benevolently:

"Thank you, Edith."

She gave a shy glint of a smile, and hurried from his presence. It was nothing, the veriest insignificant trifle, an infinitesimal fraction of an incident, but two beings had come emotionally together for an instant who probably never would so come together again.

The transient thought of the young mysterious girl living, pulsating, under the same roof with his gross, ageing self, yet millions of miles away, refined his gloom. For he was now all gloom. The buoyancy induced by the doctor's pronouncement had left him. The doctor had good reason to speak smoothly, and no reason whatever to tell the truth. The doctor was a simpleton, and how should a simpleton's views override those of the wisest men in Harley Street? And in what manner could a weak heart make the doctor into a heart-specialist? Absurd! Absurd! Mr Raingo, the realist, had been womanish enough to believe something for a few mintues because he wanted to believe it!

He went to his room and lay under the eiderdown and without intention slept.

3

The Telegram

When he awoke it was quite dark. His bedside timepiece blazed forth the hour in the blackness – seven twenty-five. He heard his wife moving about in her bedroom, which was next to his own, with an open door between them.

"That you, Adela?" he called plaintively.

"Yes, dear." Her high, bland, unconcerned voice!

"I was getting a little rest."

"I thought you were."

"The light from your room shows here and my blinds aren't drawn. There's bound to be trouble."

"All right, dear! All right! If it worries you. But really what *can* it matter? I do think the police are – " She shut the door.

How like her, that speech! Full of misperceptions and inconsequences! He arose, drew down his blinds, turned on the light, brushed his hair, and arranged the wide ends of his blue-and-white checked bow necktie. No more toilet than that, because an important article of his religion was never to be late; he would make any sacrifice to the pride of punctuality. He went into her room. She was fiddling about as usual, doing several things at once; cursed with a mind that darted to and fro and crossways like a minnow; could never do one thing at a time.

"What time is it?" she inquired indifferently.

"Your clock's stopped."

"Has it? They generally manage to stop it, dusting in the morning. I'm just ready."

She was not just ready. She was half dressed, at most.

Daily she had this extraordinary illusion of being ready when she was by no means ready.

"The car broke down outside Frinton. So in the end I borrowed a bicycle."

Her car was continually breaking down; she would drive it and clean it herself – one of her contributions to war economy in labour. He said nothing. She had quite forgotten the time-question. He gazed at the enigma of his existence. She was nearing fifty and slim; she did not look her age; in fact to him she had scarcely changed in twenty-three years. A face not uncomely, but uninteresting. Pale grey eyes that saw through you and through everything into distances. Self-absorbed, placid, tepid, vague. Above all, tepid and vague. Neither kind nor unkind. Unobservant. Untidy and disorderly. No interest nor taste in dress. Her lingerie was about as attractive as a cotton sheet. Instead of her watching over his clothes, he watched over hers. But herself, she had style and dignity and carriage. She was rarely at a loss. She talked adequately and easily – whether to a servant or to a General Officer Commanding. She had race. He hadn't. He did not quite know why she had married him, unless through nonchalance; certainly she had not married him for his money; nor from passion; for she carried nonchalance into love, and in moments of intimacy would emit such remarks as "I wonder where I left my umbrella this afternoon." She played bridge, tennis, and golf, in moderation and moderately well, and sometimes she hunted. Their son Geoffrey had been made a prisoner in 1916, and since then her war-work had been confined to British prisoners' aid. The country-side was dotted with German prisoners employed on farms, but she never even mentioned them.

"It's seven thirty-two," he said at length, determined that she should know the time, whether or not she wanted to know it. The dinner-hour in these years was 7.30.

"Aren't you going to change?"

"No."

He left her. Half-way down the stairs, he noticed that the blinds of the back windows of the hall had not been drawn.

And he noticed the thick dust on the tops of the door-frames – dust which he had pointed out a fortnight ago. Her two Pomeranians were yapping querulously on the oak bench in the hall; the hair of both was caked with mud. He drew the blinds, too exasperated and exhausted to do the right thing and summon a servant. What a house! He inspected the dining-room. Skinner, who needed a bath, had scarcely begun to lay the table. But Raingo said naught; he was resigned, beaten. Then he noticed that the room was very cold, and he felt the radiators, all four of them. Stone cold!

"Why are these radiators turned off?" he demanded, roused to revolt.

"Turned off, sir?"

"Turned off."

"Madam turned them off at lunch, sir, if you remember, and someone must have forgotten to turn them on again."

"Someone "! What a house! No comfort in it. What good was his house to him, his gardens, his cattle? He did not own them – they owned him. He recalled patting the flanks of the cattle – a purely mechanical gesture. They were not his; he had paid for them, but had failed to buy interest in them. His mouth was full of ashes. Ennui! Ennui! And the shadow of death! He always left London for Essex as for an arctic and windy hell. The service-flat in Berkeley Street was far, far better. He saw Skinner anxiously turning: on radiators, and quitted the room. In the hall he absently picked up the circular from the table. A telegram lay underneath it. Good God! How futile, in that house, his reiterated ruling that telegrams must be put to the left and letters to the right! More war news. Perhaps a complete break-through by the Germans. But the telegram said: "Prime Minister would be grateful if you could breakfast with him to-morrow nine thirty o'clock Poppleham."

Adela was coming down the stairs. Occasionally she seemed to dress with magical rapidity. He let her enter the dining-room while he was collecting his wits; then he followed her. She was seated at the table, now fully set. He smacked the telegram down in front of her.

"Read that. It's been lying under a circular on the hall table for over three hours. I only discovered it by accident."

She read the telegram, and looked through him.

"Who's Poppleham?" she asked.

Adtela to the life! "Who's Poppleham?" She rendered him speechless. He did not answer. Presently, surmising vaguely that she had not been tactful, she said: "What do you suppose it is?"

"God knows. Some circus tomfoolery, you bet."

He spoke with a bitterness that was half assumed. He had known the Prime Minister for fifty years, and detested him. After a pause he added:

"But I shall have to go. A PM's a PM, you know."

"Skinner," he said sharply, when the soup approached. '" Is Wrenkin anywhere about?"

"Yes, sir, he's doing the boilers."

"Tell him to come to me at once."

"Here, sir?"

"Here. At once. Run."

Wrenkin, ash-stained, shabby, cap in hand, arrived at once, scowling and efficient. He was a nervous and sensitive man, with a woman's intuitiveness; and he had divined some inconvenient urgency of the master's own.

"I say, Wrenkin, can you drive me to Colchester?" Raingo inquired benevolently.

"Yes, sir."

"How soon?"

"Any time, sir."

"In ten minutes?"

"Yes, sir. I must just see she's filled up."

"Say a quarter of an hour, then. Thanks," said Raingo, having glanced at the clock and at his watch.

Wrenkin departed.

"But there's no train to Liverpool Street to-night," said Adela.

"Bring the next dish, Skinner," said Raingo. "There's the Ipswich express, I suppose."

"But it doesn't stop."

The train service had been cut to bits.

"It'll stop all right when I show this telegram to the station-master," said Raingo grimly.

In ten minutes the big car was shaking on the gravel outside.

"Get my light overcoat and my big one, Skinner. But bring me some boots first."

Chewing meat, Raingo put on both coats, and stuffed a couple of apples into the pockets. At the door Adela kissed him blandly. She did not ask whether he needed anything. But he did not. He kept duplicates of all necessaries whatsoever at the service-flat. The car went ahead, curved, and threw the dimmed lights on to the gates. And then Raingo yielded himself to an almost wild elation.

4

Delphine

That same night in darkened London, Raingo went by bus to Pall Mall (there being no taxis at Liverpool Street), and visited first his club, which was apparently quite empty of members and had the air of awaiting with grim and solemn fortitude the sound of the last trump. Escaping intimidated from its twilit vastness, he walked a few hundred yards to Orange Street, and, drawing in advance a bunch of keys from his pocket, opened a door upon which shone faintly a small brass plate: "Imperial Re-investment Company." He looked about, as though for spies. Not a soul in the narrow, mysterious street. Not a slit of a gleam from any curtained window. Only the shafts of searchlights moving restlessly overhead. He vanished within.

The sea of London had closed over him. He was safe, undiscoverable. In the blackness his accustomed finger found instantly an electric switch, and a naked lamp shone at the head of a narrow staircase facing the door. An office staircase, rather shabby with worn linoleum. He climbed it, slowly. At the top on the left was a small landing with heavy blue curtains hiding a second staircase, and a glazed door on the right: "Imperial Re-investment Company." He tried the door.

"Oh! She doesn't keep this locked. But of course there's no need to."

He entered and lit the office. It had all the apparatus of an office, including several shelves of Amberg files, and it was so orderly, unsoiled and shining that it might have been a model office in some Business Exhibition. The blotting paper on the principal desk bore traces of writing. He tore off the top sheet and, examining it in the mirror of the overmantel, deciphered "Samuel Raingo, Esq." in a feminine hand. He tore up the blotting paper into small pieces, dropped them into the new waste-paper basket, left the office, and pulled aside the blue curtains on the landing.

Another lamp was burning at the head of the second staircase. The character of this staircase was very different from that of the first. The stairs were thickly carpeted in blue, with bright stair-rods, and on glistening walls hung pictures in rich frames. The lamp was veiled in a large silk shade of Chinese design. Now was business giving way to a luxurious domesticity. Sam Raingo ascended towards the bower with eager anticipation of balm and solace. He was vitalised, young. He felt adventurous and romantic. He was about to enter into his refuge from the comfortless and unsatisfying, desolate world, and to taste the reward which he had conceived and created for himself. He thought boyishly: "In another moment I shall surprise her," and he made more noise than he need have made, so as not to produce alarm in addition to surprise. At the same time he had a qualm of apprehension, thinking: "Surprise visits may be dangerous. Suppose – " The qualm was gone again.

There were two doors on the landing. He pushed a switch controlling all three staircase lights and simultaneously opened the nearest door, into a drawing-room. As he did so, a door on the right within the room swung towards him, and a young woman appeared, pale and agitated. She softly shut the door behind her and softly turned the key in the lock.

"Oh, Sam, how you startled me!"

"Did I?" he said, disturbed and at a loss. A difficult pause. "I had to come up to town on business," he said. "And I thought I'd look in. No time to let you know."

He took off his hat and dropped into an easy chair by the embers of a fire. The girl knelt at the fire and quickly tended it and persuaded it into flames. Then she rose and stood over him, bending. She was a big girl, beautiful in features and figure, not stout, but plump and tremendously developed, very dark, with black hair, large black eyes, olive skin and a faint dark down on her upper lip.

"Then you love me," she murmured, smiling.

She kissed and clasped him and bore against him, pressing him back into the great chair.

He was buried under her, lost. He ought to have been, he at his age, happy in her abandoned, enveloping youthfulness which squandered itself so generously upon him. But death was in his heart. His body made no response to hers. Surprise visits were indeed dangerous. They were fatal. He knew that when he left that room he would leave behind the one thing that rendered earth habitable, his romance. The Prime Minister's summons had suddenly become of no account whatever. Even the German attack had lost the acuteness of its menace. No wonder she had been an actress! What an actress she was! What actresses they all were!

"Why are you wearing those things?" he asked nicely, for at acting he was at least her equal.

"What things? These?" She touched her bosom. She was certainly nervous. "Oh, darling, when you aren't here...what does it matter?... If I'd known of course..."

She was wearing a very old and plain night-dress, and over it a tattered, slatternly dressing-gown. Nothing on her feet. He glanced round the room and missed various pieces of fairly expensive bric-a-brac, some costly cushions, and a Chinese rug. A formidable, a revolting thought, that in the next room, on the other side of the door there, a man – a young man – was awaiting, in bravado or terror, the upshot of her adroit acting! And he, Sam, was the old man, deceived, exploited – and humiliated. He divined all the truth. She had lied to the young man also. She had persuaded him that she was pure and therefore poor. That was why she was wearing the rags of her pre-Samuel days, and why she had hidden away the more glittering evidences of prosperity. She was full of common sense and cleverness. Folly! Frightful and ridiculous folly of an old man – no, not really old, but old in her eyes! – to believe in the rectitude of her affections! Amazing duplicity on her part! And yet was it amazing? Was it not rather the usual thing in such cases, was it not common form? All young mistresses of old men were unfaithful. All! To have imagined that his was the one exception merely proved him a simpleton.

Naturally he sprang from the state of being a simpleton to the state of being a cynic. He laughed mortally in his heart... He would clear up the situation before he departed, at any cost. Either she should confess fully on his demand, or he would go into the bedroom and face the poacher. Dangerous, but he would do it; he must do it; to do it was a necessity of his nature, for he was not the sort of person who would walk out, dissembling, and spy from the street, and, having obtained his evidence, go home and write a stinging letter of dismissal. There might in fact be a row, the police, a scandal. Instead of being with the Prime Minister to-morrow morning he might be at Vine Street. And he was an adulterer...his wife... So much the worse, but in spite of every risk he would clear up the situation. Folly! Folly! An old fool! Never mind! He had his ruinous pride.

To perfect his dissimulation he squeezed the girl with his hand. And all the while he was reflecting upon the best method of opening the attack. Should he talk quietly, or should he fly at her in an overwhelming outburst of just anger. She responded to his pressure; she kissed him.

"Sam," she breathed. "I'd better tell you. I can't keep anything from you. I've got my little sister in there, Gwen. She was in a hole and she rang me up, and so I told her she could sleep here to-night. That's really why I'm wearing these rags. And why I've hidden a lot of things. Haven't you noticed?" He nodded, non-committal."I don't want her to think – you know. I told her I was secretary to the Company and only up here temporarily in charge. You don't mind, do you?"

"I don't mind," said he, kindly, but in a tone that gave nothing away.

Ingenious liar she was! Sister indeed! He vaguely remembered that she had once mentioned a sister or half-sister, but no more than that. And no doubt he was expected to go silently away, in order not to disturb the poor tired little sister who was in a hole – and leave a man in the bedroom! Pleasing idea! What next? She had locked the door. Why had she locked the door? To protect her little sister?

"She was bus-conducting, you know. They told her to go – said she wasn't strong enough, but it was really because she was too pretty, and too young for that job. Seems a shame, doesn't it?"

"It does," said Sam, still non-committal: but he was dumbfounded.

Then she crept towards the bedroom door; turned the key with infinite precaution, very gently opened the door and peeped in. And with a smile she beckoned to Sam, and put her finger to her lips, and Sam, mesmerised, scarcely conscious, followed her and peeped into the bedroom over her shoulder, and saw in one half of the bed a young fair girl, not unlike Delphine in feature, her blonde hair spread across the pillow. She was wearing a common little chemise; one small hand lay on the eiderdown – and it was the worn, grimy hand of a bus-conductor that could not be restored in fifty washings to its rightful tints. The girl was in a deep, calm sleep. As Delphine pushed him from the doorway he had time to notice on a chair a pile of shabby clothes and a pair of deplorable boots under the chair. Delphine re-locked the door, saying:

"In case she wakes, and gets up to look for me."

5

The Liasion

For a few moments Sam dared not attempt to speak, lest he should sob – yes, sob – and he averted his eyes that Delphine might not see the wet shine on them. He made a diversion by taking off his overcoat. It was not remorse for his suspicion that moved him, but the touching sad beauty of the scene in the other room. Delphine, the- maternal sister, half proud, half shamed, wholly protective! The younger girl, fragile, exhausted from the hard, responsible labour of conducting a motor-bus, pathetically sunk in sleep! He simply dismissed his suspicions as silly, as unworthy of his common sense and of his insight into character. He owed her no apology, for fortunately she had suffered nothing through his silliness. But she rose in his esteem. He had been right from the very first about that girl.

At his city office, where he managed his estate, she had survived among others the selective sieve of his head clerk, Swetnam, in a crowd of applicants for a typewriting situation. She had been shown into his private room. He glanced at her, she at him. In two seconds the magic was begun. "You aren't quite the sort," he said. "But I might have something else for you. Call this afternoon at four." At four, he said: "Very sorry, I must go out. Walk along with me a little, will you?" Then he took her into a tea-shop. She was obviously very poor. He asked her if she was Jewish. She said she didn't know, had never heard that she was. Her name was Leeder. Her parents were dead; her father had been a head bill-clerk in a large department store. She had tried the stage and had called herself an actress, but had never got further than the chorus. Yes, she had. She had once had one line to speak every night for twelve nights. Then she had learnt typewriting. "I only asked you about being Jewish because Jews generally have an instinct for finance and that might be useful if what I have in mind comes to anything." Thus had Sam spoken, having only one thing in his mind. She was a restful companion at tea, and Sam had been living desolating days in the domestic aridity of Moze Hall. She seemed to him to have just the qualities which he needed in a woman. Next they were dining together at the Savoy Cafe. She wore a new hat and kept her nerve; but he saw that she had had little experience of the ritual of luxury; he had years earlier had to learn the ritual himself and he had an eye for the slightest signs of ignorance.

The affair was begun. He told her his age and circumstances. He used his money dazzlingly. He did not tell her that he was in love with her; but she discovered that for herself. What helped him with her was the plain fact that he was a tyro – he had never wandered from his nonchalant wife; it had never till then seriously occurred to him to do so. Delphine resisted him. She fought him on equal terms. Her youth and beauty and his passion for her, against his money. She fought illogically, and when according to all rules and precedents she ought to have yielded, she grew stiffer and stiffer. He won his victory only after a really terrible, ugly, messy affray. But her surrender was complete. She adored him without reserve. She worshipped him. She was acquiescence incarnate. They were in heaven. This happened in 1917. He installed her, or rather she installed herself unaided, save by his money, in Orange Street. The office, and the imaginary company (one of his elfish fancies or inventions), were a cover, but they enabled her on a tiny scale to play at finance, for which he convinced himself that she had some natural gift.

"We must see if we can't do something for this sleeping sister," he said benevolently.

She shut his mouth with a tender kiss.

"Darling, I won't have you troubling about Gwen. I can look after her myself, and my relations are not going to be a nuisance to you. Now tell me about yourself. I want to know. Why have you had to come up to London to-night so suddenly?"

He told her in a few words. She sat up straight.

"And they stopped the express for you at Colchester!"

"They did. And believe me, my dear, it was a wonderful moment. The train came in at such a rate that I didn't think it would stop, though the signals were against it all right. Then I could hear the wheels grinding, and be blowed if the thing didn't come to a standstill! People opened the carriage doors to see what was happening – they daren't pull up the window-blinds. The station master put me into the train himself."

"How thrilling!"

"Yes, it was."

"And what do you suppose he wants with you?"

"Who? The PM? Something he can't get from anyone else – you may be sure of that!"

"But what?" Delphine insisted.

"Give it up."

"I believe he wants to make you a minister," said the girl proudly.

"Him! He'd lose the war first. I've known him for fifty years. And he's always had his knife into me. I was in the House eight years, and I never even got the chairmanship of a Committee. All thanks to him. And that was one reason why I chucked the House. Didn't like me. Some folks said afraid of me, but I doubt that. He's physically afraid, but never morally. I'll say that for him, because I know it. I know him through and through."

As he spoke Sam had a sense of pride too; pride in his long, hostile connection with the exalted P.M.; pride in his having been important enough for the P.M. to dislike, possibly to fear; pride in so casually showing to the lowly Delphine that her Sam was something more than a mere millionaire. He added:

"Besides, what minister would he want to make *me*?"

"Well, what was that Sir somebody or other who retired the other day – illness or something?"

"Oh! Ministry of Records, eh, you think? No, my child.

No! And you may bet the P.M. wants me to do something for nothing – no kudos, no anything. That's him. And of course I shall have to do it… But a minister! I smile. I just smile an imperceptible, genial smile. Oh, not cynical! I wouldn't be cynical for anything."

"You are funny, you old silly," she breathed, smiling to herself. "And so's your silly old bow." She lovingly patted into symmetry his checked bow-necktie. "Sometimes after you've gone and I think of the funny things you've said, I almost burst out laughing. I do. But you'll see, about being a minister. You'll see."

He was exceedingly happy. Of course it was absurd about his being a minister – still, stranger things than that had happened. But it was not the off-chance of being a minister that caused him to be happy. It was their intimacy, which the episode of Gwen had somehow rendered closer and lifted to a higher plane. He liked to know about her sister; the knowledge broadened their relationship, humanised it, made her more than a mistress. He even liked her now to be wearing a shabby night-dress and dressing-gown; the shabbiness gave her some resemblance to a wife; and – astounding medley of contradictory emotions – he enjoyed the illusion of her wife-hood. And the affair was not folly; it was wisdom itself. After all, a liasion was no more an exception than a rule. She was young, but he was not too old for her. They did like men much older than themselves; they said so; he had often heard it from men and from women too; and it was true. In girls there was something morbid to which age in a man appealed both spiritually and sensually.

She was ideal – or almost ideal. She lived in him and for him. She loved him with the extreme passionateness of her temperament. She was beautiful, and so lissom; so full of life even in her passivity. She had sleepy eyes in which love dreamed for ever. She had a quiet voice, which never talked of herself but always of him. Her affectionate curiosities about him were insatiable. She strove everlastingly to please him. A word of praise thrilled her. She was neat; she was punctual; her rooms were impeccably clean and tidy. She did not yearn restlessly for pleasure, or change, or companionship. She said that she had no friends and wanted none. At night there was not even a servant in her rooms. (And except at night he never entered her rooms.) Withal she was no odalisque. She tried to improve herself, to make herself interesting to him. Did she not keep an eye on politics? She had no faults.

If she had a fault, it was a tendency towards melancholy. The war made her gloomy and pessimistic. The casualty rolls reduced her to the very depths of blank, prostrate despondency. He had to lie to her in his interpretations of military events. And her grievous anxiety as to his health was touching, sometimes to the point of painfulness. When, thinking to gladden her, he related the bright verdict of the village doctor, she pretended to be relieved, but the pretence was not very convincing. However, as he made progress in the study of her character, he was gradually learning how to deal with this tendency of hers. And perhaps also it was a fault in her that she allowed all her other interests to wither away in subservience to himself and her affection for him. She seemed to have completely lost interest in the stage; her canteen work, on three days a week, had become chiefly a tiresome task to be got through; her operations in the office below were a trifling diversion. What apparently she desired was to be utterly free till at night he arrived and she could kiss and adore him with her spirit and body fresh and unfatigued. Of course he liked her to be thus absorbed in him. But the responsibility of being her whole source of life irked and even frightened him. He would have desired her both to be and not to be what she was.

"You must go home now, dearest," she said.

"No."

"Are they expecting you at the flat to-night?"

"No."

"You must have a good night's rest. To-morrow. The strain. There's no knowing what's in store for you. Oh, darling, I do want you to do big things; but I'm afraid for your heart. And I'm afraid all this will mean I shan't see so much of you."

"Yes, you will."

"Not if it's going to tire you, I shan't."

She stood up and took the telephone from the mantelpiece.

"What are you doing?"

" 'Phone for you to the flat."

She spoke with firm decision. She was marvellously modest, having regard to her youth and beauty and his attachment to her. She accepted his ukases. She asked for nothing. She was content to lie hidden as his mistress, with no position and no hope of one, never a plain gold ring on her finger. And yet sometimes she ruled him, blandly self-reliant, in the unconscious exercise of the power of her youth and beauty.

Telephone in hand she sank back on him, supporting her shoulders against his chest. Her hair was in his eyes. He was her couch. An exquisite fancy! She said a number.

"Is that the Berkeley Mansion?... Speaking for Mr Samuel Raingo..."

When she had given orders about his bedroom, she clicked the receiver on to its hook, and still lay where she was, and sighed, and moved her head and offered her lips. Then she arose and gently pushed him out of the easy chair and helped him with his overcoat. And she stood at the top of the stairs and watched him slowly descend. She had dismissed the great Raingo. Yes, she ruled him; and he loved it. What remained in his mind, apart from the memory of the delicious weight of her soft body and the scent of her hair on his face, was her extraordinary ready assumption that he would be given a ministry. They were all alike in love, self-convinced that the potentialities of the beloved were boundless.

6

No. 10

See that young man walking down Whitehall the next morning – a bright, auspicious morning! Walking not quickly, because of his heart, and because he wished to arrive fresh and cool; but with his shoulders thrown energetically back, and his knee-joints straightened out at every firm step. No sign on his ordinary face that he was not the ordinary successful middle-aged man pretending to himself to be young; the common husband who left his wife at home on Saturdays in order by means of golf to reinforce salts and tonics in the great fight against uric acid. Nevertheless he was a youth. His youthful nostrils sniffed the air eagerly, adventurously, and his grey eyes had a glint of challenge. His brain was a whirlpool lighted by electricity. Excitement was growing in him and engendering defiance. He almost panted to come to grips with the Prime Minister and fate. The fact that through the seething night he had scarcely slept did not apparently affect him – save to heighten his pugnacious self-confidence. He had not felt so creative and so intensely alert since the morning of the day, -years earlier, when, after terrible suspense, he had made a million and a quarter in one interview over a deal in ships. All his wits were marshalled and brilliant and straining for the word "Attack."

He did not get into Downing Street without being halted , by a policeman, but his demeanour was naturally such as to inspire trust in policemen. Several young men were loafing round the door of No. 10, mean but made august by tradition. He rang, and while he waited one of the young men said to him in a tone ingratiating and brazen:

"Excuse me, sir, but are you Mr Raingo?"

"Raingo! Raingo? Do I look like him?"

"Sorry, sir."

"Why not, after all?" he asked himself. He turned, smiling quizzically at the loafers as the door opened, and said aloud: "Well, perhaps I am, but I won't answer for it."

All the young men laughed, and four press-cameras clicked. He entered No. 10 for the first time, he who had sat on the Government benches for eight years and who had known the Prime Minister from youth up.

"This clock right?" he asked the butler in the hall. "Yes, sir."

The clock showed twenty-eight minutes past nine. "The clocks here have to be right, sir," the butler added with pride and a respectful humour, on the stairs.

"Well," said Sam. "There's nothing like discipline for 'clocks and dogs." "No, sir."

He was introduced into a nondescript room set with a youngish plump lady and a breakfast table laid for three. "Mr Raingo," said the butler to the lady. "Miss Packer?" said Raingo interrogatively, when she had greeted him and they had shaken hands.

She nodded twice, smiling with a contented, contemplative expression, as though saying: "Yes, I am that celebrated woman, whom everybody governmental, of any country, has to deal with if he wants to deal with the Prime Minister. I am the Prime Minister's personal secretary; and Mr Poppleham, MP, is my washpot. And there are some who say that I rule the Empire."

She was austerely dressed in dark blue, with thin borders of white at the neck and wrists. She had brown hair, blue eyes, and the soft, downy complexion of a peach. But she was older than her marvellous complexion; she might have been thirty-four or five; the realism of a birth certificate might have run to thirty-six. She was bright as the morning, efficiently and continuously bright, bright when she spoke and bright when she listened or reflected. And her glance and carriage indicated that, unlike many personal secretaries dedicated to the comfort and convenience of great men, she was not suffering from suppressed desires. She had the air of being familiar with every variety of human character and experience and knowledge, and of mysteriously hiding a thousand secrets and a thousand personal opinions. Her brightness was a veil, a camouflage. Withal, the splendid role of efficiency and brightness seemed to lie a little heavy upon her.

"Now, Mr Raingo, do you take tea or coffee? It saves time, I find, if one can get these important things settled before the Prime Minister comes in."

Raingo laughed to himself at the histrionics of the affair. He said that he took tea, with milk and no sugar.

"Milk first? Or tea first?… Porridge? Fish? Bacon?" She was at the sideboard, conducting it with spoons and forks as with a baton.

Raingo would have a little fish – only a little.

"You aren't a great breakfast-eater?"

"No."

"The Prime Minister will be disappointed at you not joining him in porridge."

"It may suit *him*" Raingo shrugged his shoulders, moving restlessly on the hearthrug, and regarding this as the first blow in the affray. "Let him *be* disappointed!" he thought.

As a fact he had already eaten a plenteous breakfast at the service flat. He wanted no stomachic preoccupations while breakfasting with Apollyon.

Miss Packer was pouring out tea for herself when Andrew Clyth came into the room.

"Prime Minister," Raingo greeted him, rising.

The Prime Minister returned the greeting:

"How do, Sam?" he opened, with extreme geniality.: "You're beginning this wrong," thought Raingo, and?; replied casually: "How do, Andy?" Miss Packer maintained admirably her self-control.

7

Breakfast

There he was, the offspring of the Scotch father and the Irish mother; the boy upon whose front teeth Sam had once bruised his knuckles in Eccles, Manchester; the man who for years had treated him with such curt, negligent, offensive condescension at their chance meetings in and about the House! Why had Andy always, since their rise in the world, behaved so to him? Partly from envy and partly from fear, Sam had long ago decided. Envy of his riches! Andy was poor. He had no profession, and about a thousand a year or less from the estate of his cotton-broking father. He was dependent upon office for a livelihood – humiliating situation for a politician. How he must hate the legend of Sam's vast income, thought Sam gleefully!... And fear lest Sam, the other mightiness of Eccles, might rival and even surpass him in renown. That fear must now be over, for Andy, intimidating foreign statesmen, bullying War Offices, and shoving his finger into every pie of strategy and diplomacy and industry, he was at the head of the greatest empire and directing the greatest empire and directing the greatest war in earth's history. He could rise no higher. He could only fall. And there he was – Andy! – in a black velvet jacket that wonderfully set off his smooth grey hair, silver-tongued, urbane, jolly, charming, persuasive, with a background of command, of power; completely equal to the part he had to play.

And Sam could see clearly in him the Eccles schoolboy, the same lanky, scraggy, slim figure, the same big ears, the same cruel teeth that displayed themselves formidably when he laughed or smiled, the same darting yellowish eyes, the same covert glance, continually inquiring as it were apprehensively what sort of impression he was making on his company. And he wanted something from Sam that only Sam could give! And it would be something considerable, for Sam was the sole guest. Sam was having a Downing Street breakfast all to himself.

They sat down immediately. Miss Packer pushed away the brass tea-tray a little, to make room for her plate of porridge. The battle was joined. Sam was alive again, after years of coma. The blood seemed to tingle in his veins.

"Well, Sam, how's things? You look pretty fit."

Andrew Clyth seemed to have decided that the years should roll back to their boyhood. He dropped easily, and even with exaggeration, into the full accent of the past – Lancashire grafted on to his father's Lowland Scotch: an accent which the political world of London had ameliorated but never cured.

"I'm all right, lad. So are you by the look of ye."

"I suppose I am, considering. But I woke up in the middle of the night, Miss Packer."

"I'm sorry to hear that, sir."

"I must have been awake at least five minutes. A glass and a half instead of a glass, Sam. Claret, that was it. Shows how sensitive the machine is, doesn't it? You know I never wake up, and I always have to be called. You sleep well?"

"Very well," lied Sam.

"That's good. What I say is, the first duty of a statesman is to sleep well. Look at Napoleon. Gladstone. My wife says I'm the greatest sleeper she ever knew. But I'm not what I call the perfect expert in sleep, because I can't sleep in the daytime."

"Oh, sir!" Miss Packer protested against this belittlement.

"What?"

"Have you forgotten last week but one already?"

"Oh, yes, of course. I oughtn't to forget one of my finest achievements." His eyes twinkled at Sam. "You 'know we've had one or two lively nights round this way lately. Seemed to be touch and go once or twice with the old BE Well, I went to bed at seven one morning and gave orders I wasn't to be awakened. Cabinet meeting at eleven. They postponed it till the afternoon. And it didn't happen in the afternoon either. I woke at eight in the evening, much to the relief of the surrounding population. I went to bed again at twelve-thirty and had quite a good night. It's the only way. The only way. Bacon please."

Miss Packer, smiling proudly at Sam, as if to say: "What a man!" went to the sideboard with the sleeper's porridge-plate in her hand.

"Tell me," said Sam, showing no enthusiasm whatever for the unique feat of sleeping, "how do ye do for beds, you prime ministers and Chancellors of the Exchequer that have to live in these furnished houses? Do you bring your own, or are you satisfied with the mattresses of Gladstone and Salisbury?"

"Dashed if I know! I could sleep on a rail," Andy laughed heartily.

"Do you like it?"

"Like what?"

"This living in other people's houses. Same as a Wesleyan itinerant minister, eh? Change every three years." And Sam laughed.

But the Prime Minister grinned coldly, disclosing even more of his teeth than when he laughed. He had a passion for the Scottish Presbyterian Church and looked askance at any bantering at any sect that, like the Scottish Presbyterian, differed from the Church of England. In England he was a staunch nonconformist. Awaiting his bacon, he abruptly shifted without apology to another topic.

"Seen the communiques this morning, Sam?"

Sam nodded shortly.

"Dull, eh? I've tried to get some colour into 'em, but those fellows at GHQ. don't seem to know what you're talking about if you mention colour."

"I don't believe in colour in official reports," said Sam stiffly, resolute to repay Andrew for the recent snub.

"No?" Andrew exclaimed charmingly, winningly, gratefully, as though Sam had opened up to him a new vista of ideas.

"No. Colour's a snare. Look at yesterday's paper. I reckon the fellow was trying to give you a bit of colour when he mentioned those hundred prisoners."

"A hundred and forty in all."

"Well, a hundred and forty. That's worse. And then he brought in a few more in his afternoon screed."

"And why not?" Andrew's tone was the naive tone of asking for information.

"Why not? When the Boche has just been taking tens of thousands of ours. And we have to mention a paltry hundred or so! Makes the thing ridiculous in the eyes of every Englishman who reads it. I don't think those G.H.Q. fellows have the faintest notion what an Englishman is!"

"You're right, Sam. You're right." The Prime Minister yielded the point with grace, with admiration.

Sam momentarily softened towards him. A fair-minded chap, after all, open to conviction! Andy had evidently learnt a bit since Eccles. Never, at Eccles, would he have said, either to Sam or to anybody else who had contradicted him, "You're right." Then Sam hardened again, relentless. Andy was not going to come the Prime Minister over him. Besides, he had often heard of Andy's damnable wizardry of demeanour and tone when he was after something. To look at the chap now one would think from his confidential, intimate, benevolent air that he and Sammy had been as thick as thieves all their lives, and that Sammy had no greater admirer than Andy. Was the chap such a simpleton as to believe that he, Sam, had forgotten all those sterile years in the House? No! He could not be such a simpleton. He was merely relying upon the average weakness of human nature. He merely did not know his Sammy.

And yet, in that very moment, Sam felt naively proud of being thus situated with the illustrious and powerful Prime Minister, and of Miss Packer's imperfectly hidden uneasiness as she saw her Titan so audaciously and grimly withstood.

He went on to defend the writer of the communiques, who had to try to please everyone, and whose task was complicated by indirect influences from London, such as Andy's.

Impossible that the communiques should ever be satisfactory to common sense, that they should ever be other than psychologically stupid. It was part of the comprehensive stupidity of the military mind.

"What d'ye think of our propaganda, Sam?" Andy stopped him suddenly, and pushed his cup along the cloth for more tea.

A warning bell sounded in Sam's brain. The breakfast-table was a collection of remains; the interview was maturing; the crisis was approaching; drama was at hand.

"I don't know anything about it," said Sam carelessly, to conceal his excitement. The thought of Delphine shot through his brain. Women! Their devilish intuitions! No! It couldn't be a ministry; it could only be a demand for help in some special channel.

"Yes, you do. You know what everyone knows. You have international interests. You've got material for judgment, and you can judge."

"What particular propaganda?"

"Well, say in the United States."

"Well, it's obvious what's wrong there. You're directing it all from the Atlantic coast. You're giving the same stuff to the Middle West and California as you're giving to New York. No sense to it. There are three different mentalities, outlooks, whatever you like to call it, in the States, and what suits one may be absolute poison to the others. If there must be a central direction it ought to be in Chicago."

The Prime Minister tapped his teeth.

"Something in that."

Said Miss Packer in her fluting voice:

"You haven't forgotten, sir, that you yourself said much the same thing last year?"

"Did I? Where?"

"To the deputation that you sent over to inquire, just before it started."

"Well, I *had* forgotten. Are you sure?"

"Quite, sir."

"Anyhow if I did, I'm not the only person who forgot.

Because nothing's been done." Again the Prime Minister laughed heartily, as at a joke against himself.

Miss Packer rose and put cigars and cigarettes on the table. Sam negligently took a cigar. Andy also.

"If I may be excused, sir – "

"What time's that munitions affair fixed for?"

"Ten-thirty, sir."

Miss Packer departed, without a glance at Sam. Why had she been present? There had been no trace of secretarial apparatus anywhere. Nor had she received any instructions-Andy must have given her some secret sign to leave.

8

The Offer

The two men lighted their cigars, from the same match.

"And France?"

"Well," said Sam. "I'm only a business man. What do you want me to tell you about your propaganda in France – especially as I don't know a thing."

"Go on, Sam. Go on. I can see you've got an idea. Out with it."

"Even if I had got an idea, it would be no use to your people."

"Why not?"

"Because all these mushroom ministries of yours are just as sodden with the beautiful British Civil Service tradition as the Foreign Office itself. There isn't a big daily paper in Paris that can't be bought, somehow – I've proved that more than once in *my* little notations – but you're too damned gentlemanly to buy 'em. Quite as cheap in the end, much simpler, and much quicker."

"Quite. Just so. But is it so simple as all that?"

"No!" said Sam, almost savagely. "It isn't. I realize that well enough, and you know I realize it. But the attitude's all wrong and wants altering – that's what I say. Look at the results up to date. The business of your propaganda in France is to make us popular in France. Are we popular in France? Why, we're more popular in Germany than in France. If you spent a paltry half-million in direct bribery you'd do wonders – especially if besides that you hired a gang to do to one or two of their leading Anglophobe journalists what the French did themselves to Jaures."

"Sam," said the Prime Minister, smiling, "I see you've got the hang of the thing – as usual. Supposing I gave you half a million to play with, would you guarantee results?"

"You wouldn't give it to me to play with, for a start. Immediately I began to play with it I should have the Ministry of Records against me in a body, and not only them but the Treasury, and not only them but the entire Cabinet. But I admit it wouldn't be simple even if you all agreed. Still, there's a lot in what I say. The principle's right, anyhow." Sam gazed at his cigar, which he was smoking with the greatest care, in order to prove to himself, and to everybody who cared to look, that he was in calm possession of all his wits. Andy's cigar, he noticed with satisfaction, was in process of being masticated.

The Prime Minister answered:

"The principle's right. And I was right."

"What do you mean, you were right?"

"It's like this, my son. The Portfolio of Records is vacant – you know that. As you are aware the name is only a camouflage." Sam nodded impatiently. "Its sole work is to boost this country all over the world. Now, I know you. You know me. I'll talk straight. I want you to take on this job. I said you were the man for it. I've always considered you one of the finest publicity experts in England. You yourself admit you've had experience of publicity in Paris. You've owned newspapers here. In short, thou art the man, Sammy. And none other. Now!"

As he spoke, an expression of splendidly conferring a tremendous favour grew on the Prime Minister's features. He could not hide it, and had no desire to hide it. Why indeed should he? Was he not, with a single grandiose gesture, raising Sam to a giddy and unhoped-for pinnacle, picking him out of the dust of political failure and setting him on high? A Prime Minister alone could do such a mighty deed. Sam would owe everything to Andy, be in his debt for evermore. The moment was terrific. Andy had to walk about.

In a hundred financial deals, in some of which millions of money and triumph and ruin had hung in the balance for days of protracted and intricate negotiations, Sam had learnt how to wear a mask falsifying all his wishes and emotions. He prepared it and wore it now. The Prime Minister, unsurpassed for force, enterprise, originality of resource, courage and chicane, was not Sam's equal in the manipulation of masks. And Sam had suddenly been visited by a marvellous scheme. In an instant he saw the scheme complete. Triumph exceeding all hopes was his in exchange for the mere acceptance. But he had perceived the chance of doubling the triumph. The gambler in him took charge. He nodded, as if to himself, and put his lips together.

"I was afraid you were going to ask me that," he said sadly, as one who would have liked to confer an immense favour, but was prevented from doing so by circumstances over which he had no control. At high tension he thought of the phrase, "the great game," for the first time in his life fully realizing the truth of it, and feeling in his bowels that the present was a far greater game than any finance. There was no finance in it at all – there was only glory, prestige, power; chiefly power.

"What?" said Andy, obviously nonplussed, and then uneasily suspecting that depths existed in Sam deeper than he had ever guessed.

"I couldn't take it on. I can't." Despair and blank disappointment were in Sam's voice.

"But what's the matter, Sam?" The Prime Minister bent towards Sam, and almost over him; and in his rich, world-renowned voice was a tone of strong, masterful, slightly superior persuasiveness, as of one of the "saved" at a revival meeting of Sam's youth, wrestling with the obstinacy of a sinner whom the devil would not release. "This is a united call from the Cabinet. The King approves. The country needs you... We've got our backs to the wall... You can't refuse."

Sam was thrilled by the words. He looked up gravely, appreciatively, reproachfully.

"I see all that. I needn't tell you, Andy, I'm as anxious as anyone to do anything I can to help. I'd jump at the chance."

He no longer thought of the thing as the great game or as any game. At the suggestive magic of Andy's tone he saw the horrors of the Front, the slaughter of youth, the weeping of bereaved homes, the abstract grief of sensitive Delphines, the celebrated menace to civilization. His response to the mood of the Prime Minister was histrionic in origin, yet it convinced his soul and he became for the moment a genuine martyr to circumstance. He felt himself capable of a supreme sacrifice if only the sacrifice were not to be rendered futile.

"Then what is it?"

Sam explained in a few bold, effective words about his heart.

"But damn it, man, lots of us have weak hearts! You can carry on your own affairs. You can surely help to carry on the affairs of the country." The Prime Minister was now enheartening a child, a hypochondriac, mildly reproving a milksop.

"No doctor will give me more than five years – at least no London specialist will. And only that on condition that I avoid all strain. I've been particularly warned against the strain of public speaking." This was an exaggeration of a single remark to the effect that lengthy speechifying in a large hall could have no beneficent influence on a weak heart; but Sam now honestly, if temporarily, believed that he would drop down dead in the middle of any speech.

"But, my dear fellow," the Prime Minister expostulated, using a form of address unknown in Eccles, which he had picked up in converse with members of the real old official class, "But, my dear fellow, there's no question of public speaking. There can't be. Your ministry is practically the same as Secret Service. Curiosity not encouraged, just a question now and then in the House of Commons."

Sam replied impressively:

"And how am I to get into the House?"

The Prime Minister named an industrial constituency in the north where a vacancy had just occurred.

"No contest," said he. "You won't be opposed – especially at such a crisis. The Government has the right – "

"No contest?" Sam snorted. "Cready would oppose me – you can lay your shirt on it. He swore to. Ever since that Federation shindy in 1913 he's had his knife into me."

"You'd beat him."

"Perhaps I should. But I should have to carry on a regular campaign, and I couldn't stand it." He spoke with feeling as he imagined to himself all that Cready would say that he would have to answer and couldn't answer, effectively... The Cready hecklers! He saw himself a corpse on the platform, or catching pneumonia – with a heart too feeble to withstand it. "It isn't that I'm a bit afraid of the risks. ' Risks,' I say; I ought to say ' certainty.' Not a bit afraid – if any good could come out of it. If men have to die in the trenches, I'm ready enough to die on a platform for the same cause." His voice quavered with genuine patriotism.

"I'm sure of it, Sammy," said Andy, with genuine emotional sympathy... The old Eccles grit!

"But it wouldn't help you much if your candidate kicked the bucket under one of Cready's onslaughts. Now would it?"

The Prime Minister took to walking again. His cigar had vanished.

"I'm very sorry," he murmured thoughtfully, and Sam might have supposed that the great man's sympathy was continuing, had he not added: "Upsets my plans."

"Look here," said Sam. "Why are you set on *me*? There are others."

"First because you're the best man. And second because you're my colour. You see I have to run a coalition, and the balance has been going against me for a year past. I want somebody of my own party." (The great game!) "Yes, I'm sorry. I don't quite know what to do. I'm being quite frank with you."

"There's *one* thing you could do."

"What's that?"

"No, you couldn't. It wouldn't be worth while."

"What is it?"

"You might shove me into the Lords. No election. A nice homely sort of place! Club! No oratory! Just conversational. But no! I quite see all the objections to that."

This was Sam's first downright lie in the interview. He saw no sort of objection to it. He stood impartially outside himself and judged the tone in which he had offered the grand suggestion. He could find no fault with it. Indeed, the delivery had been perfect. The Prime Minister was looking through the window at the Horse Guards Parade.

"Yes," mused the Prime Minister under his breath, and then turned round abruptly. "Well, Sam," he said, as it were with stoic resignation. "You know best. I'm sorry. I'm very sorry for both of us. And I hope your case is a bittock less desperate than you think it is. Thanks very much for coming… I say, you won't mind giving us some advice, will you? Come to lunch to-morrow at one forty-five. I want you to back me against the Munitions Secretary, Tom Hogarth, you know him of course! I'm sure you *will* back me. Of course this is absolutely Masonic." He used a tone of candid, trustful intimacy.

The scene was over.

"I've won," said Sam to himself. "A peerage. Without paying a cent for it. No worry. And I can work just as well for the old country. Better!… *Have* I won?" He was uplifted high. Yes, and women were mere dots on the landscape.

9

The City

Having walked all the way along the Embankment, and then having found an empty taxi, Sam entered his offices in Bucklersbury, E.C. They were on the first-floor of a typical office-building, massive and granitic as to facade, illustrating the eternal, grim solidity of British business, with twilit, narrow stairs and small rooms inside. Every foot of space was quietly busy with various efforts to do business – each separate, self-regarding, and loftily indifferent to the rest. Forty worlds under one roof. Women passed in and out. Women had risen in the City like a flood, and no compartment was watertight against the flood; they had changed the City, in their humility, their devotion, and their disconcerting critical faculty.

At the pavement stood a handcart of the City Clean Towel Company, which had rendered housekeeping wholesale, and deprived towels of individuality, and sweetened the lives of tens of thousands of clerks, bandits, and plutocrats before lunch. No woman who set eyes on the handcarts of the City Clean Towel Company but was outraged by the horrible, insensitive practicalness of men when left to themselves. Fancy not being able to recognize in a towel an old acquaintance! Fancy using a towel and never seeing it again!

There was no name on the outer door of Raingo's offices. No inhabitant of any of the other offices in the building had ever been in them. They constituted one of the mysteries of the building; but by reason of Sam Raingo's legendary fame they were a source of pride to the building. The clerks' outer room was empty. One typewriter was open with a sheet of paper in it. Three others were in their covers, and had been for years. A forlorn room, festering in its own past. The clerks' inner room, seen through a doorway, was also empty, and had been for years.

The door of Swetnam's room opened, and a tall, thin, sad woman of about thirty-five emerged. She was quite new to Sam, doubtless one of Swetnam's enlistments; old Swetnam seldom kept a clerk for long, and lately Sam had been leaving the control of the office more and more to Swetnam.

"Good morning," said Sam bluffly. "Who are you? The new clerk?" She recognized her employer by his demeanour, and started:

"Yes, sir," she answered timidly.

"What name?"

"Blacklow, sir."

"Well, Miss Blacklow – " He stopped. "Or Mrs?"

"Mrs, sir."

Probably a war-widow. He must not take the risk of inquiring.

"Well, Mrs Blacklow, I want you to run out and buy all the French newspapers you can lay your hands on, at once."

"French newspapers," she murmured, puzzled, as though she had never till then realized that the French had newspapers like other folks. "Where shall I get them, sir?"

Sam raised his eyebrows, with conscious desire to make an effect.

"How should I know?" he demanded, acting amazement at such a question. Then he smiled. "All I know is I want all the French newspapers to be had in this city, and I want them immediately. The rest is your affair, surely."

He was not brutal nor unkind; he meant only to vitalize and inspire her. She would have to learn in whose office she was, and the sooner the better. But what was the mentality which, having received an order from the supreme giver of orders, could dream of asking how it was to be executed? In similar circumstances would Miss Packer have sought guidance from Andy? He envied Andy his bright, calm, breakfast-dispensing Miss Packer, and the inferiority of Mrs Blacklow to Miss Packer made him uncomfortably feel inferior to Andy.

He went smartly into his own rather spacious room. Not a letter, not a document, on the huge, clean, neat desk; desk of an absentee employer who was always expected and never expected. He realized that he had been asleep for five years, and indeed near death from inanition. Once those offices had been filled with clerks often working overtime. Then he had retired in disgust from politics, and the retirement had influenced all his financial activities. He had lost, unknown to almost everyone save Swetnam, considerable sums of money, so that his fortune, though very large, was less than the public imagination credited him with. And, what was more grave, he had lost the touch, the *flair*, for big buyings, big sellings, mergers, monopolies, spectacular flotations. He had lost it through fear, due to shaken self-confidence. He had been miserable at home. His heart had dismayed him. He had suffered from ennui everywhere.

He was on the way to being an invalid, a disappointed man and a failure in life when the war began. The war hid his failure and did nothing to help him morally or physically. He withdrew from nearly all risks, shut his eyes to all opportunities, and transferred the bulk of his resources to trustee securities, especially British war loan. He behaved nobly in the matter of subscriptions to British war loans. The City admired his behaviour; but nobody in the City could induce him to patronize French loans in London. He turned down all Swetnam's clever proposals for making an honest penny out of the necessities of war. He could, for example, have amassed millions by manipulating shipping interests – and did not. He was like a sick man refusing medicine. Clerk after clerk joined the army or was dismissed. Typewriter after typewriter was covered over; chair after chair was deserted and stood empty. And at length only Swetnam and a woman-clerk remained, and even their duties were a routine.

And first Delphine had stirred his coma, and now Andy Clyth had quickened him suddenly into eager life, and he had found out that his mental faculties, though they had been dormant, were as good as ever, better than ever. Marvellous fine fortune had offered itself, and he had shown the initiative, the enterprise, and the energy to exploit it to the full, to double it, to expand it to bursting. He would put the whole of himself into the Ministry of Records, whether as peer or only as commoner. He would work for the country at war as nobody had worked. His heart could not affright him. He was ravenous for endeavour. He stretched his limbs symbolically. He was buoyant, exultant, and he rang for Swetnam with gusto.

10

Swetnam

The Bell was no sooner rung than answered. Although "Thos" (as he always signed himself) Swetnam had been shut up in his own room, he had known, by magic, of his employer's arrival on the premises. He carried in his hand some cheques for endorsement, some cheques to sign, and a choice selection of letters for perusal: all of which must have been ready waiting in case of the advent of Caesar. Sam gave him a sort of Masonic nod, expressive at once of secret ties, comprehension, and friendliness.

"Good morning, sir," said Swetnam, cheerfully responding to the cheerfulness which he instantly read on Sam's face, but speaking as casually as though Sam came thus to the office every morning, and at the same hour.

"Who's this new woman you've got?"

Swetnam furnished some particulars.

"Widow?"

"I can't say, sir."

"Not a war-widow?"

"I really can't say, sir. But I'm afraid she won't do."

"Now why not?"

"Well, sir, I see she's gone out without telling me."

"I sent her out."

"Yes, sir. But you'd have thought she'd have told me, so that I could have my door open and keep an eye on the outer office." Hostility, nascent but already vigorous, was shown. "I can't have the outer office left empty – especially when you're here."

"Thos, either you're very hard to please, or you're a very bad judge of women. You're always changing 'em."

"I don't know so much about that, sir," said Swetnam, with respectful but uncompromising firmness. "But they aren't so easy to get. And since you've been leaving it to me..."

He sat down, exercising a privilege made prescriptive by years of custom. The source of Swetnam's authority was his tremendous, absorbing loyalty to the great institution known as Samuel Raingo. He was somewhat older than Sam, and Sam had inherited him from Raingo Senior. Short, stocky, plump, he looked neat and shabby, and had no distinction either of carriage, voice or speech. He was a common little Cockney, who carefully managed most of his h's, mispronounced nearly all his vowels, put in superfluous r's whenever he saw an opening for them, licked his lips, scratched his head, and walked with a marine roll. His reading was confined to *The Daily Mail, The Evening News, The Financial Times, and The Weekly Dispatch*. He knew most things about the City, and apparently few things about aught else. When, rarely, he went to the theatre, he "liked a good laugh." He had never heard of Thomas Hardy, Shelley, Beethoven, Wagner, Fielding, Dell, nor Reynolds. But he was acquainted with the names of Shaw, Wells, and Dean Inge, and by a sure instinct disliked them all.

He appeared from nowhere at 9.45 a.m. daily, and disappeared into nowhere at any time from 6 to 8 p.m. – I to 2 on Saturdays. Between these hours his devotion to the institution was complete.. During some of them he actually was the institution. There were people who said that the institution owed everything to him. But, though he had certainly from time to time put very fruitful ideas into Sam's head, and chased some very dangerous ideas out of Sam's head, both he and Sam were well aware that this theory was false. He was worth a thousand a year to the institution, and thought himself well paid with four hundred, to which were added the trifling emoluments of a few secretaryships of small limited companies. It would have been absurd to pay a thousand a year to such a shabby, neat, narrow, and undistinguished man as Tom Swetnam. He could not have carried the salary with dignity.

Withal Tom lived a double life. He was the most steady, uxorious male ever born, had been married twice, and kept the second wife and two strings of children – one still lengthening – in a tiny house and garden at Raynes Park. The wife and the two strings of children and the garden were all perfect, and the most successful of their kind. His youngest son had gained eight ounces and a tooth in the same week as his eldest daughter had won a scholarship at Bedford College. His Glaw dee Deejun roses now and then arrived in the City in Tom's buttonhole, and provided occasions for the expression of Sam's benevolent interest concerning the crowded, remote, and invisible background of Tom's Raingo career.

"How am I for ready money?" Sam asked absently while examining Swetnam's little assortment of papers. "Enough for all purposes?"

"Yes, sir."

"Sure?"

Swetnam offered no reply to this casual insult; both of them knew that he never made an unqualified statement without being sure; he might once a year-or so be wrong, but he was always sure.

"Sent that money to Clacton for Mrs Raingo, didn't you?"

"Yes, sir. I had the acknowledgment of it from the Bank this morning."

Sam, not looking up, held out his right hand. Swetnam rose quickly, unscrewed a fountain-pen, and held it towards the hand, which took it and began to sign Sam's name.

"That's the cheque for – "

"All right! All right! Doesn't matter," Sam said, briskly impatient.

There were mornings, and this was one of them, when he would refuse all attention to detail; when he would sign anything at any cost, or say "Yes" or "No" impulsively, or say "I leave it to you "; when he had to feel free, disburdened, in the shortest possible time. But whereas on other mornings his aim was to be fully idle, to-day he was ardent to concentrate his brain on a new and intoxicating task.

"One moment, sir. You're signing the renunciation form.

Aren't you going to take up the new shares you're entitled to? "' Sam's hand, holding Swetnam's pen, was over a blue document headed: "Rubber Fields Limited. Issue of new ordinary shares."

"No, I'm not. I shall sell my rights. They ought to be worth – let me see, fifteen or sixteen thousand."

"You might make thirty thousand if you take them up and hold them for a year."

"Possibly. But I won't take them up, Thos. I'm off all risks for the present. Sell the rights."

He signed the renunciation as though breaking a chain. His position was logically untenable, but he maintained it. Swetnam, in silence, watched the wilful casting away of the equivalent of nearly forty years' salary, the price of houses and gardens, the starting in life of dozens of children; and such was the force of tradition and habitual servitude that he did not rebel, nor curse even in his heart.

In a few minutes Sam had dealt with everything and handed the papers and the pen back to his employee.

"Show me the list of companies I'm a director of."

"It's in your ' A ' drawer, sir."

"Oh!"

Sam unlocked a drawer, and, extracting a paper therefrom, glanced hastily down the catalogue of the eight or ten minor enterprises from which for some reason or other he had not been able to withdraw his semi-active interest. He scarcely troubled to read their names.

"I shall resign from all of them," he said curtly. "Prepare the letters, will you?" Swetnam said not a. word, and moved to leave.

"I say," Sam called him back. "I'm going into the Government."

Swetnam's clumsy, veined face showed no change for a moment. His mental processes were slow; he always read everything through twice; and he admired his employer for nothing more than the ability to grasp the elements of a problem in a single flash. Then he smiled, partly from vicarious pride and partly from relief at finding the key to the enigma of Sam's strange mood; after all, Caesar was not developing insanity.

"A minister, sir?"

"A minister. Records. The Prime Minister sent for me. It'll be no secret after to-morrow."

He spoke just as positively as if the affair had been definitely settled. And of course it had been settled. For if Andy should refuse the peerage, Sam could still – and would – give his weak heart on a charger to Andy and offer, out of patriotism and a determination to help the Government at any cost, to accept the perils of a. contested election and all other perils whatsoever. His whole attitude, his intentions, his exhilaration assumed that the affair was definitely settled.

It was not Sam's ambition that was to be fulfilled, but Swetnam's. The thick, little, common old man was more exhilarated than Sam himself. To-morrow – the tremendous news in that house at Raynes Park! Swetnam was too happy to live. But Swetnam, in addition to being a worshipper, was a realist. He had the gift of seeing Caesar as Caesar actually was. He worshipped him, while taking account of all his clearly-seen defects and limitations.

"Will there have to be much public speaking, sir?"

Sam was startled and had to recover himself. He knew that Swetnam was not hinting at anxiety for the ministerial heart. The worshipper's concern had to do with Sam's extremely mediocre talent for public speaking. Sam was excellently fluent and effective in conversation; he could be admirable at a directors' meeting; but at a meeting of shareholders he was a quite different man, and a worse. He had sometimes made himself wonderfully ridiculous in public. For he could not stand and talk loud and keep his wits. Swetnam's tone helped Sam to realise clearly for the first time that in trying for a peerage he had been thinking at least as much of this disability as of his heart.

"There will not," Sam snapped bravely, and with finality. But he was disturbed and temporarily thrown down from his self-complacency. He had a spasm of alarm.

11

ADELA

"Oh! It's you!" said Swetnam as he opened the door to leave the presence. Mrs Blacklow was just coming in. Swetnam paused, as if to take charge of the woman himself.

"That'll be all, thank you, Mr Swetnam," Sam said. He was not going to have this taking charge of anybody or anything in his room.

"Thank you, sir." Thos departed with a grand dignity intended to overpower his enemy the clerk, who, however, through negligence or nervousness missed it all.

"Well?" Sam began.

The woman's shabbily-gloved hands were empty.

"I thought of going to Dax's, sir," she said in her weak, uninteresting voice, and then stopped; she had evidently been hurrying and was a little out of breath.

"Well, Dax's wasn't a bad scheme. So you went to Dax's. Well, you went to Dax's. And what happened at Dax's?"

He had been ready to show severity at the sight of her empty hands. But her demeanour proved her to be a hopeless case of incompetence, and moreover he had obviously inspired her with fright; so that he was content to banter.

"They hadn't got any French papers. They had Italian and Spanish, but they said no French papers had arrived since the day before yesterday. They had one old one."

"Which was it?"

"I didn't ask, sir."

"Why didn't you? I told you I wanted *all* the French papers."

"I thought – "

"That's just what you didn't do. Did you try anywhere else?"

"No, sir. I thought as Dax's said that, it wouldn't be any use me – "

"You go and make a fresh start. And remember exactly what I said – ' all the French newspapers in this city.'"

She had no capability, no style, no attraction, no energy. Swetnam was right; she would have to seek another situation. Why did such women exist? They weren't even worth being sorry for. He hated her being afraid of him; and yet he liked it.

Instead of going forth and making a fresh start, she sat down on a chair, Swetnam's chair. At this unparalleled breach of office decorum Mr Raingo really did begin to think that something strange and disastrous had happened to the very structure of society. Never before had a clerk sat in his presence without being asked to do so; he had had women stenographers who even took shorthand-notes while standing. He did not know how to act for the best. Then he noticed that Mrs Blacklow had turned pale, and it was suddenly he, not she, who was afraid. He glanced aside uneasily to see if the carafe of water was in its place on the mantelpiece.

"I'm all right," she murmured, reading his thought with disturbing insight. But he poured out some water for her.

The scene between them was now transformed. The structure of society was made whole again. And Mr Raingo perceived by a revelation that Mrs Blacklow had charm after all. She had the charm of weakness, of inefficiency, of passivity. She was made not to do, but to be done unto; to receive, and to give nothing in return; for she had not beauty – she had only an appealing, pathetic weakness. And her youthfulness was but relative; a man would have to be twenty years older than herself to regard her as young. She put the glass down on the desk, spilling some of the water on the green leather. She seemed to have blossomed feebly under his ministration; she was taking her place in the world.

"Have you ever been a clerk before?" he asked mildly, in the way of reassuring conversation.

"Oh, yes, sir. Before I got married, I had a lot of situations."

He smiled to himself. She was just the sort of clerk who would naturally have a lot of situations, possessing no ability to keep any situation.

"Your husband – where is he?"

"He's all right, sir. He was taken prisoner in 1916."

Mr Raingo thought of Geoffrey. Geoffrey would be a bond between them.

"My son is a prisoner too – since 1916 too," he said.

"Yes, sir."

"Safe, anyway."

"Yes, sir."

"Any children?"

"No, sir. But I'm going to have one." She spoke quite evenly and calmly in her flaccid voice.

"But I thought you said – 1916."

She raised her eyes and gazed steadily at him, and his own gaze shifted away from her candour.

Faithless woman! Light woman! Wicked woman! Her husband fights and suffers for his country, and she – Mr Raingo's reflections, however, did not in the least run on these lines. He was thinking with wonder, and also with soft pleasure, that some man had found her desirable, had courted her, kissed her into surrender. She would surrender simply, from a talent for acquiescence and witlessness, not from passion or carnality.

He was flattered that she had told him. There must be something in his manner, something unconscious and profound that she liked and trusted, and that had triumphed over her fear of him. He had suspected the existence of such a quality before. Never would she have confessed to Swetnam… She had a child within her as she sat there in front of him. Millions and millions of expectant mothers on earth, and yet each one was separately miraculous, imposing, confounding, majestic.

"What sort of a father?"

"I only know his name, sir. He was a lodger in the house on ten days' leave… He went back."

"How – er – soon will it be?"

"About six months, sir."

Good God! Only three months ago and she was the prize, the prey, the ravished, the bride, all soft and yielding. And now she was sitting gloved and hatted in front of him. And he had been harrying her about newspapers… And he had never spoken to her in his life before. He realized overwhelmingly the meaning of war, and felt that he was realizing it for the first time. This was the meaning of war. The meaning of war was within her… One man fast in the arid routine of a prison-camp; the other in a trench under fire. She had no home, only a lodging. The child ruthlessly, implacably growing, growing. And at the end of the war she would have to face the released prisoner, with the child. If the child did not die. Another woman, desperate, might kill the child or herself. But Mrs Blacklow would be incapable of any such deed. She must wish that the war would last for ever. And he, Samuel Raingo, was making the war into politics and intrigue. He was not aghast at his conduct, for he perfectly understood that politics and intrigue are the inevitable accompaniment, as well as in part the cause, of war. But he was deeply affected by the contrast between the two aspects of war, as shown in himself and in her. He became a speechless poet for a few minutes.

"Have you got any money?"

"Only what I earn, sir."

"But you can't stay either here or anywhere else for very Ions."

"No, sir."

"Well, I think you'd better leave at the end of next month. Give me your address. I'll see you through – so far as money's concerned, I mean." The money would be the tribute of politics to tragedy.

She did not speak; she scarcely wept, but she did weep a little. Then the officious, inquisitive, restless Swetnam poked his nose in at the door. Of course he was wondering what the new clerk might be doing so long in the boss's room, without a notebook. The fellow was as jealous as a woman in love. But Swetnam said:

"Mrs Raingo is here, sir."

Sam controlled himself. Only two days earlier Adela had said and repeated that nothing would induce her to come to London in the spring. And here she was! Always incalculable, unpredictable! Unless of course you went by the rule that if she had said she would not do a thing she would do it, and vice versa. She had a trick of "turning up" like a terrier. Sam loved to have a clear, definite programme for himself, and to keep to it; and he loved those with whom he was regularly in contact to have a clear, definite programme also, and to keep to it. He wanted always "to know where he was." But he could never know where he was with Adela. No doubt she had been wondering what could be the result of the Prime Minister's telegram, and the casual notion of strolling up to London to find out had occurred to her. He rose from the chair rather violently. He had the sensation of being wrenched violently out of one world into a very different world. Not surprising that he had to control himself and collect his wits!

Mrs Blacklow, leaving, deferentially stood aside for Mrs Raingo in the doorway – and then vanished. What was the difference between those two women? Adela was nearly as badly dressed and just as inefficient as the clerk, and perhaps just as unreliable. Nor had she more charm than the clerk; he was inclined to think that she had less charm. Yet the difference was enormous; for Adela was active, and she had authority. She was not entitled, by anything she had done, to possess authority, but she had it. He felt her authority. Put her in sacking, with rope for a waistband, and she would still have authority – and look, too, as if she had it.

"Hello, Adela!" he greeted her, and waited for the impact.

"Who was that?" she asked.

"A new clerk."

"Wears gloves, does she, at work?"

Odd remark, and how characteristic! There was no innuendo in it, for Adela was very straightforward; but it disturbed and slightly offended him; it showed an instinctive, hard antipathy to the poor creature. Should he tell her the poor creature's story? Emphatically no! She would not understand, or she would refuse to understand; she would say something dry and odious; she would tarnish the story. 'He would keep the story strictly to himself; it should be his alone.

Adela came close to him and kissed him. Her kiss had a new quality, faintly emotional. Ah! She was excited about his prospects! The snob in her was anticipating a brilliant rise – for both of them, was awaiting the moment when she would be able to say to her friends with a new pride: "My husband!" He accepted her arrival with forced resignation, but his spirit withdrew from her into the recesses of his being.

"What train did you come by?" he inquired, looking at his watch.

"I motored, dear."

"Oh! I thought your car was out of order."

"I came in yours – I knew you wouldn't mind."

"Who drove you? You surely haven't brought Wrenkin – "

"I drove myself. I'm a much better driver than Wrenkin."

"Good heavens!" He sat down. He was silenced. She was always ramming her own car into gate-posts and trees and things.

"Do you mean to say you drove all through the East End and into the City?"

"Why not? The car's outside now. I thought it might be handy for you if you should happen to want it in London."

The woman was unique. In another moment she would be saying that she had brought the car to London solely in his interests and that he ought to be glad he had such a thoughtful wife! She went on eagerly in her high voice, and her grey eyes for once were looking at him and not through him.

"Oh, Sam, it's about Geoffrey – I had a letter this morning from – "

"Geoffrey!" An absolutely new vista of conjecture opened before him. She was going to be right again, to justify her caprice in some quite unforeseen manner. He even had a feeling of guilt towards her.

"I had a letter from Jim Hylton's sister-in-law – "

"Who's Jim Hylton?" He sharply pulled her up a second time.

"You know Jim Hylton."

"I don't."

"He was taken prisoner with Geoffrey and they've been together."

"Oh, that fellow!"

"Bertha says Jim's escaped and he's just reached London. He and Geoffrey escaped together. They separated because it was safer. That's why we haven't been hearing from Geoffrey. So we may expect him any time." She stood over Sam, sparkling with vitality.

"If he's got clear away," said he glumly. He was startled, thrilled, but determined not openly to share his wife's eager excitement.

"I'm sure if Jim Hylton could get clear away Geoffrey would."

What an argument! How like a woman! How like a mother!

"You've never met Hylton. Neither have I." He knew that he was behaving like a curmudgeon and that there was no excuse for such behaviour. But she exasperated him.

"I know I haven't. But I know all about him, dearest." She was unruffled, marvellously nice. Most annoyingly she had set him an ex-ample in good manners, but she was always doing that. He scorned her for assuming that what Jim Hylton had done Geoffrey could do. Yet he himself was aware of a secret, deep, illogical conviction to the same effect.

"Better," said he thoughtfully, with a calculated, disingenuous air of solemn warning. "Better if the boy hasn't got away. He'd only be punished then. But if he's got away he'll have to fight again, and you never know what may happen." Cruel! True! But nevertheless very cruel, at such a moment! Horribly brutal!

"Oh, Sam! You oughtn't to talk like that," she remonstrated bravely, throwing back her head with resilient dignity. But she was not dashed. Nothing could lower her expectant joy at the impending sight of her son.

Sam gazed doggedly at blotting-paper.

"Why am I behaving like this?" he reflected. Adela was the mother all afresh, just as she had been long ago when she was desirable, desired. Hanged if she wasn't the wife afresh also. Their old friendly intimacy! He recalled it, but he could not rekindle the spent ashes of it.

"Well, perhaps I oughtn't," he said, relenting a little, in shame.

They talked and arranged a lunch.

"Well, I'm going on to Bertha Hylton's now, but of course I had to tell you first."

"Now do for God's sake take care of yourself in the traffic," he enjoined her as she was leaving.

She savoured his interest in her safety. She was gone. Not a word from her as to the meaning of the Prime Minister's telegram! She had completely forgotten it. And yet in a week she might, through no virtue of her own, be a baroness. How she would gloat over a title!

Sam said to himself, in a sudden whirl of emotion:

"If the kid does get back safe, damned if I don't wangle him out of the active service list and into my Ministry! Damned if I don't! Unless I'm mistaken there are one or two jobs there he could do jolly well."

12

THE LUNCHEON PARTY

The next day Miss Packer waylaid Mr Raingo on the stairs of the Prime Minister's official residence. In appearance, mood, and demeanour she was exactly the same as on the previous morning. She seemed to be immune from all the influences which hourly cause subtle changes in the functioning of the human organism; she was a woman, but above womanhood; and her baffling blandness made an invisible adamantine wall between herself and the world.

"The Prime Minister will see you privately after lunch in my room," said she. "It's along here."

She took him along a corridor, into a small room full of books orderly on shelves and books disorderly on the floor.

"I see," said Sam. "Straight through and first on the right. And am I supposed to slip out and come here on my own?" He added, moved by her uncompromisingly un-humorous nice smile to correct the colloquialism: "Initiative?" You might use such a locution as "on my own" to the Prime Minister, but not to a Miss Packer – at any rate not to a Miss Packer on duty.

"Please."

"And then wait here?"

"Please."

He wanted to say: "And shall you be here to keep me company?" But her inflexible decorum had cowed him. To trifle might be to alienate her, and he had not yet gauged the extent of her power.

"It shall be done," he said, with earnest gravity.

"They are all here," she said. "The Cabinet meeting finished earlier than was expected."

"The hell it did!" he thought coarsely. "I wonder if anything would happen if one fell at her feet in a limousine and offered her enough pearls and a flat in Park Lane. But the Queen of Spain has no legs." The ribald result, no doubt, of mere nervousness on his part.

"Mr Samuel Raingo," announced his friend the butler at the dining-room door, to reach which he had been ushered through an ante-room and a small drawing-room. Six men, including Andrew Clyth, were standing on or near the hearthrug, between the fire and the table. They turned to look at him, with the frank curiosity of schoolboys. He knew them all except one.

"Permit me, Prime Minister," said the Earl of Ockleford, tall, white, obese, stately (his was the only frock-coat in the room), putting an ash-tray neatly under the perilous long ash of Andy's cigarette.

This tiny incident saved Sam from a mistake of deportment. He had meant boldly to address Andy as "Andy." But he now perceived in an instant that, whatever Andy might be at breakfast, at lunch he was a great personage, one of the greatest in the world, the old sinner!

"Morning, Prime Minister," he began deferentially.

Andy, tossing a gracious nod of thanks to the Earl,, stepped forward and greeted him with warm, urbane patronage.

"You know everybody here, I expect." And looking round: "You all know my old friend Sam Raingo."

Sam shook hands with Tom Hogarth, in a lounge suit, short, bald, blond, and challenging, Minister of Munitions; Hasper Clews in a morning-coat, tall, dark, iron-grey, melancholy, shy, Chancellor of the Exchequer; Sid Jenkin, black, broad, shabby, canny, easily genial, Labour MP and Minister without Portfolio; and the magnificent Lord Ockleford, Lord President of the Council. The sixth man, to whom Sam had to be presented, was a Colonial Premier in military uniform, whose greeting was as punctilious as the Earl's and as genial as Sid Jenkin's.

Raingo was nervous; and, after the manner of nervous people at a party in a strange environment, he seemed to examine the sombre ill-lit room with interest and in detail, though he was not interested in it at all and scarcely saw what he was looking at. He noticed vaguely the collection of portraits, sadly mediocre, of former Prime Ministers, on the walls, and a view of a courtyard through the windows, and no more. The party sat down to meat. The Prime Minister took one end of the huge table, without giving directions to his guests. Sid Jenkin planted himself at the other end of the table, opposite the Prime Minister. Hogarth, the Munitions Minister, and gloomy Clews, the Chancellor, sat on the side to the right of the Prime Minister, and the Colonial Premier and the fine old Earl on the side to the left. One chair remained between Sid Jenkin and the Earl, and Sam modestly slipped into it.

The service was terribly slow. Sam felt his nervousness increasing. He knew that he was there to be inspected, vetted, and probably put through his paces.

Or was it really, after all, that they only wanted his advice, as Andy had said } In any case he must bear himself in a style to demonstrate that 'he was an eminently suitable candidate for the red benches of the House of Lords. The chat drooped, and Sam suddenly comprehended that if he was nervous, his presence was making the others nervous. This conclusion stiffened him and gave him heart.

"What a pack!" he thought, knowing that the derogatory appellation was unfair to some of them. "What a. pack!"

He remembered each occasion in the past when two or three of them, by the arrogance of curt nods and supercilious greetings, had made him humiliatingly feel the great gulf that separates a minister, any minister, from a private member of the House. Quite possibly that very morning they had been discussing him at length, freely, cruelly, with jibes. Let them. There was not one among them who did not envy him his wealth, reckoning it doubtless three times greater than it in fact was. (But this was a common thought with him, and a continual source of satisfaction and inspiration.)

And as for the peerage, well, he admitted that a peerage would give him immense pleasure. And why not? The prestige of lordship was still enormous. Here and there one among the pack would disdainfully smile at the notion of taking a peerage: such as Andy and Tom Hogarth: but only because it would mean banishment from the Commons, where careers lay. In old age, however, when the Commons had got beyond their dwindling powers to dominate it, they would accept a peerage fast enough, and a peerage of the higher orders, on some self-justifying political pretext or other. They always did. He knew that he was again being unfair to some of them. But all judgments with a tang in them have to be a little unfair. He caught Andy's eye.

"Prime Minister," he said clearly, inspired, and contradicting the deference of tone with an Eccles glance, "is there anybody among our friends who has specialized about prisoners?"

"Jenkin," Tom Hogarth flashed out, his face a large smile. "He's done time."

A general hearty laugh.

"And proud of it, Tommy! And 'ere I'm sitting at this table at No. 10 to-day!"

Nothing pleased Sid Jenkin better than a reference to the weeks he had spent in prison, in his fiery youth, apropos of some petty defiance of the police in a strike.

"I meant prisoners-of-war," Sam explained.

"That'll still be Jenkin," said the Prime Minister. "Jenkin is our leading authority on the Swiss organization for the welfare of prisoners-of-war,"

"Yes, I'm your man," Sid agreed invitingly.

"I've a son who's escaped, and I'm very anxious to find out what's happened to him," Sam said gravely. "I haven't heard. He may have been caught, but I know he got clear away." Sam of course was genuinely anxious about Geoffrey's fate, but at the same time he joyously realized that he had made good capital politically out of Geoffrey.

The table appeared interested, impressed, and sympathetic to the father and appreciative of the son. To the glamour of the father's riches had been added the distinction of being the only man there with a son who had had the grit and the resource to escape out of the hands of the Boche. Also the whole table was delivered from its nervous constraint.

"Good for your boy!" cried Tom Hogarth, smacking the cloth. "No, I'll have beer," he said loudly to the butler.

Sid Jenkin at once assumed possession of Sam in a private duologue, wrote down details of regiment, dates places, swore he would set the cable to work that afternoon, stated again and again that he 'ad the entire organization at 'is finger-ends; was exceedingly amiable.

(" I *am* going to be a minister and a peer," thought Sam.)

With his right ear Sam heard Tom Hogarth, at the distant other end of the table, describing at length to the Prime Minister and the Colonial Premier and whoever might care to listen how in 1899 he too had been a prisoner-of-war and how he too had escaped; he was excited and dramatic, and throughout the tale he ate plenteously in big gulps and quaffed beer.

Then the Colonial Premier quietly reminded people that he too in the same year 1899 had been taken prisoner and had escaped – from the British. He spoke very smoothly, very benevolently, understating and using no gestures. Tom Hogarth challenged him, across the attentive, enigmatic Prime Minister, on a point of the treatment of prisoners-of-war in those barbaric days. Tom grew more strenuous; the Colonial Premier grew more gentle. The argument went on and on.

"I'll lay you a hundred guineas, sir," cried Tom. The "sir" was addressed to the general in the Colonial Premier.

"Tom," laughed the Prime Minister, "you know that the general never bets – neither do I. We leave gambling to the (upper and lower classes, don't we, Christian?"

"But, really, sir… Ockleford shall decide. He knows j everything, so he must know this."

"What precisely is the question, my dear boy? "asked the Earl, who was Tom's father's cousin.

By this time Sid Jenkin had obtained all his particulars and made all his promises, and the topic of Geoffrey was closed.

"Wonderful 'ow Tommy hates Colonials," murmured Sid very low. "'E's given our friend the name of ' stroking Jesus.'"

"Why?" asked Sam. And then: "I see."

The general, speaking to the Earl, was tenderly stroking the Earl's arm.

"Jealousy," continued Sid. "That's what it is. Jealousy. And Tom's got no use either for any of us ministers without portfolios. He told me so last night when 'e' d had a drop. ' Sid,' 'e said, ' all you fellows ' – there's three of us, Hempton ain't 'ere – ' ye're only passengers, dust in the eyes of the public,' 'e says. ' I don't mind you,' 'e says and 'e doesn't. ' But we don't need any of those backwoods dagos to teach us 'ow to run a war,' 'e says. But what rings the bell with me – it isn't as I'm in the War Cabinet, though that's something as'll be remembered in the history of the Labour movement; it's that the Secretary for War isn't, and the First Lord of the Admiralty isn't, in the War Cabinet." He laughed inaudibly and winked. "Of course they says there's six of us in the War Cabinet; but really there's only two, Tommy Hogarth and the P.M. They're as jealous of one another as two comet players in a brass band, but the P.M. can't do without Tommy. Some say," he went on murmuring into Sam's ear. "Some say if there's two members of the War Cabinet, it isn't Andrew Clyth and Tom Hogarth – it's Andrew Clyth and Andrew Clyth." He grinned. "But that isn't so. Tom's on the map all right."

"Well, at any rate, you all seem very cheerful together," Sam breathed, thinking of Flanders, Amiens, the Channel coast, German prison camps, and adulterous expectant mothers.

"Well, things are better. It's not generally known yet, but things are better. *We* know that Foch is satisfied. At least 'e isn't satisfied yet, but 'e expects to be in a day or two. All this man-power business – the Bill and so on – gallery stuff! We started it. in a panic and now we've got to go on with it. Biggest piece of political camouflage ever attempted, the Man-Power Bill is. Still, it'll give the Boche something to think about."

"Quite," Sam concurred; his spirits were much raised; but he was wondering whether to feel flattered by Sid Jenkin's confidences or to condemn Sid for a general chatterer. He knew that Sid always chattered – sometimes in a most misleading manner. Still, it would be a nice thing if you couldn't chatter to a guest of what was practically a confidential meeting of the War Cabinet… On the whole he would defend Sid's reassuring loquacity. He spoke, louder, of the morning bulletin – the Prime Minister was eyeing them. Sid, too, had noticed that suspecting, uneasy glance.

"I fear I must decide against you, my dear boy." Lord Ockleford had delivered judgment, whereat the Colonial Premier bowed his thanks.

A general laugh, in which Hogarth himself was a principal performer; but Hogarth's mirth had something savage in it.

"I suppose cheerfulness is a virtue," said the taciturn and hypochondriacal Hasper Clews in his plaintive, rather quavering tone, full of implications, mild rebuke, and sinister irony.

He was eight years younger than the Prime Minister and looked a couple of years older. Except Sid Jenkin and Hogarth, he was the youngest man present, but his unconscious attitude to the table was that of an uncle to nephews. The table waited for him to continue; he said no more; he had obtained his effect.

Raingo noticed that thereupon everybody, even the Prime Minister, seemed to brace himself, to recall the sense of terrific responsibilities, and to realize the nature of the consequences, personal and general, of failure to do the job set by fate. Each face grew sterner, more, authoritative, more intelligent, a worthier mirror of the national reputation of the man behind it. And Sam's mind was suddenly filled with visions of the dazzling, dramatic annals of the careers around him. Clews had risen from the son of a Nonconformist professor of theology in a minor college to be the getter and the dispenser of millions of money per day. Sid Jenkin had worked in a coalmine, fought in sanguinary riots, quelled multitudes of his fellow-men with nothing but oratory for a weapon, and was now the head of his party and a right honourable. The Colonial Premier in his youth had commanded armies in the field against desperate odds, and then made a nation out of defeat. Lord Ockleford had been the vice-regal centre and most splendid figure in Oriental pageants of sovereignty surpassing everything else in Asiatic history. Tom Hogarth had reigned in seven departments of State, fought, written, and fought; he was the most brilliant advocate in the House, and one of the finest polemical and descriptive writers in the country; he had every gift except common sense, and he could rise victorious even from the disasters imposed upon him by an incurable foolishness.

As for Andy, Sam had known him too well in youth ever to judge him impartially in middle-age. He was as great a prizefighter as Hogarth himself, but his method was that of infighting. He mystified Sam, who could not divine how he came to be where he was. A miraculous adroitness, a unique genius for chicane, beneath a nervous and apparently trustful and candid manner! That was what it must be.

Sam considered himself the equal of any of them. He had done wonderful things. But after all he was only a millionaire and a man of business, whereas the others had the incomparable prestige which in Britain attaches to politics alone. In politics he had failed – no doubt chiefly because he could not move multitudes by word of mouth. But now he was going to succeed in politics. Once again he had the feeling of intense exhilaration.

13

Sam Exhibited

"I don't see much reason for optimism myself," Hasper Clews at last proceeded.

"Great Heavens!" Tom Hogarth burst out. "Haven't we heard this morning that Guatemala is about to declare war on Germany! What *do* you want?" Pleased with himself, Tom chuckled, looking round the table. But the smiles were restrained.

Clews pecked at the starch-free bread which he always carried with him, and went on in bland gloom:

"Of course I know the generals are optimistic. But so far as I remember the generals always have been optimistic. I should like a few sound civilians to be optimistic."

"There are some who are," Lord Ockleford put in.

"Well, that's the best news I've heard for a long time," said Clews with a grim smile. "The Paris press doesn't strike me as very optimistic, really!... My daughter's been teaching me to read French in the evenings."

"Stout fellow!" exclaimed the irrepressible Tom. "I suppose you thought somebody here besides Ockleford ought to know a bit of French, eh?"

"The French press from what I 'ear – " Sid Jenkin began.

"Raingo's got a new way for dealing with the Paris press," said the Prime Minister. "But perhaps we oughtn't to speak of it out loud." He looked at Sam as if to say: "Here's your opening."

"I quite agree with you, Clews," Sam opened immediately, thankful that he had spent the previous evening examining several files of French papers at the Club. He knew that every eye was upon him and every brain waiting to assess him. "Without actually saying so, the Paris press have been hinting, or have been made to hint, that it might be difficult to keep both Paris *and* the Channel ports – Calais and Boulogne, that is – and that Paris must be saved at any cost. Pleasing!… I call that pessimism if you like!"

"But if you had to choose, wouldn't it be better to keep Paris?" asked the Colonial Premier. "I say, if you *had* to make a choice."

"No!" roared the irrepressible Tom. "They've abandoned Paris once. Why shouldn't they again?"

"I look at it like this," said Sam judicially, glancing across Lord Ockleford with deference at the Colonial Premier. "The Paris problem is mainly psychological. The Channel ports problem is military, or rather naval, and I think on the whole more important. I think if you had to give up Calais and Boulogne you'd give up the anti-submarine barrage across the narrows and the value of every Boche submarine – I mean its destructive value – would be at least doubled. And it's four times as far to Havre. That would mean many more of our submarines needed to convoy our transports, and three or four times as much transport tonnage into the bargain – just now when we have to lend every ship we can lay hold of for American transport. And I don't say anything about the risk of Kent being invaded, or about Big Berthas being trained on Dover. The war would have been finished by this time if we'd stuck to the Belgian coast. To give that up was a capital mistake. And to give up the coast of the narrows would be still worse. The French have never grasped the naval question. Foch hasn't. Whenever they feel themselves in a real hole their instinct is to do something silly about the sea. And when they show signs of being silly it's a sure thing they're pessimistic at bottom – or even thoroughly rattled. I quite see the importance of Paris, but that's how I look at it, sir."

"Quite!" admitted the Colonial Premier, with respect.

"All that's academic," said the irrepressible curtly. "We shan't have to give up either."

Nevertheless Sam had been effective; and, with that curious naive expression which came over his face sometimes, the Prime Minister glanced about saying with his poetic eye: "Hear the man I've chosen. Hear him."

Sam gave attention to his food; the closing stages of the meal were now at hand. He said to himself that he was in a queer sort of menagerie, but after all it was no queerer than his considerable experience of the world had led him to expect. Were those the men who ran the war, men whose names filled the newspapers daily and were known to every citizen, the men who went about like gods in the departments, conscious of the reality of power? Well, they were. Only now they were not talking about what they were thinking about. Each brain held a crowded mass of details, problems, responsibilities, ever present to the secret consciousness. To know them, to appreciate their talents, you would have to be invisible and watch them at grips with their tasks, dealing with men and digesting material, balancing pros and cons, making decisions. Now they were merely relaxing, or showing off, which indeed was a favourite form of relaxation with some people. The Prime Minister was certainly brooding upon the speech which in less than two hours he would have begun in a crowded and frightened and perhaps hysterical House. Sid Jenkin, Clews and Tom Hogarth had somehow involved themselves in a discussion concerning the censorship, and Sam for a few moments was isolated.

"Your place is in north Essex, I think," said Lord Ockleford, pale and puffy, turning to him with majestic polished courtesy, and at once broaching the topic of shorthorns. He remembered, far better than Sam, the characteristics and price of a pedigree bull which Sam had sold in somewhat sensational circumstances in 1914. He had theories about breeding, about pasturage, about the value of cattle-shows and the bases of judging. It was impossible not to assume that his lordship had spent the whole of a busy life in the study of pedigree stock. Withal he was most modest, attitudinising with exquisite grace before Sam as a tyro before a master. And throughout Sam was following the discussion about the censorship.

"I say the paper ought to be suppressed," Tom Hogarth was urging passionately. "I don't care what the paper is. I said so this morning and I shall stick to it. The offices ought to be taken possession of this afternoon. Here the damned rag deliberately defies the censorship and publishes important military information – and nothing is to be done! It's an end to discipline, and discipline is the very life-blood of war." His eyes blazed; yet he was smiling as well as smacking the table.

"What does Raingo say?" asked the Prime Minister, with marked quietness of tone. The question was a command. Sam had to withdraw from shorthorns, and Tom Hogarth had to stop in mid-course.

"Well, Prime Minister," Sam began, and hesitated, looking Hogarth in the face and then looking round the room; the servants had gone.

"I was particularly anxious to get your views, Sam," Andy encouraged him.

"To me," Sam took a line, "to me the thing turns on the psychology of the military caste. You set a general an impossible task in extremely dangerous circumstances, and then you hit him over the head because he fails in it. He's bound to have defenders, and big ones. These articles are simply the revenge of the whole military class."

"We had to set him the task. The French – "

"That's beside the point. You set it. Anybody with an ounce of *nous* can see that the articles are absolutely true and can't be contradicted. There's only one thing for you to do. Stick it. Leave the paper alone. Why, if the British Government were to suppress a wealthy London Tory military paper, the affair would cause more stir than a hundred thousand dead on a battle-field – throughout the entire world! Everyone would say you were dithering with fright; it would be worth an army-corps to Germany. It isn't as if you could undo the mischief that's been done – if any. You can't."

Hogarth repeated, smacking, and red in the face:

"What I say is, discipline is discipline."

"Not always. Sometimes it's lunacy," said Sam calmly.

A pause. The outsider had at the worst demonstrated that *he* was not dithering.

"As I said in 1917," Sid Jenkin filled the pause. "You may remember, Tom, I – "

"You said a lot of things in 1917 that are best forgotten, Sid, my lad. I maintain that a lamentable lack of – er – cohesion is being shown."

"Well, if it's cohesion, we're talking about I 'ad some particulars last night about your Ministry, Tommy," said Sid, winking at Sam. "I 'ear you gave a permit to the seller to sell some engineering plant at Newcastle to a buyer, and refused the permit to the buyer to buy. That's cohesion, is it?"

"Childish!" Tom Hogarth shouted, furious at last. "My Ministry's the best run Ministry in the Government."

The episode seemed to Sam symbolic.

"They all hate one another worse than they hate the Boche," he thought, unfairly but picturesquely. The Prime Minister was the trainer of the menagerie and some of the wild beasts were defying him: that was it.

Sam waited for Andy's gesture; it was masterly. The Prime Minister looked at his watch. Tom Hogarth jumped up savagely, raised his massive shoulders to his ears, and strode towards the window. When he turned round he was humorously chuckling. Lord Ockleford spoke a courteous word of optimism to Sam about the chances of the escaped prisoner, and Sam, really pleased, thanked him with all the urbanity which he used to employ in the old days towards large shareholders in a not too prosperous company. He felt that he had been misjudging the Earl for many years.

14

The Peerage

Miss Packer was not in her room, into which Sam slipped with the illusion that he was taking part in some bustling light comedy of chicane. There must, he thought, be a good deal of careful and exact fore-planning in that house. A singular room. Besides the books it had a large easy chair, an office chair, and a very small typewriting table with a portable typewriter, a letter-basket (empty), a calendar of engagements, and one notebook thereon. Evidently, under Miss Packer, there must be a clerk who did, elsewhere, the routine work of personal secretaryship.

Sam glanced at the books. Those on the ordered shelves were calf-bound volumes such as no gentleman's library should be without, and such as no gentleman reads – complete sets of works by authors who have passed through the purgatory of criticism into a heaven of undisturbed nullity. The books strewn about were modern, and chiefly novels signed by Frankau, Hutchinson, Sabatini, Oppenheim, etc. etc., together with a Library of Standard Literature, in ten tomes of gilt cloth.

"*Her* robust taste!" said Sam, who had some notion of the difference between books and books. But, opening several of the strewn volumes, he found them all inscribed on the inside covers, "Andrew Clyth" or "AC" The Prime Minister caught him stooping at his investigations.

"Well, Sam, I've shown you the lid off, eh?"

"You have, Andy."

Andy seemed to be at his most genial, candid and sympathetic; nevertheless his yellowish, roving eyes had now the covert, inquiring look which was so marked at the previous day's breakfast, but which he had somehow put off for the Cabinet lunch.

"Now listen here, Sammy," he began in the best hearty Ecclesian vein, "we're very old friends – let's be frank with one another."

Both men were standing. Andy was appreciably the taller, and Sam did not like the lanky fellow to be looking down at him

"Certainly," said Sam. "You don't mind me sitting down, do you? Standing's not very good for me."

"My dear boy! Please!" Andy smiled eagerly, showing his bright teeth; but the suggestion had somehow twisted his opening.

Sam took the easy chair and crossed his legs.

"We want you. You are just the man we do want, and we don't want anybody else. But we can't have you in the upper House. You must be in the Commons. I'll see that you're spared in every possible way. There can't be any serious trouble in the Commons, but a question or two might arise from time to time, as I said yesterday; such questions must be answered in the Commons, and of course you'd be able to answer them quite easily. As for the by-election, if there's a contest – I don't think for a moment there will be – y >u shall have the best help I can give. You know, old chap, we all think you're exaggerating a bit about the state of your health. Natural! Natural! Prudence is always best. I know I'm a little fussy myself. But one can take one's health too seriously. Forgive me if I'm carrying frankness too far." Sam said nothing. "In any case, if you really are decided you can't go back to the Commons – then I must approach our second choice at once, and I shall be damned sorry to have to do it."

"Are you bluffing? I think you are," said Sam to himself, lolling in his chair. From the easy chair he could regard Andy's height with equanimity.

Then aloud, quietly:

"I entirely understand. But you may believe me I've not been exaggerating. It isn't that I'm worrying personally about my health. As I said yesterday, I don't mind cracking up in a crisis. What troubles me is that my cracking up would be a great nuisance to you. Moreover I should almost certainly go under before I had time even to begin. So we'll call it off. All I'll say is, it was awfully decent of you to ask me."

The Prime Minister made no reply. Sam was thrilled with the elated joy of a tussle. He sat erect. He leaned forward, confidentially, and continued in an intimate half-boyish tone

"I'm not being quite frank with you, Andy. I feel I must be. It's my wife. My wife won't let me go through an election. She won't let me go into the House of Commons. I was afraid she wouldn't."

"Your wife! What precisely does she say?"

"Oh, you know what women are. What she says doesn't matter."

"Tell me."

"Precisely?"

"Yes."

"Well, about my health she says all that I say, and a lot more. About the politics of the affair she says that obviously I'm the chap you need. She says I'm a first-rate business man, and I belong to your party, and I've some inside acquaintance with the press and so on. She says peerages are cheap to-day, and there's no good reason why I shouldn't have one. She says you don't want to give me one because you've always been jealous of me, ever since we were boys, and that sort of jealousy will influence even the biggest men. She says if I'm only in the Commons you can get rid of me as soon as my work is done and you'll have nothing further to fear from me. Whereas if I'm in the Lords you can never get rid of me, and I might make a name there, and you'd always have to reckon with me. Mind you, I'm only telling you this because you insisted. You needn't tell me there's nothing in it, because I know there's nothing in it. We've had our differences, you and me, but I'd back you through thick and thin for playing straight." He half closed his eyes and gazed steadily at Andy, and thought: "A wife can be a great convenience at a pinch." He had not even mentioned a peerage to Adela.

"Mrs Raingo is unjust," said the Prime Minister, uneasily moving.

"Man to man, did you ever know a woman that wasn't? But you won't change her, where I'm concerned. Besides, all that's a detail. The poi»t is she's determined not to let me risk a breakdown. Determined. And you know I can't defy her."

"Well, of course, perhaps I'm wrong. Perhaps the risk it as great as you and she think. If so, I should be very sorry – " And, paused, stepped forward and held out his hand, which Sam took. "I'll give you the peerage." His gesture was utterly noble.

"You mean you'll recommend me to the King," said Sam uncompromisingly.

"Naturally that's implied."

"Well, Andy, I shall do my best."

The front line of battle might have been in China instead of within hearing distance of the big explosions – so thin and unreal did it appear beyond the foreground of chicane in which Sam had fought and won. He was ecstatic with triumph. He pictured Adela's self-centred bliss and Delphine's simple, tremendous adoration, when he should tell them the news. He was a superman. But for Andy he assumed a demeanour of anxious responsibility – the true sign of the able man modest enough to distrust himself.

"There's one thing I want to tell ye, lad," said the Prime Minister, sitting down back to front on Miss Packer's desk-chair and spreading out his long legs. "Just listen to me."

Sam put himself into the attitude of deferentially listening; but he was saying to himself: "And I've got the title without paying a cent for it."

The Prime Minister proceeded:

"It's about Secret Service money. There'll be trouble over Secret Service money. There always has been. *You* have control over it, all of it, and nobody else has. It's from the administration of Secret Service that you get all your power – all I mean that's worth a bawbee. Every minister who wants Secret Service money has to come to you himself to get it. He has to tell you what he wants it for. See? Bribery, spies, expeditions. There's more goes in bribery than in anything else. You say ' Yes' or ' No' to 'em, but usually you say ' Yes.' The Treasury will make a fuss over fourpence if it's for simple straightforward propaganda; but, they say nothing at all if it's for Secret Service. They'll pay and they won't ask for vouchers either. Only, once you've ' OK'd' a thing you can't control the amount. I reckon over a couple of millions will disappear this year in SS The fact is, any neutral can walk in and get SS money for alleged information – that's what it comes to."

"I see," observed Sam judicially. The one word "Power!" "Power!" "Power!" sang intoxicatingly in his head. "Then where'll the difficulty be?"

"It's like this. Both the War Office and the Admiralty are fighting like hell to be free of Records control. But I won't let 'em. They've both been hoaxed again and again in the most absurd way, and I won't let 'em do as they like – not if I can help it. I'm running this war – or it amounts to that, my lad."

"Well, if I have your backing – "

"Ah! But perhaps you won't always have it, son. I may be forced to go against you. There'll be a lot of cross-fighting. And it may be up to you to show me how you can be too strong for me. The War Office and the Admiralty hate me. They'd love to down me – if they could. A bit complex. But you've got it." Andy gave him a searching, furtive glance.

"I have," said Sam.

"Good. I knew you'd get it. There's nobody'll understand anybody better than you and me."

"I agree," said Sam. And he meant it. "Now about propaganda."

"Pooh! Do as you like. I've nothing to say about that. It keeps a lot of people employed that might otherwise be in mischief." Andy laughed and lit a cigarette. Sam had to begin earnestly to readjust his perspective.

"And when do I start?"

"Oh! Any time. The sooner the better. To-morrow morning. Just go down to the Ministry and take charge. And don't worry me. I ought to warn you, by the way, that your notion about dealing with the Paris press isn't as new as you think it is. We've nobbled one ' great daily.' I did hear what it's costing the British taxpayer, but I've forgotten. No doubt they're doing it on us too."

"Do you mean – ?" Sam exclaimed, his patriotic prejudices somewhat flustered.

"Why not? You didn't suppose the British patrol was effective to keep the devil out of your great country. My belief is the devil was born somewhere in the City, near the Bank of England. I'll lay a hundred to one there are enemy spies in your Ministry."

"Cheerful!" said Sam. He was delighted with the phrase "Your Ministry."

A morning-coated gentleman hurried into the room.

"How do, Poppleham?" Sam greeted him casually.

"How do you do, sir?" responded respectfully the Prime Minister's principal secretary. And to his master: "You aren't forgetting the appointment for three-fifteen, sir? And here are the corrected notes for the speech."

The Prime Minister took a paper.

"Say, Raingo," said he. "Walk down with me to the House, will you? You know, of course, it's the great Man Power afternoon. Good heavens! What a circus!"

"I should like to come very much," Sam replied, curiously flattered and proud. At the same time there surged into his head crowds of new ideas for vitalizing and controlling his Ministry. Power! Power! He was a god.

15

The Walk

The Saluting began the very moment they got outside the door of No. 10. The journalists were there, in their everlasting vigil. "Click" went a camera. "The Prime Minister leaving Downing Street on his way to make his great speech on the Man Power Bill in the House of Commons." Etc. No doubt!

"I am just like a schoolboy – rather, a schoolgirl," thought Sam, noticing his own naive and excited pride at being seen in company with the Prime Minister on this historic occasion. But was he himself recognized? If only they knew that he had been given a Ministry – a Ministry all to himself – and a peerage; *given* a peerage; no hint of a contribution to Party Funds! If only they knew! And they would know!... Yes, like a schoolgirl he was. For he wanted to skip and jump. {And all the while journalists and others were mistaking him for a plumpish, middle-aged fellow.)

"You don't mind if I don't talk much," said Andy. "I've got this damn' speech in my head – not very clearly either." The strange, withdrawn, naive expression had come over his face again. You would have thought he was a poet, too simple to live, and butter wouldn't melt in his mouth. The orator was appearing. The Irishman was appearing; and the Scotchman seemed to have vanished. The instructed, the profane, and the cynical would warn you to beware specially of Andy in his Irish-poetic moods. "You may bet," they would say, "that whatever he's saying in English he's thinking something quite opposite in Old Irish or Gaelic or whatever it is."

At any rate, despite preoccupations with the damn' speech, he attended carefully to the salutes, and with punctilious geniality acknowledged every one of them. He then observed individually every person who failed to recognize and salute him; these failures somewhat distressed him. There were scores and scores of salutes and tens of failures; but had there been only one failure that one would have been the crumpled roseleaf in Andy's bed.

"You'll have to be thinking of a title, Sam," said Andy suddenly.

"My own name's good enough for me," Sam answered. Lord Raingo. Lord Raingo. Lord Raingo of – of what, Eccles? Perhaps. Rather good fun to forestall Andy in the use of the name of the district with which he had been so closely associated.

The dreamy poet, the orator, gave no reply.

At New Bridge Street one of the policemen noticed him, signalled to the others, and the whole of the traffic stopped instantly, so that Andy might cross in comfort to Palace Yard.

"I hate them to do this," Andy murmured. "But they will do it. I'd much prefer to wait with the others."

"Yes, you would!" thought Sam. "The false humility of the great man! The great Clyth waiting like anybody else for the policeman's gesture! Touching proof of the existence of true democracy!"

They crossed the road in a hush of whispers and glances. Everybody except the crudest bumpkins knew that the Prime Minister was crossing the road. The orator and poet saw nobody, nothing; absorbed in his mighty dream. Only he had a bright transient smile for the saluting policeman in the middle of the street. The schoolgirl, the nonentity almost trotting by the great man's side (for tall Andrew walked very fast) was wildly jealous of the great man's celebrity. Not a scrap of respectful attention for the nonentity; merely a faint curiosity as to who in God's name he might be! But they would know him – and soon!

Within Palace Yard the demeanour of the public was different. It was as if they knew all about Andy in Palace Yard. Even the gate-policeman's nod was a bit perfunctory.

"About a seat for you," said Andy. "Place'll be pretty full. I'll tell Poppleham to look after you, eh? But not the Peers' Gallery – yet, eh?" He smiled.

Sam naughtily resented the civil attention. Had he not sat in the House for years? Could he not look after himself?

"No. Not the Peers' Gallery. *The Press Gallery*," said Sam. "Seems the right place for the new Minister of Records – doesn't it?"

"But can you get in there?"

"I imagine I can. Au revoir." Dryly.

Sam had seen, and beckoned to, Lovesake, the sketch-writer of *The Daily Paper*; a thin, grim, grey man of fifty, with twinkling eyes and clefts under the chin and at the sides of the mouth as deep as ruts. He wrote in an ink of suphuric acid. Lovesake had been editor of a daily in the north which years earlier Sam had bought and sold over the editorial head. He had begged Lovesake to stay on, but the fellow had refused and called him a leper and worse names still. However, Lovesake was a man who understood the world and who could be just when his prejudices were not too strongly engaged, and Sam and he had remained on quite friendly terms.

"Look here, Lovesake," said Sam. "Get me into the Press Gallery, will you? I've got a reason; I'll tell it you before the afternoon's over, and you can use it how you like."

Some discussion. Lovesake swore he couldn't do it, and nobody could do it – on such an afternoon and at such short notice. But in the end he said:

"Oh, curse it! I'll wangle you in my place. I don't want to hear the old villain's disgusting patter. I'll fake up my sketch from your impressions." He laughed pleasantly enough, his eyes sparkled with fun. They ascended in a lift, and twice, before the ascent and after it, Lovesake had to perform feats of prevarication and persuasion, first with a policeman and then with a genial official in evening dress bearing impressive insignia on his bosom. The sketch-writer, obviously beloved of all, was marvellously and successfully persuasive; but neither the policeman nor the official had ever heard of the name of Raingo; which was rather humiliating for Sam.

However, he comforted himself with the thought:

If I told them what I was going to be – what I in fact am!..."

The schoolgirl again.

Sam glimpsed a shabby little refreshment-room where kindly, aproned girls were murmuring with reporters. The Press Gallery was incredibly small and incommodious; two rows of narrow seats with narrow desks in front of them. The reporters could neither have sat down, nor, having sat down, have risen up, if the desks and the seat-backs had not been hinged. A few men stood at either end, and others were continually passing in and out. A horrible lack of space; no air, no repose, no ease. A tapping, behind, of Morse instruments. The gallery seemed to be framed in elaborate wood-carving whose sharp points Sam felt on his head and his shoulder as, after ages of waiting, he squeezed himself, and was squeezed, into a front-row seat next but one to the end. He realized that Lovesake had done a miracle for him. He had no right to be where he was, save the licence bestowed by tradition on millionaires. Lovesake had his sharp knife into the abstraction of millionaires, but even Lovesake was disarmed at the sight of a concrete specimen of the hated class. Millionaires were haloed, and the nearer you came to the centre of power, the more brightly shone the halo. So it was.

16

THE SPEECH

The house lay below the future Lord Raingo. He was revisiting the glimpses of the moon, and felt very nervous and excited. Had he not got a ticket for Paradise in his pocket, he would have been humiliated to witness again, from this secret perch, the scene, so familiar and so strange, where he had failed and failed and whence he had fled in bitter, beaten mortification. But now he was uplifted, patronizing, scornful. His thought ran: "Thank God I've done with all that!"

Above, caged in the Ladies' Gallery, he descried a fashionable woman with a complexion well-tended but withering.

"Good heavens! What orientalism!" he scoffed, as if orientalism was peculiar to the miserable House.

The gallery opposite him was packed; the side-galleries were half full; the floor of the House was packed, a dozen or so members seatless and standing. He recognized many, very many, and many others he did not recognize; either they were new or he had completely forgotten them. The thing had the unreality of a play; with all the old, remembered gestures – the awkward bowings to the Chair, the slouching, the restlessness, the turning over of papers, the soundless whisperings, the deliberate histrionic attitudinizings.

There on the Front Bench lounged the gang, with Andy in the midst, and Tom Hogarth forcibly gesticulating to him. (Had Sam estranged Tom?) Every member of the luncheon party was present, except of course Lord Ockleford and the Colonial Premier, who were both conspicuous in the galleries; schemers, plotters, intriguers, formidable all…

Loud cheers startled Sam, who had been looking at the Ladies' Gallery, and idly wishing that Delphine was there. Andy was on his long legs; Andy was facing the music. Andy surveyed the assembly challengingly, defiantly, showing his upper teeth; and yet he had dignity, too, as befitted the greatest man in the world. The cheering ceased as though from fatigue and an uneasy sense of insincerity. Every eye in the House was on Andy, except those of his adjacent colleagues, who were too proud to be seen looking up at him in expectation. The House, deeply aware of a terrible occasion, was cowed, apprehensive, frightened, and very self-conscious. The British Empire had its back to the wall. Huge destinies were in the balance, one against another. The bewildered sheep on the floor of the House seemed to yearn towards Andy for comfort and inspiration.

Sam felt his heart beating, and he despised his heart for being perturbed. Andy had begun, and the grey-haired reporter next to Sam was pencilling hieroglyphics as conscientiously and stolidly as though he were setting down a speech at a Royal Academy banquet. For him, the reporter, Andy's oration was so many words in a certain order, and arbitrarily divided by time into sections of equal length. Sam perceived immediately that his boyhood's enemy had looked upon the audience and seen that they were simple sheep, and was treating them accordingly. Phrase after phrase Andy gave them, and they baa'd in unison. "We are fighting for all that is most sacred in our national existence." Loud cheers. "Our men retired, but were never routed, and once more the pluck of the British soldier, which refuses to acknowledge defeat, has saved Europe." Loud cheers. "It is idle to imagine, as some very light-hearted people seem to think, that we have got an unlimited reserve of man-power in this country" – and Andy looked round for anyone daring enough to question this profound and subtle truth. The sheep grew grave and watchful of themselves, as if saying with awe: "This man is a realist, and is bold enough to disclose to us unpleasant facts which it is supremely important for us to know. We too must be realists."

"Yes," whispered a voice behind Sam – it was Lovesake's.

"And if he told 'em that two and two made four they'd cheer his remarkable insight like hell."

"Yes," Sam murmured back. "He's putting it over."

"Hsh!" complained the reporter, who was strenuously coping with Andy's delivery.

"Sorry!" Raingo handsomely and humbly apologized.

But Andy, it appeared, was not after all doing very well. His voice, silvern when he was inspired, became rasping when inspiration failed. It was rasping now. There was no conviction behind his verbiage, and no reasoning. He would throw men of fifty to the tyranny of sergeant-majors, he would desolate homes and destroy businesses, merely because he had willed to do so and without advancing any serious argument whatever in support of the policy. The sheep were a little restive. He lost himself in some figures; colleagues were prompting him; he was in a regular mess; but he listened only haughtily to his anxious colleagues, then calmly dropped the matter, thrust away the tangle, and proceeded to his next point. It was the wisest course in the circumstances, but much strength and cynicism was needed to adopt it.

Sam admired Andy in this hour; nay, he liked him. Andy was the greatest fighter of them all. He had no scruples, no sense of justice or of decency, no loyalties; his cynicism was dazzlingly intrepid; he would have sent his carriage to the funeral of a man he had secretly assassinated. But he could fight and keep on fighting; his energy and resource were without end. He could not be beaten even by himself. He was not to-day in vein, his chief weapon, original rhetoric, had fallen from him; he had a foolish cause to defend. But there he stood, the embodiment of the will-to-win! Not a drop of English blood in him, but there he stood, dominating and bullying hundreds of pure-bred proud Englishmen. He was a fine sight to Sam.

"Power!" thought Sam. "I have had power myself; but it was nothing compared to this power."

And he longed for this power, knowing that he could never have it, but absolutely resolved to get a kind of power nearly equal to it, to blaze somehow in the public eye by the light of his great deeds, and to encounter the most puissant ministers among his future colleagues on level terms. Andy had inspired him.

(He did not care a fig now whether or not he had estranged Tom Hogarth.)

And then there was a wild, protracted storm of cheering from one side of the House. In addition to employing men of fifty to win the war, Andy had proposed to make assurance doubly sure by applying conscription to Ireland. The cheerers, however, had suddenly forgotten the war. To conscript Ireland was an end in itself, an act of justice, an act of righteous revenge. Soon not a soul in the House cared twopence about the war or about all or anything that was most sacred in the national existence. The chamber rang with cheers and howls; and Andy had to wait. He waited disdainfully. He resumed, and was assailed and supported at every sentence. He said what he had to say and sat down in silence. Not a cheer. Not a baa from the sheep. And then, after a dose of oil from a veteran, Irish oratory was loosed, furious, brilliant, ferocious, murderously passionate. Andy scarcely listened; he smiled. The sheep ran out in droves for a division in which Andy got a majority of over two hundred. Another division; a still higher majority. A third division and the second reading of the Man-Power Bill was overwhelmingly carried. The absurdity was going steadily forward to fruition.

Andy had gone, sure of the result. He had not triumphed, but he had won. His speech had reached the ends of the earth. It was causing reflection at Kaiserlich Head-quarters. It was making men of fifty to tremble, and the wives of men of fifty to weep; and people were saying that, in view of the peril to the Empire, they would not go to the theatre that night. In short, life was rather serious.

Lovesake had departed from the Press Gallery. Sam went also. He met Lovesake in Palace Yard.

"This true about your joining the Ministry, Mr Raingo?" asked Lovesake.

"It is," said Sam. "I was going to tell you."

He walked off. Andy must have given out the item.

17

The Lobby

The Incurable schoolgirl, in girlish curiosity, was on his way to inspect, at a safe distance, the House of Lords entrance, which he would soon be using as familiarly as though he had never used any other entrance. But on this occasion he did not reach it, because he was accosted by a little vivacious man who with bent head and a cigar between his teeth, and hands behind his back, was contemplatively strolling. The little man happened to raise his head.

"Hello, Raingo!" Sam hesitated. "You don't know me from Adam." There was no resentment or disappointment in the little man's low voice.

"Yes, I do. You're Rebbing. I remember you quite well, but it's how many years since I saw you? You're in the House now, of course. Went out and got wounded. Now do I know you from Adam or don't I?"

They walked together. Years earlier Francis Rebbing, then extremely young, had been sent down by the Central Office to make a few electioneering speeches for Sam. They had not met since. They were both pleased at the encounter.

"You've been hearing the show?" Rebbing asked.

"Yes. I was in the Press Gallery."

"Oh! The Press Gallery. What did you think of it – I mean the show?"

"Much the same as you do," said Sam.

Rebbing gave one of his free, jolly laughs, which transformed, but only for a few moments, his earnest, pondering, resolute face.

"I've never forgotten one thing you said to me during that election," said he, gazing up at Sam's head.

"Ah?"

"Yes. You said that the only mischief with democratic politics was that you had to govern people at their level, not at your own."

"Bit obvious that, isn't it?"

"Possibly. But it didn't seem so to me at the time, and I've never forgotten it."

"Well, said Sam, patting Robbing's shoulder familiarly." That's flattering. That's really flattering, that is. I'm not like other folks. I'm highly susceptible to flattery, especially genuine flattery. You do me good."

"I must go back," said Rebbing. "Come along with me into the Lobby."

"All right."

Sam beheld again the strange, dark Gothic interior, better fitted to be the scene of a romance-mystery by Mrs Radcliffe than the gossiping place of hundreds of high-minded statesmen, their suitors and their masters. Sam, standing apart with Rebbing, his back to the throng, glimpsed a little drive of members rushing in a body from somewhere to somewhere else. Suddenly he saw the place with a new imagination, as if, while deeply intimate with it, he had never seen it before. Members were always driving in droves to and fro, through refreshment-rooms, terraces, libraries, smoking-rooms, and grim, conspiratorial passages. Or else they were asleep. Bells were always sharply ringing, commanding instant, blind obedience. Had he not heard members asking: "Look here. Which lobby do I vote in this time? Ayes or Noes?" That was the life of the common member in this theoretically royal palace. Sheep, scurrying forward at the onrush and yelp of the trained dog!

"Yes," Rebbing was saying. "He was very well received, at first, but a few idiots can make a devil of a lot of noise. Non-idiots never cheer or make any sort of a row. Did you ever hear such cheers as when he proposed Irish conscription? But Irish conscription will never go through in this world. He's bound to drop it. And even when he's dropped it, he won't get the Bill through this week, as he swore he would do.

He may have a safe two hundred majority, but he daren't use it until he's given us an extra two days for debate, *and* he knows it!"

Sam thought that the quiet, eager, determined young man of forty was perhaps somewhat unduly teaching his grandmother Sam to suck eggs. But he admitted to himself that the had been forgetting the noisiness of fools and the silence of the other kind. There was, there must be, a considerable leaven of wholesome sagacity in this mob. Indeed, he had always known there was. Only his political failure had obscured the fact for him.

"So you're going into the Ministry," said Rebbing quietly. How characteristic of him not to have burst forth about the news immediately on meeting Sam!

"Is it abroad already?"

"Yes, it's all abroad."

"Well?" Sam waited.

"I'm glad, very glad," said Rebbing, more quietly than ever.

Sam was enheartened. He became a good man inspired by high resolves, because a good man appreciated him and believed in him. He would work to earn the approval of the silent ones. Yes, his life had lost its direction for a space, but now the direction was found again. He had had a great talent, used it, and succeeded. He had another talent; he would use it, and succeed once more. Beyond everything he wanted the morrow to dawn.

"Heard how Budstock is?" asked Rebbing.

"Budstock? Who's he?"

"Your predecessor," said Rebbing, with a faint, ironic smile.

Sam blushed. In two days the man whom he was succeeding had never been mentioned by anybody; and Sam had totally forgotten him. Sam tried hard not to blush, but he blushed – so disturbing were the implications of this swift oblivion.

18

Berkeley Street

Sam entered the Berkeley Street service-flat, his London home between six and seven that evening and he had had no tea. When in Essex he always thought of the flat as agreeable. And by comparison it was, because you knew where you were in it, and could, sooner or later, get things done for you. But, absolutely, it was a poor, mean affair. Four rooms (plus a bath-room), three of them dark, and none of them very large. Fusty, musty, grimy, impersonal, undistinguished; no better, really, than a suite in an hotel – in fact not so good. There was life in an hotel; but here was no life. The flat, like Moze Hall, was quite unsuited to his income and to his desires, and he had tolerated it for several years.

Of course the war rendered simplicity of living a virtue. But that was not the reason which had established him in the flat, nor which kept him there. The reason was Adela's lack of interest in domesticity, her dreaming self-absorption, her mental habit of living discontinuously from moment to moment. It was her business to give him adequate homes; he would have been able to inspire her in the habit of home-making, but he could not carry out the enterprise himself. That was the woman's job; he could not take it from her, and moreover he certainly did not want to take it from her, and moreover he certainly did not want to 'appear in a feminine role and look ridiculous. No! The job was Adela's; she hadn't done it, never would do it, couldn't do it; and so it wouldn't be done.

He threw down a copy of The Evening Standard on the table in the dining-room, which absurdly was also the hall. The news was in The Evening Standard. He walked from room to desolate room, turning lights off and on. Adela was not in. God knew when she would be in; it might be eight o'clock. He rang a bell, for tea, and sat down in the dining-room. Not a flower in the whole place! He would say to her, gently, when she arrived: "Couldn't we have a few flowers here?"

Then he heard the lift and the lock. The door opened. Adela! Adela with parcels and a bunch of assorted flowers in white paper. She had a disconcerting faculty for taking the wind out of his sails, for putting him in the wrong. She seemed sometimes to divine his criticisms in advance and forestall them. Not only was she home early, but she had brought flowers!

"You here! All alone?" she murmured pleasantly.

"As if we were always having crowds of callers!" said Sam in his mind, but not unpleasantly.

She came up to him and kissed him, looking through him in her dream. In a moment she had littered the room: wonderful how with so little material she could do it.

"I thought you'd like a few flowers," she said, subtly inferring that for herself she would not have troubled to buy flowers – but of course was she not always thinking of him?

"It was a good notion," said he.

Evidently she had not heard the news. She would be capable of passing through forty streets and never noticing a newspaper placard.

The waitress entered the room. Adela glanced at her with latent hostility.

"Yes?" she questioned.

"I rang for some tea," Sam explained.

"Oh, haven't you had your tea, dear? I've had mine. Some tea for Mr Raingo, please."

Now, thought that hypercritic, Samuel Raingo, the first idea of some women in these circumstances would have been to inquire whether their husbands had had tea, and even if they had had tea themselves they would have said: "I'll have another cup to keep you company." But not Adela, whose brain was never visited by such romantic ideas.

No sooner had the waitress left the room and was shutting the door behind her than Adela called:

"Waitress! *Waitress*!"

The woman returned, rather sullen; she was always being summoned back in this fashion.

"Just put these flowers in water, please. And distribute them about the rooms."

In silence the waitress took the flowers. Could you imagine a house-mistress leaving the care and placing of flowers to a servant? Was it not the special prerogative and art of wives to see to the flowers? And Adela (by fits and starts) so interested in gardening too! Thus Sam privately.

"I say," said he, as she was proceeding to her bedroom.

"Yes, I can hear you," she answered, not stopping. "I'll leave the door open."

The difficult Sam made a movement of impatience, which he checked.

"I've been talking to Jenkin about Geoffrey," he called. "*You* haven't heard anything, of course."

She returned _ instantly to the dining-room, and this time with her grey eyes gazed at him instead of through him.

"No. I haven't. Who's Jenkin?"

"Who's Jenkin? He's in the War Cabinet. You know. He knows more about prisoners and so on than anybody in the Government."

He told her all that had passed, and she put a hundred queries.

"Oh, my *dear*! But this *is* good." She had been dragged out of her dream. "If they're cabling we might hear something to-night, mightn't we?"

"No. You couldn't hope for that. But perhaps in a day or two."

"But if they really are cabling?"

There she was, with the incurable bent of her mind, implying that Sid Jenkin had promised what he did not intend to perform: thinking the worst: she always would think the worst when it was a question of motive; always, always. She sat down; no doubt she had already forgotten entirely her mission to the bedroom. But somehow Sam was touched by the naivete of her passionate maternal instinct. He saw her as she had been over twenty years earlier, with Jeff spread out on her knees. She had been an incompetent, withal dangerous mother; but indeed a mother, indeed a tigress with a cub.

And she looked exactly the same now as then – not aged by the world's contacts. She inspired respect and pity. Ordinarily she was as inhuman as a fay; but now she was human to the point of pathos. Sam wanted to see Jeff back safe and sound; he wanted it very much; he was tremendously fond of Jeff and proud of him; he probably had thought of Jeff oftener than Adela had done; but when Adela thought of Jeff her heart and mind were white-hot with emotion.

19

Dinner

Sam knew that he must tell Adela the latest political news. He hesitated on the brink of doing so, perhaps from diffidence or shyness. It was not that he feared to disturb her mood; for he might have shot the news at her before any mention of Jeff, and surely ought to have done so. It was that the news was so enormous – he could not tell it naturally; he had a feeling akin to shame. Queer! He positively had to brace himself to tell her the news.

"Well," he said at length, clearing his throat. "I'm going to be Minister of Records, and they're giving me a peerage because I told 'em my heart wouldn't stand an election and all the rumpuses of the House of Commons."

He was so self-conscious that he could not look at her, and when he did so he reddened a little. Adela turned pale. She was much moved, and could scarcely believe her ears.

"Well!" she muttered, in a high, thin tone, reacting after her fashion to what was by far the greatest surprise of her life. And she walked out of the room.

"She's as put about as I am," thought Sam.

"Sam," she called presently from her bedroom. Her voice carried with extraordinarily penetrating clearness. It would have been a terrible, torturing voice had she been of a nagging disposition, but she was not.

"Yes?" He hated these conversations between rooms; they seemed to him so undignified; yet somehow she always had dignity; also at times he copied her habit of them.

"Shall I have a coronet? Do I wear one?"

"Ask me another!" he replied grimly.

What a question! Good God! What a question! But she never had any sense of the order of importance of things. It was not that she was specially interested in gewgaws; quite the reverse, though she might be a snob in certain directions. It was simply that she had happened to think first of a peeress's headgear. He did not like it, forgetting in his self-righteousness that his own mind more than once had dwelt uneasily on the subject of a peer's robe. The chief fact, he said to himself, was that he was to be a Minister, not that he was to be a peer. But he did not say to himself that he too had been thinking more of the peerage than of the exalted office.

The waitress brought the tea and went out with four empty vases.

"And Geoffrey will be the Honourable," said Adela, coming back to the dining-room. "Let me have just a sip of your tea, dear," she said, standing close by his side.

He was amazed at this gesture. Well, the scene was strange, he thought, very strange.

"You're fearfully clever, Sam."

"I'm not at all clever," Sam protested. "I told the P.M. what I knew you'd think about things, and he immediately offered me a peerage."

"Oh! So you brought me into it!"

"I did!"

"But you never told me anything about it."

"My dear girl, you know perfectly well I told you yesterday at lunch the P.M. had sounded me about the Ministry."

"But you didn't say anything definite."

"Here, have some more tea. I didn't say anything definite yesterday because there was nothing definite until to-day – until about four hours ago in fact. I had to go to the House. The PM asked me to. And then from the House I came straight here, and I've told you." All which, while fairly accurate, was ingeniously disengenuous. But Sam was always apt to be a bit secretive.

"I see. What title shall you choose?"

He had been sure that she would ask that. About his department, his Ministry, the nature of his duties – not a word!

Just like her! She would put last things first. But his attitude towards her, if censorious, was not unbenevolent. It was made kindly by his joyful pride in the brilliant situation. He felt kindly towards all the world. And she had sipped his tea.

"What do you think of the sacred name of Raingo for a title?" he suggested, with intimate playfulness, looking up at her.

"That ought to do," she agreed.

"Well, if you think so, it's hereby settled then," said he, reflecting that he was using her with all due consideration.

"I do wish I'd been presented when I was a girl. Seems so odd me being presented for the first time at my age. My great-aunt was anxious to present me, but mother thought it wasn't worth the expense. If I'd known – "

"Ah!" said Sam. "But you didn't know."

He was like a benignant god. And in calm contemplation he beheld her past, not comparing it enviously with his own, nor snubbing it with the sneer of the self-made.

The waitress entered with the vases full of flowers.

"We shall dine at seven-thirty," said Sam to her. "Will you bring the menu?"

He did not consult Adela. He was being benevolently masterful, because she had womanishly sipped his tea. He gave her the evening paper with the news in it under a two-column head-line on the first page.

"Yes," she remarked. "He knows the war will soon be over, and so he offers you a post."

Now this was surely an astounding, unjust and indefensible remark. How had she come suddenly to decide that the war would soon be over, seeing that never had the Allies been in a worse pass, and that the war could not possibly end until the Allies had won? Yet Sam himself had had the notion that the war would, in some mysterious way, soon be ending in an Allied victory. But of course he privately condemned the notion in her. She had not the right to form such a notion. As for her aspersion upon Andy's motives, he could only shrug his shoulders at that perversity. The fact was that her mind had positively not developed since she was eighteen.

"I wish the war *would* soon be over!" he exclaimed. This was not true.

The domestic evening developed in a manner quite unforeseen by Samuel. In the middle of the *tete-a-tete* dinner, during one of the absences of the waitress, Adela jumped up, protesting against the girl's disposition of the flower-vases.

"Now do sit down," said Sam mildly. "This dinner isn't a passover."

He detested restlessness at a meal, especially on the part of the mistress of the house; and Adela could never be still. She had no sense of the proper formalism of a meal. Admitted, she moved with dignity, but the act of moving was undignified.

"Now do sit down," he repeated, imploring rather than commanding.

She ignored him; probably she had not heard him.

"The woman might have known – " she said coldly, and swept away a vase into the drawing-room, bringing another vase therefrom for the table. Before she could set it down, the waitress had returned, and saw her. Not content with this performance, Adela picked the vase up again, took it into her bedroom and put a third vase on the table. The waitress glared.

"Damn it all!" Sam was about to explode, but he restrained himself and smiled instead.

A trifle perhaps, unworthy of the notice of a statesman! But to Sam it was an awful symbol, typifying the future, as well as the past. She had after all no imaginative vision of a great event. Were not Lord and Lady Raingo, a Minister and his consort, dining together for the first time? She had never been a good hostess. Would she be equal to the position of Lady Raingo? Despite her strange, undeniable native authority she would not. She would infallibly make a mess of the position. She could not study the art of entertaining. If she entertained she would entertain untidily, raggedly. People would blame her and pity him, and ministerial dinners would be a humiliation. She would always be the same Adela. The title would be a mere ticket tied to her. Why had they no intimates, and hardly any friends? Why was his wealth futile and ridiculous? Because she would not nourish friendship. On such a night friends ought to have been dropping in or telephoning every few minutes. Nobody had dropped in, and only two men had telephoned – club friends who had no knowledge whatever of Sam's home life.

In that moment Sam relinquished part of his new ambition. Adela was hopeless, hopeless. He bore her no ill-will. His mood was magnanimous, for he had accomplished a great deed with Andy; and he was launched on an heroical voyage. So he forgave her. He even forgave her for having made not the slightest reference to his duties, to the nature of his role in the Government. All the evening he had waited for her to show some sign of curiosity on the immense subject. True, he had never in his life talked business with her or encouraged in any way curiosity concerning business. But this was not business. It was above business. However, he forgave her.' She was born thus and thus, and she was, of course, entitled to her indiosyncrasy – could not rid herself of it. After -dinner he said that he had to go out, and he went out. It was a night on which he might well have to go out. She was quite bland and full of equanimity. A world to herself!

20

The Club

He walked down St. James's Street to the Club. Searchlights were as usual probing the dark firmament over the darkened streets, but there appeared to be no sign of an air-raid. Policemen stood nonchalant. The city was timorously hoping for a quiet night. How unspectacular Sam felt, he, the King's Minister and peer-to-be, as he slipped like a common clubman out of St. James's Street into Pall Mall. Surely there ought to have been something to distinguish him from the common clubman! But there was nothing.

He had to justify to himself his visit to the Club; a Minister could not stroll casually into a club for lack of occupation. Ministers had a reason for all their goings and comings. Well, he could justify himself. Among the members of the Club were two cronies whom he knew by report to be on the staff of his Ministry, and who were said to dine at the Club almost nightly. He would meet them at the Club, he would join them in the smoking-room after dinner and chat with them quite informally, as member to member, without the least trace of ministership in his demeanour, but rather as one modestly anxious to pick up wrinkles – such wrinkles as officials of a Ministry might properly give to a new chief in the sacred confidential privacy of a club, each individual being absolutely sure that no wrong use would afterwards be made of anything said. The cronies would be flattered, and Sam would be edified, and word would get round that the new Minister promised to be pleasingly different from other ministers.

Nobody in the gloomy tessellated hall of the Club; nobody in the balconies above! Sam looked through the great sheet of plate glass into the long coffee-room, which had islands of lamplight here and there. Several waitresses standing in everlasting patience; one cashier at the pay-desk! Not a table occupied! After nine o'clock in the evening the Club seemed to be deserted. Yes, one table at the extreme eastern end of the room was occupied; he could see it by craning his neck. The cronies occupied the table; Drakefield, the youngish lame man in uniform, and Crawshaw, a middle-aged thin man. They were leaning across the small table towards each other, as though fearful lest their close secrets might be overheard by waitresses a dozen yards off.

Sam decided that he would wait in the hall until they should emerge from the coffee-room, and then either follow or precede them up the stairs into the smoking-room. He could not disturb them at dinner; he could not even accost them on the way out; they must first see him and nod and perhaps congratulate him. True, he meant to be pleasingly different from other ministers, but there was such a thing as ministerial dignity. He waited and he waited, obscure in a corner of the hall. He saw island after island of light vanish from the coffee-room. The coffee-room door swung open, and he jumped up ready, but only a waitress appeared. He peeped again through the plate glass; the cronies were still eating. He suspected that the hall-porter had an eye on his curious proceedings, and he walked straight upstairs. The great smoking-room was in darkness; club economy in the matter of electric current!

"I've had about enough of this," he said to himself, impatiently. The empty Club was getting on his nerves. He could not await for ever the tardiness of the damned cronies. He had done what was decently possible, and he was entitled to leave. In leaving his conscience was clear, except that he had the sinister sensations of a foiled conspirator. On the pavement outside he pretended to himself to wonder what he should do next; but he knew what he would do next.

He had telephoned twice to Delphine during the late afternoon, once to tell her the news and to say that he was not yet sure whether he could see her in the evening, and once to say definitely that he could not see her in the evening. It was a sense of the fitness of things that had decided him not to see her that night. He had thought that on such a night he owed something, if only a formality, to his wife; and also, unless abroad on business advantageous to his official position, it was meet for him to be at home in case of a message or summons from the Prime Minister. He ought certainly now, in pursuance of this righteous policy, to return to Berkeley Street. And yet he was well aware that he would not return to Berkeley Street. From the moment of setting out for the Club he had been surreptitiously hoping that the visit there would prove futile. Had he stayed long enough at the Club he could not have failed to encounter the cronies. He had found obscure and incoherent reasons for not staying long enough. Proof that Delphine had hold of him, and that the obsession of her was strong enough to cause him to be dishonest with himself and untrue to his conscience.

Here he was, a grown man, a middle-aged man, a man of importance and renown, a Minister with grave responsibilities, slinking off in the dark to join a young mistress who was simply nobody at all, in a dubious interior which his wealth and his passion had created for her. Incredible! And he was unfaithful to his wife, and he saw the doors of the Divorce Court ajar for him, and ignominy awaiting him in his sixth decade. Not that he felt himself to be in his sixth decade. He felt young, absurdly so, and he approached Orange Street with most of the sensations of youth. An hour in the society of the unique, soothing, tender creature, was worth a million risks. Besides, he was safe. He cast off all fears and responsibilities, and as he unlocked the entrance to his second London home and with habitual movements lighted and climbed the stairs, he gave himself completely to the thought of Delphine.

"Delphine." Softly. "Delphine." More loudly.

He went into the sitting-room, the bedroom, the bath-room, the tiny kitchen. Delphine was out. He could not surprise her by his arrival, nor hear her exquisite tones of joy at the surprise. His gloom was instant and intense. He roved from room to room, fiddling with switches, and desolation filled his heart. He sat down, picked a cigarette out of a coloured glass box and began to smoke. He was old and silly. Why had he entangled himself in such an absurd and mediocre liaison? He was in physical as well as mental pain. Now, Sam, no ridiculous, senile jealousy! You are a youth. You have confidence in your own masculine qualities. You must remember what a foolish figure you cut two evenings ago with your jealousy and your evil thoughts. She may have gone out on business connected with her sister Gwen. (Fancy having a bus-conductor for an unofficial sister-in-law!) Moreover, why shouldn't she go out? Is she to stay at home continuously lest your sublime highness may call even after he has said that he will not call? Is she to have no activity apart from you? Preposterous. You are pre-eminently a fair-minded man, Sam, and you readily admit that these questions can only be answered in one way. Of course.

But his desolation was not in the least relieved. He remembered that, at the second telephoning, he had had a suspicion of a suspicion of hearing a male voice in the background of Delphine's calling perhaps a word that might just conceivably have sounded like "Savoy." Silly suspicion of a suspicion! He had smiled at it to himself. It had not really troubled him, because it was too perfectly fatuous. And even now, as he sat smoking in the easy chair in her silken bedroom, it was perfectly fatuous. He knew Delphine; his trust in her was illimitable. And yet! And yet! How grotesque is jealousy; it has no roots whatever in common sense! Sam rose and walked again, peering round, with half a disgusting intention to spy and pry and ferret.

A drawer in the writing-desk in the sitting-room was not quite closed. He opened it; full of papers. He pulled out a paper at random. It happened to be her birth-certificate. She was born in 1889, at Hackney. 1889? She was therefore twenty-nine. Whereas she had told him that she was thirty-two. Ah! She had wanted not to seem too young for him. A woman over thirty is a suitable mate for any age. Unique example of a woman exaggerating her years! Touching! But was it touching? Was it not an indication of a deceitful habit of mind? He did not know what to think.

So he imitated his wife and thought the worst, and left the flat hurriedly.

In the dim street he glanced up and down, shamed, guilty, as though fearing private-inquiry agents, or even police-detectives. An entirely silly apprehension, and it showed his state of mind. He was not anxious about what he had done, but about what he was immediately going to do.

21

Jealousy

He walked off, bound for the Savoy. He, the dignified statesman, had yielded to the insane desire to search the Savoy for an erring mistress. He had had to yield. He realized the madness of the scheme. Supposing – a monstrous supposition – she was there, what could he do? Make a scene in the crowded Savoy, drag her away, he, the chief figure in that night's newspapers? Or just watch her from a distance and then retire? On the other hand, supposing she was not there, her absence would prove naught, would not allay his jealousy. Nothing could allay his jealousy. Never before in his life had he been jealous. Adela had frequently, in her incalculable way, gone off to spend evenings in town out of his sight, and he had not had a qualm, not a shadow of misgiving. But now he had discovered in himself the devil of jealousy; it had appeared, after lying hidden for a lifetime, and it was raging furiously within him, and he could not control it; he had absolutely no command over it.

"What a fool I am. What a dangerous fool! What a criminal fool!" he exclaimed. "Why don't I walk straight back to Berkeley Street? I have a heavy day's work before me to-morrow."

But he was crossing Trafalgar Square; he was in the Strand; he was passing what had once been, and would be again, the Hotel Cecil. He was in the Savoy approach. Still time to return to sanity and Berkeley Street. No, the sheeted doors of the Savoy revolved for him, and he was in the brightly-lit foyer, with vivacious figures moving to and fro, and vistas of glowing restaurants and sounds of music; a glittering, gay world curtained away within the dark, discouraged London world.

"I am mad! I am mad!"

He went direct and rapidly down the steps and into the restaurant cloak-room. Ordinarily he used the cafe cloakroom. The head of the cloak-room stared hard at him, as he stared hard at every man of apparent importance, took his hat and coat, and would not give him a ticket in exchange.

"That'll be all right, sir."

His lineaments were stamped for the night on the highly specialized brain of the head-attendant, and the compliment of getting no ticket would mean afterwards a shilling instead of a sixpenny tip.

As he left the cloak-room a man, entering, nodded to him.

"Hello, Raingo."

The man, whom he could not identify at the moment, looked at him curiously, half ironically, as if saying: "So you're the new Minister, are you?" but made no remark.

"If he guessed what I'm here for!" thought Sam, and went boldly down into the restaurant, which was crowded, chiefly with uniforms, girls, and foreigners of all sorts. The strolling, mysterious Italian manager of the restaurant recognized him.

"Do you want a table, my lord? Can I get you a table?"

Astounding fellows, these supermen of the great hotels! No wonder they received the salaries of ministers! ' "No thanks."

The manager bowed and passed on his rounds.

"My lord." It was the first time he had been so greeted, and the greeting was premature, but what a sensation it gave, even in his misery! He heard the echo of his wife's voice. "Shall I have a coronet?" He satisfied himself that Delphine was not in the restaurant. She might be dancing. Did they dance at the Savoy nowadays? If so, where? He would not inquire. He had known that she would not be in the restaurant. And he knew that she would not be dancing. She would be, if anywhere, in the comparative discretion of the grill-room, to which he had first taken her, and which she preferred to any other of the public rooms. He had only gone to the restaurant in order to postpone the crucial moment. He went back to the foyer and turned to the right, and looked into the grillroom.

And almost the first person his feverish eye settled upon was Delphine – there in the middle of the big, half-full room, with a young officer. He could not for a few seconds believe his feverish eye. Terrible events happened in his brain. His jealousy was now incredibly justified. A minute earlier and it had been insane, and his visit to the Savoy insane. But now he was proved wise and to have acted wisely. Now he knew. The bowels of the earth had vibrated; the lovely temple in his brain was overthrown. The war was a dream, the Ministry a delusion, titles a game of fancy-dress.

The pair were drinking champagne. Someone must have told the Italian manager of the restaurant that the new Minister was to go to the House of Lords, for that part of the news had not yet reached the papers. Those fellows went about picking up items concerning the prominent; they forgot nothing; and they never made a mistake..." Secret Service money." He could plainly hear Andy's peculiar dry Scotch tone telling him that Secret Service money would be the source of his power. Comic! His head was full of unrelated scraps. The officer seemed poor, shabby, unaccustomed to money and to the environment. Perhaps it was she who was paying – with the largesse of her elderly admirer. Such transactions were not unknown; indeed soldiers had fallen into the habit of regarding them as quite ordinary and even proper.

He glanced away. He was terrified lest she should see him; it was as if he, not she, was the evil-doer; and yet he wanted her to see him. He glanced again at the table; he could bear neither to look nor not to look. The two companions were both in profile to him. And now he saw on her face, directed to the young man, exactly the same expression of ecstasy, adoration, devotion, sweet acquiescence as he had often seen on it when her eyes were close, close to his own. Was it an unconscious trick? Was it acting? Or was she merely promiscuous, with transient but genuine passions? He was a unique specimen of a simpleton, and all that he had ever heard to the disadvantage of women was true. He turned and moved off and sat down by himself in the foyer.

No place for a Minister, the foyer of the Savoy at night! What could be his excuse for sitting there alone? Was he waiting for someone? Ministers do not wait; they are waited for. Ministers do not go to meet people; people come to meet them. Was it imaginable that any other member of the Government would sit solitary at night in so exposed a place as the Savoy foyer? Andy for instance? Or even Sid Jenkin? He smiled grimly at the wild thought of the Earl of Ockleford exhibiting himself in the Savoy foyer!

Sound of distant music. American voices. The recurrent swish of the doors. The fingers of the clock moved. Tomorrow morning, so near, he would be entering the Burleigh Hotel, so near, the seat of his Ministry, to take charge, to exercise dominion – and to receive other Ministers in search of Secret Service money. "Certainly, my dear Hogarth, I needn't say I fully approve. I wish all schemes were as sound as yours – seems to be." Urbane, with a scarce perceptible sting in the tail. And if they didn't like the sting they would have to lump it. But all was chimerical, phantasmal. The fellow had, then, been to her flat, and had called out the suggestion "Savoy," probably from the other room, the bedroom! He could feel the impress and weight of her body as she reclined on his lap while telephoning to Berkeley Street.

But of course he was now being tragically absurd. He was not, and could not be, such a simpleton as all that. And all women were not alike. The beautiful, soothing, unselfish, modest girl was as straight as a die. Impossible that she should be otherwise. In his unconscious masculine egotism he was asking too much. Was she to have had no life before she came to him? She must have had friendships, poor as she was. A girl so good, so attractive, must have had acquaintances who were admirers. And she would be kind to them. Might not a man call on her? Was it a crime to sup *tete-a-tete* at the Savoy with a worn youth emerged for a few days from the hell of the trenches? He was utterly wrong; he was coarse; he had a foul mind. But was she a virgin when she came to him? Well, and supposing she wasn't? What then? What of it? Life was life. London was not Eccles. Was he going to add to his idiocies the idiocy of being retrospectively jealous? He had a broad mind. Yes, he had a Christian mind. Was he not continually, in secret, reproaching his wife for her tendency to think the worst? He must take hold of himself, drag himself out of this slough of vile morbidity into which he had weakly and odiously slipped. And all the time she was there, on the other side of the wall, drinking champagne with the fellow, caressing him with her black, voluptuous eyes and her blasted soft smile.

22

War-time

"I suppose you're here on secret service," said a quizzing, harsh voice.

Sam started at the phrase taken from his late thoughts. The speaker was the man who had so curtly accosted him in the cloak-room. Sam lifted his head, quite composed.

"I am, Sellings," he replied, with a calm, restrained smile.

The identity of Lord Sellings, once a guinea-pig director of one of his earlier companies, had suddenly occurred to him. An old, slim, grey-moustached, well-preserved man with a questing face. Sam despised him; but Sam's rule was always to be genial in the absence of any good reason for being the contrary. Moreover he was not ill-pleased to have somebody to talk to, though at the same time he would not have been ill-pleased to feast horribly in solitude on his evil thoughts. He could not explain himself to himself.

"So am I," said Lord Sellings, and sat down. Evidently Lord Sellings also wanted somebody to talk to.

"I've just been dining at the Babylon," he began. "Eight courses and nothing to eat. One course was asparagus. I had exactly four thin stalks. What's the good of these damn' things" – he pulled his meat-card out of his pocket – "if they don't mean something to eat?"

"Quite!" said Sam politely.

"Of course we gradually get used to things, and we don't realize how serious things are getting. I'm living in Hertfordshire, and I come up several days a week – I'm helping in the censorship – letters, and a nice place *that* is! I was doing a certain job in about an hour a day. They've taken it off me and given it to a chap who spends his whole time over it, and has three assistants and ten clerks – no, nine. Fool!"

"I'm not surprised," said Sam, with sympathy.

"I took a first-class season, and as often as not I have to travel third, with about ten others in a compartment. And d'you know you can't get a morning paper now down there? I should live entirely in town, but I can't afford it. My town house is shut. And you can't entertain unless you ask your guests to bring their own food. I ask you – what about it? Mismanagement somewhere. You mustn't tell me. I'm a member of four clubs. Can't lunch in 'em, too busy. And at night not a soul there."

"I've noticed that myself," said Sam.

"Oh, you have. But have you happened to go into the card-rooms? Plenty of chaps in the card-rooms. Oh, yes, the card-rooms are all right. But elsewhere – not a soul. Personally I don't gamble."

Then it was air-raids. The Viscount knew of two ladies at Putney who had lost their reason through the continued antiaircraft barrage in the last raid. They were now in an asylum. He had put a bit of money, though he had none, into a theatrical venture, and the cursed raid emptied every theatre in London – and would keep 'em empty because people had always believed that raids could only happen in certain phases of the moon, and the last raid had destroyed that notion… Sam was about to say that he had seen the House-Full boards out at two theatres that very evening, but he refrained.

The Viscount told of a friend of his who had actually seen men burning alive in kerosene tubs in the Nevsky Prospekt. Also that unless men were sent back to the land in *all* countries this year there would be a world famine in 1920. The experts, whom the Viscount knew, had proved it beyond the possibility of contradiction. In fact…

Sam heard a low voice. Delphine and her man were passing. Delphine passed within six feet of him. He was petrified. They disappeared down the stairs, no doubt to dance, if dancing there was.

"Yes. I agree," said Sam benevolently. "Things have come so gradually we don't realize how serious they're getting."

He would not trouble himself to argue with the old fool, who soon afterwards departed. He had discounted everything that the fool had said; but still there was a lot in what he had said. Who dared assert that in a few months men would not be burning alive in kerosene tubs in the Strand, and the Savoy transformed into a doss-house? Such was his mood.

He left the hotel, having been duly recognized by the head of the cloakroom. He was forth again in the dark, silent, deserted streets… She was purity itself, constancy itself. Her gaze could not have lied to him. Either what he demanded of a woman was that she should be an Oriental slave, or she was perfectly entitled to go out to supper with anyone she chose. Nevertheless these statements and this logic did nothing at all to mitigate his frightful, resentful misery. He thought of their first meeting, his glance, something in her glance, the flash of desire upleaping in his heart, the tea in the tea-shop. He cursed the King's Minister who, in the early evening of life, had with a few unconsidered gestures forged the shackles which had so ignominiously bound him to a girl, a nobody.

23

THE MINISTRY

The next morning, walking down from Berkeley Street to Norfolk Street, Strand, Sam wore a silk hat. With that and a black overcoat and clean white gloves and a tightly rolled umbrella and his middle-aged portliness, and the military carriage which he always adopted, partly by instinct and partly by intention, when approaching an ordeal, he certainly looked the Minister. His air was authoritative, even grim. But within he was just Sam Raingo, who still tasted the mediocre bacon which he had had for breakfast, and still felt the laces with which he had rather too tightly laced up his cloth-sided boots. For years he had not had a personal servant. The late-resumed habit of fending for himself, lost since his early twenties, and the resulting close knowledge of the resources and arrangement of his wardrobe, somehow rendered unreal the millions which by a special gift for that kind of operation he had conjured out of the bank-balances of other people into his own.

He had to find, amid the ornate terra-cotta of Norfolk Street, the Burleigh Hotel, seat of his new dominion. There it was; he descried the final "tel" of a tarnished gold sign. It stood on an island site, and looked neglected; the windows had blinds but no curtains, and gave glimpses of cheap office-furniture instead of the backs of toilet-mirrors at which provincial ladies would with naive self-complacency prepare themselves for exhibition in metropolitan resorts. One of many scores of decent third-class hotels in London; forlorn; depressing.

Three motor-cars waited at the main entrance, two of them in charge of uniformed girls; at sight of an important arrival the expression on the faces of both girls subtly changed, and their faces and their whole bodies seemed to be saying: "Such as I am, I'm here, and I think I'm worth looking at; and I'm the war." Sam would not see them.

His soul hesitated but not his feet, not for an instant, as he mounted the steps. He knew absolutely nothing of his Ministry, save that two members .of the Club were on its staff. Andy had told him nothing, given him no guidance, told nobody else to tell him anything. The Ministry had been handed to him to make what he could of it, how he pleased. Were his ignorance and his freedom the outcome of mere nonchalance in the highest places, or of the alleged national bias against co-ordination? Of course he might have put himself about to get knowledge; but he was too proud to do so.

"This is their policy," he thought. "Very well. I will begin at ten-fifteen a.m. (The Ministry shall have a quarter of an hour's grace, as it'll be my first visit.) Till then I will lie completely low."

He had not even telephoned to his Ministry to say that he might be expected. But that was Sam!

The clock in the entrance-hall showed twelve minutes past ten; it was, however, three minutes slow. A shabby old hall-porter was being harshly unhelpful to a handsome lady who tried in vain to woo his favour by her youth, her sex and her lovely attire. The hall-porter in his time had probably resisted thousands of such besiegers.

Sam, behind an impressive and formidable countenance, was saying to himself: "Now it's up to you, Sam." Delphine and the unknown young officer were in his consciousness; they were profoundly there; buried, crushed, suffocated beneath a great, gritty mass of resolution. They could not stir. They might poison the roots of his being, but they could not influence his conduct nor impair the fullness of his efficiency. The old habit of energetic command, weakened by years of inertia, came back to him in strength, and he exercised it first upon himself. An enormous undertaking awaited him, looming; he could deal with it and he would deal with it, more than adequately. All his talents grew alert within him. Love, jealousy, disappointment were powerless.

He was about to affront the hall-porter, and through him symbolically to stamp himself by one sentence on the entire establishment, when the old man caught sight of him, and after a delay of a tenth of a second was transformed into quite a different hall-porter, a deferential, eager, smooth-voiced creature anxious to forestall orders by obedience.

"Good morning, my lord."

"This is all right," thought Sam, and said affably: "Good morning."

"Girl!" cried the porter in a tone like a slap in the face, to a very young girl bending over a large packet of stationery on the hall-floor. "Girl!"

The child look up, started, and flushed.

"Take his lordship upstairs."

All the grimness had left Sam's features. He nodded, still more affably than he had spoken, to the hall-porter. He felt, and was, the embodiment of good-nature, knowing that he had made a favourable impression. He, the Minister, was quite simply pleased to have pleased the hall-porter, and with his natural modesty he forgot for the moment what a tremendous swell he was in that forlorn, carpetless building. It did not accur to him that within a minute at most the tidings would fly along the farthest corridor and penetrate through all the shut, labelled doors: "The new Minister has come."

He followed the girl to the first-floor. Should he speak to her? Better not. Too much benevolence might be mistaken for weakness. As she passed a door with "Mr Mayden" painted upon it, she knocked on it thrice, quickly, but without pausing on her way. Ten steps farther and she showed him nervously into a large, carpeted, well-furnished office-room, and left him there. He took off his hat and coat and hung them up, and poked the fire.

"I'm here," he thought, satisfied with the room. "I wish they wouldn't call me ' my lord ' – yet; however, it's a fault on the right side. I wonder what'll happen next. Perhaps I ought to ring a bell."

24

Mayden

He sat down at a great empty desk, and he was about to press a button when the next thing happened; the corridor-door opened, and there entered, limping, with a sidelong and rather apologetic glance, a slim man of youthful appearance in khaki.

"Do you remember me, Mr Raingo?" he began with a smile delicious enough to undo most men, and any woman young or old.

Sam jumped up, went round the desk, and shook hands heartily.

"So you're the Mayden on the door opposite! I noticed the name, but it never occurred to me... You belong here, do you? I'm delighted. Do you know, you don't look a day older – honest."

Mayden, when the war started, had been a rising star of the hotel-world; not an hotel-manager, but managing-director of an hotel-owning company. Sam had become very friendly with him during a protracted stay, for business purposes, at one of the Company's hotels in Manchester; and he had soon discovered that in the hotel-world Mayden knew all about everything, from buying wines and cigars and checking the distribution of linen to handling head-waiters and drafting annual reports for shareholders; and indeed that the man's timid and deprecatory demeanour was nothing but Nature's mask for probably the only English-born person in England who could teach Italians how to run an hotel.

Sam's practice was to begin interviews with inferiors by interesting himself in their affairs, and he soon learnt that Mayden had joined the Army Service Corps and within a year come home with a permanently damaged leg, result of an unforeseeable long-range bombardment on Lines of Communication. The cripple had the stars of a captain.

"And what are you here?"

"Secretary-General, sir."

"Why ' general'?"

"I don't know. I understood it was Sir Henry's idea – "

"Sir Henry Budstock?"

"Yes. And I don't like it. I should prefer to drop it."

"Drop the 'general'? Not at all. Wouldn't drop it for anything. Mushroom ministries must have mushroom methods. The War Office may be content with a mere secretary, but we'll stick to our secretary-general. Will you give me one of those cigarettes of yours – if they're still the same! Sit down."

"Tell me," said Mayden, lowering himself cautiously on one leg into a chair, "if you don't mind, how did my arrangements for your arrival work out?"

Sam burst out laughing, as cheerfully as if his existence had no dark sinister background.

"So it was you, was it? They worked out perfectly. The porter fellow recognized me at once and conducted the grand entry in style. I didn't know I was so well known by sight."

"Perhaps you aren't," Mayden ingratiatingly and contritely smiled. "But I didn't know when you'd arrive and I wanted to be sure of things. So I circulated a photograph – it's a dodge I instituted in our hotels for when we were expecting the great. People love to be recognized instantly."

"They certainly do. And you told the girl to knock three times on your door as she passed?" Mayden smiled again. "I say, did you get any official notice of my appointment?"

"No, sir."

"Then how did you know?"

"I only read it in the evening paper."

"The devil you did! Well, it's a great world, isn't it? Now what is the secretary-general supposed to do in this hotel r I know nothing. Nothing. Nothing."

"I'm supposed to look after the personnel, the building, and the stores. That's all right, of course. What I don't care for is presiding at banquets to Colonials and other foreigners – I only do it because Sir Ernest won't."

"And who's Sir Ernest, if I'm not being indiscreet?"

"Sir Ernest Timmerson. He's your second-in-command, sir."

"Oh, Timmerson. Yes, of course. Able fellow," said Sam cordially, though he had contempt for Timmerson's abilities.

"Very," Mayden calmly agreed.

"Now, let me hear something about the personnel, will you?"

"Two hundred and fifty-nine on the roll at present, including forty odd women, mostly young, some barristers, two bankers, three generals, I couldn't say how many journalists, two historians, seven professors, two heads of trusts

– call them captains of industry if you prefer it, a baronet, six or eight novelists and two playwrights, a musical critic, an art-expert, two actors, a bill-broker, two curators of museums; the rest are only gentlemen. Oh! I was forgetting. There are several poets. One of them's in charge of ' Cables,' and he's the most orderly and punctual person in the building – perhaps in any building."

"But this is the most wonderful Ministry that ever was," exclaimed Sam, hiding amazement beneath jocularity.

"It's the only Ministry I know anything about. But I dare say it is the most wonderful. Whoever invented the phrase ' Ministry of all the talents,' must have foreseen it. Everything comes true in the end. And naturally for ' Records' – "

"But what's the scheme, what the idea – the organization of the Ministry?"

"It is based on what we call the ' nationals.' I couldn't tell you off-hand how many nationals we have, but there's one for every country and colony – or most colonies. Each national has charge of propaganda in his own country."

"Foreigners, are they?"

"Not" at all. They're all British. But they're called 'Nationals' – I don't know why."

"You haven't told me who sees to the finance of the show."

"Ah! His name's Locker. You know, Locker & Locker – chartered accountants, Amen Corner. But he doesn't live here; he lives in another hotel up the street."

"Well, you might let him know I should be greatly obliged if he could come and see me this afternoon at four – if it's quite convenient."

"Yes, sir. Now there's a most important question, if you'll excuse me, sir. Who have you appointed to be your private secretary?"

"I haven't appointed anybody. Yes, yes. I know it's highly unusual, but mushroom, mushroom! What's more, I haven't got anybody in mind, either. Some likely chaps here, aren't there?"

"Oh, yes."

"Well, let's have a look at two or three of 'em, shall we say at twelve o'clock?"

"Separately."

"Not a bit. I'll see 'em in a bunch. Send me some notes about them in advance. I say, how did that fellow downstairs know that I'm going to the House of Lords? It isn't in this morning's papers."

"It's about – generally. Timmerson told me."

"When?"

"Yesterday afternoon."

"What time?"

"About three."

"Well, I'm dashed!" Sam added quickly: "By the way, who's the French national?"

''Mr Eric Trumbull. He's one of the gentlemen. Has a castle-on the Loire, and talks French as well as the French Ambassador."

"And the British national?"

"They're all British, sir."

"I mean the national for Great Britain."

"There's no national for Great Britain. We don't do any propaganda at home."

Sam appeared to reflect.

"Of course not. Not necessary. I wasn't thinking," he said apologetically.

All the time he was saying to himself:

"This fellow Mayden is exactly the same here as he was in his hotel in Manchester. He becomes at once what seems to be intimate. I haven't seen him for years and years. We haven't been together here a quarter of an houry and we're as thick as thieves! He has a marvellous manner, and he must know from experience that his manner is marvellous, though he's modest by nature. He's deferential and yet he's familiar. He has a sense of fun and enjoys it. I should say he's honest. He's very able, and he knows that too. His business must have made him a good judge of character. The question is, has he judged my character, as a Minister? I gave him to understand I was in favour of ' secretary-general.' Does he think I am? And does he really think I agree that there oughtn't to be a ' national' for Great Britain? I'm going to be the British national myself. Does he think I didn't notice how he told me first he'd first learnt about my appointment in the paper, and then that Timmerson had told him at three o'clock I was to be a peer? The news of my appointment wasn't in the papers at three o'clock. What impression am I making on him? It all depends how I struck him in Manchester. I rather suspect he took me then for a rather simple soul with a *flair* for money and nothing else. As if millions were made by *flair* and flukes! That may be his weakness. I hope it is. What I want here for the present is to seem a bit of a genial simpleton, a bit raw and timid, ready to swallow all I'm told and let sleeping dogs lie and so on."

"I suppose you'll see all the nationals in turn, sir?"

"Yes. And I'll start with Mr Eric Trumbull. But I'll get you to send me in the full roll of the staff to begin with. This place seems to be stiff with celebrities."

The telephone bell rang.

"Shall I answer?" Mayden half got up.

"Don't trouble. Let me inaugurate myself," said Sam, rising. And into the instrument: "Yes. Who? Yes. Speaking. By all means. At once." And to Mayden: "Sir Ernest is coming."

"I'll go then," said Mayden.

"I'm very grateful to you for all you've told me, and also for making straight a pathway before my face," said Sam, smiling humorously.

Mayden put his hand on the knob of the corridor-door, changed his mind and went out by another door leading into another room.

"Doesn't want to meet him in the corridor," thought Sam. "Thinks Timmerson may resent his seeing me first. Some coolness between them."

Like all self-made millionaires, Sam had in his working years developed an exaggerated suspiciousness; he was obsessed by "the underlying motive." In his subsequent years of idleness he had gradually lost a lot of this suspiciousness. It had now developed a second time, and very suddenly. The strangeness of what he had heard excited and invigorated him. He was happy, without reserve, at the prospect of chicane, putting force against force, and of ultimate achievement. Also he meant to stamp himself on the consciousness of the country.

"Well," he murmured aloud in the solitude of the room "Anyhow, this is something quite, quite new. My God! What a menagerie!"

25

Timmerson

Sir Ernest Timmerson, a man of about Sam's size and a little younger, had three things large: his reddish face, his grey moustache, his white collar and wristbands. His voice was somewhat squeaky, and marred the effect of a most distinguished morning suit. He entered the Minister's room busily, importantly, and as pompously as speed and a proper regard for his superior would allow. He had papers in his hand. In greeting the Minister he would have patronized him, had he not in spite of himself been restrained by the solemn thought of Sam's wealth. Sir Ernest was in the ordinary sense of the word rich. As the head of a paper combine, he had collected for himself half a million of capital, and he drew from the business perhaps fifteen thousand a year; but in the presence of a millionaire he likened himself to a tarpon swimming by the side of a whale; financially, he knew his place; his own riches gave him a better appreciation of Sam's than the common person could possibly have; for the common person a million is a mere figure, as the earth's distance from Sirius in miles is a mere figure; but Sir Ernest could realize the meaning of a million; moreover, he appraised Sam at quite several millions. Sam also, who had once been worth only half a million, could realize, better than a clerk or a successful barrister, the true importance of Sir Ernest's half-million.

With this visitor Sam kept away from the fire; the desk was the place for the pure functionary type to which Timmerson obviously belonged. Sam put a chair for his second-in-command.

"Please, please!" the second-in-command protested, pained by this condescension. They sat down opposite each other. '

"Well, my dear Raingo," said Sir Ernest, leaning back and stroking a thigh with one hand and lifting eye-glasses from nose with the other. "Quite apart from the fact that I think the Cabinet have made an admirable choice – if you will allow me to say so, I'm delighted you're here among us. I'm relieved. I've had sole responsibility here for three weeks now, and I'm very relieved to relinquish it."

"That," replied Sam curtly (but to himself)," is a thundering lie. You hate relinquishing it. You've had three of the happiest weeks of your life, and you resent my appointment." And aloud he said with a grave smile: "My dear Timmerson, I want you to understand, right from the start, that I count on you. You must know far more about this job than I do or ever can, and I shall always rely on your service. You say you're relieved. Well, so am I. I can't tell you how relieved I am to find that you are here. Don't think I'm trying to flatter you. I know you're above flattery." And to himself: "You'd swallow anything."

Sir Ernest waved away these compliments with curves of the eye-glasses in the air.

"I hope Mayden will look after you," said he. "He will," said Sam. "By to-morrow morning I shall have the machinery of this room in order."

"Quite. I hinted to Mayden what ought to be done, and I'm sure he'll do it. He takes things rather easily, but I must say he's reliable enough. By the way, there's this." He passed across the desk a document marked ' Secret.' "Of course it's been coming to me, but henceforward it will come to you, I need hardly say."

Sam had never before seen the word "Secret" on a document, and the child in him was thrilled. The paper contained the minutes of the previous day's Cabinet meeting. Sam read them at once. No mention of an offer of the ministry to Samuel Raingo!

"Um! Yes, yes. Just so. I had a long talk with Clyth yesterday,' he murmured casually, and dropped the paper, when he tore it up, took it to the fire, and burnt the pieces, and returned to the desk. "Safe side," said he, with a solemn face.

"Do you think that's best?" squeaked Sir Ernest, impressed.

"Well, there may be spies even here."

"Spies!"

"I hear there's a possibility – I've been warned." Sam spoke firmly. The gesture of burning had delighted his sense of humour, and to see Sir Ernest impressed gave him joy.

"Er – er – there are one or two matters on which I should like to take your decision," said Sir Ernest, recovering himself, but not sufficiently to enable him to discuss the surprising spy conjecture with any confidence.

"Whatever you think best, I shall endorse."

"Well, I happen to know a young fellow in one of the M.I. sections of the War Office, and he told me last night at dinner that an order had been issued at the War Office that no officer of his section – and no doubt of other sections – was on any pretext whatever to enter our building."

Sam had a strong impulse to burst out laughing at this piece of information. Had Mayden been sitting opposite to him instead of Sir Ernest he would without doubt have laughed heartily, and Mayden also; but he was restrained by the functionary's solemn majesty and lack of humour; he knew that by laughing he might prejudice himself, the Ministry, even the successful conduct of the war, and also he would outrage the feelings of a worthy man.

"What's M.I. short for?" he asked modestly.

"Military Intelligence."

"And was it yesterday the order was – er – issued?"

"Apparently so. That was what I gathered."

Sam had a vision of a few highly-placed fellows sitting together in the vast home of the War Department, clanking spurs, and cogitating how they could get one in against these infernal mushroom ministries that were multiplying all around and appropriating sacred, traditional privileges, and having the damned cheek to try to help to win the war. Too proud to be jealous, these brahmins, and yet as raging jealous as the rivals of a favourite concubine in a harem! Germans they could understand and respect, Austrians they could like, but these dirty outsiders, from interfering Andy Clyth downwards, they detested and hated. The order was probably a hit at himself – rascally company-promoting millionaire with no father, no public-school, no style.

Yes! And he had a wider vision – of every ministry, historic or mushroom, snarling at every other ministry, regarding every other ministry as an imposed evil to be suffered as little as possible and scotched as much as possible, and ferociously determined to protect its rights and its monopoly with the last drop of its blood. The only real war was in Whitehall; the war in Flanders and France was merely a game a sort of bloody football. Sam was amused, and without bitterness. It was shocking of him to be amused, but he was amused. He had been born without the precious faculty for righteous indignation. He thought simply: "This is what human nature is."

"It's a calculated insult to another ministry," said Sir Ernest.

The portentous personage showed that he was capable of genuine indignation. In a few months or years he had grown to love and cherish his own ministry. His voice might squeak, but it also trembled. And yet Sam knew that if Sir Ernest had worn spurs and worked in Whitehall he would have promulgated with zeal just such an order as that against which he was now protesting with all the power of his soul.

"Yes," Sam breathed mildly.

"The question is: What ought to be done?"

"I suppose you couldn't go over yourself and tackle 'em about it – have it out with 'em? I'd back you," Sam suggested. "Of course you agree with me that this spirit must be checked."

"Most certainly. If only for the sake of pulling all together in the war."

"I shall remember that ' if only' to my dying day," thought Sam; and said: "Yes."

"But," said Sir Ernest, "if I may say so, I think it would be better for you to go yourself. You're the Minister."

"Quite. But that's just why I doubt whether I ought to go myself. You see, if I go I shall have to see the Minister. A minister, I take it, must see a minister."

"Quite right! Quite right!" Sir Ernest eagerly concurred.

"And I'm not sure if I ought to trouble the Minister on what's after all only a matter of domestic, inter-departmental politics." Sam added to himself: "I'm catching the spirit of the affair rather well."

Once again Sir Ernest was impressed by Sam's ministerial deportment.

"I agree," said he reflectively. "But if that's the case, as it is, Mayden is the proper person to handle it."

The great functionary was afraid; he was intimidated by the overpowering prestige of the ancient rival ministry. He dared not, on such a mission, enter those granite halls and affront the grim bearers of oak leaves and clankers of spurs. Sam was sorry for him because he had given himself away, divulged the secret infirmity of his character.

"I doubt whether I should care to leave it to Mayden," he said. Sir Ernest snapped up the subtle flattery. "I tell you what. I'll have a word with Clyth before we do anything at all."

He knew that if he chose he could call the bluff of those fellows in Whitehall. Wait till he was safe in the House of Lords. For a moment he felt grim, revengeful, malicious. What a show-down he could stage the next time Secret Service money was wanted! Then he privately laughed. He would be a minister in the grand magnanimous manner. He would rise easily above inter-departmental strife. Besides, the order seemed to him to be trivial, comic, and he did not care a pin whether it was rescinded or not. The rest of Sir Ernest's interview with his chief interested neither of them; and presently, having settled his collar and his cuffs and his moustache, Sir Ernest departed, not ill-pleased with the new chief.

26

The French National

Mr Eric Trumbull, summoned the first of all the nationals to meet the new Minister, entered as one who had heard fearsome tales of his chief. Sam saw apprehension on his pale, refined face, was both pleased and sorry, and at once reassured him. He was a very tall man, as thin as a pole, and his necktie and handkerchief showed a certain desire to obtain harmonious effects of delicate colours. About forty-five years of age, he had been born an American citizen, but had lived nearly all his life in Europe, and on the declaration of war had enthusiastically become a British citizen – in order to help. His passion was the architecture and art of France, to the study of which he had given his whole existence, with no ulterior end of achieving fame by imparting his knowledge to the Anglo-Saxon in books. He had no trace whatever of an American accent and no Americanisms of manner. Despite nervousness, he was the very perfection of deportment. Sam soon gathered that he was rich, but belonged to the type which feels no interest in money so long as it has a great deal more than it can possibly need. He had never had to get money, nor to fight for anything except pictures in sale-rooms. His admiration for French civilization was boundless.

"And what have you got there?" asked Sam.

Mr Trumbull displayed a map of France, irregularly marked with red dots.

"I am establishing committees for British propaganda throughout France," answered Mr Trumbull modestly. "You will see, sir, that some districts are rather blank at present, but I already have committees in one hundred and twenty-three towns, and my ambition is to reach two hundred. I want that map to be red all over – except of course in the occupied territories. I think I shall do it," he added.

"If the war lasts long enough," said Sam, with a kind but enigmatic smile. "What are your committees supposed to do?"

"Well, sir, we supply them with material, and they use it in the way they think best, according to local peculiarities. Of course I often make suggestions to them. I happen to have travelled in every part of France. I've been wondering whether it wouldn't be a good plan for me to make a personal tour. I think I could promise that if I did that map would look very different within a few weeks. You see in the neighbourhood of Grenoble, which I know intimately, there is scarcely a dot. I could – "

"Um!" Sam murmured, stopping him by inattention, and pretending to examine the map with minute care. (What he did examine was the marvellously manicured finger-nails of Mr Trumbull's hand holding one side of the map.)

Here was yet another war, Mr Trumbull's own war, and the operations thereof were shown by masses of red dots. Every red dot was a victory, and Mr Trumbull hoped to win two hundred victories. Mr Trumbull had invented this war, and in the activity of his mind there was no other war; all the other wars were phantasmal for Mr Trumbull, who in a frenzy of military ardour having taken out his British letters of nationalization, was now by pertinacity and sheer faith daily fulfilling an honourable ambition. And withal he could find time to attend gloriously to his finger-nails! Mr Trumbull was no ordinary man.

"And what kind of material do you supply to these committees of yours?"

"Oh, all kinds. It depends – "

"Well, give me an example."

"Well, at the moment I am having prepared an illustrated article on English gardens. You see, the educated French have contempt for what we call here ' landscape gardening.' They think that a garden ought to be formal, as of course according to all tradition, French, Italian, Spanish, even German, it ought to be. They don't know that England possesses some of the very finest specimens of formal gardens in the world, and I intend to enlighten them on this point."

Sam could not completely hide his amazement. He thought:

"Somebody has gone mad in this room. Is it me? Here we are in the worst period of the worst war in history, and – and – !"

No, he could not continue even to himself. Mr Trumbull's own private war was too fantastically absurd to be discussed.

"But do you really think – " he stammered.

"That such an article will do good in the relations between the two countries?" Mr Trumbull loftily finished Sam's sentence for him. "Undoubtedly. Propaganda, if I may say so, is an extremely subtle enterprise. Whatever else it may be it must not be crude, which is another way of saying that it must not be direct. I venture to conceive that anything which increases the respect of the French intelligentsia – a very numerous class indeed – for us cannot fail to do good – and lasting good." Mr Trumbull spoke with firmness, with authority. He had ceased to be nervous. His refined, somewhat finicking tone exhibited, subtly, a certain condescension towards Sam; seemed to imply that he, Mr Trumbull, belonged to the intelligentsia, whereas the excellent and worthy Sam did not; seemed to be saying: "Here is another poor barbarian who does not understand."

Sam was rebellious; he forgot that Mr Trumbull was born so and was entitled to the idiosyncrasy of his individuality; he wanted to crush Mr Trumbull by the exercise of autocratic power and fling him into the street; he yearned to restore ordinary British common sense to her throne in the French department of the Ministry. But the autocrat was a little intimidated; the barbarian uncomfortably felt that possibly he was indeed a barbarian. Supposing that there was after all something in Mr Trumbull's superfine theories! Anyhow, Mr Trumbull, if subtly insolent, was without question subtly courageous.

"I say," Sam began in a new tone, pushing away the map. "You keep an eye on the French daily papers?"

"Yes, sir."

"You've noticed how Anglophobe some of them are?"

"I'm sorry to say I have."

"You've not tried to do anything about it?"

"Well, sir, what is there to do?"

"What about bribery? Is there a paper in Paris that can't be bought?"

Mr Trumbull did not quail for one instant before the terrible word.

"I should say there most decidedly was, sir. But in any case I have nothing to do with those methods. They're a Secret Service affair, and I have no information."

Sam spoke more gently:

"Did you ever make a collection of the most outrageous of these Anglophobe utterances that everybody seems to take as a matter of course?"

"No, sir."

"Well, I did. Here it is." Sam drew from his pocket a long slip of paper with cuttings pasted on to it. "Just read these."

Mr Trumbull, glancing at his chief with a new, uneasy eye, took the paper.

"Yes," he murmured, when he had finished reading. "Yes. Deplorable."

"I'd like you to have a good lively translation made of all that, Trumbull. By three o'clock. If you can oblige me."

"Yes, sir. I'll do it myself."

"I'll be grateful." And Sam stopped Mr Trumbull as he was leaving the presence. "You might get out a scheme for that tour of yours," he said with much geniality. His notion was to exile Mr Trumbull from England and especially from the Burleigh Hotel.

"Did I score or did he?" Sam asked himself, when he was alone. He could not definitely answer the question. He might exile Mr Trumbull with an almighty gesture; he might run British propaganda in France according to the dictates of British rough, bluff, common sense. But. was Mr Trumbull right with his sutleties, and was Sam in the way to be a coarse blunderer? Sam turned to the question of the ministerial secretariat.

27

On the Embankment

Between half-past one and two, after a morning of almost sensational excitements borne with praiseworthy exterior calmness, Sam had to satisfy an empty stomach. He felt lonely. He had not asked anybody to lunch with him; and of course nobody had dared to ask him to lunch, it being naturally assumed that the great man would have mysterious and important appointments in the highest places. So that he was left forlorn, hungering for companionship, and full of the envious, unhappy feeling that everyone in the Ministry had human ties except himself. Once more he was failing to achieve the dreamed-of ministerial ideal.

However, he managed to walk out of the building with brisk dignity, as one knowing exactly whither he was bound and what he had to do. But because he, in fact, knew neither of these things he dismissed the waiting car which he had allocated to himself, smiling very amiably at the tight-clad girl in charge of it, and turned smartly down to the Thames Embankment, where he could make a decision in peace.

Already he felt as if he had been in the Ministry for weeks. He had had practically no previous experience of administration except the administration of his own private affairs. For, although he had bought and sold vast undertakings, he had learnt little about any of them beyond what might emerge from a ruthless, critical examination of their books of account; and he knew that one might even for a brief period preside over the destinies of an industrial enterprise as Chairman of the Board and still remain ignorant of the daily human realities which were the material of its success. Nevertheless he considered that he had begun to get the hang of the Ministry, to envisage it as an entire organism and understand its mode of functioning.

He had selected a secretary, an assistant-secretary, and a nice, soothing, plump stenographer. He had mastered the system of "Minutes" which circulated from section to section, adding to themselves marginal notes in black and marginal notes in red, and which stood for all time as a record of what particular official had decided or suggested on a particular question at a particular moment. He had dictated minutes; he had dictated a letter. He had surveyed the diary of the conferences which apparently formed a large share of the activities of the Ministry. He had carefully read through the brilliant roll of the staff and had a chat with one popular novelist and with the austere, precise poet who was in charge of "Cables." Various other persons, male and female, had been presented to him, and he had had encounters in corridors. He knew what the interiors of the offices looked like; he was acquiring the vocabulary and idiom of the place; he was separating in his mind the cheerful from the grumblers, the willing from the unwilling, and those who could think straight from those who could not. A full morning, at the end of which he was saying to himself, as he reached the Embankment:

"*No!* New brooms must not sweep clean. *No*! New brooms must not sweep clean."

He saw the delicacy and the difficulties of his task. He saw "that he must moderate the eagerness of his ambition. He had supreme power, but there was no such thing as supreme power, and indeed all his wariness and force would be needed to prevent the nominal master from becoming the slave of the Ministry.

"Shall I lunch at the Savoy or at the Club? " he asked himself, hunger increasing. But he knew that he would lunch at the Savoy; the self-consciousness of the newly-appointed Minister would keep him out of the Club. Everybody would discreetly glance at him, while pretending not to do so, as he entered the Club coffee-room, and he would not be natural; he might blush. Besides, the cronies would be there – he had met one of them, Drakefield, during the morning – and they might expect him to sit at their table, and he positively would not sit at their table. He wanted to be alone and not to be alone, or he wanted to be with people who did not know that he was a raw Minister. But, on the other hand, the Savoy! The Savoy was equally impossible. He could not, after the previous night, bear the Savoy.

So he walked to and fro, secure from observation in the traffic, still persuading himself that he was undecided, and affecting to be interested in the phenomena of the thoroughfare. At any rate in the street you knew by a hundred signs that the country was at war. The contents-bills of the papers – printed, because of the paper-famine, on old sheets of the papers themselves, just as in former days at Eccles – proved that. Whereas within the self-absorbed Ministry – except for an occasional uniform – there was no symptom of war; all was administration, conferences, minutes, literary composition. In three hours and a half he had scarcely heard a mention of the war.

As he entered the foyer of the Savoy Grill he saw Sid Jenkin coming out of a telephone-box.

"'Ello, Sam," Jenkin greeted him. "I was just giving you up." This was the first time Sid had addressed him by his Christian name. Sam felt flattered, and disliked being flattered. "I 'phoned you at the Ministry, and they said you'd be sure to be either here or at your club."

"Oh!" said Sam, wondering by what right anybody at the Ministry was entitled to divine so accurately his views on resorts; but underlings by some magic always know everything about your movements.

"Yes. So I rang up the club. You weren't there. So I came here, and you weren't here either. Let's have a bite, shall we?"

28

Sam's Lunch

Sid Jenkin tossed his grey hat to a menial and, putting his thumbs into the waistcoat of his creased tweed suit, strode in front of Sam into the grill-room.

"I've never been in 'ere before," he remarked loudly.

Sam thought:

"Has Andy sent him to find out how I'm getting on?"

But he was glad to see Sid. Sid was the solution of the luncheon problem.

"*She* was there last night," he reflected, looking at a certain table as they sat down. But he tried to put the thought away from him, as being melodramatic or sentimental; the room must be only a room and the table only a table. Moreover, though the place was much fuller than on the previous evening, and though there were many women, of all sorts and all degrees of attractiveness, it was not under the sinister dominion of Aphrodite as at night; eyes were not speaking equivocally to eyes, nor gestures to gestures; colours were severer, languor was absent; the atmosphere was astringent, bracing, unfavourable to the mysterious works of the goddess. Further, the morning's work had had the effect of somewhat calming Sam's secret agitation and softening his resentment. And yet he was still in a dangerous state; the lava was still darkly boiling far down beneath the crust apparently so firm.

At a neighbouring table sat an old man, far older than Sam, with a youngish,' stylish woman. But the old man was sure of himself, had no visible consciousness of the difference in their ages; that was because he was very slim and moved his head and limbs youthfully; and Sam thought:

"I wish I was slim."

The desire to be slim was passionate in him for a few moments: such was his state.

The two Ministers received at first no attention whatever from the staff. Sid Jenkin, fretted by his sense of importance, grew restless. At last he called out sharply in a voice so loud that quite a number of people turned to look at the disturber of restaurant conventions. A shocked member of the upper caste of waiters sprang forward with a glance half soothing and half protesting. As if the caste had not already enough to worry them with the twice-daily performance of the miracle of the loaves and fishes, and the pain of asking important, wealthy customers to produce those humiliating food-cards!

"See here, mate," said Sid Jenkin, with a sudden smiling geniality that entirely nullified the sharpness of his summons: "My name's Jenkin. Sid Jenkin. I'm a member of the War Cabinet, and I'm expecting an important telephone call. See that there's no delay with the 'phone. And we want something to eat quick. 'Ave ye got any asparagus?"

The hieratic Italian bowed with immense respect, and respectfully greeted Sam, whom he knew by sight. In another moment waiters were fussing round the table like flies.

"I'm not expecting any telephone call at all," said Sid to Sam. "But it's a good way of letting 'em know who y'are. I 'adn't used to be so refined – I mean refayned. I'd tell 'em who I was, straight out. But I'm learning. Oh, I'm learning." He was obviously enjoying himself. He went on: "I'm the only member of the Cabinet as goes about freely. P'raps its part of my job. All the others keep themselves mysterious. Not my line. I've often said I'd come 'ere one day. And 'ere I am. I've worked on the coalface and gone 'ome black and 'ad me bath in me kitchen, and now 'ere I am 'aving a bite with a millionaire, and I'm in the War Cabinet and 'e isn't. What about it?"

Impossible to be offended by Sid's crudity. Nothing that Sid ever said ever offended anyone, and he would say anything and everything.

"This man is living in a wonderland," thought Sam, and he liked him the more for living in a wonderland. He had reached wonderland less by his brains – though he could make marvellously adroit and telling speeches in difficult situations – than by his individuality.

Sid wanted asparagus, and in due time he got it – six thin stalks were held to be a portion in the midst of a so-called food famine. He began to eat it with his fingers.

"I never use them things," he said, pointing to the special utensil for handling asparagus. "I find as it isn't done. I was dining with Ockelford t'other night, and he didn't use them. I only learnt about asparagus not long since, and now I make a point of losing no opportunity of getting used to it. I took some 'ome in a bit o' paper to my missus the night before last. ' 'Ere's a bit o' sparrow grass, missis,' I said. Slavey came in while I was eating it, and caught me picking it up with my fingers. Next morning she says to my missis, so missis told me, '

'Ow does master eat 'is sparrowgrass when 'e's out with company, mum?' says she."

He laughed. Sam laughed heartily. He guessed that Sid had ordered asparagus solely in order to give full value to the story. Nobody knew better than Sid the importance of introducing a good story properly.

"And why are you and I lunching together to-day, Sid?" Sam demanded quietly, but grimly.

Sid's eyes glinted.

"Well, lad, I thought as ye might like a bit o' moral support on your first day. I knew damn' well Andy hadn't given ye much."

"So he repented and sent you along, eh, to see how things were going?"

"He did not," said Sid, firmly and seriously. "But I told 'im I might look ye up, and 'e was quite willing. Ye know, Andy believes in ye. It was 'is own idea choosing you. 'E respects ye. 'E says he knows ye'll come through. 'E don't much like this peerage business, but now it's decided 'e wants it finished up quick. It's going to be in to-morrow's papers, perhaps in the Gazette to-night. 'Ow did ye get on this morning?"

'I got on all right," said Sam. "But how about the peerage business? What do I do? Who makes the first move? Do I? Has it anything to do with the College of Heralds? I'm quite ignorant."

"So am I. But listen here now. I shall be at No. 10 to-night. You come with me, and we'll put Poppleham or someone on to it."

"But surely the PM doesn't keep open house at night. I can't go unless he asks me."

"Rot!" said Sid shortly. "I'm like the old King of Denmark. I go about unattended among the people. Andy's like Lewis the Fourteenth. He loves to 'ave his court around 'im. And you're from Eccles too! And I might 'ave something to tell ye about that son of yours to-night. Oh! I've got it in 'and, trust me. I might 'ear any minute. You come along o' me to-night and you'll 'ear nice things about the Man Power Bill! Such a mess! Andy's furious. But you tell 'im just what ye think."

At that moment a waiter came up to inform Sid that he was wanted at the telephone. Sid was startled and his gaze questioned Sam's. While he was gone Sam argued with himself whether his dignity would permit him to go to No. 10 uninvited and as the protege of Sid Jenkin. He decided that it would. He wondered whether he dared to try to find out from Andy why Andy had waited till the year 1918 before enlisting the services of the man whom he so liked and respected.

"The old lady is seriously ill," Sid murmured very excitedly, returning. "Who?" "Mrs Clyth." "His wife?"

"Bless ye no! His mother. She's staying at No. 10 and she's 'ad one of 'er attacks – don't know exactly what they are. 'E worships her – fair worships 'er.

A fat lot 'e'll care for 'is Man Power Bill now! Look 'ere. I must slip off sharp. It's your lunch, isn't it?"

"Yes," said Sam. "It's my lunch all right. To-night will be off, then?"

"Of course it won't be off. 'E'll want everybody to call and see 'ow the old lady is."

"Very well, then. Ring me up. As far as that goes I've known Mrs Clyth for fifty years if not more."

Sam was impressed and a little disturbed by the almost violent effect on Sid Jenkins of the news about the old Mrs Clyth. He had a dim memory of her in the late seventies, and he seemed vaguely to recollect that even in those days the bellicose boy Andy had a special attitude towards her. Sam had completely forgotten her; had probably assumed that she was long dead; in the earliest days he had never thought of her as other than old. And here, across the immeasurable stretch of time and marvellous change, she was surviving – and so influentially! Sam was awed.

As he paid the bill, with a negligently magnificent tip, his soul went back to the narrow houses of Eccles, and the goodly virtues for which Mrs Clyth had stood and doubtless still stood. The susceptible fellow was inspired anew to serious and wholehearted endeavour. He regretted the idleness of years. He must do his very best with the Ministry; his methods might perhaps prove to be questionable to the old-fashioned, but his aims would be above reproach. He had ordered the French translation for three o'clock. He would be back in his room at a minute to three and at three o'clock precisely he would ring for Mr Trumbull.

29

A Table for Two

At the end of a very active ministerial afternoon Sam said a cheerful good-bye to Sir Ernest Timmerson on the steps of the hotel. Sir Ernest had almost fully recovered the sense of his ability to guide towards triumph not merely the Ministry but the entire operations of war. Sam had closely examined the financial system of the organism over which he presided: the secretaries had proved sympathetic. The two cronies of the Club had paid him a visit, separately. And in general Sam, though anxious to criticize himself and the Ministry adversely, had to admit that the day had been satisfactory. But he had, as he foresaw, been forced to adjust his ruthless ministerial ambitions to the plain facts of the interior of the Burleigh Hotel; a process which pained him at first, and soon afterwards gave him a pleasing relief. He perceived the folly, and also the impossibility of setting the Thames on fire; he despised the simple Sam of the previous afternoon.

Further, he had a new feeling of responsibility, which frightened him. Several times in his life, in the midst of temerarious negotiations on a very large scale, he had been frightened by glimpses of ruin out of his left eye; but never half so frightened as now, after a placid initiation into his Ministry. The responsibility grew upon his mind; it was terrific. However, it had the effect of freeing him from the more general responsibility of a citizen. He said, lightly scanning the still formidable war news: "Ah well, that's *their* affair! I can't be bothered about it. They've got their job and I've got mine, and mine's all I can manage." He washed his hands of everything else.

At the flat the maid, who was tidying Adela's bedroom, gave him a message, in a rather melting, compassionate voice which implied all her hostility to Adela, that her mistress had failed to get him on the telephone and had returned to the country.

"Yes, I was afraid she might have to go," Sam lied, accustomed to Adela's vagaries and to the diplomatic task of making them seem quite natural and proper to the world. He liked the idea of being alone, but was apprehensive of what being alone might involve for himself.

The accumulated mail of the day comprised a considerable number of congratulations – some from people of whom he had not heard for years – and a few appeals for posts in the Ministry; also a letter, conceived in odiously submissive terms, offering either to make his peer's robes or to lend him robes on hire; also a thick green bundle of press cuttings, which he read with the greatest care and then put away in a drawer. He had nothing to do till half-past nine. There was no alternative but to go to Orange Street. It was Adela's fault. Had she stayed by him – instead of wandering off to the East Coast to discuss (with dignity) that peerage among her bridge-playing and golfing acquaintances – he would have stayed by her. But now he must positively go to Orange Street. Although he dreaded going more than he desired to go, he could invent no excuse for not going. He owed it to himself to go.

Night had completely fallen in Orange Street. He had the same sense of unwisdom and shame as on the previous evening – he the responsible Minister carrying on a liaison with a poor little nobody, etc. etc. – but to-night the discomfort of his conscience was intensified. It was intensified, strangely enough, by the thought of old Mrs Clyth and all that she stood for – all those forgotten standards of right and wrong. What would old Mrs Clyth think of him could she know? And it was intensified by the thought of his high resolves to do his very best in the role to which he had been called. And lastly it was intensified by the thought of the years – especially the war-years – which he had spent in idleness, sulking, yes, sulking! He was alive now; he was born again. Was his new life to be soiled...horrid, silly, sentimental! He must go, because in Orange Street he had a responsibility, not only to Delphine but to himself.

He furtively unfastened the door and climbed the flights of stairs. And he trembled for the upshot of the visit. He was far more perturbed than when, two nights earlier, Delphine had locked the bedroom door behind her. He hesitated on the landing at the sitting-room door. Ought he not to warn her by some noise of his arrival! He always did so. Yet why should he? This was his home. She continually insisted that it was his home. She loved him to refer to it as his home. A man was entitled to enter his home as he chose. He opened the door quietly, and saw in the sitting-room a table charmingly set for a meal for two.

Jealousy leapt up furious and gigantic, and instantly killed everything else in his mind. It had lain there, growling, or in silence sullenly watchful from side to side, ever since the previous evening. Now it was rampant, and far more powerful than he could have imagined. The sensation of its tyrannic mastery was appalling. The Minister was dead; righteous aspiration was no more; shame was no more; old Mrs Clyth was a silly legend. This girl then – had she the damnable impudence to arrange to entertain her young officer in Sam's home? Did she count so surely, and with that lack of the sense of danger so characteristic of women, upon the absence of her lawful lover?

He had not written to her; he had had no communication with her since the brief talks on the telephone twenty-four hours earlier. What exactly had he said to her? He tried to recall the very words. Certainly he had told her that he could not come on the previous evening. That had been quite clear. But had he said with equal clearness that he could not come on the day following, or had she understood him to say as much! That was it: she had got the thing wrong on the telephone; and she was relying on his habitual cast-iron adherence to programme. Was the young jackanapes with her now in the next room? He took off his overcoat – gesture symbolic of a boxer tripping for a dust-up.

Hats and overcoats had to be hung on the landing. There was no place for them in the poky little hall itself. Not a foot of space to spare! Here was a grievance against her. Why should his chosen and spoiled mistress insist on living in two rooms, plus a preposterous dwarf kitchen and ditto bath-room, with a half-time domestic, when she might have had every luxury of space and service? She had given the war as an excuse for her obstinacy. War be damned! She would have shown the same obstinacy had there been no war. Because she was like that! Adela had no ambition, and Delphine had no ambition. He supposed that a man always, by some unfathomable instinct, selected women with the same characteristics! He had read that somewhere. He did not see the monstrous absurdity of his idea. No two women could have been more different from one another than Adela and Delphine. But for Sam in that moment they were alike.

Having disposed of his hat and coat, he returned into the room. And immediately afterwards Delphine appeared.

30

Dinner

She had a tray in her hands and was wearing a foolish, fluffy white apron, about the size of a fig leaf, a stylish, alluring conventionalization of a parlourmaid's apron. And Sam, even in his wrath, could not deny that it was indeed alluring. He was conscious of extreme agitation, and, beginning at once to act a part, he winked slyly at her, as a man who has not a care and is utterly content. She smiled sadly – he could see that she was in one of her dark moods, put down the tray on a chair, clasped him in her arms, and kissed him. He did not kiss; his considerable power of acting would not go so far; he allowed himself to be kissed.

Here she was, round about him, with the amplitude of an epical heroine or a goddess, with her curves and' her bare forearms, and her fingers ringed in his costly jewellery, with her faint sweet odour, with her passionate, strong individuality burning secretly beneath a contemplative languor... She shut her eyes and kissed him. Well, whatever else she might be, she was a marvellous phenomenon.

Strange: jealousy had deprived him of the faculty of judging evidence; jealousy had nothing to do with reason, and it would not suffer the operations of reason. Ordinarily he could see and hear a person and weigh pros and cons, and bring to bear his experience of human nature, and arrive at a decision concerning the problem of that person which fairly satisfied him and which he would maintain unless and until further evidence persuaded him of error. But now he could arrive at no decision. He knew she was guilty; he fancied she might be innocent. He was convinced she was acting; it was impossible that she should be acting. Her demeanour implied one thing, but it also implied the opposite.

The sole certainty in the situation was that he was extremely, torturingly unhappy and fearful – as pathetic as an unhappy child. Yet he would not, if he could, have wiped her out of his life. The awful affliction which she caused was precious and vitalizing. To remove it by violence would produce a void still more excruciating.

"Is this for us?" he asked lightly, quizzically, pointing to the set table.

"Of course."

"But you didn't know I was coming."

"Yes I did."

"But I didn't know myself half an hour ago."

"Ah! But I *knew*."

She was another of your mystical women, with secret, psychic sources of knowledge. The frequently-proved unreliability of these sources never weakened her faith in them.

"I can't stay. I have to see the Prime Minister."

"But you must eat."

"Yes. I suppose I must eat somewhere."

"If you hadn't come I should have done the same to-morrow night. And I shall – every night, unless, of course, you say you *know* you can't come. You won't be able to go to restaurants so much now – I understand that. So I want you to feel there's always a meal waiting for you here. I'm just going to warm the soup. Everything else will be cold – but I think you like that."

She disappeared into the bedroom. In her absurd flat the kitchen could be entered only through the bedroom, and the bath-room only through the kitchen.

Alone, he saw clearly that his suspicions about the destination of the dinner were completely preposterous. She could not conceivably have been expecting anybody else. He had been wrong, and ridiculously wrong. The realization of this gave him ease for a moment, until he remembered – where was his presence of mind? – that the allaying of the suspicion about the dinner could have no effect upon the far more serious suspicion concerning her rendezvous at the Savoy on the previous night. The more serious suspicion remained intact and terrible, and nothing could possibly allay it. Why, if she was innocent, had she not told him instantly of her visit to the Savoy? Well, he must give her a chance... But of course she would not tell him instantly; it would be necessary for her to prepare the ground, so as to make the rendezvous seem the most natural thing in the world... Supposing she did not tell him! That would be the end of all.

She brought the soup in two bowls, one in either hand. She untied her foolish apron.

"Fold it up, darling, and hide it under the cushion of the easy chair." She smiled exquisitely.

He took the unimaginably flimsy thing – part of herself – and did as he was told. A damnably clever notion of hers for quickening intimacy! Guilty, she was determined to surpass herself in the craft of ravishing him. They sat down. Stretching out her arm she extinguished one of the lamps. There were moments when, despite the courage of her beauty, she loved twilight.

"Now tell me. You've been working too hard."

"No."

"But I say yes."

"How do you know?"

"Your eyes are tired. Oh! Darling i sensible."

"I shall be sensible."

"But will you?"

There was intense solicitude in her tone. But naturally she didn't want anything to happen to him. He was her support. She had no other. She needed his money to be hospitable to her *young* men. Horrible minutes! When was she going to tell him of her visit to the Savoy? Would she tell him in the next sentence? Or the next after that?

She inquired minutely concerning his day. She rained questions upon him. But of course this was her old trick, the well-known feminine device of feigning an insatiable interest in the man and pretending that her own doings were of

I do hope you'll be the last unimportance compared with his great, enthralling works.

And also she was very discreet; they always were. Her curiosity was confined strictly to himself. She never referred to his wife; she would not worry him. As for Geoffrey, he had had no opportunity of telling her about the hopeful rumours concerning Geoffrey. He replied to her questions rather grudgingly, but lightly.

Did he feel anything wrong with his heart? Was he sure? She made him promise that he would see his London doctor every week. But he promised as it were under duress and did not hold himself quite bound. When, if ever, would she tell him about her visit to the Savoy last night?

The meal was attractive. After the soup, fish mayonnaise. A cold chicken, entire. (How had she wangled that?) A salad. A fruit-tart. A creme-caramel. A tiny cheese in silver paper. Some claret. She must have got everything ready cooked at some stores. He drank the soup, but only coquetted with the fish. The chicken he looked askance at. She was alarmed.

The fact was that beneath his light demeanour he was too miserable to eat. His appetite was gone. To swallow made him feel sick. She came round the table to him, put an arm round his neck, speared a bit of chicken on a fork and enchantingly offered it to his mouth. He had to accept it. Another exquisite gesture; but of course all part of the siren business. When would she make up her mind to tell him about her visit to the Savoy?

He asked about Gwen. Oh! Gwen would be all right. Gwen was to have a situation in a shop at Kingston. She did not encourage his curiosity about Gwen; nor, later, about her canteen work. His state grew worse. Time was passing; he foresaw the moment when he would have to leave her without having heard a word from her lips about the visit to the Savoy. He could not bear to contemplate that moment. He refused to contemplate it.

31

Washing-up

He took a cigarette. In a second she was striking a match for him. He pulled himself together for a supreme histrionic effort, and, smiling at her through the smoke, with the cigarette between his lips, he said to her casually and agreeably:

"I hear you were at the Savoy last night in the grill-room."

She had not told him. He had had to force her to an avowal. His happiness was for ever ruined.

"Yes," she answered, with a sudden note of sadness in her voice, but unhesitatingly and simply, "I did go. For supper. With a man I used to know. He started in the ranks, but he's just got a commission – he didn't want it, only he thought he oughtn't to refuse it. He's going back to the front to-night again. I met him just outside in the street here. Yesterday afternoon. I asked him up. Of course I had to tell him I was secretary to a company. That was just before you telephoned to me the second time. In fact he was here when you telephoned. If you'd telephoned a bit later I shouldn't have gone with him because I shouldn't have known you weren't coming. I wondered whether you would think I was rather queer on the telephone. But you see him being here, in the room – I had to be careful, hadn't I?"

"You certainly had," Sam agreed.

She had given him an account of the affair which at any rate fitted the true facts so far as Sam knew them. But why had she not told him earlier? And why had she offered no explanation of her failure to tell him? Would she ever have told him, had he not compelled her to do so? He was too proud to ask her for the explanation of her secretiveness. There might be a good one, or at least a plausible one, but he could not bring himself to demand it. He waited. She seemed thoughtful, and said nothing. His suspicions were somewhat lulled, but assuredly not killed. Women in her case were so clever, persuasive, so skilled in wearing the mask of innocence.

"Who told you I was there, Sam?" she questioned, again quite simply. "Is there anybody knows I know you?"

"Ah!" said Sam, roguishly and benevolently, raising a finger. "Wouldn't you like to hear? Well, nobody told me. I saw you there myself. I had to go to the Savoy on some business, and it just happened I saw you – one glimpse. I was sitting in the entrance hall and you and your friend went past me. That was all."

Naturally he would not tell her the whole truth. Part of what he told her was true, but it was highly misleading. While expecting perfect candour from her, he held himself justified in having misled her; for he was still by no means convinced of her candour. She had beyond any doubt deceived him, for instance, as to her age. Perhaps from a fine motive. But perhaps also from a base motive. She might have argued with herself that had he known her to be as young as she actually was he would have turned from her before it was too late, in a fright at the immense difference between their ages. In his mind suspicion bred suspicion at a tremendous birth-rate.

"Darling," she murmured, sitting down plump on his knee, and burying her nose in his cheek. "You don't object to me going out like that, do you?"

He put his head back and looked her in the face.

"*Object!*" he chid her, kindly. "Of course I don't object. Why should I object?" He hated her to suppose him capable of so mean a thing as jealousy; he so large-minded, so much her superior! And he followed the train of thought by which he had excused her to himself on the previous night. "I should be awfully sorry if I thought you didn't consider yourself free to have your own friends and to live your own life. A nice thing it would be if I insisted on cutting you off from the world! What sort of a fellow do you take me for"

She kissed him in silence.

His own words had reassured him about his nice-mindedness and freedom from pettiness. He now wanted to believe in her absolute honesty, and he did believe in it, by an act of will; and by an act of will he drove away every suspicion. She kissed him again. Bliss rose: clouds of a delicious drug that sweetly overcame him. He thought: "I ought to fight this influence." But he would and could not fight it. A marvellous relief filled the whole of his being. He was happy. He became playful, and without moving his body drew the foolish apron from under the cushion.

"What's that for?"

"She must clear away the things. Stand up, please."

He tied the foolish apron round her waist, and she stood happily, eagerly acquiescent while he knotted the strings at her back.

"I suppose the charwoman washes up in the morning?"

"Oh no! I always leave everything straight and clean for her before I go to bed. I'm like that, Sam. I shall wash up after you've gone."

"Oh no, you won't, my lass."

"Why not?" '

"Because you'll do it now."

"But why?"

"Because I feel as if I should like to see you washing up."

She entered into his mood. He helped her carry the things into the kitchen, and then stood in the doorway between the kitchen and the bedroom and almost beatifically contemplated the movements of her splendid limbs as she worked. This was life for him. It was the summit of life for him.

"I do wish this war was over," she said unexpectedly, in a dissatisfied, gloomy tone.

He understood then the origin of the melancholy which he had noticed in her on his arrival. She was worrying again about the war.

"Look here," he said teasingly. "Do you want me to strike you, you chit? You can't have the entire earth. The war *will* be over. It's going on better now. And if you've got any other idea than that in your head about the war, pull it out and throw it down the sink." She smiled.

"Oh, Sam, you are funny sometimes! You almost make me laugh sometimes, you do. But you are silly." "Not so silly as you think," said Sam.

Then he told her the enormous news of the peerage; he had not mentioned to her before the probability of a peerage, because he always preferred to make his effects with sudden brilliance. And naturally he had not told her earlier in the evening while she lay under suspicion. Of course she believed the news, but she could scarcely credit it all at once. She had to assimilate it gradually. She was amazed, delighted past measure. At first she could not speak.

"And you standing there watching me wash up!" she murmured at length, regarding him as a god. She sprang forward, rubbing her wet hands on the foolish apron, and dared to kiss the god. The god become mortal.

As he was leaving she stopped him at the outer door. "I want to tell you something," she said gravely. Sam was afraid, of he knew not what. "Yes?"

"I love you. You're a terrible dear." She laughed with quiet glee.

But outside, on his way to meet Sid Jenkin, he kept on wondering what her earlier relations had been with the unnamed officer friend. He might have asked her, but as usual he had been too proud to ask. And why had he had to compel her to confess the visit to the Savoy? Why? Why? She was exquisite, but... Well, he had wanted to believe in her implicitly, and he had believed in her. He had fought on her side against himself.

On reflection he regretted his humorous remarks to her about the war. Though they had succeeded in their purpose, they were not in good taste, for they took no account of the daily torture of millions of young men, including Delphine's own promoted ranker. Of course it was the thought of that youth returning to the horrors of the front that very night that had induced her gloom. Was he, had he ever been, anything to her?... Still, she always had a general tendency to gloom: sometimes it came near to melancholia: a defect in her. So to-night's gloom might have been general and not particular.

He wished he had told her, what he had heard on authority at the Ministry, that no air-raid was expected to-night. He hated the idea of her all alone in the house during an air-raid. But she would have it so. She would put wet cotton wool in her ears and lie under the bedclothes and wait. Sometimes she would go off to sleep thus. There were certainly people with an instinct for solitude. He was aware of an extreme tenderness for her.

32

The Image of Mrs Clyth

As Sid Jenkin and Sam rang at No. 10, Downing Street that evening, the door opened and a visitor was shown out.

"Hello, doc!" Sid greeted him. "I must have a word with you."

"You must come with me in my car, then. I haven't-a moment," said the other briefly, after a slight hesitation, in a slightly nasal voice – a voice of authority which matched his mien and which evidently belonged to a man to whom ministers were not a bit more impressive than plain persons.

"Right, doc!" Sid agreed, in a surprisingly serious, acquiescent tone. And to Sam: "Shan't be long."

The doctor eyed Sam for half a second in the dim light thrown from the interior of the house, and walked quickly to a waiting car, Sid following. Sam had to enter No. 10 alone; he was annoyed to find that he felt nervous thus suddenly deprived of Sid's high protection and sponsorship. The grave welcome of the butler's manner somewhat reassured him.

The butler suggested finding Miss Packer, and Sam followed him through the arcana of the house. Two minor members of the innumerable Government came down the stairs and Sam met them on the landing. The greetings showed reserve. Through an open door Sam glimpsed and heard the martial Tom Hogarth haranguing and hammering at two Staff Officers whose red-tabs were no protection against him. Tom paused for half a second as he caught sight of Sam, but gave no sign of recognition. The urbane Poppleham came down a passage playing the perfect Prime Minister's private secretary to two very self-assured and rather noisy ladies whom Sam did not know. The house seemed to be strident or murmurous with conspiracies.

Miss Packer was not in her room, but she appeared outside the door of the room in which Sam had originally breakfasted with the Prime Minister. She wore evening dress, and might almost have been called effulgent.

"I'll see," she said softly and mysteriously in her blanched voice, as she shook hands.

The next moment Sam was delivered into the breakfast-room, which that night Andrew Clyth was evidently using as a lair. Andy was lounging with bent head in an unassorted easy chair in front of the fire.

"How is the dear old lady? I thought I'd just look in to inquire," said Sam, with apparently intense sympathetic solicitude, as he advanced quickly towards the chair.

Andy moved and lifted his head as if out of a dream. He was wearing the velvet coat; his silver hair was in disorder, and he was both unkempt and unwashed.

"My dear fellow! My dear fellow!" said Andy emotionally, raising his hand to take Sam's. "This is most kind of you. I appreciate it more than anything. And I like you to be from Eccles. Such a relief from all those finicking Londoners. Doctor's just been. I hardly dare think she's over it, but the doctor says she is. At first, at the beginning of the attacks, they always warn me she cannot possibly get over it. But she always does. She's a marvellous woman. So quiet and gentle, you wouldn't think she had it in her to fight, but my God! – can't she fight!"

"I'm very glad," said Sam. "You know, Andy, I suppose I haven't set eyes on your mother for over thirty years, and yet I can see her as clear as anything. I always thought a great deal of her."

"And she hasn't changed!" Andy exclaimed with animation. "She hasn't changed! That's the astonishing thing. Sit down, lad. Draw that chair up."

Sam pulled a chair from the table and sat close to Andy. It was not a comfortable chair for gossip, but Sam was quite happy in it. There they were together, two boys, alone together in the half-lit room, with the image of an ageless old woman in their minds, a woman without ambition for herself and surveying the world kindly, lovingly, forgivingly, optimistically, from the threshold of death. All her character came back to Sam's memory. He felt himself to be spiritually very near to Andy. He positively liked Andy, had no rancour against him, and would have done anything for him. Old Mrs Clyth was in the room, a presence unseen.

Andy gave some particulars of the illness, and then, leaning closer towards Sam, he said: "I'll tell you something, Sammy. You know – you know when I was casting round for someone for Records, it was she who put you into my head. 'Why don't you get Sam Raingo?' she said to me. She always had a soft corner for you, lad."

"Did she, by Jove!"

"She did. It was like a stroke of lightning for me. And she gave her reasons too. How you were – well, this, that, and the other – I won't tell you what she did say, I decided instantly. I saw she was right. As far as that goes she's never wrong. She's uncanny. And ever since I see better and better how right she was."

They sat silent, religiously contemplating the venerated image within them. In that moment Sam could understand the worship of God. Here, then, was the explanation of his call to office. No chicane in it, no deep scheming! It was a mystical explanation. Never would he have divined it for himself. His appointment sprang from a favourable impression which, unknowingly, he had made when he was a youth, in the brain of an old lady who judged the fundamentals of character by infallible instinct. He was awed. He was ashamed of his sins. All the impurities of ambition, greed, vindictiveness, egotism, slipped away. The desire to do the very best he could in his office flamed and burned within him. He laughed at his weak heart; his weak heart should be his servant. His years dropped from him; he had the pure ardour of a boy. He could see nothing but the good side of Andy. Was not Andy the son of his mother? Was not Andy engaged in the most terrific task that ever burdened a man, and should he not give his very soul to the helping of Andy?

Yes, and should he not cherish Delphine with a tenderness far surpassing any compassion that had ever inspired him? He would make his relations with Delphine such that old Mrs Clyth herself might bless them! "And I'm fifty-five and a fat lump of a man," he thought, puzzled.

"I needn't ask you if you're getting on all right, because I know you are," said Andy, passing his hand over his hair, and smiling.

"Shall I tell you what worries me?" Sam answered. "And I didn't think it would."

"What?"

"The responsibility of the thing," said Sam. He was going to say "the damned thing," but the image of old Mrs Clyth chastened his tongue.

"Pooh! That's nothing. You'll soon forget that."

"Well, I don't know. I feel as if I shouldn't sleep very well to-night, any how."

"But do you like it? Do you enjoy it?"

"I suppose I do," Sam admitted, rather sheepishly.

"Of course you do. You were made for office. As for the responsibility, the work is work like any other work. It isn't a nuisance if you take pleasure in it. Can't be. And all this talk you hear about being only too willing to ' put down the burden of office ' is insincere nonsense. It makes me sick. Look at me. Look at my responsibility. I'm game for it. I love it. World-war and so on – it's wine to me, it's women and song to me, lad. There are no public worries. There are only private worries. If my mother's ill, the world-war can go hang, and I don't want to help it. It was only because I had a feeling mother was going to have one of her attacks that I didn't quite come off yesterday afternoon. I didn't, did I?"

"I think you came off very well," Sam said dishonestly, and at the same time he thought momentarily of Delphine.

"You did!" Andy clutched at the reassurance. "I'm glad. Very glad."

"Considering," Sam added.

"Considering what?"

"Well, the material you had to handle. Especially conscription for Ireland."

"Oh, we shall have to drop that. I knew before I had sat down."

"But nothing you said was received as well as conscription for Ireland. By far the loudest cheers."

"Yes, but whose cheers? What sort of cheers? I know that sort of cheering. I say, Sam," Andy's always changing tone was modulated into quite a nice key of seriousness. "Been reading that fellow what's-his-name's attacks in The Sunday *Times?"*

"Who? Oh, him! Yes."

"Pretty damaging, eh?"

"You leave him to me," said Sam without any hesitation, full of loyalty.

"Oh! You think you can. But they're fairly stiff, aren't they?"

"You leave him to me. He's in my department," Sam insisted, though he had no idea how he could effectively deal with the foremost military writer in Europe. He shook his head defiantly, challengingly. Andy smiled appreciatively, as at a good boy.

"I didn't say anything to you about salary, Sam."

"No, sir, and you'd better not, if you'll allow me to say so." He became inexplicably respectful, formal, in his repudiation of the notion of taking a salary.

"But there are others, for instance me, who can't quite afford not to be paid for their services."

"Then let them be paid, sir. I've no objection. But you'll never persuade me to accept a penny." There was a faint note of rancour in his voice.

"Enough said! Enough said." Andy yielded, pretending humorously to have been bullied.

33

BROTH

The door opened slowly and quietly, and Miss Packer entered, bearing a basin. There was something splendid and yet sinister in the spectacle of this elegant, majestic Juno playing the handmaid.

"She's asleep," murmured Miss Packer.

"Thank God!" Andy ejaculated with fervour, as it might have been at the news that all the German armies were driven into the Rhine.

"What's that you've got there?"

"Some broth, sir." She smiled aside at Sam, and then tenderly at the Prime Minister.

"I didn't order it. I don't want any broth."

"Please, sir," she pleaded. A hint of commanding and assured determination in her tone contradicted the "sir." Andy took the basin and smiled aside at Sam, rather foolishly. An odd domestic scene. Yes, it was clear that Miss Packer ruled the empire.

"I say." Andy stopped her as she was going out. "You might tell Mr Poppleham that I want him to see our friend here to-night."

"Certainly, sir."

"I say," said Andy, like a spoiled child, after noisily absorbing a mouthful of broth direct from the basin. "Just taste this, will you, and tell me if it really isn't bilge-water. I haven't used the spoon."

Miss Packer had gone. Sam took the basin on its saucer, thinking: "Prime Ministers are entitled to these caprices of behaviour, no doubt."

"Seems to me splendid broth. Scotch, of course." Sam licked his lips.

"Funny!" Andy murmured meditatively. "Whenever my dear mother's ill my sense of taste leaves me. Some obscure kind of nervous reaction, I suppose." He spoke as if secretly proud of such a reaction.

"Dashed if I don't have another sip!" said Sam half roguishly.

At that moment, as he was taking a second mouthful, the door opened and Tom Hogarth was seen looming in the shadow of the doorway. Sam turned.

"Here!" Andy exclaimed. "You needn't have all my broth, and you're going to upset the blooming basin if you don't take care."

Sam caught Tom Hogarth's blazing eye for a second. The man was thunderstruck.

"Come in, come in!" said Andy impatiently to Hogarth, rescuing his food.

Tom Hogarth obeyed, leaving the door ajar. Sam saw in a flash that Tom Hogarth was astonished and aghast at the degree of intimacy which existed between him and the Prime Minister. He, Sam, had been seen drinking the Prime Minister's broth. Sam felt triumphant. He comprehended that political power sprang as much from intimacy as from anything. The minister who was on a footing to share the Prime Minister's broth was on a footing to influence the Prime Minister with peculiar, perhaps unsurpassed, force. He had known the truth of the abstract principle, which was no more Oriental than Occidental. He now witnessed the concrete illustration of it in the new glance of Hogarth's eyes partly curious and partly respectful. And the situation had arisen solely out of the way in which Sam had first entered the room and greeted Andy, winning his sympathy at a stroke. Hogarth was evidently sizing Sam up entirely afresh.

Sam was delighted, but he was also alarmed – at the implied revelation of his own naivete in the political game. He had sat for years in the House of Commons, but rather as a solitary. He had been nominated to an occasional committee; he had attended Speaker's dinners, party dinners; he had listened to the harangues of whips, and of single-taxers and other monomaniacs, but of the inside of politics he had no practical experience – save in regard to the electioneering of his own party in the Midlands and the North and a little in East Anglia. This he did know, with some intimacy and understanding. Now, however, he had disturbing perceptions of factors of all sorts to whose existence he had scarcely given a thought. Similarly with the war! What did he know of the realities which underlay the appearances of the war? Nothing but what his common sense and his genuine knowledge of human nature could hint to him. And yet, without any initiation at all, he had been put in charge of an immense and delicate organism whose exploitation specially demanded the knowledge which he did not possess and which he must pick up discreetly, gingerly, bit by bit. He was fearful. He saw vague perils and menaces everywhere around him.

"Here's Tarporley," said Hogarth in a low voice, almost apologetically to this chief.

"Tarporley? Tarporley? Who's Tarporley?" the Prime Minister asked sharply, though he knew well who Tarporley was.

"You know – "

"Oh, one of the Military Intelligence fellows."

"*The* one. The newest broom." Hogarth shrugged his shoulders, placatorily, and laughed.

"What's he want?"

"Oh, nothing. He telephoned me he'd like to see me, and I told him to come here, and *I'm* through with him. He said if he might just meet you… I'll tell him he can't, eh?"

Hogarth knew his chief. There were moments when Andy could not bear not to be all things to all men. And especially he had an eye for careerists.

"Oh, well, if he's here – "

In ten seconds Hogarth came back with Major-General Tarporley. Sam noticed that Andy had slipped again into his unconscious trick of glancing sideways, or under dropped eyelids, to see what effect he was producing.

Four people were now in the room, and each of them was an audience, for Andy was always an audience to himself. He rose slowly and languidly, in the manner of a poet, exaggerating strongly the contrast between his own demeanour and that of the very smart, full-bodied military gentleman, all khaki, red, brass, steel, leather, and ribbons. He deliberately roughened his hair.

The general, cap under arm, bowed and clicked, and in a thin voice said something about "the honour" with excessive deference. He was in a state of super-plenary sartorial correctness. His thin chin was blue-black and as smooth, and glistening as ivory. Apparently he must shave, or be shaved, about every two hours. He looked as if he was all ready to descend into the lists for a mortal joust, which he would take airily, as a cup of tea. Sam thought of the hard, continuous labours of the batman whose patriotic role in the great war was to maintain General Tarporley in immaculate personal splendour.

Andy paid the general a poetic compliment and then said that he meant to pick the general's brains at the earliest opportunity. All was vague, non-committal.

"Do you know Samuel Raingo, the new Minister, shortly to be Lord – *what* did you say you were going to call yourself, Sam?"

"Raingo?" said Sam.

The two men bowed, measuring each other.

"You may be of use to one another," the Prime Minister added.

"Why?" thought Sam – and he would have thought earlier had he known his job, "it may be this chap – if not, one of his friends – who's made that order forbidding his people to enter my Ministry." He had a wild impulse to tackle the general on the spot about the order, but caution held him back. He would mention it to Andy afterwards. No, he would not mention it to Andy. He would deal with it himself when the chance came. He was convinced that not even the newest star of the War Office Secret Service could beat him in chicane. He assumed an air of modest and naive innocence, and smilingly said something artless. Tom Hogarth was marching up an down the room. What Sam respected in the oiled military dandy was the imperfectly concealed background of his excessive deference to the Prime Minister – a background of hard, uncompromising reserve, which Andy tried in vain to dissipate.

"Well, sir, what's your summing up of the MI merchant?" asked Tom Hogarth, twinkling, as soon as the general had taken leave.

"Tom!" said the Prime Minister, as if pulling up to the surface and exposing a subject which had been disturbingly sprouting in the depths of his mind. "Here's Sam says he won't accept any salary." He drank the broth in quick gulps.

"What do you mean, sir, won't accept any salary?"

"I prefer not to," said Sam sharply.

"Too high-minded, I suppose," answered Hogarth. And to the Prime Minister: "Of course he needn't *keep* it, sir. You won't object to him doing what he likes with it after he's got it; he could give it to the Home for Lost Dogs or the Hospital for Orphan Kittens, but I assume you'll insist on his taking the salary attached to his post?"

"Why should I, if I prefer to save the country the expense?" Sam demanded, and his own words seemed to ring false to him.

"The country be damned!" said Tom Hogarth, chuckling; and putting his thumbs into the armholes of his waistcoat. "It would be in the papers before you could say knife that Lord Raingo had nobly refused to take a penny of the poor distressed country's money – whereas the rest of His Majesty's Ministry were raking in the shekels in the usual manner. Inference obvious. You know you're only making a noise like a millionaire, my dear baron. It's easy for you – you're getting richer every year because you can't spend. But what about us? I'm a man that has to live on the country – I've nothing else to live on. I work sixteen hours a day seven days a week. My sole distraction is presiding at uneatable banquets given to or by profiteers and other common objects of the Whitehall gutter. I have to stand up every day of my life to be shot at. At the end I may just contrive not to be hung, but I'm certain to be thrown out of office – we all are – and I shall have to fight an election and no doubt lose it on what I haven't saved out of my salary, and I've two boys at Winchester and a girl at Roedean, and debts in every corner of the parishes of St. James's and St. George's, Hanover Square; and I'm to be made to look like a money-grubber because you're so stinking with riches you have to hold your own nose. I wish to God this war had bloomed in the eighteenth century. If I'd had my present job when Charlie Fox first entered Parliament, I should be making a million a year out of it. There's a lot to be said for the Augustan age. You can't give forth this noisy noise of yours, Sam. You aren't going to be allowed to. Of course, sir," he turned to Andy, "I'm speaking for myself alone, I needn't say. Naturally the decision rests with you."

Tom was quite good humoured, but with grimness and even with ferocity. The force of the man beamed out of him. He approached Sam and stood quite close to him. Sam laughed. Andy laughed.

"And I'm nearly in the same boat – not quite," said Andy.

"I hadn't looked at it like that," said Sam.

"Then why the devil hadn't you?" Tom Hogarth demanded, rather less pleasantly.

"You needn't take the money, Sam, but you'd better sign for it, and it can go into the pool."

"And my miserable share of it will pay for Roedean," said Tom Hogarth, smacking his lips. "Ha, ha! I spend five millions a day sometimes, and at night my wife asks me for a fiver and I scrape it together in ten-shilling notes and some silver. Keep the home-fires burning." He marched away to a corner of the room in triumph.

"All right," said Sam. "As you please, sir."

He had a base feeling of throwing pence to ragamuffins. He knew that he was envied; he liked to be envied; and he hated to like to be envied. The image of old Mrs Clyth was somehow fading. He grasped after it, but it eluded him.

34

The Article

The wearied, worried, resigned, sedate Mr Poppleham came in. He wore a dinner-jacket. Tom Hogarth was in a shabby tweed suit, and Sam himself had not troubled to change – at Sid Jenkin's suggestion. But Poppleham, who never knew what ceremonial he might have to take part in of a night, must follow the rules, even if doing so shortened his dinner-hour. Poppleham had no surcease, and while possibly Hogarth worked sixteen hours a day, Poppleham worked eighteen. There was little mercy for Poppleham. He bore in his bony white hand the galley-proofs of some printed matter.

"Perhaps you might like to glance at this, sir. It's just come in."

The Prime Minister took the slip with interest. And Tom Hogarth, interested immediately at the sight of newspaper stuff, peered without any shame over the Prime Minister's shoulder.

Sam, who was close by them, could scarcely avoid reading the title: "French Press Criticism of Britain" His heart made itself felt instantly. The slip was a proof of the article which he had caused to be put together that day at his Ministry. He was alarmed. By what underground agency had it reached the Prime Minister? He saw himself in a net of spying whose existence he had not even suspected. Was there a traitor in his Ministry? Obviously there was a traitor in the office of the newspaper, which was understood to be uncompromisingly hostile to the Government and which had just been openly defying the Government and risking suppression. Yes, his eyes were being opened to the realities of politics in war, and he was alarmed. The article was sensational; he knew it. The article might have repercussions throughout the world.

Curiously the Prime Minister's interest in it was not maintained; he read some of it with care, but the latter part of it he did not read at all.

"Um!" he murmured with a faint smile which might or might not have been expressing amusement.

The fact was, as Sam divined, that Andy was preoccupied with his mother; in this lay the explanation of his attitude of indifference towards the salary question. Tom Hogarth, on the other hand, read with the maximum of intensity though with extreme, almost incredible, rapidity. The whole of his tireless, greedy, tremendous brain was operating on that slip of paper.

"What newspaper, Poppy?" Tom demanded. Poppleham raised his eyelids and was about to reply when Sam snapped out the answer. The tired eyelids relapsed on the tired eyes.

"You know about it then?" said Andy. "Considering that I did it," said Sam laconically. He made no reference to the machinery, or the machination, responsible for the arrival of the proof in Downing Street; nor did anyone else. The prudent policy of letting a sleeping dog lie evidently appealed to all of them.

Tom Hogarth looked straight at Sam with blazing eye and was about to speak but checked himself, no doubt feeling that he must tread carefully with a man who shared the Prime Minister's broth. Firedamp was in the air Poppleham alone was concerned.

"Well, what do you think of it?" Sam asked nobody in particular, soothingly.

The Prime Minister said naught. For the moment Sam was the Prime Minister's pet lamb, the protege for whom he was responsible to his colleagues; and if he could not defend, at least he would not criticise.

"It's madness!" Tom Hogarth fiercely ejaculated. "Why is it madness?" Sam demanded, still gently. "It's asking for trouble – obviously."

"There won't be any trouble," said Sam. "America will be delighted, and some other places too. France can't say anything. And I'll lay you what you like you'll see a difference in the tone of the Paris press from now on. I've thought the thing out pretty carefully – needless to say."

"And in that paper!" Tom Hogarth exclaimed passionately.

"Who does this fellow take me for?" thought Sam, content. "Does he imagine I've stepped out of the nursery into the Ministry?"

He recalled some of his more brilliant feats in the manipulation of public opinion regarding certain limited companies. He had yielded once that evening. He would not yield again. He was in a mood not to care a fig for Tom Hogarth, or for Andy either.

"My dear fellow," he said aloud to Tom, "surely you can see that I chose that paper deliberately. It's notoriously against the Government. Hence Paris can't suspect that the Government's had a hand in it." He turned to Andy. "Isn't that plain? Further, if I may say so, incidentally I've nobbled the paper. I fancy I've got the blessed paper in my pocket now – anyhow for a few weeks. Not without difficulty."

Miss Packer appeared, and everybody looked at her. Andy jumped up as out of a lethargy.

"She's awake now. She'd like to see you – just for a second. The nurse thinks you oughtn't to stay."

Andy flew, Miss Packer holding the door open for him. No doubt in one corner of his mind he was weakly glad to escape from a tiresome dissension. Both Sam and Tom Hogarth forgot him.

"Here one day we've practically decided to suppress the paper, and the next we're asking it to help us!"

"And what of it? It is helping us." Sam saw that Hogarth could not possibly maintain the position into which he had blundered.

"It ought to be stopped! It ought to be stopped! It's bound to confuse our relations, and it ought to be stopped!"

"Well, you're entitled to your opinion, my dear chap. But the thing's in my department, and I'll take the responsibility of not stopping it."

"That's all very well – all very well. The responsibility is collective. That's what we all have to understand. Collective."

Tom strode out of the room. Sam stood hesitant.

"The Prime Minister wished me to speak to you about the procedure as to your peerage, sir," Poppleham began, in his flat, half-saintly voice.

"Yes. But I've had no sort of official notice of it," said Sam with a short laugh. "From anybody! I was expecting – "

"No, sir. You won't get any notice at this stage. It will be in the papers to-morrow morning, and that will be the first intimation."

Mr Poppleham then entered upon what seemed to Sam to be a long rigmarole in which the Privy Council and the Heralds' College played incomprehensible parts.

"Yes, yes. Quite." Sam agreed at intervals.

"Lord Raingo of – er – where, sir?"

"Eccles in the county of Lancaster."

Mr Poppleham wrote.

"Did the Prime Minister happen to mention the question of photographs, sir?"

Up to this point the conversation had not laid hold of Sam, absorbed as he had been in the clash with Hogarth. But he was now startled into full attention.

"No. Not a word."

"The Prime Minister thinks it advisable for you to have some new photographs taken. Several. There will be a demand for them, of course."

"There has been. But I couldn't supply it. I haven't any – except a few old ones," said Sam, who hated photographers and had not submitted to them for many years.

"Old ones would scarcely do in any case. The Prime Minister thinks it important that you should not look too young. I said ' several,' because the big dailies, and even some of the weeklies, prefer to use exclusives. Perhaps you might be able to send for more than one photographer." Mr Poppleham went on quietly. "And there's your necktie, sir, if you'll pardon such a detail. Your necktie is of course well known. But blue in a photograph is apt to come out white, and so the white spots would not show properly."

"My God!" said Sam, cheerfully mocking. "Here is a complication that hadn't occurred to me!"

"So that if you could wear black-and-white instead of blue-and-white, of course only for the photographing, it might be a good thing. But the same shape at the ends, sir. If you could get one to-morrow."

"But, Mr Poppleham, do you know where these neckties come from? Eccles."

"Where, sir? Oh, yes, Eccles."

"Had 'em from there – same shop – for something like thirty years, my friend. However, I'll see what can be done. I'll see."

"It was thought there ought to be no doubt about your special neckties in the first photographs, sir. You see, it will give something to the caricaturists to fasten on to."

Sam left the room solemnized by the gravity of the issues which Mr Poppleham had just put before him and which in his simplicity he had not even dreamed of. The complexity of politics struck him afresh, and Andy's all-embracing watchfulness forced his admiration. "All St. Stephen's is a stage," he reflected.

As he went downstairs – Mr Poppleham had suggested that it was needless to await the Prime Minister's return – he saw that the door of the room where Hogarth had been talking to the officers was still open. He stopped and beheld the figures of Hogarth and Sid Jenkin standing close together, each holding a glass.

"Oh, you've come back, Sid."

"I say, old man, one minute. Half a mo', Tom," cried Sid, rushing to Sam in the corridor. "I've had that message I was expecting. It's not quite so certain as I hoped for, but it's *practically* certain – he's got clear away. I shall know more in a day or two."

"Geoffrey?"

"Yes. I was just coming up to tell you," Sid finished proudly.

35

Elevation

"The King has been pleased to confer the dignity of a Barony of the United Kingdom upon Mr Samuel Raingo, Minister of Records." This announcement, under various head-lines in all newspapers, definitely marked a stage in Sam's life. Everybody now addressed him as "my lord," except those sufficiently high up in the world to say "Lord Raingo," and those few who (with self-complacency) felt that they could still say "Raingo," and those still fewer who went on saying "Sam" as though nothing had happened. The demeanour of the staff at Berkeley Mansion showed that the Mansion was naively delighted and proud. And it was the same at the Ministry, where the most pleased, excited, and fussily deferential of all was Sir Ernest Timmerson himself.

"Well, my lord," Delphine greeted him, tenderly roguish, when he called to pay her a hurried visit.

"Well, my lord," were his wife's first words, when, without warning, she entered the flat in the early evening of that day. (The coincidence disturbed him.)

After seeing Sid Jenkin at No. 10 he had gone himself straight to the always-open telegraph office at Charing Cross and telegraphed the news about Geoffrey to Adela at Moze, and she had received the message at eight-thirty a.m. He saw at once, as she coldly kissed him, that with all her mysterious aloofness, outwardly so tranquil and indifferent, she was in an acute state of nerves. She seemed to be living withdrawn in communion with Geoffrey, living *on* Geoffrey. Sam was touched at the sight of her. There she was, ageing, desiccated, dignified, destined perhaps never again to arouse passion in any man (but you never knew) – and yet inwardly burning in a flame of maternity. Sam too was elated and kindled by the thought of Geoffrey free, but his excitement could not match hers. She worried him with questions which he could not answer, for Sid Jenkin had suddenly gone to the Continent, without warning and without trace. (Sam was gradually putting Sid into the class of half-unreliable dash-abouts, as Sid's individuality took more definite shape in his mind.)

At the same time Adela worried, even exasperated Sam with trifling points concerning the title. She spoke at length of new notepaper, of the coat-of-arms, of the necessity of instructing country servants in the right forms of approach to members of the peerage and their wives. She reminded herself and him that Geoffrey would be "the Honourable." All, these matters, which for the most part she had mentioned before, on the first tidings of a peerage, struck Sam as petty in the circumstances. Was the peerage anything but a device to help Sam to help his country to the fullest possible extent? He sought to restore her perspective, for she was by no means a fool, as he kept on saying to himself, despite her wandering, darting mind. He spoke vaguely of vast plans for the improvement of the Ministry as an organization. She immediately said that she could see in his face that he was overworking. He soothed her with fibs. He was utterly determined to work hard. He was convinced that he could do so without detriment to his health, and he was mad for work.

His plans were indeed vast. Sometimes he wondered what was the quality that set him above even the best members of the staff, who knew so much more about the technique of propaganda than he did himself. He soon perceived that his superiority lay in a higher degree of creative enterprise and of the courage to execute. The staff was timorous. The article on French Press criticism, which had caused Timmerson and others to tremble, had precisely the success which Sam had predicted for it. But this success did not cure the cowardice within the Ministry. When he sketched to Timmerson, Mayden, and his secretaries and the financial director, a scheme for bringing the outlying departments together under the main roof – the book-department, the foreign-press reading department, and the British and foreign press reception department – Timmerson led the revolt of prudence and discretion. May-den alone, in his airy, imperturbable, sympathetic way, was ready for anything. Sam said that there was plenty of space in the hotel for all, and that rooms must be shared and clerks crowded together. Timmerson feared dissatisfaction in the staff. Sam damned the staff – and suggested commandeering a larger hotel. Timmerson then feared the press and the Treasury. Sam damned the press and the Treasury.

The climax came with Sam's hint that he meant to try to get hold of all Government propaganda whatsoever – that of the Admiralty, the War Office, the National Service, the Munitions – even Mayden was a bit flustered then, and at this sign Sam laughed off the hint as a dream. But it was more than a dream; obviously all propaganda ought to be, and must be, under one sole direction. Such a logical arrangement would do away with overlapping, amateurishness, positive contradictions, dangerous discrepancies, avoidable expense, delays through lack of the co-ordination of material, and the fantastic consequences of inter-departmental jealousy. And chiefly it would centralise power in the hands of the person best fitted to wield power, Sam himself. It was the very crown of his living vision of perfection in propaganda, and his heart did not relinquish it. Indeed the next day he began privately to take the first steps towards realizing it.

In the meantime he devoted much effort to the elaboration of daily and hourly hospitality of every kind to the British press and the correspondents of the Allied and neutral press. He filched another floor in the building up the street where this hospitality, mental and material, was practised. He talked to the pressmen once and occasionally twice a day in English and in French. He invited very small parties of them to lunch at the Savoy – he knew that he could not handle large parties. He engaged a suite for himself at the hotel, and the chosen were invited there. He abrogated the rule against giving out advertisements of War Loan to newspapers which, while not disaffected, were inclined to behave uncomfortably. He had the knack of winning over journalists; he had always had it – was born with it. His sole enemy was an excessively tall, excessively thin, bearded foreign-affairs expert, who would listen to his somewhat ragged discourses with a calm, condescending mien, as one who said: "I know more than this tyro, with all his special sources of information." The down-flowing white beard made him feel nervous, and a lunch-party at which the beard assisted was a sad failure. "Well," said Sam doggedly to himself. "He does know more, curse him!" He would have assassinated the fellow, had assassination been within the rules of the game.

Sam's propagandist care for journalists was not to be confined to Britishers and the resident correspondents of the Continental and American press. His predecessor had initiated a project for bringing to London a few of the leading editors of the Dominions and the United States, which project seemed to Sam to be half-hearted and meanly conceived. He transformed it, multiplied it by ten, and lifted it up to a plane of splendour and costliness unprecedented in the. annals of the art of capturing the organs of public opinion – an art of which, he remembered himself, in earlier days he had had some very satisfactory experience. The English-speaking press of the entire world was to be entertained in the grand manner. Money was not to be spared; it was to be squandered. Mayden had charge of the hotel arrangements, and Mayden was told by Sam himself, and in a tone full of significance, that economy would be counted against him as a sin. Mayden replied that he understood, and soon began to prove that he had understood. The enlargement of the original scheme had to be »- carried out by cabling: which added to the general zest. The H whole Ministry grew excited about the visit of the Dominions and

American press; and Sam at least as much as any of his staff. Word was passed that the Minister was excited, and so excitement reacted on excitement.

And yet all the time, Sam, who had been despising his "wife and the heads of his staff for their infantile interest in the details of his formal elevation to the peerage, found in the mysteries of his soul that just those details obsessed him far more than any ministerial work – even the organizing of the tremendous press-visit. Somehow his supreme mental preoccupation was the ceremonial preliminary to the peerage. Beneath an ironic demeanour he took with an extraordinary worried seriousness such details as sitting for his photograph and the proper attire therefor. If he watched over cables to New York, Chicago, Milwaukee (especially Milwaukee), he also watched over telegrams to Eccles about neckties. The Heralds' College became for him the most important and formidable institution in the kingdom; the Heralds' College made him nervous. In the end he rivalled and surpassed Adela in his minute concern over note-paper, envelopes, crests, coat-of-arms. He almost trembled with apprehension when he learnt that the formal supplication had been sent to the Lord Chancellor to receive him, and when the Lord Chancellor grandiosely replied that the suppliant would be received on a certain date, he still trembled.

The summit of the high ordeal loomed now close above him, and he was more nervous than a student about to sit for an examination. In vain he repeated to himself that he was being merely childish. Elevation to the peerage, the honour of it, the publicity of it, the majesty of it, was a terrific event, and he was capable of neglecting nothing connected with it. He, Sam, of Eccles, was to be a peer.

He made mistakes – and two serious ones. Both were inexcusable. He had to have two sponsors to introduce him into the House of Lords. Lord Ockleford was the Leader of the House and a friendly and urbane colleague, and Sam thought that he would like to be sponsored by Lord Ockleford, and without consulting experts he wrote to his lordship to ask for his collaboration. The earl's reply was a masterpiece. "Greatly as I should esteem the privilege which you offer to me," wrote the earl, and went on to point out that a peer must be introduced by his equals in rank, and that as Sam was to be a baron, whereas an earl was an earl... Sam's humiliation was intense; he blushed in solitude as he read the courtly letter. He had been caught in a frightful solecism. There was absolutely no escape from the quandary. He had demonstrated publicly – for Lord Ockleford could not be expected to keep the titbit to himself – that he belonged to the type of the new rich. "What the devil does it matter?" he cried superiorly; but it mattered.

The second serious mistake was in regard to his peer's robe. He ordered it to be sent to Berkeley Street instead of to the suite in the hotel. His wife happened to be in the flat when it arrived. She had already smiled at his decision to buy a robe (at a cost of nearly *£200)* in preference to hiring one for about fourpence. And when he had said stiffly that he would enter the House of Lords in no hired reach-me-down she had smiled again. Indeed her behaviour was incomprehensible and annoying. But as she asked his permission to take the gorgeous garment of scarlet and ermine out of the shell in which it had arrived she appeared to be commendably serious. She shook away its creases, admired it, and gravely asked him to put it on. He put it on. She then gravely asked him to walk to and fro in it. There was no reason for Sam refusing to do so, though he felt somewhat self-conscious. He obediently walked to and fro in the trailing thing. And Adela suddenly burst into laughter, loud and hysterical. Sam was extremely and foolishly cross.

36

Induction

The day came when Samuel Raingo, the Eccles boy and millionaire, preceded by two of the very highest officials in the historic hierarchy of Parliamentary ceremonialism, walked slowly in the red-benched chamber towards a Lord Chancellor seated on an unrecognizable woolsack. Sam was flanked by two barons – not barons descended from the defiers of King John at Runnymede, but common barons of no lineal prestige, mere acquaintances who not much earlier had been as plebeian as Sam himself and whose elevation had been due to causes perhaps far less avowable than Sam's. All were gorgeously and absurdly clad. Sam felt at once an ass, a cynic, and a conqueror.

"This is nothing but a form, and will be over in five minutes," he said to himself; but he was horribly nervous – and yet naively proud. He was aware of a few peers sitting on either side of his procession, leaning back, sprawling their legs, yawning, digging hands into pockets, murmuring politely to one another tepid observations (" the latest cut-throat" was a phrase he thought of as being applied by them to himself), and as bored as Russian boyars watching the manoeuvres of a troupe of gipsy dancing-girls. The procession halted at a word from another official, less exalted but more domineering than the others. Sam was now rather worried by the insubordinate antics of his robe, and he had almost -completely forgotten the lesson of the rehearsal which only a few minutes before had taken place in an ante-room. Instead of collecting his wits like a man, he was criticizing the architecture of the chamber and comparing it with that of the House of Commons, or studying the hairs at the base of the Lord Chancellor's nose. But the angels had charge over him.

"Bow," said the sergeant-majorish official behind him, in a no-nonsense voice loud enough (Sam thought) to be heard across the chamber. Sam bowed.

"Sit down," said the unashamed voice, and it was as if he had said: "Sit down, damn you!" Sam sat down. "Stand up," said the voice. Sam stood up. "Bow," said the voice. And so on until Sam had bowed, sat down, and stood up thrice. He felt like a recruit, a conscript, in the grandeur of the dim chamber.

"And this, too, is part of the war," he thought, with a sort of insane detachment. His uneasy mind ranged over the immeasurable panorama of the war; the ministerial departments contending with one another in secret, the altercations in the Commons, the clangour of the factories, the bland disdain of imprisoned conscientious objectors, the private agonies of the parents of young conscripts, Mrs Blacklow waxing with a baby not her husband's, his wife toying with the idea of being presented at court, Delphine dreaming in loneliness of love, submarines under the sea and ships on the sea being blown up, all the blood and mud and roar and shrieking of the battlefields, and beyond the battle-fields the veiled lands where the enemy planned more destruction or yearned for peace at any price, and his son Geoffrey, who had had the guts to escape from those lands and was now – somewhere.

"And here am I performing in a red dressing-gown that cost me a hundred and eighty pounds!" thought Sam. But not quite so crudely as it might seem, for he well realized, beneath his nervous cynicism, that the most preposterous contrasts are capable of rational explanation, and that it takes every kind of phenomenon to make a world. He saw through the back of his head the picture of Pitt dying in his robes in another House of Lords. He was impressed, intimidated, confident, scornful, and resolved. Of the taking of the oath he had no recollection afterwards. When the Lord Chancellor, a lawyer who had quarrelled violently with him years ago about the conduct of an immense financial action – when the Lord Chancellor benignly shook hands with him, tears came into his eyes. He could not have uttered another word. Strange! Strange!

"I bet Adela's here," he thought suddenly, though she had said naught about attending the ceremony. "I wonder what she'll say."

In the ante-room again he threw off his robe, shook hands with and thanked various persons, and returned to his right mind. The next minute he went swiftly, as it were defiantly, back into the chamber, a completely initiated baron, a baron entitled to stand sponsor for later barons, and sat down on the front Government benches, the ambition of a lifetime accomplished – more than the ambition of a lifetime. Lord Ockleford took his hand in the friendliest welcoming manner. Of course he was still very self-conscious. And having come through one ordeal he began to fear the next and greater ordeal, a speech in that house, in the presence of those boyars.

37

The Right Honourable

Sam had not yet kissed hands as Minister, nor, of course, had he been inducted into the Privy Council. He arrived at the Palace early on a Tuesday morning, in his Ministry car driven by a girl who pleased him because she used her horn far less than any other chauffeur he had ever known. The girl drove past guardian policemen into the precincts with that curious pride that the whole of the Ministry staff seemed to feel in Sam's elevation. Servants led him to an ante-room peopled by two other candidates for the degree of Right Honourable (a certain wholesale quality about this Privy Council, thought Sam), and by four ageing officials, calm and yet fussy, dignified yet comic, who were all evidently animated by a sincere, passionate, transcendent belief in the vital importance of ritual in politics. Two of the officials minutely instructed him in the role which he was about to play, and as they talked, in low tones, with occasional weary smiles, like a clergyman to a bridegroom and bride in a vestry, he noticed the groovy lines of ritual in their faces, and in their eyes the vain meanness of obsequious habit. They left the room, the tremendous lesson ended, and Sam talked to the other destined Right Honourables, whose nervousness had the effect of curing him of his own. Moreover, he observed that he had the best new frock-coat in the room.

Then at length he was ushered into the audience chamber, a small, dark apartment which vividly reminded him of the office of an unsuccessful company promoter in New York; ornate decoration, a bright carpet of vexatious pattern, a desk which was not used, chairs which were not used, walls without significance. He knelt before the fountain of honour, a hand was placed on his extended wrist. He raised it and kissed it. He took the oath, of which little was clear to him except that he swore to hear no evil spoken of the King. He rose, with an aching knee, and backed away and was led out of the room – but only to be led in again and hear a deep voice referring to details of his own career and expressing vague hopes for his success in office and recalling the seriousness of the times.

He was now, by virtue of these brief, smooth, fantastic ceremonies, not merely a peer but a Minister. But no seals were delivered to him, for though a minister, he was not of that higher order of being, a minister of state. He could not sit in the Cabinet; he could only be summoned to give counsel to and take orders from the Cabinet. It was small solace to him, indeed rather an insult, to be told that he would be a member of the Imperial Cabinet, a body created for the comforting of Colonial politicians, which discussed tremendous questions of no direct importance, and did nothing. Sam hated and mistrusted the word empire and its adjective, for he had always heard it in the mouths of self-seekers and vapid rhetoricians. The sole material proofs of his dizzying rise were a tawdry red box containing his patent of nobility and receipts for substantial sums paid to the Clerk of the Privy Council and the Garter King-at-Arms. There is no rose without a thorn, and no triumph without a hurting disappointment.

He descended the steps of the august portico into the beautiful morning of the real world and waved to his waiting car.

"Please, sir," said a woman's thin voice at his side. For a tenth of a second he did not recognize the poor, ineffectual figure of Mrs Blacklow, the temporary clerk in his City office and the detested of Swetnam. She proffered an open telegram in her shabby-gloved hand. He knew that something grave had happened, and probably at Moze. Only from Moze, and by somebody unfamiliar with his new habits, would a telegram have been addressed to his City office.

"Get in, Mrs Blacklow," he said, and to the driver: "The Ministry."

Then he read the telegram: "Serious accident to Lady Raingo. Your presence necessary. Wrenkin." He noticed the time of dispatch and of delivery. Wrenkin! Yes, Wrenkin the outdoor man, had taken charge: the strong individuality was bound to come to the top in a crisis. Sam noticed that as his open car drove slowly through the loose crowds in the front of the Palace, nobody seemed to recognize him. Perhaps the figure of Mrs Blacklow confused the public gaze. He read the telegram again, putting it in his pocket, saying savagely to himself:

"I always knew that woman would kill herself one of these days – always driving in a dream!"

"How did you find me, Mrs Blacklow?" he asked, in a very quiet, friendly voice.

"It came while Mr Swetnam was out, sir – the telegram did. So I asked the hall porter to keep an eye on the office, as I couldn't lock it up, and I took a taxi straight to the Ministry, and they sent me on here. When I told the policeman he let me through and showed me the way. The footman at the place where the car was waiting told me that you'd be out in a minute, and you were, sir."

"Not so ineffectual, after all," thought Sam, and said to her aloud: "You did very well."

Mrs Blacklow's eyes shone with devotion. She seemed less pathetic and a little more self-reliant than before.

Sam began to organize his mind. At the door of the Ministry he said to the driver: "I want you to get some sandwiches, enough for me too, and be back here in a quarter of an hour. You'd better fill up. I shall want you to drive me to Moze at once, and quickly. We'll go along the Lea Bridge Road and through Chelmsford and Colchester. You understand. A quarter of an hour from now."

"Yes, my lord," the somewhat dandiacal girl answered smartly. And her eyes, too, shone with devotion. Mrs Blacklow had doubtless informed her of the nature of the telegram.

"For service" thought Sam, "give me women."

38

The Accident

When Lord Raingo arrived at Moze he found Wrenkin at the gates, shabby and curt as usual, but more communicative than was his wont. Every window blind was impressively drawn down.

"I saw your car down the hill, sir – my lord. I thought you'd be coming. The body's lying in the house." That was how Wrenkin began.

"Come this way and tell me about it," said Sam calmly. He preferred Wrenkin's account to any other.

"You can take the car round to the garage. It's behind the house on the left. Mind how you back in," Wrenkin gruffly instructed the chauffeur, without consulting his master. Then he followed Sam towards the copse on the upper slope of the hill, beyond the gardens.

Adela had left London on the previous day, alone in the big car, having told Sam on the telephone that she had decided to accept a telephone invitation to a bridge party at Frinton that evening. She had persisted for many days in driving Sam's big car. Wrenkin had discovered the car, in the early morning, overturned in a ditch, and Adela crushed underneath it, dead. The car's lights were then still faintly burning.

"Disfigured?"

"Not the face, sir. I got Skinner and the boy and between us we jacked up the car, and pulled her ladyship out. I sent Edith down for the police and the doctor, and as soon as I could I telegraphed for you. I'd no idea her ladyship was coming to Moze at all. She hadn't warned any of 'em in the house."

"And the car?"

"The car's still there, my lord."

"I never saw it as I came up."

"No, sir. It's on the Flittering road. That's what I couldn't make out, if she was coming from London."

"She wasn't," Sam explained.

Evidently Adela had driven straight from London to Frinton, and when the accident occurred was returning to Moze to sleep.

"She must have been going at a rare pace," said Wrenkin. "I know that car. It wouldn't turn over at any ordinary speed, and the ditch isn't deep. It happened at the bend in the lane just after you've passed the block-house at the corner of Adams's big field."

"We'll go and have a look at it," said Sam.

"Her ladyship has been a bit queer lately, my lord. Never spoke to me when she came. Nor to Skinner either."

"Lady Raingo was very worried," said Sam.

"About Mr Geoffrey, my lord?"

"Yes."

"No news, my lord?"

"Not yet. There may be news at any moment."

"A nice home-coming for him when he does come!" Wrenkin observed resentfully.

They left the copse and the grounds, and walked down the hill facing the estuary.

"Those are my children," said Wrenkin, when they came in sight of the car. "I set 'em to watch the rugs and the timepiece and things. The sergeant said I'd better not move anything yet. I kept 'em from school."

Sam ignored the two little sentinels. The car lay with its wheels in the air, like a great maimed animal that had fallen and been struck stiff; an object most distressfully forlorn. Two of the wheels were twisted, and the front axle and the radiator. The clock was going, as indifferent as a god to human woe.

"Um!" Sam murmured.

"Her head was – "

"All right! All right! I understand," Sam stopped the description.

He pictured Adela under the car, lying there all through the night, with the lamps burning patiently around her, like the candles of a bier. For a moment he could not speak. Then he gave a shilling apiece to the boys, one of whom could not restrain an "O-oh!" of ecstasty at the incredible gift. He returned to the house. Old Skinner was in the darkened hall, dusting his coat with bony hand. Tears at once began to run down Skinner's cheeks. Two housemaids were in the back hall, one of them Edith. Edith sobbed when she saw her master.

"Come, come!" Sam expostulated sadly, and, noticing the servants no further, walked brisk and erect to his study.

"Send Wrenkin to me," he called out.

He was full of the thought that the affair was very complicated and must be thoroughly organized. He sat down and wrote: "My dear Timmerson. My wife has been killed in a motor accident. There will have to be an inquest and I must stay here for several days. I leave the Ministry in your able hands. But I wish to be kept *au courant* by special messenger of all that goes on. If necessary commandeer all the Ministry cars you may need, and send your news by men whom I can talk to confidentially and who know what is being done and why. Collins, for instance. And Dacres or Millingham. I should like Mayden, but probably he can't be spared. Please send also my typist and her machine and stationery. Have my mail collected from Berkeley Street and the Savoy, as well as anything in the Ministry, and send it on, will you? We are in the middle of most important work, as no one knows as well as yourself, and my private affairs must not be allowed to delay it for a moment. Before I left London I telephoned myself to the Postmaster-General and asked him to see personally that I had the telephone installed here. There is a post office telephone at Hoe, a mile and a half off, but of course none here. I see no reason why a field-telephone should not be installed to-morrow, pending something more permanent. I shall then be in touch. Please see to this. Yours sincerely, Raingo."

"I say, Wrenkin," he looked up. "Go and see that my chauffeur is being looked after. Let her have some petrol and tell her that I shall want her to go back to town at once. Then I'll get you to run down yourself to Hoe with some telegrams. And while you're there telephone to those undertakers at Colchester and ask them to send a man over here immediately, and he is to bring some samples of coffin plates and funeral cards."

Wrenkin returned in a moment.

"Dr. Heddle is here, sir. Will you see him?"

"I'll see everybody that comes. Tell the cook I'll have some tea and bread-and-butter and an egg. Remind her: three minutes and a half. I'll have it in here. I'll come out to Dr. Heddle."

He wrote a telegram to Swetnam to start for Moze at once. And then he wrote a short letter to Delphine, which he put in his pocket. Ultimately he confided it to the doctor to post; he would not give it to the trustworthy Wrenkin.

"Well, doctor," he said calmly in the hall. "It's good of you to come up like this at once. I wanted to see you very much."

39

The Bed

That evening Sam went to see his wife for the second time. The first visit, formal and brief, had been more for the satisfaction of public opinion in the house than for his own. He unlocked the door of her room, lit the chandelier, lit the bed-lamp, and then extinguished the chandelier. The shade of the bed-lamp kept Adela's face in shadow. It was true, what Wrenkin had said – the face was not disfigured; the rest was hidden.

Sam had none of the uncanny feeling commonly experienced by those who are alone with the dead. If he turned his back to the bed he did not foolishly fear that the corpse might be looking at him by stealth. The sensation which he had was one of possession, of monopoly. "This is mine!" he thought, and bolted the three doors of the room. No one would disturb him, indeed he had sent the household to bed. He had Adela and the night. She lay in dignity and at rest. So she would lie in the blackness of the coffin, at everlasting rest. Nothing could annoy her, for ever and ever. It was thus that his imagination pictured her, and all visions of a future life seemed to be repellent. He wanted simply to think of her as at rest through endless ages.

He examined her lined, dry features, her rather wispy greying hair. Viewed close, she looked rather older than her years, yet at a little distance quite young, almost girlish. Suddenly he recalled her when she was a real girl, when she was carrying Geoffrey, and his own excited interest in the mysterious and somehow awe-inspiring progress of gestation. He would follow her about, guarding her like a porcelain vase that a rude touch might shiver. She never lost her dignity, even of carriage, during those months. Pathetic for her – it appeared to him now – that his interest had not been in herself, but in the unborn. For him she was the expectant mother of his child. For her, he was the indispensable originating preliminary to motherhood.

After Geoffrey's birth his interest in her drooped and died, and hers in him. When Geoffrey went away she lived in a dream, pkyed bridge in a dream, drove cars in a dream. Her home was part of the dream, seen dimly and negligently. She was a cold woman, and the habit of life with her made Sam cold too. He had forgotten love, until Delphine set him on fire. Adela was exasperating in her dreamy, careless calm. She was queer... (But were they not all queer? Look at Delphine with her melancholia. He remembered a man saying to him one night, passionately emphatic: "*All* women are queer." It was so.) He felt only compassion for Adela. He mystically understood her at last. He had no resentment against her for her lamentable failure to make their home beautiful and comfortable and resistlessly attractive with constant solicitude and hospitality and agreeable friends. He had desired such a home more than anything; but she could not create it for him; she could not. She did not want to create it for him. She had rendered his wealth futile. Not her fault; nobody's fault.

He saw his home, this very home, refurnished as only a woman of taste with a vocation for the home could furnish it; shiningly clean, impeccably orderly, luxurious in every detail; maintained by contented, disciplined and efficient servants; frequented by friends who came with eagerness and left with regret; himself basking in it and in the companionship of a woman young, lovely, ardent, and filled with a striving ambition to succeed in pleasing. The young creature took the shape of Delphine... No! On this night he did not in his mind's eye see all this; he was too moved, too decent, too weary, to see it yet. But he foresaw the distant day when he might with propriety begin to visualize it. So far and no farther did his fancy go.

He opened the drawers of her desk, dismissing the notion that he was spying upon her. Someone must sooner or later delve into them, and he was the sole person to do it. A frightful disorder! Of course! Adela could seldom find anything when she looked for it. There were unopened letters; opened letters from acquaintances congratulating her on the peerage, saying what a wonderful man Sam was, sharing her hope that she would soon be presented at Court, giving addresses of marvellous dressmakers; a few bills; proofs of photographs of herself from Bond Street (she had said nothing to him about being photographed herself); samples of note-paper with crowns – or should they be called coronets? – in the top left-hand corner; envelopes to match; particulars of a hair-wash; seven packs of cards: aspirin, phenacetin, bicarbonate of soda, in phials; some orange sticks; eau de Cologne, no other scents; no rouge, no skin-foods (such as the youthful Delphine had); valuable jewels lying loose; three watches; a locket with an unrecognizable early portrait of Sam in it; thick packets of letters from Geoffrey, each most carefully tied up in violet ribbon; a little album filled exclusively with portraits of Geoffrey... Yes, he was spying.

He shut all the drawers and moved away from the desk. Compassion! Sadness! Weariness! And again compassion? On the bed lay the symbol and summing up of all the war-grief and fatigue of the world. The universe was old and spent. The war continued desperately – but mechanically, of its own inertia of desperation. Where was Geoffrey? Where was her wandering boy to-night? Sid Jenkin had vanished. He, Sam, had come late into the war. Many who had come into it early had retired. Millions more were dead. But many who had come into it early were still doggedly and cheerfully labouring. Andrew Clyth, for instance. That man was astounding, a giant, with his mother, and his unseen cypher of a wife, and his Rosie Packer, and his Scotch broth. He deeply admired the fellow. The clock on the mantelpiece went ting-ting. Sam had been with his wife for three hours. He was desolate, weak with fatigue and emotion. But he thought that he was as good and as tireless a fighter as Andy Clyth, and he would prove it. He unbolted and' opened the principal door, extinguished the bed-lamp, extinguished the chandelier, went out and locked the door on the outside.

40

Geoffrey

"You'd better have a look at me, doctor," said Sam, glancing at his watch. "We've got nearly a quarter of an hour." He took the doctor's arm and they went into the study, where Mayden, who had been "spared" from the Ministry, was at work. "You needn't go, Mayden. You know my friend, Dr. Heddle, don't you?"

"I brought my stethoscope," said the doctor, disconcerting Sam somewhat by the implication.

All three men were in formal black, and the doctor held a silk hat. Sam loosed his waistcoat and lay down on the sofa, which he thought was not a great deal more comfortable than the terrible sofa in Heddle's surgery. Sam had decided to be examined, not because his heart was giving him disquiet, but because he had heard from Delphine that morning – a short letter in her enormous handwriting which reminded him of his promise to her to have himself examined every week. He felt that he ought to be very loyal to Delphine. She had kindness; he was her whole world; she trusted him.

In the three and a half days since Adela's death all had been done that had to be done. And yet Sam was not conscious of overstrain. He had directed others, kept an eye on everything, and been careful to do nothing himself but talk to people and make quick decisions upon data which he insisted should be stated briefly. Mayden, so debonair, sympathetic, and tranquil, had been the success of the affair, and Swetnam the failure. Admirably efficient and resourceful in Bucklersbury, E.C., Thos Swetnam lost his head in the strange environment of Moze, and Sam had to invent an urgent mission to London in order to send him back to his fixed habits and the domestic background of Raynes Park. Swetnam's downfall in the vast improvisation was not surprising, for the activity had been tremendous. The service of couriers by car and by train from London; the callers leaving cards; the deluge of telegrams of condolence, including one from the King and another, rather too elegiacally turned, from the Prime Minister; the incessant telephoning on the field-telephone worked from an understaffed village post office; the policeman, the coroner, the local jury; the journalists, including photographers; the undertaker's men, the archdeacon and other clergymen. All these factors amounted in total to something positively prodigious. Moze Hall did not know itself in the ordered turmoil. The entire district was in a state of acute excitement. And the entire country was reading front-page illustrated stories of the tragedy in five hundred newspapers.

If Sam had not had the first news as he was emerging from the King's presence public interest might have been less; but that chance detail, followed by the anecdotic news that the Minister, undeterred by private grief, had contrived to go on with his invaluable official work by dint of practically transferring the ministerial head-quarters to Moze Hall, had achieved for Sam in forty-eight hours a celebrity rivalling that of Andrew Clyth himself. Everybody in England and America and the Dominions now knew who Lord Raingo was, and what a terrific manner of man he was, and all about him. At that moment, while the doctor's ears caught the unsteady rumour of Sam's hidden heart, Mayden was classifying great piles of press-cuttings which had arrived from London at short intervals by courier. And in another room Miss Newman, the plump, soft, ministerial typist, was making long lists of senders of telegrams and letters, senders of wreaths, and callers. There was nothing that was not organized. And Sam was as well informed of the doings of the Ministry, especially in relation to the overseas-press visit, and of the true meaning of the minutes of the Cabinet meetings, as if he had never left London for an hour.

"I've come through," he said to himself, lying on the sofa, pleased with the aspect of affairs. And he wondered how soon he would be able to see Delphine. The thought of Delphine was his balm.

"Urn!" mused Dr. Heddle deferentially, straightening his back. "It might be worse, Lord Raingo." His tone was not very reassuring, but Sam rejected his tone and accepted only the words.

"Ready, Mayden?" said Sam, buttoning his waistcoat, and adjusting his frock-coat.

In the hall waited the funeral guests; three ladies, including a sister of Adela's (who were not to attend the ceremony), three of Adela's male relatives, and the General Officer commanding the district, a great admirer of Adela's bridge playing. Sam had determined to have the funeral most strictly private, but he had not been able to evade the honour of the GOC's presence. The coffin was lifted from its trestles by Wrenkin, the decrepit Skinner, and two hired men, and put into the hearse and eclipsed in great masses of scent-giving flowers. Adela had left the house for ever. Wheels crunched the gravel of the broad drive. At the principal gate two policemen held back half the population of the peninsula. The postmaster's daughter ran in breathless with a telegram which Mayden opened and put in his pocket. The GOC rode with Dr. Heddle; the three relatives travelled together, and Sam, irregularly, took Mayden in the chief mourner's coach. If Delphine was his balm, Mayden was his stand-by; he could not dispense with Mayden, who had never even set eyes on Adela. Wrenkin touched his best hat at the window of the coach.

"Shall I have the blinds drawn up, my lord?"

"Please do."

"What was that wire?" Sam asked, as the carriage rolled out of the demesne through the bareheaded crowd of country gapers.

"Private audience at the Palace on Monday morning at eleven," answered Mayden, producing the telegram,

"I don't want to see it," said Sam, and began to put on his black kid gloves.

Half-way down the hill towards Hoe church the procession surprisingly stopped. There were no onlookers here; nothing to be seen but the curving, narrow road and the hedges and the sloping fields with a tiled roof here and there bright in the chilly sunshine of noon.

"What's up?" Sam demanded, impatient at this flaw in the perfection of the arrangements.

Mayden glanced out of the carriage window. A young military officer was peering into the carriages. He came to Sam's carriage. He was tall and emaciated, with prominent eyes that had a permanent childlike stare of wonder at the world, and unruly hair that stuck out under his cap. His uniform, with the stars of a captain, did not fit him. A band of crepe was loosely pinned round his left arm.

"Dad!" he breathed.

Sam could not speak for a second, so shocked and frightened was he by the intensity of his own emotion. At length he said quietly, casually:

"Get in, Jeff. Jump up. Don't let us keep her waiting here."

Mr Mayden slipped lamely out by the other door, without a word, and joined the G.O.C. Geoffrey sat down by his father's side. The procession moved on. Geoffrey hid his face in his hands and sobbed.

"Is this more than I can bear?" Sam asked himself, afraid.

Geoffrey controlled himself and put his hands on his thin, pointed knees. Sam took the boy's right wrist and gently squeezed it. He thought again: "Can I bear this?"

Geoffrey began to pull nervously at the front of his khaki collar, twitching his neck again and again to the right.

41

NERVES

In the afternoon, when the funeral and late lunch were over, Geoffrey went out at once into the garden, refusing coffee. He almost ran into the garden. He had said nothing in the coach, either going or returning, and very little during the meal. Father and son had, indeed, talked about the weather. As soon as Sam had completed arrangements with Mayden for the departure to London, he put on his hat and started out with as matter-of-fact an air as possible to join Geoffrey.

He had decided that something was very wrong with Geoffrey, and he was debating with himself how to handle him for the best. He saw the boy as an intricate mechanism that was not functioning properly and that might stop or explode at a maladroit touch. He was frightened by the boy's manner, by his glance both dull and defiant, and by the altered tone of his voice. The boy seemed to be more boyish than ever, with his big, wondering eyes and his wiry, disorderly hair, and yet he seemed old too. He began again to fidget with his collar and twitch his neck to the right – rather like a bird on a branch that will make the same gesture a hundred times.

"If your collar isn't comfortable, Jeff, I might – "

"It's quite comfortable, thanks."

"Then why do you – ?"

"Oh, I can't help *that,"* said Geoffrey, with a sort of cold, calm resignation, as one who regarded himself quite objectively. "Can't you see it's a nervous *tic?* I've had it for six months.'"

Sam made no reply except: "Sorry!"

"Tell me about mother."

"Yes, I will. Let's go into the house. It's a bit chilly."

"No, no!" Geoffrey snapped. "Not inside. I had as much of that as I could stand with the ride to the church and back."

"All right, lad. Let's go for a walk then, shall we?" Sam suggested quietly, not at first catching Geoffrey's drift – or not caring to catch it. Sam's fear grew. He perceived that for Jeff he was not a father, but just some suspect individual whom Jeff happened to have met.

"I can't understand how you came to let her drive about by herself," said Geoffrey critically, when Sam had told all he knew and had heard.

"But, my lad, what was I to do? You know as well as I do that your poor mother always did just as she liked."

"You ought to have stopped her."

"Well, perhaps I ought. I don't say. But you must remember I was really very busy all day and every day at the Ministry."

"At the Palace, you mean. I've read all about you in the papers at The Hague. And I'm the b – y Honourable, I suppose. I'm surprised you should be working for that scoundrel Clyth. Responsible for all the mismanagement of the war! He only got where he is because he happened to have someone over him who wouldn't stand up to him. All the best men thrown out, one after another. And look at the new lot. Good God! What a crew of circus-performers, liars, whore-mongers and millionaires! I saw some of the land defences here as I walked from Harwich. It's enough to make you laugh."

At this point Geoffrey suddenly sat down on a stile. Sam submissively halted and stood by his side.

"Thank God that's still there," Geoffrey added, gazing at the muddy ground.

"What?"

"That sea."

Beyond the creeks and banks of Mozewater was a faint blue line.

"Oh!"

Sam could think of nothing to say. He was amazed at the force and crudity of his son's views on things. He had thought that young soldiers were men who fought passionately for country, took orders, obeyed orders, and enjoyed themselves wildly when they could – and didn't argue nor reflect. Now he stood like a tongue-tied criminal at the judgment-seat of his fierce and dangerous son – yesterday a boy, to-day an old, damaged, disillusioned man. He could not answer back, he could offer no defence, partly because to do so would have angered the judge, and partly because the judge was a suffering victim whom it would be cruel to put in the wrong. Geoffrey was somewhat sacrosanct. And Geoffrey kept twitching at his collar and writhing his neck. Sam had foreseen nothing of the situation in which he found himself as he gazed sadly and hopelessly across the beautiful, wide landscape – and could have foreseen nothing.

"Got a gasper?"

Sam hadn't,

"Oh, never mind. What does it matter?"

The hope of the Raingo family, the darling of his mother and the pride of his father, the young man scientifically educated according to the best and latest educational theories, stood up and shook his slacks and spat, glowering.

"Did you get any cigarettes – over there?" Sam asked, determined at any rate to achieve some small talk and hoping to lead Jeff to an account of his adventures.

"Not enough."

"I expect you had some roughish times."

"Oh, that's nothing. They treated their own fellows just as badly as they treated us. And their men hated them as much as we hated "em."

"You saw that for yourself, eh?"

"Did I see it for myself! I should say!"

"How?"

"How? Because you had me taught German and Germany a damn' sight too well. When I got away the first time, and stole a regular outfit of clothes from a shop in Gronau and they bagged me in the middle of some infernal river or other, they took me for a German deserter. I suppose I must *look* German! Anyhow they would have it I was a Boche. That's how I know the way they treat their own fellows and what their own fellows think of them. I've lived in a German military prison for Germans. I know what it is. And I can't say I cared much for it. No doubt it was all right, but the fact is, I haven't got a natural taste for prisons or for trenches either. Not as a permanent residence. The food might have been better; also the company. Now *you* might like solitary confinement. I didn't. But you might. Shut yourself up in your bath-room for a week and try it. Only the water must be turned off of course. Should be worth trying as an experience. Then you'll be able to talk to me, dad."

Sam's soul fastened on to the word "dad," which he had not heard since the morning. The glimpse of his son's odyssey in the land beyond the faint blue line fascinated and appalled him. But he dared not ask for more. What perfect German his son must speak!

Sam mentioned his own work, but Geoffrey obviously felt no interest in it. His casual "Yes" showed disdain as well as indifference. Sam accepted the unfilial affront with a gentle smile, thinking: "Poor fellow! Perhaps it's good for me." He recalled the Sermon on the Mount, and observed the changes in himself with strange curiosity.

Then he tried again for details about Geoffrey's adventures. Nothing was vouchsafed to him. Similarly about the lad's original capture in the field: nothing. Similarly about the companion of his escape, Jim Hylton: not an enlightening word! Geoffrey did not at first even trouble to open his mouth when Sam said that Adela had tried to see Jim but had failed because Jim had left London and nobody seemed to know where he had gone. After a few moments Geoffrey remarked sardonically: "I'm not surprised."

"I've got to have a smoke," Geoffrey burst out, at the end of another pause, and jumped up.

"Plenty at home," said Sam soothingly.

Geoffrey set off in silence towards the house, Sam keeping by his side.

42

Claustrophobia

As they entered the grounds Sam asked as to Geoffrey's kit.

"Haven't any kit. What I'm wearing I had to borrow."

"I'll give orders then."

"You needn't. It doesn't matter."

"And I'll see to your room. I'm the housekeeper for the present. I never succeeded in persuading your mother to have a regular housekeeper. I shall have to get one from somewhere." He smiled gravely.

"Shan't want a room."

"Of course you will want a room," said Sam firmly.

Geoffrey turned on him:

"I can't sleep in a room."

Sam was dashed, more alarmed and perplexed than ever.

"Then where shall you sleep?"

"Oh, anywhere. In the garden. Under the big cedar."

"But look here, they'll think you have taken leave of your senses."

"So I have."

There was a box of cigarettes in the hall. Geoffrey seized a dozen and slipped them into the pocket of his tunic; Sam took one, and they both smoked, standing aimlessly in the large hall with the front door open.

"I say, sonnie," Sam began to plead ingratiatingly. "Don't sleep outside; to please me."

"Oh, all right!" Geoffrey answered gruffly, but with the first touch of good nature that Sam had noticed in him. "I'll sleep here in the hall, near the front door, and have the door open. That satisfy you?"

"Claustrophobia," thought Sam apprehensively. But the slight change in

Geoffrey's voice eased his mind somewhat. The lad was not quite insensible to an appeal.

"What a deuce of an ugly place this hall is!" said Geoffrey, glancing round. "But of course the mater never had any taste. She couldn't help it, but she had no taste in these things." He spoke quite kindly, if realistically.

Sam was astonished, and very pleased thus to see traces of himself in the boy. This was the only hint he had ever had that his son cared for interiors or had a critical attitude in such matters towards his mother. "Yet why should I be astonished?" he asked himself.

"I was taken to a lovely house at The Hague," said Geoffrey, with a smile. "By Jove! They understand furniture, the Dutch do! But it must have taken a couple of hundred years to fix up that house." "Tell me about it." Geoffrey complied. Sam's mind was still more eased.

"I wish you'd refurnish this place for me," said he eagerly. "Can't." Geoffrey's voice was rough again. "Why can't you?"

"I shall have to report for duty," he said, with savage disgust. "Not you?" "Of course I must."

"I can see to that for you," said Sam with assurance. "I dare say you can, but it wouldn't do." Geoffrey's tone, however, was not very positive.

"Perhaps it wouldn't," Sam diplomatically agreed, determined nevertheless that Geoffrey should not serve again. He went on, dropping the subject: "Afraid the maids will disturb you here in the morning... I'll stop 'em."

"Let 'em all come," cried Geoffrey. "I like to hear 'em talking. That was the one blot on my otherwise charming holiday in the land of lager beer. Never heard an English girl talking. I'd have given my eyesight to hear that sometimes... I'll tell you the worst thing that happened to me in Germany. I was sitting in a full tramcar and an awfully nice young female Boche got in. I was just jumping up to give her my seat, but I remembered I was in Germany, where they don't do such things, and if I'd got up for her I might have been copped for an Englander. So I had to see her stand. It was awful." He banged the hall-table furiously.

Sam was pleased, but alarmed again. Why all this fuss about not standing up in a tramcar for a fraulein? The boy's mind was sick. Claustrophobia. And what else? He looked at his son foolishly.

Then Mayden came into the hall. Geoffrey moved to the doorway and turned his back.

"There are two journalist fellows to see you, sir. They've been waiting some time. I haven't said you'd see them."

"I'll see 'em," said Sam, and to Geoffrey, approaching him and putting a hand lightly on his shoulder: "See here, brother. I'm off to London early to-morrow morning. Must. Will you drive up with me?"

"No."

"Sooner stay here, eh?"

"I don't know about sooner stay here. But no London for me, till I've got to."

"Anyhow, I'll see you at tea-time." Sam felt as though his own brain was giving way before the enigma of Geoffrey's mental state. Geoffrey absorbed him in the most painful manner. Adela was scarcely buried. Till the appearance of Geoffrey he had been absorbed in retrospective compassion for her. But now he could not keep his mind on Adela for a moment. She had vanished away from him, and seemingly from Geoffrey too.

"I must go and have a look at mother's room," said Geoffrey, and went off crying. The transient scene was terrible. Sam glanced at Mayden for sympathy. Mayden softly met his gaze... Politics! Titles! Propaganda! What odious, contemptible tinsel and mockery. Here was the war itself, tragedy, utterly distracted fatherhood.

43

The Half-sisters

When Sam went back to the Ministry of Records the sympathetic woe of his staff was rather difficult to bear. He wanted everybody to behave to him as though nothing had happened. After all, the Ministry was the Ministry, and his domestic affairs private to himself. But nobody would. With scarcely an exception – the chief exception being Mayden – all seemed determined to treat him as a creature set apart and afflicted by heaven; they adopted a special tone of voice for him, and in argument agreed with him too quickly and often quite insincerely; he might have been a sick man whom it was advisable to humour lest his illness should get the better of him. Sam well knew that he was under a severe strain, that he had as much anxiety and distress as he could cope with; but he felt equal to the situation if only those around him would conduct themselves naturally and cheerfully. Moreover, there were compensations, or at least there was a compensation – the existence of Delphine.

The worst sinner was Sir Ernest Timmerson, who indeed did appreciate the importance of cheerfulness, but whose cheerfulness was even more desolating than all the well-meant exhibitions of sympathetic grief. Sir Ernest monopolized Sam. He insisted on rendering to Sam an exhaustive account of his stewardship, which, however, had been no stewardship, seeing that Sam had not for an hour during the week lost directive touch with Ministerial activities. And in Sir Ernest's demeanour was latent some implacable jealousy of the favourite Mayden, which had to be soothed. Finally, Sir Ernest invited Sam to a *tete-a-tete* dinner that night at his flat.

"Couldn't we make it to-morrow night?" Sam suggested, instead of saying positively and instantly, as he ought to have done, that he had another engagement.

"To-morrow I have that Rumanian dinner," said Timmerson. "I'd like you to come to-night."

"Well, you must come and dine with me at the Savoy," said Sam.

"If you prefer it," Timmerson agreed, hurt. "But I've not yet had the pleasure of entertaining you, and in these sad circumstances, I should have liked just to show – "

Sam, nervously exasperated, had a tremendous impulse to abandon discretion and even decency, and shout: "Oh, go to the devil with your sad circumstances. I intend to dine tonight with someone I'm very fond of, and so now you know!" But he controlled himself by a great effort, shuddered inwardly at the revelation of the state of his nerves, and said eagerly, with a gentle smile:

"My dear fellow, of course I'll come. It's most kind of you. But you'll let me leave early, won't you?"

Sir Ernest displayed his deep, flattered satisfaction by fussily arranging his wrist-bands.

Sam telephoned to Delphine that he would be with her at ten-thirty. The sweet, agitating sound of her voice lived in his cars. He listened to it, summoning it back when it left him, throughout the arid afternoon of hard, detailed work. At last he said to himself: "I must see her beforehand. I can't go through with that dreadful dinner unless I've seen her. And I won't." And he got Timmerson to fix the dinner for nine o'clock, saying mysteriously that he had had an important summons. At half-past six he dismissed his chauffeur and started for Orange Street. He let all affairs of State fall out of his mind. He even forced the harrowing thought of Geoffrey aside and concentrated his whole soul upon the image of Delphine. He yearned painfully for the solace of her presence, her soft gaze, the touch of her hands. And yet, as he crossed Leicester Square in the lowering twilight, he was afraid, and unconsciously slackened his pace.

A difficult encounter! He had been an adulterer, and though he was so no longer, he was in effect leaving the fresh grave of his wife to join his mistress. The nicest tact on the part of both himself and Delphine would be required, to preserve that first meeting from offence. Joy, even if secretly felt, would be out of place if it found expression. The sad compassion which lay in his heart for Adela must dominate the scene. Yes, a difficult encounter, and while longing for it he feared it and would be relieved when it was over.

Nor was that all. There was something baser in his trouble, something that he hated to acknowledge to himself. He had not warned Delphine that he would come earlier than the hour of the rendezvous. Horrible and unjust thought; supposing that she were not alone! Here he was, loving her, wanting desperately to be with her; and yet jealous, and yet mistrusting her! The truth was that he had never entirely recovered from the shock of seeing her with the young officer at the Savoy. The obstinate suspicion was a monstrous insult to her; it convicted him of illogicalness, unreason, and viler faults. But he could not help it. Jealousy, the most terrible affliction possible to a human being in love, was too strong for him. He suffered in shame. And the real basis of his mental disorder was the inability to believe that he, middle-aged and worn by life, was capable of holding and satisfying her youthfulness. How could he rationally have such bold confidence in himself? Youth wanted youth, and he was middle-aged, inelastic, not bubbling with vitality and zest. Useless to say: "Nerves! Fatigue!"

He unlocked the front door in Orange Street, and climbed the first flight of stairs. And through the door of the office on the first floor he distinctly heard the murmur of voices. He pushed at the door fearfully, as though his doom lay on the other side of it. Delphine was stitching at a familiar old green dress, and she was crying; he could see the tears rolling down her cheeks under the electric light. And near her was standing a younger girl, with no frock on, her bosom half exposed. After a second's hesitation he recalled her; it was Gwen, Delphine's half-sister, whom he had once seen for a moment asleep in Delphine's bed. Both women screamed, and then Gwen, blushing painfully, began to cry also, in her affronted modesty. How odd and out of place they looked amid the masculine, business-like office furniture. The desk was covered with dressmaking litter, and there were bits of stuff on the floor.

"Sorry! Sorry!" said Sam, just as disturbed as either of the girls, and drew back on to the landing. But he felt happy; the torture of jealousy, frightful from the moment when he heard voices till the moment when the interior of the room was revealed to him, had gone.

44

Delphine's Sympathy

"Go upstairs will you, Sam?" said Delphine, showing her head. "I'll be up in a minute." She seemed to be quite calm. Sam obeyed.

"But why was she crying?" he thought apprehensively. And in a moment jealousy, from no apparent cause, began once again to invade his mind.

"This jealous feeling is a disease," he said to himself, and tried to master it. "I won't have it," he said to himself. He was standing in the drawing-room when the half-sisters arrived, laden with the green dress, some pieces of stuff, and the sewing-gear. Sam was self-conscious, and the two girls felt much more so. Sam did not like the situation, he felt out of place. Tenderness for Delphine had left him. He had come for solace, and had found only a new complexity in his life.

"Gwennie," said Delphine, "this is Lord Raingo. Come now, put those things down and shake hands with him."

Gwen was tremendously abashed, having never to her knowledge set eyes on a lord before, still less shaken hands with one. Sam smiled, and warmly clasped her thin, rough, delicate hand. She made a very sharp contrast to Delphine. She was short, slight, fragile, very fair, and much younger than Delphine. The two were alike in one point only: they were both beautiful. Gwen was certainly the more beautiful. Her beauty was surpassing, and its fragility made an unconscious appeal to the beholder, almost painful in its intensity. Every man who saw her would have an instinct to befriend and protect and save her from the assaults of the world. In the brief, shadowed glimpse of her, as she lay asleep, Sam had failed properly to appreciate her physical qualities. The notion of such a girl being a bus-conductor, or even a shop-assistant, was monstrously offensive. Sam could scarcely bear to think of it. Something must positively be done for her. There she stood, over-faced and dumb and apologetic in her plain brown dress, without a jewel, without an ornament, and by right of the contours of her cheeks and lips and the exquisite curves of her ears and nostrils, and her large, wistful frightened eyes and superb blonde hair, she was entitled for her advantage to adoration, power, and the costliest luxuries of attire, precious stones, and environment that worship could offer.

Delphine, effulgent and mature beside her, had the air more of an aunt than of a sister. Sam was glad of this; it aged the glorious dark Delphine, and thus helped to justify the relation between Delphine and himself.

"I'm dreadfully sorry I disturbed you like that, without any warning," said Sam, benevolently retaining the slim hand. "You must excuse me."

"Oh, that's all right," Gwen murmured, with a short, nervous laugh, blushing afresh.

"Run into the kitchen, dear, and see how our bite of supper's getting on," said Delphine. It was an invitation to Gwen to leave her sister and his lordship alone together.

"Yes, I will," said the young girl, with eager deference. How could she not be deferential to an elder sister who so familiarly addressed a lord as "Sam!"

When she had gone Delphine still stood away from Sam, in constraint.

"Sam," said she. "I hope you don't mind – I told her about us. She's all right. She knows what things are. You needn't be afraid."

"I'm not," Sam answered. "You did well. Why shouldn't she know? She seems an awfully nice sort."

"Well, I couldn't help telling her. I thought you said on the telephone half-past ten."

"So I did. But my dinner's put off till nine, and I thought I'd come here first." He smiled oddly, like a boy.

"Oh, Sam," she exclaimed, running to him and putting her arms round his neck and kissing him gravely. "I am so glad to see you. I haven't seen you for years. I suppose you know that. Years." She went on, withdrawing her face, and gazing at him and shifting her arms to his waist: "We were altering one of my old frocks for her, and I thought it would be less messy if I did it downstairs. You don't object, do you?"

"Is it possible," Sam mused, "that this wonderful creature is as fond of me as she seems?" For Delphine seemed to idolize him more than ever, to be gloating passionately over his reappearance. He said aloud: "If you ask me any more questions like that I shall have to smack you, my child." She smiled, making a faint gurgling noise in the throat.

"Delphine, why were you crying when I came in?" he asked seriously.

She hid her face on his shoulder for a moment, and then, without raising it, replied semi-articulately: "I was telling her all you'd been through. I couldn't help crying. But I'm awfully sorry I *was* crying. I *did* want to comfort you when you came, and there I was crying! I don't mean I wanted to be jolly and happy and all that. I knew you couldn't be very cheerful – it wouldn't be quite right, would it? – I only wanted to be a. bit of comfort to you in your sorrow... As if it wasn't enough you being told of your wife's death just as you were coming out of the Palace! And then, on the top of that, your son meeting the funeral procession! Sam, what you've been through! And your son's adventures in Germany. Him wanting to hear an English girl's voice, and not daring to stand up in a tram for a German girl because German men don't do that sort of thing."

"But who told you all this?"

"Why! Isn't it all in the newspapers! When I read it in one paper I went out and got some more to see if there was anything else in any of the others. But they were all the same." She lifted her head and pointed to a pile of papers on a chair.

"Of course," said Sam, who had seen every daily in London morning and evening.

It was wonderful how the information which he had amiably given to some journalists on the previous afternoon at Moze was spread abroad in a few hours throughout the land, and no doubt throughout the world. But news items of such quality were, he knew, rare enough in Fleet Street.

"Why!" said Delphine. "There's nothing but you in the papers to-day!... Excuse me a minute, Sam. I must just see Gwen isn't spoiling the – " She hurried away without finishing her sentence.

Sam thought:

"That wasn't what she was crying for. She was crying for something else, that she doesn't want me to know about, and she's gone out to tell her sister what she said to me, so that there won't be any bungling when her sister comes back. That's it... What a beast I am, though!" But the jealous, horrible thought stuck in his mind.

45

The Mystery

"Lay another place, Gwen," said Delphine.

"But I can't eat here," said Sam. "I'm dining out."

"But not till nine o'clock."

Gwen hesitated, waiting for a decision by the two high beings.

"Still, I can't eat two dinners."

"I'm not asking you to, darling. But you can eat *something* here, and a bit less at the other place."

Delphine spoke with a loving appeal – an appeal, however, in which there was authority, and such authority as she had never before shown. No doubt she had the human weakness to display in front of the humble and frightened Gwen her power over the great man; but there was more than that in Delphine's tone. There was the obscure consciousness that she was now the sole woman in Sam's life and hence that she had the right to influence him for their common good.

Sam, far from resenting this altered attitude, liked it. He liked to see her dominating him and to yield to her command. He even liked to be so openly called "darling" in front of the young girl. And he was very pleased to see Gwen's adoring awe of Delphine. Delphine seemed to have much more individuality than Gwen.

He had another vision of Moze Hall splendidly and tastefully refurnished from top to bottom, and Delphine the mistress of it. The vision of it appeared to be nearer now. Nor did it strike him as unseemly that he should be entertaining such a vision so soon after Adela's funeral. Would Delphine, he asked himself again, be equal to the part? Could she hold her own against those ministerial wives of whom, when he was; in the Commons, he used to hear such strange, quaint, piquant,, contradictory tales, but about whom, since his ascension to office, not a word of gossip had been uttered to him by anybody? He decided in Delphine's favour. Already she had learnt a lot, and she could learn a lot more. He toyed with the idea,, half seriously.

Gwen laid the plate, and they sat down to a meal which reminded him pleasantly of meals in Eccles in the eighties.

"I showed Gwen your picture in *Punch*" said Delphine.

"And what did you think of it, Gwen?" Sam asked. He felt quite at ease in a sort of old Eccles atmosphere.

Gwen was flustered at the call to take part in the conversation.

"I don't know," she stammered. "They've made your necktie too big."

"Ah! But you see you must exaggerate in a caricature."

"I don't think I like caricatures," said Gwen simply.

"But fancy having your picture in *Punch*!" said Delphine,. not quite pleased at Gwen's dislike of caricatures. "My word,. Sam. You *are* in the papers!"

Sam said nothing, but he admitted to himself that he indeed was in the papers – no one more so, except Andy. He was. eager to examine the packet of press-cuttings which would arrive the next morning. At the same time his publicity was-due so much to the drama of private affairs that he did not care to dwell on it. In fact he was secretly ashamed of it,, though he had brought it about only in the interests of the Ministry, which to be effective could not be advertised too. extensively. Delphine read his thoughts, and changed the' conversation.

"Gwen's only here because the shop's closed."

"Kingston?"

"Yes. The proprietor's going to be called up – he's forty-six, but he'll have to go – he's been told. There's nobody to take his place when he does go, and as he had an offer for the business he's selling at once. The shop's closed for stock-taking, this afternoon. He'll be nearly ruined. It does seem a shame, doesn't it?"

The conversation flowed sombrely, as was meet. The shadow
of the war had darkened the room.

Then Gwen had to leave. Sam was told that she must be back in Kingston by eight-thirty. He suspected that Delphine had instructed her to leave early – perhaps that was the reason of the visit to the kitchen. The half-sisters held a colloquy on the green frock, which was made up into a parcel. Delphine gave Gwen the parcel. Sam shook hands, and both girls went downstairs.

When Delphine returned Sam said:

"I say, you really must let me do something for your sister. I like her. She's very nice, and the prettiest thing I ever saw in my life. I'm sure she's no ordinary young woman." He strongly desired to help Gwen. It seemed to him odious, unbearable, that so much of his income should remain futile, heaping itself together for no end, when Gwen was wasting her lovely youth in a shop at Kingston. He knew that it was

the business of everyone to work, but if Gwen was to work he wished her to work in ideal conditions. In truth, however, he did not wish her to work at all. He could not bear to be happy with Delphine while her sister was out unsheltered in the world. He wondered whether he might find a place for her in the "Ministry – no, that wouldn't do. Or perhaps at Moze.

"Yes, she's a nice child," Delphine answered absently.

She put Sam in the arm-chair and sat herself on the arm of the chair, and laid her hand as it were diffidently on his shoulder. Then she rose and extinguished all the lights except one, and returned to the chair and laid her hand again in exactly the same place on his shoulder.

"Oh, Sam!" she breathed. "When *will* the war be over? I don't feel I can stand it much longer."

An unexpected remark! Her melancholia! He could feel the dark mood creeping upon her. Apparently she didn't want any answer to her question.

And beneath her melancholia was something else. He did not know what. By one of those intuitions which are certainly not the monopoly of women he divined that she had a secret from him, that her attitude was subtly prevaricating. *Why* was she crying when he first saw her? Could a woman love two men at once? (For he was sure that she was fond of himself.) Could he love and respect her and yet believe her capable of duplicity? Strange! He could! He felt descending upon him the balm which he had longed for. It came through the mere touch of her hand on his shoulder. Not from her eyes, for she was looking fixedly at the glowing bars of the electric stove. He thought of the complex variety of his life; publicity, fame, official power and work, Adela newly in her grave, Gwen laboriously getting back to her prison _ in Kingston. His wealth, his schemes, his chicane, and this beautiful woman here sitting on the arm of his chair and somehow deceiving him. But he was solaced. His heart grew larger, till it was large enough to hold every experience in kindliness. He must await with indulgent fortitude whatever might come. The hour was marvellous, and he was thankful to be alive.

46

AFFLOCK

Sam had another marvellous hour, of quite a different kind, when Colonel the Right Honourable Sir Rupert Afflock, Baronet, MP, JP, FRS, and a whole string of other affixed abbreviations, entered the Minister's room at the Burleigh Hotel by telephonic appointment on a certain afternoon.

Sam had known Afflock slightly in the House of Commons, and he knew him to be a man of many parts. But a special study of *Who's Who*, wherein his biography was given at great length and yet in a highly condensed form, showed that the parts of Afflock were much more numerous than Sam had supposed. Educated in England, the United States, France and Germany, Sir Rupert had gone early into politics and into the House, had inaugurated various international movements – as, for example, the movement for the preservation of languages falling out of use – and presided over scores of international committees. He had edited journals and written books. He had invented an automatic brake and a propeller for ships, and a patent medicine, and a system of phonetics. He had travelled over all the world. Eleven foreign orders had been bestowed upon him (and three on his wife). His colonelcy (of Yeomanry) was a mere ornament, but an elegant one, and useful. He was a recognized authority on forestry, rotation of crops, wireless telegraphy, mediaeval manuscripts, international law, physics, the Far East, Parliamentary procedure, and half a hundred other subjects – not including, until recently, military administration. Hence, in accordance with the British tradition against employing experts in the high offices of state, he had been made Secretary for War.

He was the most prodigious worker in the Government – with the probable exception of the Earl of Ockleford. He had also the reputation of being, after

Andrew Clyth himself, the most finished and dangerous plotter and schemer on the Front Bench. At the moment the blight on his life was that he had not been included in the War Cabinet.

Perhaps his greatest gift, not counting industry, application and natural talent, was that he knew how to wait. When he had waited for something and got it, he at once, without wasting a moment, began to wait for something else.

Sam went half-way to the door to meet him and greet with bright smiles and deference, as the biggest nob that had ever entered that room in Sam's time. He was a little, black-haired, dark-complexioned man, in a long frock-coat, with a quiet apologetic style, and a trick of raising his black eyebrows. Sam stood over him during the first exchanges. Sam, being a biggish man, had a theory, ignoring the instance of Napoleon, that little men had little minds, and the theory now warmed his heart. He knew that Afflock was held to be dangerous, but he did not care. He defied danger and was thereby uplifted. He had the august and tiny War Minister in his parlour, and the War Minister was the first of the major ministers to venture into his parlour. Sam was no longer a widower, a lover, a father. He was a statesman; he was the holder of the rich purse of Secret Service money, and Sir Rupert, head of the vast and bullying machine for war on land, wanted some of his money and would have to ask for it. Sam feigned to be impressed and nervous.

"My dear Sir Rupert," said he, when they had both sat down. "May I offer you a cigarette?"

"Thank you. I don't smoke. I'm sorry."

"Shall you mind if I have a gasper?"

"Well, if it's a gasper – " said Sir Rupert, and took one.

They lit gaspers from one match.

"First of all," said Sam, "I owe you an apology."

"Surely not," protested Sir Rupert leniently. "Surely not."

"Well, then, say an explanation. Somebody in one of your MI sections telephoned up here yesterday to ask whether we could send a man down to the War Office to produce documents giving certain information which we have in our possession. Our reply was that perhaps the officer in question could spare a moment to step in here and examine the documents on the files." And Sam, assuming his eyeglasses and beaming timidly over them at Sir Rupert, added to himself, "Yes, you piccaninny, that was our reply to the infernal impudence of your Whitehall circus."

"That seems quite a proper and reasonable suggestion," said Sir Rupert, twinkling darkly.

"No," said Sam. "It was neither proper nor reasonable. And that is why I owe you an apology. We had forgotten that there is in existence a War Office order forbidding officers of the M.I. to enter this building under any pretext whatever." And Sam added to himself: "I also have known how to wait."

Sir Rupert at once broke into placatory and diplomatic smiles.

"I assure you," he said, "I have never heard of such an order."

"I am convinced of it," said Sam, with smiles rivalling Sir Rupert's own. "It would be absurd to expect you to deal personally with all the details of inter-departmental procedure. Besides, I dare say that your M.I. people had very good reason for issuing the order. After all, what are we – in this hotel? Mushrooms, my dear Afflock."

"But are you sure about this order?"

"Quite."

"How did you know of it?"

"Ah! Knowing is the speciality of this hotel. Either we know – or we are nothing."

"But I really – "

"I'll send for Timmerson. You know Sir Ernest Timmerson. He's really the brains of this place. I'm only a learner."

"Timmerson! Known him for years, of course! We've sat on more than one committee together. I remember I was chairman – "

Sam rang for a secretary and said he would be glad to see Sir Ernest if Sir Ernest could make it quite convenient to come along. He noticed that the War Minister's benevolence of demeanour had not diminished; neither was he cast down; on the other hand he had quite lost the apologetic air which had marked his entrance.

Timmerson, as the guardian of his own dignity, knew better than to run in immediately at Sam's summons, and while they were waiting for him, Sam said to Afflock, in a confidential,, trustful tone:

"I'm very glad you've come to see me, Afflock. I had thought of mentioning this matter of the excluding order to-the Prime Minister. I was pressed to do so, here. As you know, I'm one of Clyth's oldest friends – in fact, I'm the-oldest friend he has. But I really don't want to bother him about it – at any rate until you'd seen me. I felt quite sure that you and I would soon come to understand one another." Every phrase was a dart that stuck in Afflock's. susceptible hide.

"I'm convinced we shall understand one another," Afflock agreed firmly. "As I say, I never heard of the order till you. told me about it."

"Just so," said Sam, and to himself: "That naturally is a whopper. But never mind."

Sir Ernest and Sir Rupert met with the loving exuberance of fast friends whom destiny had long been cruelly separating. They called each other Rupert and Ernest amid delightful shows of mutual affection. Sir Ernest related his information about the order, treating it as a sort of family affray between much-attached cousins, and not to be taken seriously. Sam had instructed him in the method of approach.

"Now, of course, Rupert," said Sir Ernest, raising a playful finger, "you're not going to ask me to name names. In the circumstances that wouldn't quite do, would it?"

"It would not!" Sir Rupert admitted bravely.

"I ought to tell you, Afflock," Sam broke in, inventing interesting details to enliven the case, "that I've got to sand away those documents that your people want to see – to-night. If your people want them urgently, perhaps you'd like to telephone yourself now and give instructions for someone to

come along, without delay."

"Yes," said Sir Ernest. "Tell 'em to ask for me. We're

only too anxious to be of service to *any* other Ministry."

While Sir Rupert was telephoning in an august and autocratic voice that went ill with his stature, Sam winked at Timmerson. The minister in him, indeed, the whole man, was exceedingly happy. "A moment like this," he thought joyously and recklessly, "is what I have lived for," and added, recalling with a start his high resolves: "It also makes for efficiency in the conduct of the war."

Within a few weeks he had become one of the leading figures in the newspapers – the very darling of the press. The number of his press-cuttings was increasing 'weekly. The state of the war was improving. The *morale* of the country was improving, and the improvement was attributed quite as much to the activities of the Minister of Records as to the operations in the field. He was a peer dealing with a commoner. He was fighting the battle of the mushroom ministries against the overbearing jealousy of the older ministries – and he was winning it. Everybody in his own ministry would soon know what was now passing and would revere him and rejoice accordingly. He was proving the strength of his qualities, and the reality of his power. He exulted.

He exulted even in the risks which he ran-in humiliating so ingenious and patient a person as Sir Rupert Afflock. He knew that if Afflock had not shown fight it was probably because Afflock was waiting for a better tactical position. But he deemed himself as clever a tactician as Afflock; in the meantime he had scored, and the victory would mean prestige wherever statesmen, parliamentarians, officials, or organizers, were gathered together. His exultation flowed triumphantly over private griefs and anxieties, and over the apprehensions and the gloom of the patriot in him. He was gloriously living, and if his heart played him false and he dropped down dead that minute, his last thought would be: "I have lived." He knew now all the fascinations of office save one – the oratorical triumph, which he did not hope for.

At the end of the telephoning he said, sunning himself in Timmerson's gleeful gaze of admiration:

"Possibly you might care to send a chit, Afflock, to say that either the order never existed or has ceased to exist." He went on quietly, giving Afflock no chance to say Yes or No: "And now what can I do for you, my dear Afflock… Don't go, Timmerson… I have no secrets from Timmerson… Sir Rupert wants our authority for some Secret Service money."

Whereupon Afflock gave a sketch of a scheme for a spying expedition into Austria, to be carried out by disaffected Austrians who had brought with them into Switzerland bad memories of unjust treatment under German commands and a conviction that the brightest hope for Austria was a quick peace at no matter what price.

"I needn't ask you if you're sure of your tools," said Sam grandly; and to himself: "More money going to be wasted by these military simpletons! But who cares?" And after a little more talk he graciously accorded the official permit, and Sir Rupert Afflock, departing, had to assume the demeanour of one who has been granted a very considerable favour.

"There's an enemy there," said Timmerson uneasily, when Afflock had gone.

"I agree," said Sam. "But he asked for trouble before we did. It's a pity he's such a dwarf – they're so damned cunning – especially when they don't say much."

47

Rift

Lord Raingo went into his Club for lunch one day. He had called in at Christie's to see how Geoffrey (who had been granted indefinite leave and had put himself in the hands of a psychoanalyst from Cambridge) was getting on at a sale of antique furniture. Geoffrey, with unlimited credit behind him, was almost passionately engaged in the refurnishing of Moze Hall; he would not quit the sale-rooms either for lunch or anything else.

The hour was half-past one, and the great coffee-room of the Club was nearly filled with lunch-habitues. Sam stood hesitant just within the east door. An old head-waiter, who never forgot a face, a name, or a dignity, greeted him:

"Good morning, my lord."

This was his first visit to the Club since his elevation and immense notoriety in the land. The tone of the head-waiter reassured him somewhat, but not enough. He felt instantly, as an actor might, the attitude of the public of the Club, and knew that it was curious and critical rather than sympathetic. Various tables were occupied by groups of intimates who met there four or five times a week, each group a little world, and whose ideal of conversation was ruthless, cheerful freedom to say whatever happened to come into the head. Sam caught them slyly glancing at him and then making remarks to one another. Celebrity and prestige in the land counted no more in the Club than in the House of Commons. In particular, millionaires and famous statesmen were not received with any excessive gusto unless, as happened but rarely, they had established themselves first as clubmen. Sam had never been a marked success in the Club, not because he did not want to be, nor because he assumed those airs which a club resents, but because despite certain quiet, uncultivated social gifts, he was a solitary by disposition and was anyhow more at home with women than with men. Moreover, he was handicapped by front-page publicity in the popular press; a phenomenon always regarded with suspicion by a collection of men familiar with the inside of things.

He walked about looking for a chair. He passed the cronies from his own Ministry, Messrs. Drakefield and Crawshaw. At their table was an empty chair. They nodded to him, but did not suggest that he should join them; perhaps they lacked courage; certainly Sam lacked the courage to join them. At length he sat down at a table for four where were two men whom he did not know and who apparently did not know him. They ignored him – not even a club nod, not even the passing of the menu-card. He wrote out his order which, as was meet, was zealously taken charge of by the head-waiter himself. Sam ate alone and forlorn in the buzzing room. Half-way through the meal the head-waiter arrived again and, bending down, said in Sam's ear:

"Mr Sid Jenkin is asking for you, my lord."

"Bring him in, will you?"

Sid Jenkin was brought in, smiling and twinkling. On the way to Sam's table he shook hands with several men. He beamed with ingenuous and yet shrewd pleasure at finding genial, welcoming acquaintances in the historic coffee-room. His eyes seemed to be saying: "Sid Jenkin is at home anywhere."

Sam rose.

"Had your lunch?"

"I'm just going to have it," said Sam humorously.

"Take Mr Jenkin's order, please," Sam said to the head-waiter, grasping Sid's rough hand. The other two men gave quick, interested glances at the pair; and Sid's eyes seemed to be saying: "Two of His Majesty's Ministers, one of 'em a lord, and the other plain, proletarian Sid Jenkin, lunching together."

"Sid, you've got a special knack of tracking me down," Sam said. He laughed, but he was beginning to be uneasy about Sid Jenkin, considered as a schemer. Nobody at the Ministry knew where Sam was lunching. Spies? Detectives? Sam smiled to himself at the richly comic thought.

"Ah!" drawled Sid, with a face of mystery. "You're a very great man now, Sam, and you can't 'ide your light under a bushel." Then he laughed and became confidential. "No! I'll tell you. I rang you up at the Ministry – "

"After I'd gone out – as usual."

"As usual. And they said you'd probably be at Christie's."

"The deuce they did!"

"Yes. The deuce they did."

"Very indiscreet of them."

"Perhaps. But they couldn't deny Sid Jenkin. I told 'em I'd got to get you – and quick. And quick they gave you away. Off I went to Christie's and found Geoffrey there. Never been in there before. Quite a place! 'E's looking better,

Geoffrey is."

Sid had insisted on making the acquaintance of Geoffrey. Implicit in all Sid Jenkin's relations with and talk about Geoffrey was the extraordinary assumption that he, Sid, had somehow been the instrument of the lad's safe return to England. Instead of being apologetic to Sam for remissness and futility in the Geoffrey affair, Sid without saying a word took much credit for his actions; which annoyed Sam, especially as Geoffrey evidently liked and admired the illustrious tribune, whose attitude towards him was avuncular.

"Yes, I think he's better," Sam agreed.

"Well, Geoffrey didn't know where you'd gone, or if he knew he wouldn't say, the rascal. But I put two and two together. ' Christie's,' said I. ' Club,' said I. ' A hundred or two yards between 'em. 'E's at 'is Club,' said I. And I was not very far out, was I?"

The other two men at the table dropped napkins on to chairs and departed.

"About that question in the 'Ouse this afternoon?"

"But I gave you the full answer yesterday. There's nothing else for you to know."

It had been decided, with the approval of the War Cabinet, that questions in the Commons concerning the Ministry of Records should be answered by Sid. The arrangement suited Sam well, and he could find no fault with Sid's adroit, placatory, and indeed masterly methods of dealing with spoil-sports, cranks, and real enemies. Sam's own answers to one or two questions put in the House of Lords were not often on the same high plane of efficiency as Sid's.

"I know you gave me the full answer," said Sid Jenkin with a grin. "But I 'appened to be talking to the old man this morning – "

"What old man?"

"Andy – his worship – the lord god."

"Oh!"

"And 'e seemed a bit – not scared but wavering like, filmy – ' filmy's ' a good word – about any more commandeering."

"But he told me to do as I liked."

"When?"

"Last night. And I have an appointment with him this afternoon."

Sam spoke rather defiantly and suspiciously. Andy might be the Prime Minister, but he wasn't going to have any Prime Minister interfering in his department. His department was definitely a success. He, Sam, was beyond question a source of strength to the Government. The Government could not afford to cross him, and if the Government did try to cross him he would jolly quick present an ultimatum. Sam indeed, though he did not know it, was suffering ever so little from the disease known as *folie des grandeurs.*

"Well, lad, you won't see 'im this afternoon, because Vs gone into the country – to think, 'e says."

"Who told you?"

"I saw 'im go with me own eyes."

"But I was going to Downing Street straight from here."

"Yes, they told me at the Ministry you were to be there at three. But you needn't trouble, lad."

"He ought to have let me know."

" 'E never lets anybody know – except Hogarth."

Sam had a qualm. He was thrown down from greatness. He saw nets being spread to entangle his stumbling feet. He saw crevasses, shifting surfaces of treacherous snow. Only last night he had been the boon companion of Andrew Clyth, and Miss Packer was soft sweetness itself. And now…! Who was against him? Who wanted his scalp? Had Andy developed jealousy of his creature? The mention of Tom Hogarth as being favoured beyond all others annoyed him and bade him be wary. No! He could not defy the entire War Cabinet. An ultimatum would be too dangerous. No doubt Sid Jenkin had been sent to give him pause, or perhaps to gather material for an attack on him. He must go slow. Supposing that he had actually gone to Downing Street full of easy confidence, and been turned away by the smooth butler with the information that the Prime Minister was out of town! What humiliation! What a blow in the face!

"When will the PM be back?"

"God knows. Perhaps the day after to-morrow."

"Well, I've got to see him about interviews with those damned overseas journalists. That's certain."

The overseas editors had begun to arrive. Those who had arrived were saying, and those who had not arrived were cabling, that they must positively see Andrew Clyth, Andrew Clyth, Andrew Clyth – that was the name on all their lips. They everyone wanted to go back home boasting that they had had personal, private speech with Andrew Clyth. Nobody else mattered to them. Andrew was the greatest man in the world. Sam had already carried through several such interviews, and others had been decided on.

" 'E's getting a bit fed up with your journalists," said Sid Jenkin. "Says 'e ain't going to see any more. Says 'e's got something else to do than waste his time listening to the gabble of a lot of prairie reporters. 'E's fretting, Andy is. I thought I'd tell ye."

"But what's he got to fret about? The war's going much better."

"It ain't the war as is troubling 'im. 'Is Man-Power Bill isn't panning out as 'e said it would. There's a lot of 'em getting at 'im about it. And 'e was obliged to ask the Privy Council to postpone conscription in Ireland. That made 'im wild, you bet. 'E don't want any more trouble along of all this commandeering of yours, my boy."

"Have I been absolutely blind?" Sam asked himself. "Are they all cleverer than I am? Am I only a beginner?" Sid Jenkin's tidings staggered him, by their revelation of the unimaginable duplicity of his boyhood's friend and enemy. Had then the value of old Mrs Clyth's sponsorship dwindled to nothing?

They discussed a long time the precise form of Sid's answer to the afternoon's question in the House of Commons, and eventually it was transformed into something very different from what Sam had intended and originally laid down. Sid summoned a waitress.

"Get someone to order a taxi, will ye, miss. Say it's for Mr Sid Jenkin." And to Sam: "I must shunt it." The tables were now all empty. And yet Sam had scarcely noticed anyone go. The room was desolate. And Sam was desolate – and rebellious.

48

Dictators

On his return to the Ministry of Records, at least an hour earlier than he was expected – indeed he had told the privileged individuals on the steps of his throne that he might not be back till late, if at all – Sam had the sensation of one who has been found out, who has something to hide, who must pretend to be what he no longer is. What a fall from his gay mood that day when he had cornered Afflock! His first impulse was to act the tyrant and, as it were, lay waste the entire hotel and spread terror from floor to floor. He rang, a lengthy, hard push on the little knob, -for a secretary, and seemed to count the seconds till the summons was answered.

"Send General Slessing in to me at once, please," he commanded grimly.

The changed look on the secretary's face flattered the instinct for cruelty which sleeps in every man of authority. Sam took a special pleasure in giving orders to generals, no matter what kind of general they might be. In so doing he satisfied the popular prejudice, which he sometimes for fun allowed himself to share, against the whole tribe of red-tabs and brass-hats. General Slessing was a Colonial officer, over sixty years of age, whose rank was dear to its bearer because it enabled him to receive salutes from colonels and to hear at the end of every sentence the word so fraught with prestige: "General." He was high up in the "Cables" department.

"General Slessing," announced the ministerial watch-dog and guardian of Sam's room.

"Yes, Raingo," said the tall, gaunt old man, striding lankily into the presence, and saw the watch-dog shut the door, and waited.

Suddenly, and apparently for no reason, Sam perceived that he was about to take the wrong tack. He recalled the wisdom of a modern philosopher:

"Never show a wound." The very last thing he ought to do was to endanger further a damaged authority by using it roughly. Everybody would guess, if he gave wiggings contrary to his habit, that he had received one. No! He must be smooth, courteous, lenient, and even gay.

"Awfully good of you to come so quickly," he said, smiling and indicating a chair. "I hope I haven't taken you off anything very urgent; but I want you to keep an eye on the broadcasting message to-night. I expect you know more about feeling in the Antipodes than anybody else here – "

He continued, inventing when necessary as he went along.

The General smacked his lips over the honey, not dreaming that Sam had it in mind to scourge him for trying to interfere in the composition of the nightly world-message. Sam knew that he might be laying up trouble for himself later, but he did not care; he could secretly appoint someone else to counter any possible foolishness on the part of the General. Then he rang again for the secretary.

"General Slessing has very kindly promised – " he began to the secretary, thus publishing the General's rise in favour. The General departed, very content.

"Yes, that's the tack," said Sam to himself. "What an ass I might have made of myself!"

He took a letter out of a drawer. It was from Mr Eric Trumbull, the French "national," dated Grenoble, and gave a clear, succinct and modestly triumphant account of Eric's activities in the way of forming Anglophile propagandist committees in Central France. Sam had been gradually coming to the conclusion that Anglophile propagandist committees in France were not worth the trouble they made; and further that Trumbull was too clever and reliable a man to permit to be absent from the Ministry. He could find more important work for Trumbull. The next minute he was composing in quiet tones to Miss Newman, the plump, bland stenographer, a letter which she stroked and dotted in her notebook as calmly as though it had been an order for stationery instead of a semi-imperial ukase destroying the elaborate plans of an exceptionally brilliant brain and changing the trend of an international policy. As the fair but lumpy young woman silently left the room, Sam thought how strange it was that such a great deed could be so simply and casually done.

"This amounts to a dictatorship," he thought. And somehow the incident threw light on the eternal enigma of the Prime Minister. Everyone had agreed that Andy had attained to the position of Dictator of the British Empire. Yet Sam had never heard him dictate, had never even heard him talk at length in private. The dictatorship was in the secret processes of Andy's energetic mind. He reflected; he hesitated; he gave play to his instincts. Then a laconic word, and the

course of policy was thrust into a new direction, and there was nothing more to be said. This was power. The only difference, save the difference of degree, between Sam's method and Andy's was that Andy seldom read anything and never wrote anything.

The watch-dog entered. Sam looked up through the lighting of a cigarette.

"Can you see Lord Winton any time this afternoon, my lord?"

"Who the devil was Lord Winton? Ah, yes! Of course!"

"No."

"Very good, my lord."

The watch-dog entered again.

"A Mrs Blacklow is on the telephone, my lord. Can she come to see you?"

"Ask Mrs Blacklow to take a taxi and come at once. She didn't say what it was about?"

"No, my lord."

"Never mind."

"Very good, my lord."

He could not imagine how the expectant mother had found the courage to ask for an interview – he had not been to his office for days – but Mrs Blacklow was his protegee, and therefore he could not deny her.

"I say, Stewart."

"Yes, my lord."

"Tell the hall porter that when she comes Mrs Blacklow is to be shown up at once. And, Stewart, ask Captain Mayden to come to me."

"Very good, my lord."

49

The Confidence

Mayden was Sam's confidant at the Ministry.

"Mayden, my poor friend," said he, when the Secretary-General had limped in and gently deposited himself on the chair opposite to the throne at the great desk, "I want to talk to you."

But an instinct – pride, vanity, or prudence – prevented Sam from being completely candid even to Mayden, his pet and his pillar. He had meant to be completely candid, yet no sooner had he opened his mouth than he felt that such a course would be impossible to him. How could he tell Mayden that he, Sam, was in disgrace, that he had had a near escape of going to Downing Street with a definite appointment and being turned away with the news that the Prime Minister had left for the country? He could no more tell this to Mayden than to Timmerson himself. Nobody on earth could be permitted to share his secret humiliation.

Mayden watched smiling.

"It's like this. We can't keep on bothering the Prime Minister with these editor fellows from God knows where. It takes up too much of his time. We simply can't expect him to do it. There'll be about four hundred of them by the time they're all here. They all want to see him alone. Give 'em twenty minutes each. That's a hundred and thirty-three hours – not counting the fitting in. You only have to look it in the face to see how absurd it is. He's seen six or eight – and I wish he hadn't."

"Has he been complaining?"

"*Oh, no!*" said Sam, as if shocked at the notion. "I was with him last night and he was most obliging. It's true that I've heard a rumour indirectly that he isn't absolutely mad on meeting the fellows; but it's up to us to protect him.

After all, there's a war on, isn't there? The question is, how are we to protect him?"

"We've made a bad beginning, sir."

"That's it. We've made a bad beginning. We've established a precedent. You may bet that all those who have seen him have taken steps to inform the entire world of the fact. Of course he must see some of 'em."

"Yes. He'd better see the stupid ones. They must be sorted out."

"He must see the really big guns," said Sam firmly. "You and I'd better go through the list."

"I don't think the big guns matter a bit, as such," Mayden stuck to his point. "If they're intelligent and decent they'll understand – however big they-are. If they're stupid and conceited they won't understand and they'll feel insulted and their sables home will be coloured accordingly."

"There's something in that," said Sam blandly, laughing. "But perhaps not as much as you think." "Perhaps not, sir."

"No. You mustn't be too ingenious, my boy. It never works." Mayden smiled wistfully and apologetically. "We'll just mingle the very biggest guns – the fifteen-inchers – and the masterpieces of stupidity, and cut the number down as low as we can, and try that. The rest of 'em he can chat with at the banquet. I only hope he won't go out on strike before we get to the end of our list."

"If he does, we might turn them over to Mr Sid Jenkin to handle."

"Jenkin won't satisfy any of'em."

"Oh, no! I meant that he could take them to the Prime Minister." Sam was hurt.

"D'ye mean he'd get 'em through?"

"I should say so, sir. The Prime Minister would never refuse him."

Mayden put so slight an emphasis on the "him" that Sam could not be quite sure whether he put on any emphasis at all. But Sam was disturbed at this frank, almost crude, suggestion from a valued ally that Sid could accomplish what he himself could not accomplish with Andy. It seemed plainly to indicate that Sam's position *vis a vis* the core of the Government was by no means what he had been thinking it was. The sense of his insecurity was increased. He had no thought now of marching straight on and defying the Government. He was extremely uneasy.

The watch-dog entered.

"Mrs Blacklow is here, my lord."

"Well," said Sam. "We'll think it over. Come and talk to me about it to-morrow, will you?… Show Mrs Blacklow in, Stewart."

50

Warning and Reassurance

Mrs Blacklow presented her usual meek, shabby, mended appearance – well typified by her worn gloves – but she had lost much of her diffidence, and she was quite cheerful. He had noticed some change in her demeanour when she had met him under the portico of the Palace; the change was now more marked; certainly he had not before seen her so cheerful. There was no visible change in her figure. Sam responded to her mood and, to his own surprise, became cheerful also.

"Well, Mrs Blacklow," he began. "Sit down and first of all tell me how you are."

"I'm very well indeed, thank you, my lord. I've never been so well in my life."

"That's fine," said Sam warmly. "You look well." He was full of benevolence towards his protegee, and it was his benevolence that made him happy. He waited for her disclosures.

"I thought I ought to tell you that Mr Swetnam says I must leave on Saturday. It isn't that I mind, now you've been so good, and of course I can't blame Mr Swetnam in any way, because he doesn't know what's happened to me. But I thought I ought to let you know, for fear you might come into the office, one day and find me gone."

"Then you've not told him?"

"Oh no, my lord. I wouldn't tell him without your permission. I wouldn't tell anyone. I'm not afraid to tell him. T should like to tell him. Sometimes I feel I *must* tell him. I should like to tell everybody. I'm not a bit shy now. I think I'm rather proud, in fact."

"You're quite right. But if I were you I wouldn't tell Mr Swetnam – yet."

"No, my lord. Very well, I won't. It's just as you think best."

Sam was moved, partly by her simplicity and partly by her absorption in the greatest experience of her life. She was not worrying about her future, or that of the child far from being born; she was not even to be cast down by the thought of having one day to meet her betrayed husband. She had forgotten the child's chance father. She was wrapped up in her supreme role and the marvels that were obscurely passing within her.

And also Sam was once again flattered by her trust in him.

She had only spoken to him a few times, and yet, quite easily and naturally, she opened her heart to him as she might have done to an aged, benignant priest. He admitted to himself humbly that he had never understood women and, now, that he never would do. He had never desired that Delphine should be a mother, but now he desired this. He had a most touching vision of Delphine, strong and massive, plenteously nursing his child. If from no other motive, he would marry Delphine, and all the world should see her in her growing physical splendour. His sensations before and after the birth of Geoffrey were but the pale precusors of what he imagined in that moment.

"There's no reason why you shouldn't stay on in my office another month, is there?"

"I think not, my lord."

"Does Mr Swetnam know you've come to see me?"

"Oh no, my lord. He went off and left me to lock up. I didn't telephone you till he'd gone."

"That's all right, then. I'll speak to him. I may or may not tell him. If I do, he'll understand. He's very much of a family man, Swetnam is."

Miss Newman came in with some letters for signature, interrupting Mrs Blacklow's reply. The Ministry was strangely functioning just as usual, regardless of the wondrous scene at the desk. When they were alone again, Sam said:

"Anything else?"

"Well, there was something else, my lord, and that's really why I came. I could have written the other."

Mrs Blacklow then began to apologize for prospective temerity, and Sam encouraged her therein, somewhat impatiently. Of the two Sam was perhaps the more nervous, certainly the more apprehensive. She said in her weak, now pleasant voice, that on the previous night, travelling homewards in the Tube, she had sat next to two middle-aged military officers and had gathered from fragments of their talk that they worked at the War Office. One of them had opened an evening paper, and Mrs Blacklow had just been able to distinguish on the front page a small portrait of Lord Raingo.

"Yes. That's right," said Sam. "There was one."

"One of the officers just showed it to the other. He didn't quite show it. He lifted it up so the other could see it. And he pulled a face, and the other one said, ' I wonder if he knows he's going to be done in.' He only grunted it, so you could scarcely hear what he was saying, but I did hear it, my lord. I heard it quite clearly."

Sam smiled, partly to Mrs Blacklow and partly to himself.

"That all?"

"Yes. They never spoke another word – at least not while I was in the carriage."

"What grade were they?"

"The one nearest to me was a major. I couldn't see what the other one was." She went on, more eagerly and earnestly, without waiting for Sam to say anything: "I wanted to tell you, sir, because it was so queer. I thought I ought to tell you. Me being there next to them, just then. I might have taken another train. I was a bit later than usual because I stopped to buy some oranges. And when they got in at Westminster Bridge there was just those two empty seats by us and no more. And it wasn't a smoking carriage either. I can't bear the smell of smoke now, and I never get into a smoking carriage; but officers almost always go smoking. And him unfolding his paper just then, and so that I could see it. No! I couldn't rest satisfied till I'd told you, my lord. It must have been meant for me. You can call it what you like, but it must have been meant for me. And it was a call for me to tell you. It couldn't be anything else. We can't understand these things. I know that. I'm not religious – well, I don't think I am, but I always believed in Providence, and who could help believing in Providence after that? That's what I say. And I hope you'll excuse me, my lord."

Sam had not the heart to reply: "Pure coincidence." He had not even the wish to say it, nor the conviction necessary to say it. Her implications were enormous. They influenced him despite himself. They shook his very sturdy rationalism. Who could deny that the universe was moved by mysterious forces of which men knew nothing – or were only just beginning to suspect the existence? Blessed are the meek. To the simple is given wisdom. Rationalism was as dogmatic as mysticism and superstition – must be, in the last resort.

The love of superstition which is dormant in the most rigidly rational was aroused in Sam. He was overset by the evident power and pure sincerity of Mrs Blacklow's belief. He could even credit that because she was carrying a child special faculties were granted to her by Nature. How strange it was that while talking of these tremendous matters which transcended all common experience she should be mindful of ridiculously petty distinctions and address him as "my lord." Her lord! Good God!

"I'm much obliged to you for telling me," he said.

"Thank you, my lord. But that isn't all either. Oh, my lord, I hope you'll excuse me, but I couldn't go to sleep last night because my little one was uneasy. And I knew that was a sign too."

Sam felt constrained, and looked away. Surely she was going foo far. But then women never had a genuine sense of decency.

After a pause, she went on:

"I take Gerald into the parks as often as I can."

"Who's Gerald?" Sam interrupted her.

"Why! My little one, sir. But if it's a girl she's Rose. Only I think it's a boy. I take him into the parks so we can smell the flowers. It's good for him. And we go to the Abbey too, and to St. Paul's. And we've even been to the National Gallery to see the Madonnas. But that was for me more than for him. He's always been a happy child. That's why I've been getting happier and happier. I'm so proud of him already. But he was very disturbed last night. I didn't notice it till I was in bed in the dark. Everything's been so harmonious for him, since I told you about him and you were so kind. But it wasn't harmonious any longer last night. I don't think he likes Tubes. I don't think they're good for him. And of course he'd felt all that I felt. He feels all the time. He felt last night that destruction was in the world. My brain was too active. He doesn't like my brain to be too active. He likes it better when I just feel – quietly. I said to myself I must control myself. I tried to soothe him all I could. I whispered the Lord's Prayer again and again. And then I said ' One, two, buckle my shoe, three, four, shut the door.' That was more for *him*. And at last I got him soothed. That was when I saw that destruction would destroy itself. And when it's destroyed itself there's an empty place, and good creeps back again bit by bit into the empty place. So I feel it'll all be all right in the end, my lord. I'm easier in myself now I've told you. And so's he."

Sam could not speak. He was awed; there is no other word. And he was using this miraculous shabby creature, this fearless trafficker with the most secret forces of Nature, as a clerk! And Swetnam had told her she must leave his service on Saturday! He felt the full weight of her warning news, and the menace of his invisible enemies in Whitehall. But he was not daunted nor gloomy. He could not meet Mrs Blacklow's quiet, assured smile and feel gloomy.

51

The Summons

"The Professor's broken out in a new place," said Timmerson, coming into Sam one morning with a marked newspaper in his hand- Timmerson's demeanour had a veneer of jauntiness covering apprehension. Sam did not notice this, or he willed to convince himself that he had not noticed it. Anyhow he never attached importance to Timmerson's demeanour, except in regard to matters which might affect his personal relations with Timmerson. Those relations he took much care to keep sweet, for though Timmerson might be a fool he was a well-established fool, and a breach, or even friction, between them would cause far more trouble than it could possibly be worth.

"The Professor" was the nickname given in the Ministry to the military writer who had been attacking the Government, and the Prime Minister in particular, in a Sunday paper, and whom Sam had promised Andy Clyth, on the memorable evening of Scotch broth, to deal with effectively. Sam, having nosed into the private affairs of Fleet Street experts in the art of war, had discovered another military writer of some weight, who had quarrelled with the Professor, and presently a short series of counterblasts to the Professor's stately diatribes was appearing in a morning sheet of vast circulation. Sam was rather proud of the results of this scheme; but his hope of some expression of appreciation from Andy had been disappointed. At their meetings Andy had said not a word about the soon-notorious counterblasts, and Sam's pride would not allow him to angle for praise.

He now glanced preoccupied at the top of the page. The newspaper was the very one which at the beginning of his career as a Minister he had debauched by getting it to print the translated extracts of French Anglophobia.

"You've seen it, of course," Timmerson squeaked apologetically.

"No, I haven't," said Sam curtly. He noticed his own curtness, almost a presage of irritability, and instantly took stock of himself. His thoughts ran like lightning: "This means fatigue. I'm tired. I must watch my sleeping. Two nights I've had night-sweats. What does that mean? I haven't been to the doctor this week, either. I'm never irritable except when I'm tired. I don't feel tired – at least I don't think I do. But I must be. Am I overworking?"

He turned with a smile to the man of ample and starched linen:

"Excuse me, my dear fellow. I wasn't thinking. What is it? Yes. I'll read that before lunch. Public's tired of it now, anyway. I'm glad you've come in. I wanted to explain to you about Trumbull. He's on his way home. But I'd like you to cable him to stop in Paris long enough to see the Ambassador. We've got to square that fellow, and Trumbull's the man to handle him. Do you think so – or don't you? Tell me frankly."

Timmerson squeaked away; of late he had been squeaking more frequently. Sam longed for him to leave the room.

"If this chap doesn't clear out I shall have to chuck the paper-weight at him," thought Sam. His irritability was increasing, but he successfully hid it, and in the end dismissed his second-in-command in a mood of restored confidence in the goodness of God.

Since the visit of Mrs Blacklow Sam had been on the whole blithe, despite the feeling of being surrounded, at a distance, by inimical machinations. Like a child he trusted Mrs Blacklow's assurance that all would end well. It was very strange. Of course the staff of the Ministry had copied his attitude towards affairs. He really ruled the Ministry now. Gone was his affectation of being a simpleton who desired to learn and who believed everything he heard from his men. He was getting to be an autocrat, but an autocrat beloved. He was beloved because he contrived to be an elder brother to all, and because he was a success with the public, and because his schemes seemed to succeed; also because, after a terrific, frightening outburst, which Timmerson, Mayden and two secretaries had witnessed, he had cashiered a railway director whom the staff hated for his incompetence and meddlesome arrogance. That scene had given the keenest pleasure to everybody except the railway director. Four different versions of it, all highly coloured, were current within the building, and perhaps four and forty in the great world beyond. It had inspired Sam to permeate with his individuality every room in the hotel. And more than anything else it had helped to rid him of the exaggerated painful sense of responsibility which had disturbed his initiation into office. He could treat propaganda now as lightly as Andrew Clyth said he treated the entirety of the war.

He loved his work; he had developed a passion for it. He smacked his lips over conferences, press-audiences, press-lunches, minutes, finance, cables, broadcasting, films, intimate banquets for foreign nobs. And all these were nothing in his mind compared with his large comprehensive scheme for unifying every kind of propaganda under one roof and his own headship. Sid Jenkin's warning against commandeering had not deterred him – so much momentum had he acquired. And further, little by little, he was collecting knowledge about the war in general – the altercations between ministries, the more serious altercations between Allies, and the still more serious troubles between Britain and the Dominions.

Where he fell short was in the pursuit of close, familiar relations with important ministers, the men of paramount influence. His trouble lay in the absurdly limited number of hours constituting a day. He knew that here he was running a risk, and he was always trying to remedy the defect in his activities and never satisfactorily succeeding. Tom Hogarth he had scarcely seen; and his rare chats with the Prime Minister had been too friendly, too much on the Eccles plane, and not sufficiently significant in an official sense. Moreover he had scarcely set eyes upon the Prime Minister since Sid Jenkin's incursion into the Club. His extensive memoranda submitted to the War Cabinet were all duly answered by the secretariat, but the more recent replies had shown a certain tepid vagueness.

He looked at the clock, which showed a quarter to twelve. He had squandered nearly half an hour in undirected reflection. "There must be something the matter with me," he thought. At noon was appointed to take place the important weekly conference, at which he presided, of heads of sections and other important members of the staff in the big room in the basement. He had not a moment to spare, for his absolute punctuality on all occasions was famous throughout the building. Nevertheless, he felt that he must read the Professor's article. He was suddenly apprehensive about the article; it might need special attention.

He took up the paper which Timmerson had left for his august notice. As he studied it he wished that he had ignored it for a little longer – anyhow till after the conference; for it alarmed him and induced disorder in his mind, which he had tidied up for the conference. It amounted to a demolition of the rival expert, and put the Government in a worse plight than ever. It was written with authority and force – even with indignation, and it demonstrated that the Professor stood easily first among military experts in the press. Also it was brilliant and made fine reading. Perhaps the most annoying thing about it was its attack on the Prime Minister for an interfering, restless amateur. It would want some answering, if, indeed, it could be effectively answered at all. Sam wished to heaven that he had not so gratuitously and lightly offered to deal with the Professor. He imagined Andy's sensations on reading the accursed thing.

"Well, there it is, anyway. Damn it!" he ejaculated aloud, and rang the bell for secretaries.

In the next five minutes he gave one of his most dazzling displays of dispatch in transacting business, devolving all small points upon others, deciding larger ones in a moment, refusing to consider details, and spreading responsibility around.

"Give me the agenda of the conference," he said. "And my notes. Didn't I specially ask you to have a wider margin? I suppose I must speak to your typist myself."

Then another secretary ran in, like the bearer of supreme tidings on a battlefield.

"The Prime Minister on the telephone, my lord."

He hesitated.

"Put me through then, quick."

He took up the receiver.

"Is that the Prime Minister?"

"Is that Lord Raingo?"

"Speaking."

"Kindly hold the line, my lord."

He held the line, he who always made other people hold the line! He held the line for more than a minute, tapping his foot. It seemed like a quarter of an hour.

"That Raingo?" came the telephone-transformed voice of Andy.

"Yes, sir."

The secretaries stood waiting by his side.

"I hate to trouble you, Sam, but could you come down to No. 10?"

"Now, Andy:" He said "Andy" for the benefit of the secretaries. A paltry ostentation of which he was immediately ashamed.

"Yes. If it isn't inconvenient. I want to consult you."

"Consult me?" he repeated. Another paltry ostentation. Somehow he could not renounce these effects.

"Yes. About one or two matters."

"I've got a rather important conference – just beginning."

"Ah! Then I mustn't trouble you." Andy's voice was that of a spoiled child.

"Oh, but I'll come, of course."

"Now?"

"Now. I'll be with you in less than ten minutes."

"You're very good, and I'm grateful.":

"Not a bit. Not a bit. The reverse." Sam replaced the receiver violently.

Why had Andy chosen to telephone such a simple message himself? Well, you never knew why Andy did anything.

"Ask Sir Ernest to preside at the conference. Give him my notes and help him all you can. Get my car... Stewart!" he cried through the open door. "My hat."

52

Sam's Fright

A magnificent car stood at the door of No. 10. A watchful policeman raised his hand suddenly to stop Sam's car from approaching near enough to prevent the magnificent car from having to back in order to leave. Photographers stood about, shooting, and beyond the photographers a small crowd of gapers who had somehow forced the barrier at the end of the street. A very aged and rather diminutive spectacled lady was being helped into the car by the Prime Minister himself. Andy wore a morning coat, and his grey hair was brightly glistening in the sunshine and the ends of it waving in the breeze. The brakes of Sam's car squealed; the car halted with a shock, and Sam actively jumped down.

He recognized, across forty years, old Mrs Clyth, Andy's .mother. She had somehow changed; in particular she was much smaller than his memory of her; but substantially she was still indentical with the mistress of the Clyth house at Eccles. .As he stood waiting for attention he noticed the extraordinarily soft, delicate cheek which once as a child he had kissed. He was moved, as by the magic of some beautiful miracle. With what filial solicitude Andy took a hot-water bottle from the butler and stowed it under her honoured little feet, and then arranged the mohair rug and affectionately tucked it in.

The old lady glanced casually through her dark spectacles at Sam, but how could she be expected to see in the middle-aged, full-bodied man of importance the child, the schoolboy, or the hobbledehoy of Eccles?

Sam did not venture to intrude into the tableau. The cameras clicked again. A spectacle for the public: " The Prime Minister sees his mother off from Downing Street for a drive in the park." The magnificent car swerved and vanished silently amid salutes into Whitehall. Andy turned and started, as if out of a dream.

"My *dear* fellow! Is it you? Why didn't you give a sign? My mother would have been delighted to see you again. Delighted! She'll be quite cross with me when I tell her she missed you by so little."

Sam said something modest and polite.

"Yes," he thought. "The old lady would have been delighted to see me again, and I should have liked to speak to her. But you saw me all right, and you didn't want me to speak to her. You were afraid that if I spoke to her she might have made a fuss of me, and it would have given me a standing you don't intend me to have." He felt "sneaped," as they used to say in Eccles. He divined that he was in disgrace, and began to examine and improve his defences.

"This is politics at their subtlest," he thought as, in front of the amiably chatting Andy, he went into the house.

They sat in the breakfast-room, and on the way thither saw not a soul except the butler.

"I've formed a partiality for this room," said Andy, sitting down in his own chair before a spent fire. "I can't keep out of it. I hate the drawing-rooms. I hate the Cabinet-room, and who wouldn't? Sit down, lad. Take a cigar." He spoke affably, but Sam, gloomy and resentful, believed that he was acting.

By the side of a cigar-box on the table behind the chair was a copy of the paper containing the Professor's article, Sam thoughtfully opened a cigar, saying to himself: "I may as well get this thing over at once."

"You've seen that article?" he began, jerking his head in the direction of the paper.

The Prime Minister nodded.

"Might have been better if we'd let that fellow alone," said he indifferently, showing his teeth in a determined smile, and looking warily at Sam, just as if Sam could not see him looking! Astonishing how the man could not resist so ingenuously watching his effects!" He's a bit too heavy metal for your
chosen bruiser, Sam."

"It's not over yet," said Sam defiantly.

"I'm sure you've done your best – by the way, I suppose you didn't know this screed was going to appear?"

"How could I?"

"Oh, I don't know how, but some people do get to know things, and I thought you did. You remember you told me to leave it all to you, and so I dismissed it from my mind. It's
only by dismissing from one's mind the things that are dismissible that one can carry on. You know that, Sammy, with all your experience. However, as I say, I'm sure you did your best and nobody can do more. And if there's some damage we must just stick it – that's all. Don't take it to heart, my lad. I won't try to influence you, but if you asked me my opinion I should say that it isn't

worth bothering about any more. What's a newspaper article? We might go farther and fare still worse." He laughed again. "But do as you think best." Every phrase was a condemnation, despite the always genial but continually varied tone.

Sam said to himself:

"He's fixed it so that he can blame me whatever happens. He's fearfully sick over it, and he had the paper put there on purpose. Damn him! He thinks he's talking to me like a father, and I'm the stupid boy. I wonder what sort of a mess the sublime Timmerson is making of my conference. I ought to be there, dominating everything, instead of puffing here at Andy's second-rate-cigars and being lectured."

"Well," he said aloud, "it's very decent of you, Andy, to eave it to me. I'll think it over."

"That's quite all right," Andy reassured him. "I shouldn't have mentioned it if you hadn't. I think absolutely nothing of it, *really*. It wasn't in the least about that that I wanted to see you."

"Oh!" Sam cocked his ear.

"Of course not. I wanted to give you a hint that we've made an enemy."

"Who?'"

"Afflock."

"You mean *I've* made an enemy."

"I say ' we ' because we stand together. But I expect you-did it. He didn't very much care for your attitude over his last demand for Secret Service money – so I hear."

"But I gave him his money without a word. Without a word."

"Well, apparently he was offended."

"Listen here, Andy," said Sam, sitting up. And he related fully the interview in which Afflock had had to withdraw his; own order on Sam's telephone in Sam's presence.

The Prime Minister ought to have laughed at the predicament in which Sam had placed Afflock. But he did not. He gave a faint, insincere smile, and allowed Sam to see plainly that it was insincere. An infernally clever chap, thought Sam,, and was much impressed by the skill in intercourse which Andy had acquired since the old crude days of Eccles. In those days Andy would have flown out and cursed Sam to hell, and given him ten good chances in five minutes. Now he enclosed himself in a sort of block-house, and there was nothing doing. He clearly conveyed his thoughts, his censure, his displeaure, while; offering not one opening for an effective riposte.

"I gather there's going to be a question, or perhaps a motion, put in the House of Lords. All about you, my lad."

"What sort of a question?"

"Don't know. I thought you might be able to tell me.. But you may bet it won't ostensibly deal with what they're objecting to."

"Who are 'they'?"

"War Office. Admiralty. FO War-Aims Committee..."

"God knows what all!"

"But – "

"One moment. There are two matters. One is Secret Service. They all want control of their own Secret Service-supplies. They all hate to have to come to a mushroom Ministry for that. The other is your scheme for getting into your own. hands all propaganda."

"But – "

"One moment. We shall have to make some compromise, – give 'em something. Now I won't yield over Secret Service. I always said I wouldn't and I won't. I mean to keep my hold on that – through you. The centralization of propaganda is another matter."

"But my proposals have had your full approval – the approval of the War Cabinet."

"Not all the War Cabinet, and don't think it!" the Prime Minister smiled sardonically – a long smile. "Your scheme is perfectly logical. It means more efficiency. There's no answer to it – except human nature. I've got to keep the peace. Peace is better than efficiency. Half the gang is up – or will be up."

"You never mentioned it before."

"I didn't know of it. And even if I did know I expected you'd know more."

"I've been too busy to bother about intrigues."

"Doubtless! Doubtless!" The Prime Minister said naught else; but "doubtless" implied: "More fool you!"

Sam saw his centralization scheme shivered to bits and cast away. He wanted to show defiance and dared not, could not.

"And there's this," added the Prime Minister. "You've made yourself so popular. There's such a thing as being too popular. They're jealous of you."

"So are you," thought Sam. "I lay anything you're more jealous than anybody. And that's the explanation of the entire business."

The Prime Minister began to discuss in detail the coming affray in the House of Lords, which (he said) nothing could prevent and which threatened to develop into what is called a full-dress debate. They talked till the clock showed five minutes to one. Sam was lost in suppositions of attack and suppositions of defence. But his heart was full to overflowing with one terrible alarm, which, however, was utterly unconnected with the loss of his centralized scheme, or even the jealousy of his fellow-ministers, or even the possible loss of his office. He was indeed more frightened than he had ever been in his life.

The door opened.

"What is it?" the Prime Minister demanded sharply.

Miss Packer stood in the doorway.

"I wouldn't let the servants come in. But I thought the fire ought to be seen to."

"Don't trouble. The fire's quite all right," said Sam, "And it's a warm day."

Miss Packer glanced at the expiring fire and smiled to herself, and came into the room. Sam jumped up and shook hands with her. Her demeanour was not quite as warm as the day. She made up the fire; smiled again, nodded, and left without another word.

"She's his boss anyhow," thought Sam.

Ten minutes later he departed, amid jolly, odious exclamations of mutual esteem and affection.

53

The Statesman's Wife

That Evening, on the plea of indisposition and excessive fatigue, Lord Raingo asked Sir Ernest – the second request of the day – to take his place in the chair at a small dinner to & visiting deputation of neutrals. Sir Ernest, much flattered and still mildly glorying in his chairmanship of the conference in the morning, broke an engagement of his own in order to oblige! Sam's fatigue was not after all excessive, nor did he feel noticeably indisposed; but he had a most powerful desire, which he could not resist, to escape out of the world and repose himself on the soft cushion of Delphine's tenderness. His longing for solace was scarcely tolerable, and at any price of dereliction of duty had to be assuaged. He had not seen Delphine for several days and he wondered, apprehensively, whether she was keeping her resolution to have a meal prepared for him on the mere chance of his coming without previous notice. He might well have warned her, but had purposely refrained from doing so. From some obscure, naughty, inexcusable motive of jealousy he wanted to take her unawares. He had several of the maladies of love, and knew it not.

The meal was ready. Delphine was waiting in one of the absurd trifling aprons of her housewifery. There she stood in .all her physical and emotional splendour, and greeted him with her quiet, enfolding love. She stole away his hat and coat. The lamps glowed. The table shone. The blinds and curtains were drawn, though night had not yet quite fallen. The small room had a faint, agreeable odour of stuffiness. The door was shut. Not a sound from the street. No war! No world! Only the haven of a room, and her tenderness! Sam's relief was intense. He could feel tears of relief in his eyes.

"Come here, child," he said in an uncertain, throaty voice, after she had kissed him and retreated nervously to verify the correctness of the table.

"Have you got a cold, darling Sam?" she asked with sudden anxiety.

"No," he answered. "Come here."

He was pulling a case from his hip-pocket. She came close to him, obedient, expectant, acquiescent – magnificent, massive, as tall as himself within half an inch. He clasped round her neck a superb jade necklace, which he had bought, at great cost, tempted by a shop-window, in the course of a circuitous reflecting stroll from Downing Street to his lunch.

He was happy in the gesture, in her large yet childlike pleasure, in the brilliance of the stones on her bosom. He would have had the moment endure for ever. He was ready to imitate the sublime, ignominious madness of a Boulanger or a Parnell, and eternally shame himself by abandoning all duty for passion. (No, not that; but nearly that.) She laughed with glee as she thanked him by word and deed and ran to the mirror.

Nervous now with delight, she excused herself and hurried through the bedroom into the little kitchen to begin the serving of the meal. He followed her, and back to the sitting-room, and back again to the kitchen, and finally to sit down opposite to her at the table. She did not remove her futile apron – sign of an increased, more delicious intimacy.

"I've had a knock, my dear," he said, and related the great episode of the morning. He told it in much detail, but rather jauntily. Even to her he could not boldly show a wound. And of his terrible alarm at the prospect of a full-dress debate in the House of Lords he said nothing, because he simply had not the courage to confess it. He must maintain his prestige in her sight. She listened. She understood. She grasped the situation, and the origins of it. He was pleased with her. She said:

"They've never forgiven you for refusing to touch your salary."

Here was a point which he had forgotten, and he appreciated her shrewd, realistic feminine perspicacity. How many women were her equal in political sense and the weighing of human motives? She was astonishing. Was she not astonishing? Then she said, indignantly:

"The truth is that politics is a trade union and you aren't in it. They'd sooner help their enemies that are in the game, than you."

She was more than astonishing; she was miraculous. In two sentences had she not summed up the basic psychological truth of the affair, more daringly, more bitterly and completely than he could have done it himself? He had always perceived that she had sagacity, and a sure feeling for the significance of things. Now she had proved it, now she surpassed herself.

His love for her flamed up even brighter and hotter than ever before. She was the only woman. None could match her. How right had been his first instinct in choosing her from all the other women in the world! How wrong his regrets that she was what is called a nonentity. She possessed the fundamentals; everything else could be acquired. He had wanted to admire her without reserve, and he admired her without reserve. He had a second and a lovelier, more intoxicating vision of her as the mistress of Moze Hall, playing with his child, his children, bearing more children, having learnt her profession of wife, mother, and hostess, speaking shrewdness to impressed, envying guests, adroit, modest, kindly, always furthering a political career which would extend for years beyond the end of the war.

He had made a mistake in not consulting her daily, at every turn of his work. He might never have been in his present mess if he had consulted her. (Fancy consulting poor Adela!)... However, she would now help him to save himself. She might show him the way to convey, without humiliation, to Timmerson, who had always opposed the great centralization scheme, the news that it would be abandoned. He thought, with rapture, and quite heedless of his troubles:

"I am terribly and finally in love with this girl. In all things she is absolutely necessary to me. I cannot do without her. I am the most fortunate of men. Millions of men would sell their souls to feel as I feel now."

It was true. But he wished to heaven he was slim, like the old man with the young creature at the Savoy that day at lunch. In her presence he was ashamed of his girth, which made him too old and unworthy to possess her physical magnificence. He hoped she would grow stout. No! Such a hope was base. She must remain for ever perfect, and he must put up as best he could with his size – which after all was perhaps not too marked!

"You're the goods, my dear," he began, a little nervously. "And I want to talk to you seriously."

She knew that he meant to praise her brief remarks on the situation, but she pretended not to understand, even while smiling her pleasure.

"Why!" she exclaimed. "What have I said now? You're teasing me, I suppose."

"You know quite well what I mean. Any woman as clever as you are must know just how clever she is. There's no such thing as unconscious common sense. I mean, you understand politics, and you know you do. And it's a very rare quality in women, believe me."

"Oh, Sam, I don't. I like to read about politics, because you're interested in them."

"That's true," said a voice within him. "She's only interested in them because I am. They're all alike, these passionate women are."

But he ignored the voice, and, leaning across the table, he put his hand playfully on her mouth to silence her.

"Mum-um-um-um," she affected playfully to talk through his hand. She was delighted by his unusual gesture, and the touch of his hand. She might have withdrawn her face, but she did not, pressing rather her mouth against his hand.

"Will you? Will you! " he menaced her. " Will you spill your gibberish all over me when I've told you I'm going to talk seriously to you? " She kissed his hand, and leaned back in her chair.

"One day," he said, " I don't mean now, but when the right time comes, we must get married."

"Sam! " she interrupted quickly and diffidently. " Not that! I couldn't. Me your wife! "

"I say," he continued masterfully, confidently, " when the right time comes we shall get married. You hear me – married."

U T–"

"Be quiet. Don't interrupt me, or I shall have to choke you, and I don't want to go to extremes. There'd be no end of a mess if I did. I'm having the house at Moze refurnished. Geoffrey's seeing to it for me. I dare say it'll cost twenty or thirty thousand: but as it's all old stuff he's buying it doesn't mean any diversion of labour – except of course for transport, and that's nothing. The war'll be over this year, bound to be – there's been a mutiny of German soldiers in Brussels, and I'm the only person that's heard of it here. And when the war is over I'll take another house in London, and I shall stick to politics and you'll help me. You'll be an absolutely ideal help for a politician – let's say statesman. Now don't infuriate me by telling me you aren't equal to it. You are equal to it. You'll have a thing or two to learn, but there are places where you can learn those. I assure you you're out of sight better than the wives of half the politicians I've met – out of sight. If you knew Mrs Jenkin, for instance! My God! Oh! And lots more! You talk nicely. You know how to dress. You can keep your head. You're beautiful. You never want to do anything silly, or say anything silly either. Everybody would like you. *And you understand.* That's the point. Nine women out of every ten never even begin to understand. That's why the successful men in my new line of business simply leave their wives out of count. I shouldn't. I should count on you, and what's more I'm going to start in counting *on* you at once. We're going to talk politics a lot more than we have done in the past – a lot more, my child. You'll soon see how you'll get on."

He was pleased with the convincingness of his little speech. He saw his conception of the future complete. There was no flaw in it. She was the perfect figure to fit it. She had every quality. He adored her, but he saw her (he thought) with the most impartial detachment. Only his poetic creative fire was suddenly damped by the change in Delphine's face.

54

DEFEAT

She stared at him with large, alarmed eyes; her full lower lip bulged and fell; tears ran down her lovely cheeks; her head sank into her hands; she sobbed.

He went round the table to her; but she was tragic; she pushed him away, and would not be comforted, nor cajoled, nor comforted. For her the crisis which he had in his ardour so swiftly precipitated was very grave; it was vital. He was terribly dashed; he did not know what to do with himself, whether to stay where he was or to move away. At length, crestfallen and lugubrious, pitched down from heaven into hell, he resumed his own chair, and absurdly feigned to eat.

"You mustn't ask me," said Delphine, controlling herself and looking at him courageously. "I will never do it. I sh'd be miserable and it would kill me. I know it would. I'm not that sort. I'm quite happy like this – except for the war and I don't want anything else. Me the wife of a lord!" (How the phrase grated his susceptibility!) "Let me stay as I am, please, Sam. Please!"

She came to him and knelt at his feet abjectly, and raised her wet, imploring face. He could not bear to look at her, but to calm her he stroked her hair with a casual, patronizing hand.

"Promise me, Sam, you'll let me alone."

"Very well," he murmured sadly, half disdainfully.

He had essayed one of his brilliant effects and failed. In three minutes a battle had been fought and lost, a dream shattered, a reed broken. Instead of being succoured, he must succour. Instead of receiving, he must give – give – give. He saw the truth as if for the first time, though he had seen it more than once before. She had every quality except that of ambition. She had no ambition at all, save to please him in her own way. Her temperament was not active but contemplative, and nothing could change it. He doubted not that he could by persistence persuade her to his will, but to do so would be worse than useless, for the cherished plan could never succeed. He saw that as clearly now as a few moments earlier he had seen a triumph for it. She had definitely forsaken the world for his .arms. She could swoon into him and wear his necklaces with grace, even with majesty. No more!

Throughout their friendship she had constantly shown her limitations. She would not have a large flat. No, she would not. She had fought for a small home, a "nest." Damnable word! He well remembered how she had irritated him by her insistence on a ridiculous modesty of material environment. And he reflected that of late he had heard less and less of her canteen-work, and that the financial office, which had been her favourite toy for a space, was now fallen to a dressmaker's sewing-room.

He yielded. She had the invincible strength of the dreamer. She was far stronger than himself. She would never yield; could not. She would only pretend to yield. He immediately, characteristically, began to readjust his ideas for the future, his own future. Yes, she could only help him in her own way, and with that he must be content. He was as indissolubly attached to her as ever. And he must take her as she was, for he could not live without her. He knew it – and she knew it. He tried to piece the old happiness together again.

And then jealousy startlingly reappeared, stabbing him, piercing him. Causeless jealousy. But was it causeless? Why should she not marry him and take her rightful role? Not because she could not fulfil it, but because she would not. She desired to be free – for that mysterious man. She loved him, Sam, but she loved the other more: the other was young, of her own generation, and he, Sam, was old and fat. She was all goodness and affection; but she was capable of the deepest duplicity. Every woman was capable of duplicity.

She had returned to her chair now, weeping softly, and she sat wiping her eyes, and forlornly smiling (the smile of the victor, though) – and she was deceiving him. And when one night she had sunk into his lap as into a sofa and telephoned for him to the Berkeley Street flat – even then she had been deceiving him. But he was still hers, despite all her past, present and future deceptions, and would ever be. He, the popular minister, the great newspaper figure, the autocrat over hundreds – the conscious dupe of a typist girl! He hated her; he hated the jade necklace on her incomparable neck. He loved her. "This jealousy of mine is insane and disgusting," he said to himself.

"Oh, Sam," she whispered to him afterwards, with her arms tight round his neck as he sat in the easy chair. "If you wanted a mistress for your large houses, you ought to have chosen Gwen. She's the one. She isn't really timid, you know; she only seems timid. She's always wanting to do things, Gwen is. And when she was at Hanlopes, she *did* see some big houses I can tell you."

"Hanlopes? What Hanlopes? *The* Hanlopes?"

"I suppose so. Davies Street."

"Yes, that's it. You never told me she'd been at Hanlopes."

"Yes, she was. Sempstress. You know, fitting carpets and things. They turned her off and a lot more. The war's half ruined them… Gwen's the one."

Extraordinary how they liked to belittle themselves in favour of another. They never meant it. More duplicity.

"How's Gwen getting on?"

"Oh, fair – she says. But I think they'll sack her at Kingston. Not enough business. The new boss is afraid. She's downstairs now."

"Downstairs now!" he exclaimed.

"At least she was when you came. I told her to do out the office – it was getting awfully dirty."

"But she hasn't had anything to eat, then!"

"Oh, yes, she has."

"How do you know?"

"I told her if she heard you come in she was to finish the room and then get a bite at Gaycock's opposite, and come back, and, if she didn't see you go, or I didn't come down and fetch her before nine o'clock, she could go home. She's gone by now I expect. Of course if you hadn't come she'd have eaten up here with me."

What a capacity for planning, for scheming – all carefully thought out! What duplicity! And how hard on the beautiful Gwen!

As the evening passed Delphine dropped more and more into her exciting, pensive melancholia. Incomprehensible! Well, perhaps it was the result of the shock which he had given her. He had to try to raise her out of it. She was very loving in her melancholia.

55

Dinner

"Sam, you're very merry, but the famous burden of office is beginning to make its mark on your boyish eyes," said Tom Hogarth, with a jolly, half-brutal laugh; his broad shoulders shook.

"I wonder what *you'd* look like if you had to organize an overseas press visit to this city, with no help from any of your fellow-ministers," Sam replied lightly. "No, Sid," he added, turning to Jenkin, "I mustn't forget you. Sid does help me. He wangles interviews for my editors with the P.M. I'm damned if I can get 'em myself. But nobody else helps me. Not that I care! But I may tell *you*, Tommy, that munitions is nothing compared to my job."

"I'll swop with you," said Tom Hogarth challengingly.

"So will I," said the gloomy Hasper Clews, sardonic and kindly, Chancellor of the Exchequer.

The four were assembled in Sam's opulent, lofty sitting-room on the river front of the Savoy. The low roar of County Council trams came faintly up from the Embankment through the open window. The room was full of the preliminaries to a dinner given regardless of cost and perhaps somewhat regardless of the rules of the Food Controller. A high priest in the guise of a specially chosen *maitre a 'hotel*, and his acolytes, showed by their important and hushed demeanour a consciousness of being in the presence of the very great.

Sam, Tom Hogarth and Sid Jenkin were drinking cocktails. Of late Sam had discovered the tonic value of a cocktail. Hasper Clews, abstinent, was unwrapping at the table a paper containing his indispensable starchless bread. The other three had each a second cocktail. Sam was undoubtedly gay – and he was dominant. He had had, and was still having, difficult hours; he was still menaced; but what a difference, for him, between the atmosphere of this assemblage and that of the lunch at Downing Street which he had attended in order to be vetted by these same men. He had surpassed them all in the affections and gossip of the people, and they knew it, and that was perhaps the most significant fact for all of them in the situation.

The dinner was a sudden growth. In the morning the Prime Minister had rung up Sam to say that he would like to see him. Sam had instantly suggested the dinner, and the Prime Minister had surprised him by an amiable acceptance – through the lips of Rosie Packer. Sam had had the idea of reuniting the luncheon-party, but the Colonial Premier was out of England on a mission, and the Earl of Ockleford had declined, most urbanely, on the plea of a previous engagement. "Never mind," Sam had said to himself, "I shall be the only peer at the table."

It was a quarter to nine; the dinner was fixed for eight-thirty; they were waiting for the Prime Minister. At five minutes to nine Sam telephoned to Downing Street. The next moment he said to the high priest:

"We'll begin, please." And to his guests: "This dinner seems to be proceeding quite according to custom. Andy can't come. Prevented at the last moment, Miss Packer says. Says she's been trying to get me for the last twenty minutes. I wonder." He maintained his gaiety, which indeed not even the rebuff could overset.

Hasper Clews glanced at him with sad, humorous eyes.

"Prefers a quiet evening – dictating, oh yes, dictating," Tom

Hogarth murmured, in a voice too low for the waiters to hear.

He gave a soundless laugh, letting his head sink into his shoulders.

I saw 'im at seven. Said 'e was coming then," said Sid Jenkin.

They sat down, and the meal began. All, except Hasper Clews, ate quickly – partly from war-habit and partly because, unconsciously, they wanted to get the waiters out of the room in order to be able to talk freely. And Clews, the most deliberate masticator in the Government, ate so little that he could easily keep pace with the rest.

"How's the French getting on, Hasper?" asked Tom teasingly.

"*Est-ce que qa vous regarde?*" Clews retorted.

"Oho!" cried Tom, while Sid Jenkin tried to look as though an ignorance of French was to his credit as a proletarian.

Gaiety persisted. They were no longer ministers, but boys giving their brains some well-earned repose and indulging in a crude general rag. The champagne helped. Clews drank nothing, but he managed to be unusually cheerful. The fact was that the progress of the war helped more than the wine.

"When's your show coming off in the House of Lords, Sam?" Tom Hogarth questioned.

"I expect you know better than I do," said Sam.

They glanced at one another, playful and yet dangerous, like two tigers not quite sure of their mood. The implications of Sam's retort were plainly horrid.

"I'll tell you the minute I do happen to know," said Tom. "I hear the attack is to be personal. I wouldn't conceal anything from you, my dear; and I tell you frankly I hear it is to be very personal." He sniggered happily, quaffing champagne.

"Who told you?"

"Oh! It's about. Nobody in particular."

"Don't you let 'em rattle you, Raingo," said Hasper Clews. "They're keeping you on tenterhooks day after day in the hope of getting you rattled. They're relying on upsetting your nerves before they start."

"I know that," said Sam evenly. And he did know it. "I'm expecting the blow in the next day or two. I think it's about that that Andy wants to see me. If so, Andy's expecting it too, and he'd know."

Apparently there was no attempt to disguise the fact that the Cabinet, or at any rate part of it, was divided between the desire to preserve the full prestige of the Government and the desire to see Sam in a mess of his own, and that on the whole the latter desire prevailed over the former.

"It's my damned popularity you hate," said Sam with the utmost geniality.

And not even that astounding remark could mar the jolly atmosphere. Clews shot at the host a sympathetic and admiring look, which Sam appreciated, and repaid with a glance of thanks.

"And now I've got something to tell you," said Sam the moment the waiters had gone, leaving the old cognac, the coffee and the cigars. "There's been a mutiny of German soldiers at Brussels." He gazed around.

"Oh rats!" exclaimed Tom. "I've heard that before."

"You've never heard of *this* mutiny before, my boy," said Sam. "I heard of it a fortnight ago and I've not mentioned it to a soul" – (he was forgetting Delphine) – "I wanted to make quite sure about it, and I've made quite sure."

"And 'ow did ye get 'old of it, Sammy?" asked Sid Jenkin.

"A Pole – "

"Aha! The usual Pole!" Tom Hogarth shouted, spluttering in malicious glee. "Sam, I'm surprised at you. What's his name? Phillipowski, no doubt, or something like that."

"I don't know his name. I only know what he calls himself. Noganski. He's probably forgotten his real name long ago. But if that fellow hasn't told me the truth I'll eat Tommy's swelled head. They seized the ringleaders pretty quick and lined 'em up to be shot, but the soldiers wouldn't shoot. Then they covered 'em up with sheets or something, marched off the firing-party and got a fresh one – and gave a fresh order to fire. But there was still no shooting. Then they bundled 'em all back to prison again, mutineers and non-shooters together."

"And then?"

"I don't know any more. But you can see for yourselves what a thing like that must mean," Sam finished exultantly.

"I suppose your Pole saw it all himself?" said Tom.

"He didn't see it. But he was in Brussels, and you may take it from me it happened all right. I only finished my inquiry this afternoon."

Sid Jenkin and Hasper Clews were impressed by Sam's air of strong conviction; but Tom Hogarth and his champagne and cognac obstinately and pugnaciously took another view. Tom had been doing fifty per cent, of the talking throughout the dinner, and his percentage now rose to ninety or ninety-five.

"Just listen to me," he said, "and I'll put you wise about German mutinies in Brussels."

He was lively with wine, but still master of all his renowned dialectical skill, of which he at once opened a marvellous display, reinforced by his extraordinary detailed knowledge of every aspect of the war. Sam sat back, and Sid Jenkin and Clews sat back, until Tom Hogarth had talked himself out, whereupon Tom poured out another glass of cognac.

"Don't drink it, Tom," said Sam, taking a fresh cigar.

"You're a nice sort of a kind of a host. Why not?"

"Because if you drink another drop you'll be drunk."

Tom sprang up, overturning the brandy bottle, whose fall knocked over two glasses. The sound of broken glass and the spectacle of precious ancient cognac making a pool on the cloth seemed to bring the night to a dramatic climax. Sam did not move.

"I'm going to get the PM to see my Pole himself to-morrow," he said quietly.

Tom hesitated, and sank into his chair. Then the thin, insinuating ting-ting of the telephone bell was heard in the stillness of the room.

"Andy wants me to go down to him at once," said Sam, having visited the instrument. Hasper Clews leaned across the table and saved the poor remainder of the cognac.

51

Winning the War

Sam found the Prime Minister once more in his favourite room, not in evening dress, but wearing the favourite velvet coat. His silver hair was spectacularly disarranged. He sat in his own special chair, huddled over some despatches, nervously settling his gold-rimmed eyeglasses as he frowningly and eagerly read. Mr Poppleham, MP, and Miss Packer stood with solemnity about him.

"Was this effective tableau arranged for my benefit?" Sam asked himself as he entered.

"Hello, Sam!" said the Prime Minister, looking up casually for half a second and then bending again to the page. "Sit down, will ye?"

Miss Packer gravely shook hands; Mr Poppleham, being farther off, only nodded – but deferentially. Sam sat. Not a sound in the room, save the rustle of a turned page, and the stir of coal in a fire which had just been lighted.

"Well, what of it?" Andy cried suddenly, and as it were reproachfully, to Mr Poppleham, pitching the despatch on to the table. "This news might be ten times worse than it is and there'd be no need for us to get excited. It's only this spring that we've had the first real test of our grit. We've got to take the general curve, not tear our hair over every little down and up. We must whip 'em, and we shall whip 'em, till they're unconscious. Labour's ready to stick it anyway. And from the bit of a kick-up in the House this afternoon, it doesn't seem as if people are very anxious to change me for anybody else just yet, eh?"

Miss Packer gave a serene, confident smile.

"Poppleham, telephone to Sir Rupert Airlock to come along here at eleven-thirty to-night."

"Yes, sir."

"Thank you, Miss Packer. D'ye mind passing me the remains of my broth before you go?" Andy was showing his teeth; his yellow eyes roved defiantly; his voice rasped; he ran one hand through the tangle of his hair. Sam did not know what had happened; he had never been told anything really secret or interesting, and he was to be told nothing now. But he gathered that somebody had been disturbed by the course of events at the Front, and that the dictator in Andy was tigerishly functioning. Authority, masterful and overbearing, seemed to exude from Andy's person, and Sam himself felt small, nearly as small as Mr Poppleham and Miss Packer.

"No!" The Prime Minister repeated, casting a swift, covert glance at Sam. "They don't want anybody else but me yet." His tone was truculent, challenging, utterly intrepid – the tone of the man who had overruled commanders-in-chief in matters of military strategy and who stood by his decisions.

Sam thought:

"I have caught him in the very act of winning the war by will-power."

He both admired and feared Andy. Strange: all the food that Sam had eaten, and all the alcohol that he had drunk, were suddenly and completely digested.

"Sorry I couldn't turn up to-night, Sam," said Andy apologetically, when they were alone. No explanation vouchsafed. Andy did not furnish explanations, unless it might be the wrong ones. He was putting the spoon into the basin.

"No!" he exclaimed impishly. "You needn't look at it like that, my son. There isn't going to be any broth for you to-night." The Irish poet in Andy was speaking.

Sam laughed heartily, and Andy smiled with friendly roguery; but both felt the significance of the symbol.

"Well, how did the dinner go off?" said Andy lightly.

Sam was about to reply that the dinner had been great, but he checked himself.

"We missed you."

"I only wanted to tell you, Sam, I picked up a bit of gossip this morning, and I think there's something in it. They're going to tackle you in the Lords about your failure to counteract pacifist propaganda in the country. Alleged failure, I should say. Alleged failure. They're late of course. They always are. If they'd begun to make a fuss before the German push started they might have had something to talk about, but the push did for the Germans because it practically killed pacifism in this country. However, that's nothing. It's *your* head they're after, Sam. Pacifist propaganda's as good a pretext as any other. They don't want the fall of the Government – naturally. Only yours."

"Yes," said Sam. "I've heard it's going to be personal."

"And don't count too much on your press – on that press of yours, my boy. You've nobbled the working journalists all right, and even the editors. But the press-lords will have the last word, and they have their own axes to grind. Don't *I* know it! You might find the whole popular press change in a night. The press-lords only support popular favourites as long as it suits 'em to support 'em."

"We shall see about that, my big Andy," thought Sam. "Anyhow, you aren't the only person now that makes people nudge each other when they catch sight of him in a restaurant or in the street. And I've crowded you off the front-page quite a lot of times. And that's what's the matter with the joint of your nose." Aloud he said, smoothly: "The press-lords are your affair more than mine. I don't meddle with them. What interests me is the members of your Government who are engineering this push against me."

Andy laughed loud, his Scotch laugh; and he said nothing.

"Yes," Sam continued, still more smoothly. "Master Afflock, Bart., in particular. Perhaps I know a bit more than people think I know." (He did not.)

"I told you at the start I should stand by you," said Andy. "And – "

"No, you didn't." Sam stopped him. "You said I might find myself in a position where I should have to fight against you – and win."

"But I have stood by you."

"Oh, I know you have. Please don't imagine I think anything else." His tone was soothing and trustful. "You liar!" he said to himself. And aloud again: "I'll just explain to you the line I mean to take."

"No, you won't!" Andy cried. "You must talk to Ockleford – at any rate you must talk to Ockleford first. I've got myself into quite enough trouble with Ockleford as it is." Sam did not understand the allusion. "Ockleford's the leader in your House, and it's him you've got to settle things with. You can talk to me afterwards if you like – if we get a chance. I'm quite easy about you. I know you aren't the man to go and make yourself ridiculous."

"All which means," Sam addressed Andy in his heart, "you're taking me for a simpleton. The idea of you wanting to stifle a purely private conversation out of regard for Ockleford and the etiquette of the House! All you want is to sit on the fence till the thing's over. Then you'll drop down on the comfortable side. You aren't at all sure I shan't make a fool of myself. You know I'm not a good speaker. If I were you'd be all over me. If I'm ridiculous you'll drop me like a hot coal." His tongue merely said: "Of course! Of course! I wasn't thinking. I'll see Ockleford." And to himself: "' I won't say another word to you about it. Nor to Ockleford either – unless he comes and asks me."

"There's just one thing," Sam resumed, "and it's rather important." He related in detail the Pole's circumstantial story of the mutiny in Brussels.

The Prime Minister listened intently at first and then grew restless.

"Very interesting," he said casually at the end.

"I want you to see the man yourself."

"Oh, no! No need to do that. If you're satisfied."

"But I should like you to see him. I think you'd be convinced. I'm pretty sure you would."

"If you're convinced, that's enough for me. I quite appreciate the importance of it. Quite! You'll send along a chit of course in the usual way."

Sam persisted, and they argued for some time, Andy making it more and more clear that he entirely disbelieved the tale.

"Well, we'll see," said Andy at length, rather patronizingly. "I haven't got a moment to-morrow – *or* the next day." He rose and smiled benignantly. "I needn't tell you I have to ration myself. I'm going to send you in an account of the hours I've spent on your world-journalists, my lad – and especially on your Canadians. It was nice of you to drop in. I'm awfully sorry about the dinner."

In the hall Sam came upon Tom Hogarth, Sid Jenkin, and Sir Rupert Afflock, laughing and murmuring together, as thick as thieves. He chatted lightly with them for a minute, in the most colloquial and intimate manner, grinning appreciatively at one of Sid's stories.

No butler had appeared. Sam dismissed his car, and walked home along the Embankment, deserted even by the homeless. Only a few dimmed motor-cars and trams redeemed the thoroughfares from perfect darkness. The river and the bridges were nearly invisible.

"Andy can't help it," thought he, ruminating on the interview. "He's got human nature to deal with, including his own. I had a silly, footling idea that a world-war would change human nature. For all human nature cares a world-war is just like company-promoting. And my human nature's not better than theirs. He might, if he'd had time and if his human nature would have let him – he might have put me through an intensive inside course of politics, but he's more important things to think about. And I couldn't learn politics in three months more or less – nobody could. I've got to do the best I can and avoid moral indignation, and go through with it. We shall see what we shall see, Andy."

"Good evening, my lord," said the porter at the Embankment doors of the hotel.

"I'm a peer till I die, anyhow, and you can't alter that, Andy," said the human nature in the Minister of Records as he returned the porter's greeting. His heart was grim, sardonic, and yet kindly; subdued and yet purposeful. He wondered if Delphine was asleep.

57
The Motion

When winning entered the Upper Chamber on the afternoon of the anti-Raingo motion his self-consciousness and his stage-fright were intense. He walked to his seat with the quasi-military carriage which he always by instinct adopted on important occasions, but he was incapable of a single natural gesture. Neither his wealth nor his popularity was of the least service to him in the ordeal. He dared not look at the benches, and yet he could not help looking at them. The House was small, and the attitude of the few members present, as he felt rather than saw, frigidly civil. He held himself with the constraint of one upon whom all eyes are set – and set with hostility; nevertheless the detached witness in him knew that the eyes of most members were avoiding him, partly from an affectation of indifference and partly out of a decent desire not to incommode him, – for the House undoubtedly had manners; he was convinced also that the hostility would be tempered by a highly developed sense of fair play.

"Am I very pale?" he asked himself.

He was ashamed to think that he should be pale in the presence of these titled nonentities. What was their power to whiten his cheeks and constrict his throat? He scorned them, but in their collectivity they still overfaced him. He was dressed in mourning, with, however, a black-and-white check bow tie. He wished now that he had confined himself to strict black. Adela's death had deprived him of the celebrated blue-and-white neck-tie; but after a few weeks something had compelled him to imitate the blue-and-white in black-and-white (as first used for the sittings to photographers) – he could not forgo his label by which the world was used to recognize him; it would have been better, he now surmised, to return to plain black for the solemnity of this starched afternoon; unfortunately he had had no one to consult on the delicate point. Still, what could a necktie matter? But a necktie did matter – to himself.

"Why was I such a fool?"

As he sat down he had the illusion that the entire House was criticizing the taste of the mushroom minister who so soon after his wife's death could attend a debate with white in his necktie; if one member turned murmuring to another the murmur was surely about the offensiveness of his necktie. He had encountered Sid Jenkin in the precincts. Sid had evidently been told off to report to Andy upon Sam's performance. Sid was most friendly and encouraging, without any note of patronage towards a tyro; but he had given Sam a queer look before speaking: was the look an animadversion upon the necktie? And so on. Then Sam completely forgot his necktie and never thought of it again.

The House was discussing a local Electrical Power Bill. The speeches were brief, conversational, and not perfunctory. Members seemed to be saying: "This affair is a trifle, but let us be just and conscientious towards it." Sam wished that the debate would end; he wished also that it would last for ever.

He glanced around, trying to copy in his demeanour the urbane boredom of the rest of the House. He watched the Lord Chancellor, who with little movements of the head over a motionless body simulated a grave interest in Electrical Power. The officials were gloomily bored, gazing back in their hearts upon a past, and forward at a future, of ennui. But they were proud of their posts, too, in the august assembly.

There was Lord Lingham, whom Sam would have to answer; an old man, hero of agriculture and hunting-fields, with a kindly, courtly, honest face. The opposition could have selected no better spokesman for their purpose; for he was respected, utterly sincere, not a fool, and could be relied upon not to weary and annoy the House by any exhibition of undue intelligence. Sam scarcely knew him, scarcely even recognized him, but he had recently learned enough of Lord Lingham to know that his previous estimate of him, formed during years of hearsay in the Commons, as a violently prejudiced and foolish reactionary partisan, had been grossly unfair to the noble viscount.

Lord Ockleford, leader of the House, entered, with due ceremony, but in a sort of gravely apologetic haste. He sat down by Sam and gave him a stately, courteous smile, whose perfection was the fruit of as many generations as the perfection of a lawn in an Oxford College. The electrical debate stood adjourned. Sam nerved himself for the assault. But two other Electrical Bills came up for a third reading, and Sam was reprieved. The third readings were accomplished in the winking of an eye.

Lord Lingham gathered together his aged, athletic limbs, stood up, and cleared his throat. He was untidy and ungainly, but what a style he had, what natural distinction of tone and department! What a contrast to Eccles – and

Sam could feel "Eccles" written all over himself. The motion to which the noble viscount spoke was thus conceived: "That this House regrets that stronger measures have not been taken to combat the various agencies in this country which are serving the interests of the enemy."

Lord Lingham spoke with the ease of an old and honoured man who had made thousands of speeches in all sorts of conditions – and never one really good and never one really bad. He had the ideal combination of qualities for consistent success in British politics – character, mediocrity, and a hale common-sense. He spoke of the British Empire having its back to the wall with as much emotion and sincerity as though the phrase had never been used before. It was as if he actually felt the wall behind his own back and saw the horde of enemies in front, and as if he was grimly and pugnaciously enjoying the desperate situation, secure in the absolute conviction that he never had been beaten and never could be beaten. He was not bitter, even against pacifists, but he condemned them and thought strongly that they ought to be silenced, and that since mild measures had not sufficed for this purpose severe measures should be employed.

What he feared more than anything was a peace by negotiation. He did not say, but he implied, that if the positions had been changed and it was the enemy that had its back to the wall, he might have been willing to negotiate, but as things actually were any negotiation would be a shame and an everlasting disgrace. He ended with a warm appeal to the Government to be more active in safeguarding the country against mischievous groupings, coupling this with the assertion, which he challenged anyone to deny, that the great heart of the people beat true. Only one thought made him angry – namely, the thought that, in the midst of a paper famine, seditious sheets were allowed to buy paper while Government propaganda was hampered by the lack of paper. That this should be so was, he confessed, an insoluble puzzle to his simple intelligence. (Cheers.) The speech contained no personalities and showed no rancour.

Then up rose the breezy and gallant retired general who was to second the motion. Lord Garsington was nearly eighty and always the youngest man in any company in which he found himself. He was the chief orator and stand-by of the peace-at-no-price party, and his position with the country was tremendously fortified by the fact, which he did not cease to proclaim, that all his pre-war warnings had come true. If Lord Lingham had made thousands of speeches, General Lord Garsington had made tens of thousands, and to make them he had travelled – it was computed – three times the distance between the earth and the moon. He had never had a day's illness in his life, and never had a tooth out. He would say whatever came into his head, and justify this breeziness by the plea that he was a soldier and a plain-spoken man. His friendships were steadfast and everybody liked him, though his jokes were outrageous and he would sacrifice anything and anybody to get them out.

But to-day his mood was far from jocular. He was simply appalled by the lethargy of the Government. He was simply appalled by the gullibility of the working-classes (who nevertheless, he admitted, made the finest infantry in the world and in the history of the world, and whose great heart, he agreed with the noble viscount who had preceded him, beat true). He wanted to know, he insisted on being informed, where the pacifist organizations got their money from; and if no one could tell him he was prepared to tell everyone that in his opinion the pacifist organizations got their money from Germany. He attributed the failure of propaganda throughout the country and elsewhere to a lamentable tendency on the part of the Government towards over-centralization. The fighting services were not allowed to do their own work in this connection, or at best they were hampered in the doing of it, by departments which, however excellent in intention, were without tradition and actuated by a spirit foreign to the British spirit, – the spirit of the fighting services. He employed the phrase "fighting services" several times, and by the emotional emphasis which he put upon it showed plainly the origin of the inspiration which now vitalized his attack. He warned the Government – he whose warnings had never once yet been falsified by events… He suddenly sat down, amid cheers which would have been called tepid in the Commons, but were deemed enthusiastic in the Lords.

58
The Ordeal

Sam was horribly taken aback by the suddenness of Lord Garsington's down-sitting, for he had been expecting the noble and gallant lord to continue for quite another ten minutes. Scores of discreet and desperate thoughts ran through his mind. About his insomnia. About his night-sweats. The carefully composed sentences of his exordium, which he had learned by heart and repeated, with various intonations and stresses, in his room at the hotel and on the Embankment at early morn. Why Delphine was not in when he called to see her. The artful malice which had caused "them" (the real originators of the debate) to select the very day of his great press-banquet for the day of the debate. His own proud foolishness in not asking for another day. His own rash foolishness in telling Andy, on the afternoon when Andy gave him the ministerial appointment, all his ideas about Andy's motives in wishing to keep him out of the Lords. There had been no personalities after all. Why grown men – barons, viscounts, earls, marquises and even a duke – should applaud such an ingenuous speech as Garsington's. Where could Delphine have been. when he called to see her and found the flat empty? Not that he was jealous. No. Jealousy had gone from him. He had not heard from her, but he had written to her while driving in the car. No chance, in the great rush, to telephone to her. His heart. Eric Trumbull's demeanour to him on his return from France...

He felt the Lord Chancellor's gaze upon him, and a certain expectant uneasiness in Lord Ockleford's posture by his side – and he saw that the House had considerably filled up, not only with members, but with -spectators. More were now coming in. Excitement was in the air of the usually somnolent chamber. If not quite a full-dress debate, the affair was rather like one. This was practically his maiden speech.

"Well," he thought, "I'm up. My back is to the wall. I wonder what sort of a hell of a mess I shall make of it all. I wonder how I shall be feeling half an hour hence."

He fixed his eyes on Lord Lingham, as upon a comforting phenomenon of decency. Every gaze was upon him. He was alone and naked in infinite cold space.

"Can I say the first word?" he thought.

Ages passed. Well, he could not keep them waiting for ever. Why had he ever entered politics? No reward could compensate for his racking torture. He began with calculated humility by apologizing for his inexperience as a Minister and for a natural nervousness at addressing at length for the first time their lordships' historic and august Chamber. He heard his own voice. Was it quite like his own? He was suddenly conscious, with terror, of hidden reporters taking down, pitilessly, every phrase he uttered. Once said, no word could be altered, improved, destroyed. Each sentence was unchangeably there for ever. A frightening thought! He regretted the word "august." It laid on flattery with a trowel. "Historic" would have sufficed alone. But there "august" was, fixed certainly in Hansard and probably in *The Times*! Apart from that, he had made a good start; he could feel that he had impressed the House favourably.

He generously praised Lord Lingham for the sincerity of his patriotism and Lord Garsington for the effectiveness of his oratory in propaganda. Then he smiled contemptuously at pacifism. He related how a pacifist in a large northern munition works had been thrashed into hospital by angry fellow-workers. He deplored violence, nobody could deplore violence more then he did; but the incident showed that the citizens could deal with pacifism unaided by Government departments, and that pacifism was indeed scarcely worth official notice. As for the pacifist press, it was, Britain being a free country and the war being a fight for liberty, surely entitled to a fair share of that scarce commodity, paper – so long as it did not transgress the law. If it transgressed the law, then the matter was one for the police (Hear, hear!), not for the Ministry over which he had the honour to preside. He then, without a note and entirely from memory, gave a long series of colossal figures to show what the Ministry of Records had done in the way of circulating literature under his gifted and regretted predecessor and also under himself. The closely listening House was still more favourably impressed. He was doing very well. He saw the safety of the shore; which was getting nearer, and he was swimming strongly.

Turning to the charges of over-centralization made by the noble and gallant lord, he denied them completely. "The noble and gallant member for the fighting services" – A mistake! A horrible mistake! *A double and a triple gaffe!* Sam's occasional Puck-like humour had surprised and got the better of him.

Also his tone was wrong; the spirit of defiance which now and then would stand up audaciously to the most formidable opponents rang now in his voice. No! He was not a good public speaker, because he could not depend on his apparatus.

He at once felt the House react against his ill-timed pleasantry. The atmosphere was changed, and the change grew more marked. Friendliness became indifference, resentment or hostility. Why had he been such a fool f There it was. The words were irrevocably and ineffaceably down in the note-books of the reporters; nothing could draw them back. He longed to be able to fade away, to cease to exist, to be erased from the memory of men. But he had to continue. He said, more smoothly, that no modification whatever had occurred or been planned in the organizing of propaganda, beyond an amicable arrangement between himself and the National War Aims Committee in regard to the exploitation of cinemas. True, the general ground had been explored; but all decisions were in the hands of the War Cabinet, and he might say for himself that he had not the least intention of attempting to impair the independence of other departments. And on and on. But it was useless. He was not being convincing. His grip was gone. The House was not listening, or listening only to condemn. He swam laboriously. The shore was hidden by great waves.

Then he had the misfortune to catch sight of Geoffrey among the spectators. The startling vision unnerved him. Why was Geoffrey there? He had said nothing to Sam about going. He had openly and bitterly despised politicians and the machinery of politics. He was gazing straight at his father. Sam's mind became a complete blank, as regards the speech. He could not speak. He was in danger of collapse. He thought of the story of the German mutiny in Brussels. It seemed to be his one hope. "Before I sit down I should like to tell the House some facts of which I can guarantee the authenticity." He related the story at length. The House was held, thrilled. Every head was turned towards him. He was making a sensation. In ten minutes, he thought, the story would be cabled to the ends of the world. No doubt he ought not to have done it, for he had consulted nobody as to the advisability of doing it, and he was saddling the Government with responsibility for an item which the Prime Minister had refused to credit. But he did it. After a poor, brief peroration he sat down, saved. (Cheers.) Many members left immediately to spread the news.

A peer belonging to the Opposition and an ex-minister spoke quite amiably about the Government, and there were other speeches, none of which was listened to. Finally Lord Ockleford, august leader of an august House, rose, and in a long piece of elaborate oratory made nothing clear except the fact that he was not supporting Sam. He was so close to Sam that the tail of his frock-coat rubbed against Sam's elbow. A positive malice against Sam glinted out at intervals from the smooth grey contours of his polished sentences. Sam, amazed, smiled to himself acidly. The noble earl sat down. Lord Lingham's motion was by leave withdrawn.

The House rose and emptied. The demonstration was over, having served its purpose of a warning note to the Government in general and to the Minister of Records in particular. Lord Ockleford, departing, gave him a very gracious smile.

In the precincts Sam was accosted by many, all anxious to learn from him, if possible, further details about the dazzling mutiny. Lord Lingham was among them. Whatever Lord Ockleford might have said, or thought, Sam was beyond question the hero of the moment and the observed of every eye. He was very excited by his reception, but unhappy. He felt thirsty and tired and had a faint, nervous cough.

"I must lie down and get a sleep," he said to himself. "If I don't have a nap I shall never manage the banquet to-night."

59

The Reception

The Press-banquet occupied the largest ball-room in the hotel, with a large reception-room adjoining; and it now shone with the utmost magnificence that war-conditions would permit. The finest procurable food, champagne, port, cigars, abounded. The greatest editors in America confessed amazement at the profusion of hot-house flowers and hot-house fruit. A week or two earlier a teetotaller who smoked a pipe had raised a question about the national ability to pay for certain unheard-of luxuries – wines and cigars – supplied by a spendthrift Government to a group of overseas journalists on a visit to Glasgow. When asked whether there would not surely be trouble over the prodigious cost of the Savoy banquet, "That will be all right," said Sam, who had determined to bear the entire expense himself.

The Prime Minister arrived early. Sam had procured four members of the Government to speak: the Prime Minister because he was the Prime Minister and the most famous man in the world, and because he wanted to come; Tom Hogarth to display the bellicose pugnacity of John Bull in unsurpassable oratory; Sid Jenkin to prove that Britain was truly democratic; and the Colonial Premier because he was a colonial. Andy took his place by Sam's side near the entrance to the reception-room. His demeanour to Sam was very genial and somewhat noncommittal.

"You look a wee bit tired, Sam," said he. Not a word about Sam's performance in the afternoon.

Sam replied by mercilessly administering to him on the spot such a dose of overseas journalists as no Premier had ever before had to swallow. Droves of editors, each autocratic in his own sphere at home, swept into the great room, and Andy had to be the most famous man in the world to every one of them.

And he successfully was.

The visitors, though indefatigably fresh, were really sated with hospitality. Each during his visit had had what he desired to the full. Those who wanted sociological inquiry, including the study of vice, those who wanted the aristocracy, those who wanted sight-seeing, those who wanted prize-fighting or sports, those who wanted religion, those who wanted the stage or the cinema, those who wanted the society of acquiescent ladies, – all had been humoured and satisfied, by experts in the various branches of activity. Their free and sometimes condescending criticism had been heard with respect and a promise to try to do better, and their praise stoically endured, by Britons whose secret conceit, compared to the ingenuous self-complacency of overseas, was as Mount Everest to Snowdon.

Now was the climax and zenith of the epical visit to the senile, worn-out country, and every Briton in the room knew that every traveller from overseas was knocked silly by the spectacle of what the sangfroid of the land of his fathers could accomplish in the midst of the most desperate altercation in history.

And it was Sam's night. Sam was once again shining in the foreheads of all the evening papers, by the great light of his German mutiny story, which had put a new complexion on the progress of the war – which indeed had in effect announced to the whole universe the impending downfall of the enemy, and brought smiles to the faces of millions. Sam knew it and felt it. He knew also that every journalist in a room crammed with journalists was expertly appreciating the news-value of the story, and setting him up as the very prince of newsmongers. What mattered the awful slip in his speech, the frightful narrowness of his escape from collapse? Naught! He stood far higher than ever in the admiration of peoples. He was a rival even to Andy himself. Withal he found opportunity to be particularly agreeable to his own men, who adored him for his comradeship and impatience of all extra-ministerial obstacles – to the returned Trumbull, whom he put in charge of French-speaking Canadians; to Mayden, who arrived later after super-adding to the labour of organizing the banquet the labour of fitting nearly a hundred officials from outside buildings into the restricted spaces of the Ministry: to Sir Ernest Timmerson, whose praises he sounded into the ear of the richest editor in New York.

The last of all the nobs to arrive was Sid Jenkin. Sid drew Sam apart.

"A bit rough on you this afternoon, Ockleford! Eh:"

"Pooh!"

"I suppose ye know why?"

"Because I hadn't asked him to patronize this paltry banquet, no doubt."

"Not a bit of it. Because 'e's the leader of the Lords and Clyth didn't consult Mm personally before 'e appointed ye. Ocky 'as a great notion of the importance of maintaining 'is own discipline in the Lords."

Sam saw a sudden light in the darkness in which as a minister he had been compelled to exist. Nobody had ever told him anything worth knowing. He had been treated always as an intruder. He regarded it as symbolic that he had never even seen the Cabinet room of No. 10 Downing Street. And imagine the courtly Ockleford secreting his wrath for months until a supreme occasion arrived for venting it!

Never mind! Though Sam had prudently given up his project for centralizing all propaganda in his own Ministry, he had other projects, and they were maturing and he would carry them through because he was a power, and a popular idol, and destined to triumph. Mrs Blacklow had foretold that all would be well. All, in fact, was well, and very well.

"Who's that dark fellow just in front?" Andy privately asked him as they were moving into the hall of the banquet. "I seem to know his face. I must have met him somewhere."

"I doubt if you've met him," said Sam, amiably smiling.. "He's only one of your numerous ministers. I won't tell you his name. Your mind mustn't be burdened with trivial details.""

Andy had to laugh.

"You look a wee bit tired, Andy," said Sam; and to himself; "I shall pay for this, I expect."

But he never did pay for it. On this evening he got something for nothing.

The company slowly took the appointed seats at dinner. Sam as chairman had the middle seat at the north table, and Andy, opposite to him but far off, the middle seat at the south table. Twenty different varieties of nasal accent filled the grateful air.

60

Apotheosis

Towards the end of the evening it had been established and many times ratified by libation that the English-speaking peoples – that was to say, Britain and her far-flung broods, including, of course, the people of the United States, whose representatives were present duly admitted, while not exulting in, their parentage – were God's chosen and the possessors of all fine qualities, and the sole salvation of the world (excepting, of course, the Continental Allies, who also were the possessors of all fine qualities and the salvation of the world); whereas Germany, with her misguided friends, existed only to prove the principle of evil and to be smashed to pieces by the righteous. Even war had become glorious – and the men in the trenches were not forgotten.

Amity reigned. Everybody loved everybody else. Sir Ernest Timmerson himself and Captain Mayden himself had got together and were chatting like David and Jonathan; Sir . Ernest's unique evening shirt, one of the most wonderful phenomena in the huge, glittering room, was considerally disarranged. Sam had left his presidential chair and was moving along the tables in snatches of conversation. The richest editor in New York came after him.

"Say, Sam," said he (they had got thus far in intimacy). "You're wanted back."

"Am I, Teddy? But the programme's over."

"Not on your life. Come along."

Sam obeyed. He knew what was coming. He had struck out of the draft programme of toasts any reference to himself, partly because he shirked a set speech (hitherto he had had to say little beyond a general welcome, and summonses to others to speak), and partly because he could not hear himself being praised in public without being victimized by a strong, humiliating desire to disappear into the bosom of the earth. Now, however, and in a flash, he saw that he was no longer his own master, but the slave of the excited assembly. As the tall, slim, white-haired New Yorker rose in his place, waving the assembly into silence with a fresh cigar, all the rovers slipped hastily into chairs – the first chairs handy, no matter whose – and not a sound was heard for a few seconds.

"I rise to perform a duty, and to call upon you to perform a duty, which is also the keenest pleasure, and the neglect of which would amount to nothing short of a public scandal. I mean, proposing and drinking – I say drinking – the health of our host, the Minister of Records. Lord Raingo – Sam, in fact." What immediately followed was not cheering, but a sudden sharp, explosive, deafening noise, like a broadside of guns – an overwhelming revelation of feeling. Then a tattoo of cutlery on tables and heels on floor, prolonged and prolonged. Andrew Clyth had dazzled the company by a first-rate specimen of his expert wizardry; Sid Jenkin had warmed all hearts by his genial tact and artful artlessness; Tom Hogarth had laid a magic spell on the room by a wondrous exhibition of pure and impassioned oratory; and one or two of the finest overseas after-dinner speakers, including the Colonial Premier, had well upheld the honour of the broods in speech. But none of them had called forth a demonstration comparable to that which the New Yorker now evoked with fifty simple words. The speaker waited.

"I say that no man – I make no exceptions – has done more than Lord Raingo – or as much – or as much – in the last few weeks to nourish that spirit of friendship and mutual understanding among Allies which closes up the ranks, puts shoulder to shoulder, and wins wars."

Sam listened, with bent head. He did not hear everything; there were moments when the clear voice of the man by his side was rendered inaudible by strange occurrences in Sam's head. But he felt throughout the throb of intense sincerity which vitalized the sentences and destroyed all memory of the laudatory and optimistic hypocrisy that had disfigured the oratory of this banquet as it disfigures the oratory of every banquet. Yes, he believed every word, because he had to believe it. He tried to pooh-pooh every word but could not...

"Gentleman, I give you the health of Lord Raingo." The assembly jumped to its feet. An uproar, formidable and terrific! Tables, the floor, the room itself shook. Sam, his head still bent, glanced from under his eyebrows, and saw amongst hundreds of upraised arms and glasses the arm and glass of Andy Clyth and Andy's lighted, beaming face. And he looked down again.

"For – "

"He's a jolly good fellow" (in tremendous unison)*..." Hoorah! Hoorah! Hoorah!"*

The ends of the earth were united in esteem and affection for Sam. He arose and beheld the mess of the disordered tables, and every flushed, admiring, enthusiastic face aimed straight at him. The applause would not cease. He felt like a small, timid boy; and, staggered by the thunder of his own apotheosis, he trembled, and tears came into his shamed, happy eyes.

"I should only make a fool of myself, if I – " he stammered, thanked the assembly brokenly and very movingly, and sank back into his seat.

The affair was finished. Angels and archangels became men, with prosaic ideas about getting home, what they had drunk, possible headaches, the tiresome duties of the next morning. At the doors Mayden was waiting for the hero. "Can I do anything for you, sir?"

"No, thanks. No, thanks. You must be very tired. See you to-morrow, my boy."

Sam ignored everybody else, took the lift to his rooms, got a hat and coat, and went privily and swiftly out on to the Embankment. Rain had fallen, and there was still a slight drizzle in the air. He chanced on a taxi and drove to Orange Street. He had drunk little after the cocktails and felt very thirsty. His throat, irritated no doubt by smoke and odours, relieved itself occasionally by a faint, dry cough. And a headache was beginning.

He wanted to be with Delphine, not necessarily to recount the evening to her, but simply to be with her, to taste the reposefulness of her presence. In five minutes, in one minute as it seemed, he was switching on the light and climbing the stairs at Orange Street. He could not wait till he set eyes on her. He called out. At the same moment he heard a door open and a footstep. But it was Gwen who stood watching him from the head of the stairs.

"Hallo, Gwen!" he greeted her. "Where's Delphine?"

"She isn't in," said the pale girl. "I thought she must be out somewhere with you."

"Not in!"

"No. I've been waiting here four hours. I wanted to sleep here."

"Was she expecting you, my dear?"

"No. Not exactly. But she always knows I may pop in any evening. I haven't been for three days."

"Neither have I," said Sam.

They stood together, hesitant, on the landing, the girl looking up at his great bulk with her lovely, frightened eyes.

"Oh well," he said firmly. "She's bound to be in soon. Let's sit down, shall we? And can you get me some water?"

He put on a good front, but fear was in his heart. Fear! He sat down in the drawing-room and Gwen served him. What a sudden contrast between this scene and the scene he had just left! The banqueting-room would not yet be emptied of the mighty influencers of public opinion; and here he was, the admired and illustrious Lord Raingo, in the nest of his illicit love, with a little ex-bus-conductor! He was somehow ashamed. Into what inglorious situations would not passion force a man! If the richest editor of New York, with his firmly-expressed, harsh views about the open incontinence of London, could have seen him at that moment, with that young, shabby, beautiful girl, in that room!

An unopened letter lay on a table at hand. He glanced at it and recognized his own handwriting on the envelope. Proof enough that Delphine had not been at home on the previous night! Gwen was crying. And Sam could have cried too, had it not been for the tradition that important, big, middle-aged men do not cry in the presence of weak, beautiful girls.

Part Two

61

Conspiracy

When, after a swift journey from London the next morning, the car curved round along the weedy gravel and stopped with its door precisely opposite the front-door of Moze Hall, Sam was a little surprised to find that he was too indifferent and too tired to trouble himself about descending from the vehicle. He shirked the physical enterprise and exertion which would be necessary in order to get out. He just sat back, leaning, and waiting for something to happen. The driver tooted her horn, and immediately the unkempt Wrenkin appeared, from somewhere, glaring inimically at the girl, as if saying: "Can't you keep quiet with your horn in my garden?"

Sam had to be helped out of the car, and the gingerly manner in which he set his foot on the ground reminded him of Mayden lowering himself into a chair. Was he stiff from the ride, or was he weak? Stiff, he thought.

"All right! All right!" he said rather sharply to Wrenkin. "I can walk."

Wrenkin loosed him. Sam turned to his driver.

"Thank you," he smiled. "Have some lunch before you start back, will you?"

She nodded, gave him a long smile, and said naught.

"Why the devil does she look at me like that?" he thought.

"Bring in all those newspapers," he said to Wrenkin, "and the press-cuttings. The green things."

Newspapers and press-cuttings littered the floor of the limousine. He watched Wrenkin methodically pick everything up. He had meant to take his usual course of papers and cuttings in the car, but he had not done so; he had wanted to reflect; he had not reflected. "When I'm settled I'll reflect."

"Mr Geoffrey had gone off to Colchester about some glass before your message came, my lord," said Wrenkin in a low, grumbling voice.

"My message! What message:" he was about to say, but refrained. He had sent no message. He stood staring around, vaguely. It had rained, soft summer rain, and would perhaps rain again.

"Miss Thorping came in the day before yesterday, my lord," Wrenkin continued.

"Thorping? Thorping?"

"The new housekeeper Mr Geoffrey – "

"Oh yes! I think Mr Geoffrey did mention it to me. Pretty good, isn't she?" He was falling at once into the old vein of being confidential with the slatternly, gruff, and efficient Wrenkin. They were man and man once more.

"Yes, my lord. She's a Hoe woman. She's always been very well spoken of. Housekeeper in Belgrave Square before the war."

The front door opened and old Skinner appeared, in a new cut-away morning coat and striped trousers, but with his prewar dirty finger nails. Wrenkin entrusted to him all the literature.

"Don't drop any of 'em," he curtly enjoined Skinner, just as though the employer were not present.

Yes, Wrenkin was acting up to his own ideal of himself as the most remarkable man that ever lived. He touched his shapeless cap to Sam and went his ways, knowing that under the new jealous regime of the nevertheless friendly Miss Thorping he must not enter the house save for strictly engineering purposes – such as stoking the hot-water furnace.

Sam nonchalantly greeted Skinner, whom he pitied for an ageing inefficient, and stepped into the hall. The door leading to the drawing-room on the right and the door leading to the dining-room on the left were both wide open, and the rich vistas of antique furniture, curtains and carpets, thus suddenly presenting themselves, startled Sam, who had not seen the house for a month, and filled him with paternal pride in Geoffrey.

"That lad's no fool," he thought, passing his hand over a walnut table that was certainly entitled to call itself a museum piece.

And Geoffrey had evidently been buying pictures, too, and bric-a-brac. The interior, so far as Sam could see it, was very complete. The soiled walls had not been renovated because Geoffrey had agreed willingly that labour must not be employed, but they looked quite respectable, and even dignified, as a background. Of course refurnishing one's house in the midst of the very crisis of the war…

"War be damned! I like it; it's fine. And if it's given the boy something to occupy himself with… It may be the saving of him!"

So ran Sam's thoughts. At last he had a home and he did not care what anyone said! But, by Jove, the thing must have cost money. All the better! It was time a bit of money should be spent. He anticipated the bills with positive pleasure. Few of them had yet come in.

Dr. Heddle, hat in hand, appeared round the corner of the staircase. What the devil –

"How d'ye do, Lord Raingo? I heard you were coming, so I thought I'd pay a call. Just been up to look at your bedroom. Hope you don't mind. Wonderful change here your son's made."

The excellent, hale man, still in his khaki, hastened down the last steps to shake hands. He was too deferential, as usual, and in addition a little nervous.

"Glad to see you, doctor," said Sam; and to himself: "What's all this?" He had a sensation akin to that which disturbed him when he felt the mysterious circumambient plottings of Andy and Company embarrassing his plans.

"You've got a cough, I see," said Dr. Heddle. "Slept well? Had a good breakfast this morning?"

Sam's replies were defiant, feeble, and unsatisfactory.

"You look tired. The drive, I expect. It's close weather. I think I'd better take your temperature."

The tradition and magic prestige of his profession were now behind the simple Heddle. He was the medical adviser, and could not be withstood even by the conqueror of the House of Lords, the hero of four hundred overseas editors, and the darling of the public. Sam was reduced to the patient. A strange, annoying transformation of roles! As the patient, Sam meekly followed the simpleton upstairs.

"Seems to me you know more about this place than I do," said Sam, as the doctor led the way across the landing straight to the bedroom which had been Adela's, and which Geoffrey had decreed should henceforward be his father's, Sam's old bedroom being transformed into a dressing-room.

The landing, carpeted with rugs, had almost the appearance of a room; it had completely lost that bleakness which was so characteristic of Adela's ideal of furnishing. The style of the large bedroom was now Empire, of the late, ornate period. Geoffrey had said that Empire was the only really masculine style, and therefore best suited to a man. The chamber glittered with bronze crowns, swans, claws, wreaths and sphinx-heads. Geoffrey had said: "Never be afraid of ornament if the lines are good." Sam exulted in the rich majesty of the room. He said to himself that he had longed all his life for such an environment, and now, thanks to the surprising and silent-working autocratic Geoffrey, he had it.

"I wouldn't mind being ill for a bit in a room like this," he thought, as, yielding himself to the doctor, he lay down on the magenta silk coverlet. The examination was exasperatingly lengthy; and Sam, very impatient and anxious – (" Suppose I am going to be ill after all! ") – unjustly judged that the doctor, with a millionaire-celebrity under his thumb, was making himself important.

"Did you ever have rheumatic fever as a child?" asked the doctor, after he had used the stethoscope over Sam's chest and back.

"Yes."

"You never told me."

"No. Never thought of it."

The doctor abruptly stuck a thermometer into Sam's mouth.

"A touch of fever: but nothing to make a song about," said he, at the window, peering at the thermometer.

"Yes, but the heart?" Sam questioned, trying to seem indifferent but not succeeding.

"Well, I can honestly say that it is no worse than it was," the doctor answered, with his ingenuous smile.

"Oh!" An intense relief filled Sam's mind. "And how's your heart?" he inquired, and, slipping off the bed, he stood up. He felt better again, and indeed, though he had had to be helped out of the car, he had walked up the stairs quite easily.

"Ah! I take care of *my* heart. I'm a humble sort of a person. *I* don't make speeches in the House of Lords and take the chair at banquets. We humble persons give our hearts a chance."

The doctor's tone was curious, proud, a little obsequious, and disturbing. Sam felt ill again. He sat down in an easy chair and put his hands on two bronze sphinx-heads which terminated the arms. He said nothing.

"Now if I were you I should rest for a while," the doctor proceeded. "Lie down. Get *into* bed. Only for an hour or two. You need it."

"Take my clothes off?"

"Why not?"

The doctor pulled aside the coverlet, and Sam saw that beneath the coverlet the bed had been turned down. He also saw a suit of pyjamas. The sensation of being trammelled in a web of conspiracy recurred. It would be easier to acquiesce in silence, hiding his suspicions; and he acquiesced. More than ever he wanted to reflect, and in bed he could reflect exhaustively.

' Shall I speak to the housekeeper myself about your food?" I think you ought to stick to slops."

"Oh!" said Sam, with mock plaintiveness. "Do exactly what you like with me. I know one thing – I'm a model patient, always have been."

"Well, I hope you are," said the doctor, as if he was not quite sure. A strange saying!

"By the way," Dr. Heddle turned round as he was leaving the room. "I suppose you wouldn't care for me to send a nurse over for you from Clacton?"

"A nurse! What on earth for?"

"A night nurse. That cough – it might be troublesome. It's always nice to know there's somebody handy; in case – "

"No thanks," said Sam dryly. The idea of a night nurse fidgeting around revolted him. And in God's name why a nurse? No doubt because he was a millionaire and a great celebrity! Rot!

"All right," said the doctor. "I only mentioned it. Some patients *like* to have a nurse. And as there's no lady in the house. However, there's no absolute *need* for a nurse… Good morning. Afraid I can't look in to-night. But I'll be along in the morning."

Why should the fellow dream of looking in again that night?

62

Housekeeper and Nurse

At half-past eight that same morning Mayden had most startlingly limped unannounced into Sam's bedroom at the Savoy Hotel.

After leaving Gwen alone in the Orange Street house Sam had passed a night both physically and mentally torturing.

On the mental side, he was convinced that Delphine, faithless to him, had decamped with her mysterious ranker-officer. He remained in this conviction (of which he had neither cared nor dared to give the least hint to Gwen) for a space, and then it had been utterly destroyed as outrageous by his conviction of Delphine's honesty and passionate love. But his inability to conceive of any other credible explanation of Delphine's disappearance left a vacuum in his mind and the old conviction surged back into the vacuum. So the night had wearied itself out. Of course Delphine might have been the victim of some street accident, but in that case news of the affair must have reached Gwen or himself, for the girl naturally never went out without a bag, in which were her cards, and if the accident had been fatal the papers would have had word of it. No! The theory of an accident was in no way tenable.

On the physical side he suffered from the dry, hard, faint cough – he who never coughed, and from a recurrent pain in the ribs; also his breathing, though scarcely difficult, had become a conscious function; and at intervals he shivered. He would have sworn that the night had been entirely sleepless, had not Mayden's advent very obviously wakened him with a jump.

He had pulled himself together for the benefit of Mayden, who was fresh and bright and so healthfully young and made such a contrast to Sam's tired middle-age. On the previous evening Mayden had shown exhaustion, but all signs of it had vanished; the night had restored him to perfect condition. Not that Sam could admit illness. By no means! He was only unwell and very fatigued – as who would not be at the end of so terrible a night, following so strenuous a day.

Mayden had implored his chief, as a favour to himself, to take a day's holiday, if possible a couple of days. That was why he had ventured to call so early. And Mayden was irresistible. Mayden had stayed and done everything for Sam – prepared his bath, put studs into a clean shirt, selected a tweed suit, ordered breakfast, ordered his car. It was touching. Sam could not eat, but he thirstily drank a lot of coffee. Sam gave him the Orange Street telephone number and asked him to get it. But the exchange had said that no answer could be obtained. Sam was reassured. Gwen had somehow received the solution of the mystery, and had gone out to meet her sister. If she had had no news, or if the news had been untoward, Gwen would never have left the flat without ringing him up. She had not rung up because she had gone out early and wished not to disturb him. It was clear enough.

And yet in a moment it was not clear at all. Perhaps he ought to have driven round to Orange Street; but lassitude, a strange, transient indifference, as well as a certain delicacy about directing the girl-chauffeur to Orange Street and using his latch-key in her presence, prevented him from doing to. It was all odd, dream-like.

Besides, what could twenty-four hours matter? He could telephone from Moze. A day and a night in the country would put him to rights. Mayden's advice was very sound. The man was a jewel. And thus Mayden, smiling hope and encouragement, had seen him off from the portals of the hotel.

Now, as he lay on his Empire bed, his eye lighting continually on beautiful things, the newspapers and press-cuttings on a table by his side, he was at leisure to reflect, to see all matters in their due perspective and proportions. But he could not reflect in an orderly manner. His mind was not under control; a. score of topics jostled together in his mind, and first one came to the top in the affray and then another. He felt better. He said again that he was not ill, only unwell. The pain in his side was easier, the cough also. He thought he had slept. He had mentioned the pain to Heddle, and Heddle had offered no comment. Heddle was changed. Hitherto he had held Heddle to be incapable of concentration. But to-day Heddle had kept to the point of his patient's condition. Not a word about the war, or general topics! And Heddle, after a little preliminary nervousness and over-deference, had seemed to show a new authority and firmness. Did this mean that Heddle thought him ill, or merely in danger of being ill? No medicine had been prescribed. Adela had lain in that bed. No, of course not in that bed, but in a bed on exactly the same spot. She might have been dead for years, so completely had the impress of her personality upon the house been got rid of. Sad! She was a dignified creature, who inspired respect. Even her Pomeranians, whose yapping had brought them very near to death at the hands of Geoffrey, were given away to her relatives. He wanted to see Geoffrey and yet was shy about seeing him, because of his being in bed. Geoffrey was evidently a masterful man, and he was not sure how Geoffrey would treat him, what Geoffrey would say of the House of Lords debate. Had Geoffrey reciprocated his mother's passionate love? Geoffrey was a mystery. Mayden must have thought Sam really ill or he would not have called so early and packed him off with such speed. But Mayden could not have thought him really ill, or he would not have packed him off alone on a seventy-mile drive. He dwelt on his new schemes for the Ministry. They were not mature; they were far from mature. His conscience was not at ease, for instance, about Eric Trumbull. He had destroyed Trumbull's plans in France, by an autocratic ukase, because he had instinctively decided that Trumbull had a brain capable of a wider sweep than was needful for the care of any single country – even France; but he had done so before settling what the man's new post should be. He had left Trumbull disappointed, probably resentful, at a loose end. He must reflect, reflect!

A great triumph, the previous afternoon and night! At the memory of it he thrilled to an immense satisfaction. He had taught Andy and the War Cabinet and the famous fighting services a lesson. He longed for more press-cuttings. His appetite for press-cuttings was gluttonous. Yes, a dazzling triumph. But what a fool he had been that morning – to leave London without calling at Orange Street! What the hell could it matter what the girl-driver would have thought? Delphine was all right. .She must be all right. She was now, at that very moment, with Gwen. She must be. A telegram might somehow come at any instant. Skinner might walk in with a telegram from Delphine in his skinny fingers before the timepiece with a gold cock on its summit struck three. She would telephone to the hotel and learn that he was at Moze and then she would telegraph, or she might even telephone. Trust her to get at him! All would be explained. A delusion! A fool's paradise!... The timepiece somehow struck four... She had run off with her young man. All young mistresses of old men were alike. He had said it to himself before. Nature would have her way. There was a knock.

"Oh, well, of course they won't leave me alone," said Sam to himself, like a pettish invalid who was determined to be a martyr! A telegram? He was forgetting. No! It was not Skinner's knock. Was it indeed a knock at all? The knock was repeated. He sang out a cheerful cracked summons to enter.

A thin, spectacled woman, with wispy greying hair, showed herself in the doorway. She wore a neat dress of dark blue, and was very self-conscious, very conscious of her sex.

"I'm the housekeeper, my lord. Mr Raingo engaged me." Mr Raingo? Who the devil was Mr Raingo? Geoffrey, naturally. He had never till then heard Geoffrey called Mr Raingo.

"Come in! Come in!" he urged her, brightly. "Come in, Miss Thorping. How do you like being back again in your own part of the world?"

She simpered a little, flushed, was delighted with the welcome. "I'm very glad, my lord."

He knew he was making a conquest of her. He thought, as she crossed the space between the door and the bed under his gaze: "One of those women that carry virginity to the point of fanaticism and think about men all day and all night." But he had already had evidence that she knew her business of housekeeping. Her face was lined by responsibilities and conscientiousness. As with respect and some surprise she took the august outstretched hand, she started, scarcely perceptibly, as though she had touched hot metal unawares.

"Is my hand hot?"

"Oh no, my lord," she protested hastily. f' A little warm."

"She fancies I am very ill," he thought. But he would have none of her fancies.

"Are you comfortable here?" he asked her, with brisk interest in her welfare. "Domestic staff all right? Marketing not too difficult? Different from Belgrave Square, eh?"

"Oh, very comfortable, thank you, my lord. I'm sure it's a beautiful house." She seemed to be inhaling his kindly welcome like a sweet and .tonic odour. She was his. Her self-consciousness melted away in his sunshine, and as she preened herself with minute movements, she showed frank pleasure in the situation; but mingled with her pleasure was a responsible anxiety about his condition, as if she herself would have to answer personally for his well-being.

"I thought you might be wanting to see me about your food, my lord. Dr. Heddle didn't say whether this arrowroot was to be made with milk or water, and I didn't think to ask him. But cook and me agreed it would be safest with water. I hope it was to your liking, my lord." She picked up the empty basin from the table by the bed.

"Very nice," said Sam casually, looking at the ceiling. He was tired now of welcoming her, and he frowned.

"I hope you aren't in pain, my lord."

"Oh, no! Nothing. A bit in the side, that's all. I must have caught a chill."

"Yes, my lord. Shall I send you up some tea?"

"Yes, if you like." ("Don't bore me.") "And some lemonade. Lots of lemonade. Lemons and sugar and water, nothing else in it."

"Yes, my lord. And I've sent for some ice and some grapes." Grapes! That was always their one idea. Why grapes? But ice! When they ordered ice, that was always proof that in their opinion illness was in the house. "Has Mr Geoffrey come back yet?" "No, my lord."

"I want to see him when he comes." "Very good, my lord."

"Oh, here's the nurse, my lord, from Clacton." Nurse! But he had distinctly told Heddle that he didn't need a nurse and the doctor had concurred. And now there was a nurse here! A conspiracy; that was what it was. They were all in a conspiracy together. They were playing with him. No wonder the virgin's voice, announcing the nurse, was queerly self-conscious in its attempted casualness! Well, he wouldn't have a nurse. Yes, he would, because he couldn't fight them all. At least, he could fight them, but it wouldn't be worth the trouble; it would be too boring to fight them... The duplicity of that apparently simple, ingenuous fellow, Heddle! Well, let the nurse stay, and be damned to her! Never in his life had he had a nurse. They didn't have nurses in Eccles in his day. But she must let him alone; she mustn't worry him with any of her blasted fuss. He had to think; he had to reflect. Then he turned charmingly to the nurse as she approached him:

"Well, nurse, so it's you, is it? I'm bound to tell you I'm the worst patient in the world. You're asking for trouble, coming here."

The nurse and Miss Thorping smiled at each other happily. "I can see you aren't very ill," said the nurse without formality, and laughed. She had a blank chart and a small case in her hand.

63

The Most Dreadful Word

Nurse Kewley had left the room. In answer to Sam's question she had told him her name, and, without being asked, that she came from Ramsey in the Isle of Man. As soon as she was out of sight Sam slid from his bed and went to the mirror over the dressing-table between the pair of front windows.

"Surely I'm a bit grey," he thought, regarding himself. "And I've got a sort of worried look."

He glanced at the fields in the afternoon light, and they seemed for ever unattainable; he could not now just put on his clothes and walk forth free and enjoy the fields. He was fast. He returned to his bed with a relieved feeling of having accomplished a dangerous adventure fortunately without any mishap. The nurse returned with both arms full of fresh, white pillows.

"It's hard work breathing. I suppose you won't deny I'm very ill." He spoke lightly, teasingly, but badinage involved him in a considerable nervous effort. He was breathing more and more quickly, – "*Ah*-ha-*Ah*-ha-*Ah*-ha."

"You'll be quieter with those under you," she replied; and lifted him up, till he was leaning against a bank of pillows.

The starchy white surface of the pillows was exquisite to him; the two pillows with which he had begun the day were already, it seemed to him, frowsy and secondhand. Another thing that pleased him was the exceedingly white starchiness of the nurse's cap, cuffs and apron; the apron showed all the longitudinal and latitudinal creases of the laundry, an unimaginably immaculate apron, large, practical, enveloping, an apron at which you could gaze in satisfaction for hours; he liked the way in which the broad band of it bound her blue print dress tightly about the waist.

"My lips tickle me," he said. "Is it pimples?"

She examined his lips.

"Little pimples," she said negligently. "We call them vesicles." Then, without asking permission, she softly wiped sputum from his lips, and put the swab on the dressing-table.

"I could do with fresh pillows about once an hour," he said.

"Yes, they're a comfort," she said.

Then she sat down. Nothing else to be done for the present. He had had tea. The lemonade and the ice had been brought; the grapes had not arrived. She had taken his temperature and his pulse, and written on the chart. Geoffrey had not come. No news from London. Na news from anywhere.

He was too weary and gloomy and uneasily expectant to play a part now, or to get into relations with Nurse Kewley. Plenty of time for that. She was about Miss Thorping's age – say forty-five, tall and buxom, with a ravaged, determined face and some humour in her eyes. He thought she was all right. At any rate she had enough sense to respond to his mood, not to worry him, not to be damnably bright when he wanted silence and stillness. He shut his eyes.

Someone knocked at the door. No cheerful summons to come in, now. The nurse rose from her chair, and without a sound crossed the room and cautiously opened the door a few inches. She reigned over the room, and none might even enter it without her licence. Sam heard murmuring. She shut the door.

"Telephone message from Sir Ernest Timmerson – if that's the right name? – to say that everything's going on well at the Ministry, and he hopes you'll take a good holiday, and if he wants your advice he'll be sure to let you know."

"Oh!" Quickly. A monosyllable deftly inserted between two respirations.

Another knock at the door. Another message.

"Telephone message from Mr Raingo. He went on to London from Colchester this morning to look at some glass that he had heard of. He only saw in the evening papers that Lord Raingo had gone to the country for a couple of days' rest, and he will come back by the six-twenty-eight from Liverpool Street to-night." This message had been written down and the nurse read it aloud.

"That's good. I expect it's Waterford glass he's on the track of. That's good."

Sam wondered whether he ought not to give orders about Geoffrey's dinner being prepared and a car to meet him. But to give orders concerning such complicated matters seemed a troublesome enterprise, and he said nothing more. Miss Thorping and Wrenkin between them would see to everything. Why should he exert himself? He could not. He had enough to do in directing the enormous business of respiration. He dozed, and had brief fragmentary dreams about the Ministry, Waterford glass, Geoffrey's twitching, Delphine and Gwen chatting together, the front pages of evening papers; yes, he had reached such a pitch of celebrity that the wiping of his nose would constitute a news-item; the next moment he could feel Delphine reclining on his lap as she telephoned to Berkeley Street for him.

At intervals he looked at the window and wearily saw the light reddening at the approach of sunset. The grapes came and he refused to touch them. Everything came. The doctor came, entering without a knock. Nurse Kewley started up to rebuke the impudent intruder who would so unceremoniously enter; but as soon as she identified the doctor she was transformed into an obsequious slave, and stood sharply at attention.

"I had to make a call in the village, so I thought I might as well look in after all," said the doctor with bright casualness.

But Sam was not deceived. An old dodge, this happening to be in the neighbourhood and so looking in! The fact remained that the doctor was coming twice a day. Serious! Or the simpleton thought it was serious. No! The deferential simpleton was more likely heightening the importance of the case on account of the patient's tremendous importance in the world. A rare bit of luck for Heddle to get hold of such a patient! That was what it was. Human nature, of course, and therefore pardonable. The patient gave no sign that he saw through the tactics of the simpleton. Nor would he deign to challenge the fellow about his mystification in procuring the nurse.

"Very good of you, doctor," said he feebly. "But you needn't have troubled. I'm very well looked after." He generously tossed this testimonial to his nurse. No doubt he was indeed being well looked after, but really he didn't know.

"How do you feel?"

"Oh! So-so. Not bad. Pain in side. Headache. Bored."

"Your breathing isn't much better," said the doctor cheerfully, producing his stethoscope. More sounding of the chest, and more elaborate even than before. The doctor glanced at the nurse's chart and she showed him the piece of cotton-wool that she had put on the dressing-table. Sam saw that it had a rusty colour.

"Um!" murmured the doctor, and dropped the cottonwool into a receptacle.

"Well," said he, smiling at Sam. "You've got a touch of pneumonia. Good thing we have you safe in bed before it's got far. I wish all pneumonia cases were as wise as you've been. Things would be simpler. There's nothing to worry about."

"But you've said the most dreadful word in the language," Sam retorted grimly.

"Oh! What's that?" the doctor laughed humouringly.

"Pneumonia."

64

THE SITUATION MADE CLEAR

The Most atmosphere of the room seemed to be quite unchanged. Sam lay high on his pillows; he breathed rapidly and with difficulty; his cough was worse, and the pain in his side was becoming more severe. But he apparently had energy left for the maintenance of cheerfulness and even of detachment.

"Tell me something about this pneumonia," said he. "It's only a name to me. Don't you think I'm entitled to know what it is that's got hold of me?" His voice was weak, eager, and the phrases came out in separated fragments.

"Fairly simple. The lungs are engorged – congested with blood. At least, one of them is, in your case. The air has to make room for the blood, and so the lung is put partially out of action. This means that the part that isn't out of action has to work harder. That's why you're breathing quicker. And it's the heart that has to bear the .strain. That's about all there is to it."

"It seems very romantic," said Sam, looking reflectively at the ceiling, upon which he painted pictures of his heart and handicapped lungs calling upon each other for sublime efforts to supply their master with all the oxygen he needed.

"Romantic?" repeated the uncomprehending doctor, at a loss. He was a plain man, and to him pneumonia was pneumonia, and the reverse of romantic.

"And what's the treatment? Tell me exactly. The more I'm told the more I shall help you all I can. I suppose you want me to help you?"

The impulse to exchange a glance was too strong for doctor and nurse.

"I don't mind telling you," the doctor answered, when he had somewhat recovered from the strangeness of Sam's remarks. "I shall give you a sedative for the night. And some digitalis to help the heart. And you must have a drop of brandy every few hours. And an antiphlogistine poultice – that's to reduce the inflammation and ease the pain in your side. And you needn't talk a lot. Your temperature's rising, and talking won't do it much good."

"Right! Right! But what about getting the medicines?"

"That'll be my affair. You haven't got to worry about a thing. I'll speak to Wrenkin. I saw him driving your son to the station this morning in the big car, so it's evidently been repaired. There's only one thing, and you mustn't misunderstand me. I should like to call in a consultant. Your case has no complications; it's quite straightforward; but you're a sort of a public invalid, and I don't care to act alone. The look of the thing... I'm only a village doctor, you see. You see my point, don't you?"

"Appearances!"

"I thought if you agreed I'd telephone for Sir Arthur Tappitt. He's about the best there is."

"Why! That's the Canadian fellow – Prime Minister's magician."

The doctor laughed uncertainly at the designation.

"Royal Family too. I was at Guy's with him, but he was my junior. If he could come – "

"Oh! He'll come fast enough. Trust him. He's fine at writing bulletins. Very well, let's do the thing in style, Heddle. Let's do it in the grand manner. I'm ill – I'll *be* ill."

The doctor turned to the nurse, murmuring:

"I'll try to get another nurse for to-night."

"You needn't, sir," murmured the nurse, casually. "I can star on duty to-night. In the morning will do."

The doctor at once casually assented.

"You're an exceptionally good patient, Lord Raingo, if you'll allow me to say so."

"Yes," said the nurse, in a new, assertive voice, after she had held the door open for the doctor and shut it upon him. "And you told me you weren't a good patient. But I didn't believe you."

"You wait. You wait."

"Nurse," called the doctor, putting his head into the room. She went quickly out to him.

Sam felt that he was in a world new to him, where an employee thought nothing of adding to her day a sleepless, active night alone with a sick man. What was the reward of this selflessness? A miserable pension when, in a few years, she would be too old to work? Yet she seemed to be content with her lot. A contrast with the everlasting self-interest of all those ministers, with his own self-interest! Mysterious creature! What was the secret of her content? He had glimpses of all that he had missed in the depths of living. He felt like making her a present of a thousand pounds for her casual renunciation of a whole night's rest; and then he was ashamed of a gesture so gross, so humiliating to himself and to her.

He had made a fine display of courage and wit on the doctor's declaration of his malady, but it was only a display, a proud piece of showmanship perhaps unworthy of so solemn an occasion. Nothing but despair and self-pity lay behind it. He knew himself for a sick man; the whole of his being was stricken; there was no health in him anywhere. He realized that the finest of all earthly possessions was a healthy body, and it was no longer his – it never had been his. The poor, ageing, plain nurse was healthy, was going steadily about the daily business of existence. He alone was the prisoner of disease, and suffered the spiritual shame thereof. Everybody was his superior. Everybody would soon be condescending to him. He might flare in the newspapers, which would record day by day the successive phases of his illness; but the world's exclamation would be: "Poor fellow!" Negligent and forgetful, the world! He had fallen wounded in the battle. A glance of preoccupied commiseration – and his comrades would press onwards. How could they stop? Andrew Clyth would go ahead with his chicane and his will-to-win and his ruthless egotism; the Cabinet would meet and wrangle and decide; the Ministry of Records would function, and all the other ministries and departments; the soldiers would fight – and he was laid away futile and corrupted on his bed. God had decreed ruin for him, in order to prove the vanity of his wealth and of his great fame.

Twenty-four hours earlier the debate in the House of Lords was safely over and the banquet was about to begin – his apotheosis was preparing. Now he was cut off. Life was very illogical. No (he smiled philosophically in his pain), it was not illogical, it was merely long and had a long memory. Half a century ago, – some carelessness on someone's part, and he had got rheumatic fever! He recovered, but not his heart. His heart had implacably waited for him, waited for another bit of carelessness. He had been warned and warned. Too stupid to take the warning seriously! In defiance of common sense he had strained his heart, continued to strain it. He had left no margin for accidents, and the accident of pneumonia had arrived. He had thrown open the gates of his city to the foe. The foe had entered. That was all. Nothing illogical in it. His life had unity, and the disaster of to-day was just as properly a part of it as the triumph of yesterday. His life was really all of a piece. He knew he was finished, and that he deserved to be finished. He had eaten the cake; the cake was gone; it was not in his cupboard. The transaction of his life was as fair and as just as arithmetic. Still, it was a damned shame.

Pneumonia! He had always known that the successful issue of pneumonia largely depended on the soundness of the heart. He had always known that its serious onset would be a terrible menace to him. You would have thought that he might for his own sake have studied a little the characteristics of this disease and the way to treat it. But he had omitted to do so. How human, and how negligent! He knew about pneumonia only what the doctor had just told him, and that it was termed "the enemy of middle-age." He thought he had read somewhere that more than half the cases of pnuemonia in men over fifty ended fatally. (But even of that fact he was not quite sure.) And many of the cases were not handicapped by a weak heart. What chance had he, then? None. He was sentenced. Yes, he had the chance conferred by great wealth. He could and would receive the finest treatment which the world of medicine could offer. In that particular his riches were not in vain. But what was treatment against an unsound heart? And there wasn't a pin to choose among doctors. The most celebrated of them were merely the creations of fashion. Mountebanks! Charlatans! Ingenious self-advertisers! In pneumonia a sound heart was worth a hundred specialists.

A knock at the door. The nurse instead of opening the door called "Come in." Edith, one of the housemaids, entered, bringing a tray. Sam was under the impression that she had left. But there she was, and a very different girl from the girl in the dirty apron whom he had summoned one day in spring. Clean, neat, smart. Miss Thorping had had an eye on her. She was highly self-conscious as she bore in the tray. He had had human relations with her once for a few moments. He had merely to greet her: "Hello, Edith," and she would turn her head and blush with responsive pleasure. But he could not bring himself to greet her. It would be too much of an effort, and moreover he was ashamed of his condition. And so he let her pass with her downcast eyes.

"In there, please," said the nurse softly, pointing to the doorway communicating with the next room, formerly his own bedroom.

And Edith vanished through the doorway. The tray no doubt held an evening meal for the nurse. The nurse followed it. Edith did not return through the sick-room. He heard her and the nurse murmuring together, and then there was silence; Edith had gone out by the other door. She was healthy. She was brimming with health. She might be clean, neat, smart; she might be young and pretty. That was naught. The one important, attractive, enviable thing was that she was healthy and going her ways. And she didn't know it. She simply was not aware that she possessed the greatest thing in the world. Similarly with Nurse Kewley. The nurse was healthy; she had been looking forward to her meal. She went her ways. She could calmly anticipate a night of duty and no sleep – so healthy was she! And she made nothing of her luck!

The light was fading. The fields would be darkening, which he would never see again. The Ministry was closed now – save perhaps for a few late workers. The shadows were collecting furtively in the corners of the room and under the furniture. He knew the room by heart now. And he knew

every bit of the bed; it was all so odiously familiar to him that he might have been lying in it for a month instead of only for a few hours. The sheets might have been weeks old from the laundry. The pillows might have come soiled out of a shop with a Hebrew sign in Houndsditch. It was a bed of ennui, pain, corruption, shame; and he would never escape from it. Prisoner for life, for death! He wanted to cry. How much longer would his heart be able to keep up that laborious pumping? When would it abandon in exhaustion its awful, vital task?

He suddenly remembered that he must make provision for Delphine, and by direct gift. His will, executed years earlier, was in order. It provided that if Adela had predeceased him, everything should go to Geoffrey. (Geoffrey might be back ,at any moment now.) He would give Delphine twenty; no, thirty; no, fifty; no, a hundred thousand pounds. Why not? His wealth had been automatically increasing for years, and it was nearly all in the very soundest, most commonplace securities, the dividends on which became, as to a large part of them, additional capital as half-year succeeded half-year. Delphine should be very rich. She should be dazzled. And Gwen should be rich too, because she was Delphine's sister and .beloved by Delphine. Gwen should have the means to exploit her beauty. And he would not forget Mrs Blacklow. Mrs Blacklow should have ten thousand; which might help to smooth the relations between her and her husband when he returned. Bearer-bonds, – that was the device to be employed. There were heaps and heaps of them,. Mayden! He must have Mayden down to-morrow. Damn his duties at the Ministry. Mayden must be his secret agent, not Geoffrey. It would not be quite nice to employ Geoffrey in such matters. .And then, after no preliminary knock, the door opened and

'Geoffrey appeared.

65

THE WILL-TO-WIN

To Sam, Geoffrey seemed to rise over him like a cyclopean monolith. He had apparently grown not only in girth but in height. His khaki was tight on him. He had an air of great strength. Indeed, a man. But his short, wiry hair, and his staring, somewhat bulging eyes, always looking out at the world as if in surprise at what they saw, made him at the same time boyish and rather wistful. Sam was touched and impressed. This was his son – and Adela's; and he wondered where the youth had come from. It seemed strange, nearly incredible, that he had come from Sam's loins and Adela's womb. Sam had an intense feeling of pride in the miraculous Geoffrey.

Though they had scarcely talked together for weeks – Sam's policy had been deliberately to leave him alone – Sam did not now offer to shake hands. In business and in politics Sam was as lavish in such gestures of goodwill and friendliness as an Englishman can be. If the Colonial Premier stroked, Sam for his part was given to patting shoulders. But these habits were merely acquired. In Eccles handshaking had never been quite good form; it was regarded as effusive. And in his illness and in this private meeting with his own son, Sam was somehow back at Eccles. He kept his hands under the sheets. He now had to play an Ecclesian role, to hide the shame of his illness, and of his corrupted, enfeebled body, and to affect the terrible impassivity of the northern Midlands. He divined that the boy was rendered nervous and constrained by the startling spectacle of the hard-breathing, decrepit, changed creature on the bed.

"Well, my boy?" he manfully quavered between respirations. "I must say you've done very well with this house, I like it."

"That's good."

"Get your glass all right to-day?" Then the pose failed, and he went on, without a pause: "I'm very ill. I'm very ill indeed. I've got pneumonia. And with my heart you know – "

He cried. He could feel the tears on his hot, dry cheeks. He was no longer ashamed. He cared not what he looked like. He was filled with the immense megalomania of the sick. He had become in an instant the centre of the universe, and nothing on earth mattered in comparison with the supreme business of curing his disease. And yet he had leisure in his brain to hope that the nurse would not disturb them. She did not disturb them; she had gone out, after her meal, by the door of the next room, and was unaware of Geoffrey's arrival.

"Yes, you're ill, dad," said Geoffrey. "I wish I'd known earlier. I should have been back earlier. I thought you looked a bit queer in the House of Lords yesterday afternoon."

"What did you think of my speech? I saw you." He half resumed the pose.

"All right. It knocked 'em. I thought that fellow Ockleford was a. dirty cad."

Sam sniggered with joy at the boy's warmth, but he still cried.

"I'm very low," he said. "I've got to be looked after. And I've only you, Jeff. I'm glad you've come. I was beginning to think you were never coming." But even while he spoke he admitted to himself that his "I've only you" was a sentimental exaggeration; for he had Mayden also, and in some ways he would trust to Mayden more than to Geoffrey.

"I say, Jeff. Where are you sleeping now?"

"In the garden."

"Well, you must stop indoors to-night. I ask you to. You're much better. Your twitching's lots better. It's almost gone." He was the ruthless invalid again, but he was also the father, who saw in the present occasion a fine opportunity of breaking the boy of his claustrophobia.

"Oh, I will if you want me to."

"Well, I do."

"I keep my things in the room next to your old room. I'll sleep there. By the way, Tappitt's coming down to-morrow morning. I've just heard on the 'phone. It's all arranged. Everything's arranged. I've seen Heddle too. I shall look to things myself. So you needn't worry. You'll be all right."

Sam tried to speak his thanks, his appreciation, his relief; but he could not articulate. He was crying like an infant.

"You see how weak I am," he murmured at length, thickly, with an extraordinary, shameless detachment.

"Oh, that's nothing," said Geoffrey tenderly. "I've seen that scores of times in France." He was referring to the tears. "Don't let that trouble you. It's purely physical."

"I should damned well think it was physical!" Sam burst out with sudden power, and laughed, hysterically. And the enterprise of his breathing went laboriously on.

In a corner of his brain he was thinking:

"That boy really is getting better. And he's the right sort."

The change in the boy since his escape was very marked. Cynicism and bitterness (though there was bitterness in his verdict on Ockleford) seemed to be dropping away from him. His tone was sound; it showed authority and it showed kindliness and was reasonable; and he had proved in the house that he could carry through a scheme. Yes, the refurnishing of the house had saved him, or was in process of saving him.

It was at this juncture that Sam recalled his quite gratuitous undertaking to the doctor to help all he could towards his own cure. He had entirely forgotten it, and he had been behaving like a coward, losing his hold on himself, yielding up hope, disgracing himself before his son whom he so much admired. He was betraying the doctor and the nurse and his son. He had gone over to the enemy, death. And for no cause. After all, nearly half the pneumonia patients of about his age did recover. And why should not he? He would recover. Everything possible would be done for him. The chief agent of recovery was always the patient himself. Andrew Clyth in his case would recover by force of the will-to-win. And Sam would recover. He grew calm, grim, worthy again of his son. Even his breathing went easier, and the pain in his side. He appreciated in his own person the virtue of resolve and the dominion of the mind over the body. The mental act of thought had in a few seconds influenced his tissues and the very muscles of his heart. He became cheerful and collected.

"I'm better," he said. "You've done me good."

Geoffrey nodded.

"There's someone here wants to see you," said Geoffrey. "But if I were you I wouldn't see 'em till to-morrow morning."

"Who is it? Not Mayden – from the Ministry?"

"No."

"That reminds me. I want you to ring up Mayden – Captain Mayden, it is. He lives at the Connaught Club. Tell him I want him to come down and see me to-morrow as early as he can. Don't forget. He'll come. Who is it wants to see me?"

"It's a young woman."

"What?" Sam controlled himself, remembering his resolve.

"I saw her at Hoe station. It took me some time to get out of the train because of my glass. The station-master told me someone was asking for Moze Hall. So I spoke to her. She said her name was Leeder and she wanted to see you."

Delphine! Sam's demeanour was a masterpiece of acting. But was it

Delphine?

"What sort of a woman – dark or fair?"

"Very blonde – and very pretty; So I brought her along in the car. I couldn't see what else to do. I couldn't leave here there."

"She's here now?"

"Yes. Old Thorping's looking after her."

"You go and bring her up here this minute, my lad."

"But look here, dad. Hadn't you better – She can wait. You're tired now… Seems a shop-girl sort of a person."

Sam's eyes flashed and glared at his son.

"You needn't tell me what sort of person she is. I know her, and I must see her. Fetch her in."

Gwen in the house all that while, and he kept in ignorance! He didn't care what Jeff or anybody else might think of the situation; he would see her. The tension was maddening. But still he controlled himself. His will and the will of Geoffrey met in conflict; Geoffrey's was defeated. The nurse inopportunely entered, and she had been fortified by a meal.

"Nurse, this is my son."

"How d'ye do, nurse. There's someone come to see father on urgent business."

"Lord Raingo ought not to see anybody," said the nurse quietly.

"I must. I must. Jeff, run along and fetch her."

"I shan't take the responsibility," the nurse said, with amiable firmness.

"No one's asking you to take the responsibility. I'll take-the responsibility. Anybody might think I was dying. Please pass me my hair-brushes."

The patient dominated the room. The nurse said nothing more, and to maintain her dignity, while Sam was brushing his hair, she turned on one light in a corner and began to draw closely all the curtains. There was a pause. Geoffrey, who had stood hesitant, departed to obey his father.

66

GWEN'S TALE

Gwen looked haggard and rather shabby; but her beauty, youth, litheness, remained in their full allurement and power. Sam motioned Geoffrey to leave, and told him to see that the nurse kept out of the room. Geoffrey nodded, and, with a strange, lingering glance of protective compassion at Gwen, departed a second time. Sam asked himself what "they" thought – meaning everyone in the house who had cognizance of Gwen's visit, but especially Geoffrey and the nurse. His conscience was at work. He was no longer a man desperately fighting for life, nor even a sick man, nor a minister, nor a millionaire, not the darling of the public – he was the lover of this young girl's sister, whom he had seduced, and this young girl was aware of the relationship and therefore in a sense guiltily compromised. But nobody in the house knew of the existence of the young girl's sister; only the young girl herself was known. Would they think evil? What else could they think? The young girl on her mysterious errand had not the figure of an emissary from the Ministry, of a secret service creature, nor yet of a secretary or a clerk. What could they think? His conscience was putting evil thoughts into the minds of the household; that was it. No! They could not think evil. Geoffrey in particular did not and could not think evil; and after all Sam was only interested in what Geoffrey thought. The purest innocence was inscribed on the young girl's face, that shone palely in the half-lit room. He, Sam, would by his own thoughts shield the young girl from the evil thoughts of all persons whatsoever. These ideas flashed through his brain with unimaginable rapidity, so that they seemed not to impede for the hundredth part of a second the onrush of his ravenous eagerness to learn what the young girl had to tell about Delphine.

Horribly nervous and distracted, Gwen sat down on a chair which Geoffrey had placed for her by the bed. She looked round to assure herself that she was alone with Sam, and burst into sobs. Her tears gave Sam strength and calmness. He put his burning hand paternally for a moment on her soft hair to soothe her.

"Then she hasn't come back?" he asked. Gwen shook her head violently, to dismiss a notion so impossibly sanguine.

"And you ill, too!" she muttered.

"Why, have you heard that Delphine is ill?" He had hope. Gwen shook her head again.

"No, no! I only meant – you being ill and her gone, just at the same time. And me out of a situation as well!"

"That's nothing – you being out of a situation. I shall look after you, of course," said Sam, to whom it seemed that his first duty was to solace and inspirit the young girl rather than to dwell on his own woe. "Why did you go out so early this morning, my dear?"

"I didn't go out at all this morning."

"But I rang you up about nine o'clock, and there was no answer."

"I must have been asleep."

Ah! She was young. She could sleep through a reiterated telephone call in a small flat. She could sleep in the midst of her grievous anxiety.

"I sat up waiting for Delphie till four o'clock, and then I thought I'd better go to bed for a bit, but I must have dozed off in the chair just while I was thinking of going to bed. I didn't waken till ten o'clock. It was Mrs Cartright woke me – the charwoman, you know. She only comes every other morning now because she's got so many other jobs. Delphie does the rooms herself when Mrs Cartright doesn't come. So you see Mrs Cartright didn't know that Delphie wasn't at home yesterday either."

"And did you say anything to the woman – about things?"

"No. I wasn't going to have *her* knowing Delphie 'd been out two nights – if not three. I just told her I'd come in very early and Delphie 'd had to leave early on canteen-work. I remembered just in time the bed hadn't been slept in, and I said I'd made it myself, thinking it wasn't her morning for coming. It *was* lucky I thought of it. She got me some food, and I stopped till she'd gone away again. If Delphie had come in while she was there I should have had to let her know on the quiet what I'd told Mrs Cartright. If it hadn't been for that I should have come to find you sooner."

Sam, carrying on his difficult respiration now almost unconsciously, pictured to himself the strange secretive life of these women so apt and resourceful in deceit. Delphine had never said a word to him about the charwoman only coming three times a week. He supposed she thought that his mightiness should not be troubled with such sordid details of existence. Then they had been living on that plane of laborious meanness while he, their protector, so anxious to maintain them in spacious luxury, had simply not known how to spend his huge income! At any rate Delphine, if unfaithful, deceitful and crafty, was magnificently not venal.

"Gwen, my dear," Sam began persuasively, "you've really no idea where she can be?"

Gwen shook her head, looking down at the disordered bed-clothes.

"No idea at all?"

"No. I've racked my brains for hours to think."

"Now you must answer me this. It's very important to me. You remember that time when I first saw you. You and Delphine were sewing in the office, and you were crying – both of you."

Gwen nodded.

"Why were you crying?"

Gwen's tears fell once more.

"She'd been telling me about Harry Point," said she, hesitating and slowly flushing.

"Who's Harry Point?"

"He's the young man she used to be engaged to – before she met you, sir." She cried freely, sniffed, and patted her eyes with a tiny handkerchief which she drew out of a cheap bag.

So Delphine had been engaged! The first he had heard of it!

"Was she fond of him?" He pursued the cross-examination gently, holding himself painfully together, the most dreadful despair in his soul. All his everlasting, unsubduable suspicions justified! The jealousy had not been a species of madness.

"She was only fond of him because she *had* been fond of him – you see, sir, she was so sorry for him. But she'd thrown him over because she really didn't like him, but he was that gone on her he nearly went off his head while he was at the Front. Then he had some leave and she met him by accident, and she did try to be kind to him, in a nice way, if you know what I mean. Oh yes, it was all *right!* But she said they had a terrible scene when he left again for France. She said it was that terrible she couldn't believe it had happened." A pause. "She was so sort of tormented in her mind about whether she oughtn't to have stuck to him even when she knew she didn't care for him and wouldn't be happy with him."

"Now, Gwen, you and I must be straight with one another. Delphine told me that evening that you'd been crying because she'd been telling you about *my* troubles and misfortunes."

Gwen jumped up from the chair and hid her face in her hands, and then very astonishingly dropped on her knees.

"I know! I know!" she wailed. "She told me she'd told you that, so I shouldn't make any mistakes. And now I've let it out. You said I must."

She sobbed afresh. He could feel her head pressing the bed-clothes against his side,

"My dear, you mustn't stay like that. The nurse might come in any moment. Get up. And dry your eyes."

He touched her arm. Gwen walked about the room. Having yielded herself to grief, she was now certainly neither nervous nor intimidated.

"Where is she? Where is she?" the young girl moaned, her long, thin hands working.

"She's gone away," said Sam gloomily. "She's gone away. She couldn't stand me any longer. My dear, I was too old for her, and she was too kind to tell me so. If I wasn't sure she'd gone away of her own accord I should put the police on the business."

Gwen stopped and faced him with a mild gesture.

"She couldn't have gone away like you mean. I looked, arid she hasn't taken any of her clothes, and her boxes are there too. She wouldn't go away without anything, and she was frightfully fond of you, sir. You should have heard her talking about you – when I asked her. She was dotty about you, and so I'm telling you, sir."

But Sam was not in a mind to admit evidence against his theory. He *knew* that Delphine had deserted him, and jealousy horribly exasperated his heavy sorrow: so much so that he forgot that he was ill.

"Did you look in the drawers of her desk?" he asked suddenly.

"Yes. I looked. There was nothing in them in the way of papers and letters and things except one photograph of herself. She'd just had it done."

"She didn't say anything to me about having a new photograph. Not a word. Of course she'd destroyed all her letters and so on. And she's left the photograph on purpose, for me. I should have thought it must have been plain enough to you she's gone."

He was triumphant in his sorrow, and Gwen was abashed. His explanation of the disappearance of all letters and papers from the drawer of the desk had not occurred to her simple mind. There was silence between them because nothing more could be said. He felt the strangeness of the situation. Before the greatness of the catastrophe the popular minister and the young girl with nothing but her beauty were as equal as two human beings could possibly be. He was still ashamed of the sinister, awkward appearance of their relationship; but he was not ashamed in regard to Gwen herself. The fact that he had been Delphine's lover was admitted between them; Gwen accepted it with the utmost naturalness; it did not seem monstrous to her, nor immoral, nor in the least offensive; conventions did not trouble her simplicity; and Delphine was so much older than herself, so much a mother to her, that the difference in age between Delphine and Sam was nothing to her. That was how it was. She was overwhelmed in her own grief and Sam in his; and their griefs joined them together. Moreover she liked and respected Sam because Delphine had loved and respected him and because he had been kind and generous to Delphine; and in the stress of the crisis she had lost nearly all her awe of his grandeur.

The nurse entered impassively from the next room. She had food for the patient.

"Come along in, nurse," he said, affecting cheerfulness. She smiled, gently superior, as if to say that she had no need of anybody's permission to enter the room of which she was the indisputable mistress.

"Now, my dear," said Sam to the young girl. "There's no more to be done at present. You must stay here to-night – you can't go back because there's no train. Tell the housekeeper, or my son, that I say you are to stay and they are to look after you."

Gwen gave a frightened smile of obedience and went. Sam was alone with the nurse, wondering guiltily what she thought. She stuck a thermometer into his mouth.

"Have I gone up?" he asked in a culprit's tone, when she had taken the temperature.

"Of course you have," she replied (but gently), and she wrote on the chart.

"But it always goes up at night, doesn't it?" he argued.

"Generally," she admitted.

Geoffrey came in, with no purpose but to observe.

"I say, Jeff, that girl's a protegee of mine, and she's very anxious about her sister. You'd better telephone to London – she'll give you the number. I've forgotten it – and see if you can get an answer."

"Right!" said Geoffrey, carefully casual. There were vestiges of Eccles in Geoffrey, though he had never seen Eccles. The boy left his father unsupported to the dominion of the nurse.

Some time after Sam had eaten and drunk, the doctor arrived to administer digitalis and see to the antiphlogistine, and to examine the progress of the malady. His third visit in nine hours! It was understood in the room, without being stated, that the patient was somewhat worse. Faces said it, and Sam knew it. His heart was now fearfully engaged in a tremendous and perhaps forlorn effort to energize the respiratory apparatus. Grief, anxiety for others, jealousy, were driven into the background of his thoughts. At a quarter to ten Geoffrey reappeared, and, after a glance at the nurse, said:

"Took me over an hour to get on. No answer. Mayden's coming down to-morrow morning."

Sam nodded, without looking at him. Geoffrey left. No good nights. The patient was too absorbed to be bothered with an unnecessary word. The nurse was beginning her night vigil. She had had a large screen brought in, and had arranged a little corner of privacy for herself.

67

IN THE NIGHT

Night. The middle of the night. Sam could have looked at the Empire clock of which he had now and then caught the faint, refined, sardonic, Gallic tick on the mantelpiece, but he did not because in order to do so he would have had to twist his head, and he did not want to twist his head. He could hear the scarcely audible movements of the curtains of two of the three windows as the night-wind disturbed them. All the windows were open behind the curtains, but the blinds closely drawn in obedience to military regulations; nobody wandering in the night could guess that vigil was being kept in the sick-room.

He saw, or thought he saw, the nurse placidly reading, only half hidden by her screen. She sat in an easy chair, the sole light, shaded, on her left hand. She was wearing large rimmed spectacles, but he had not noticed her put them on. She read steadily, she read for ever and ever, turning over page after page without a sound. The wonder was that she did not fall asleep: but she had by now established herself with Sam as a creature who had no need of sleep, and as the most mysterious and enigmatic of all creatures.

He really could not be quite sure whether he was awake, or half awake, or delirious, or dreaming. But he felt fairly sure that he had heard now and then the tones of his own voice, saying things of strangely profound significance, things that he ought to remember. He was under the influence of the sedative which the nurse had given him after changing his pillow and performing the last intimate little ministrations for the night. He-"was under various influences – those of the digitalis, the brandy, the poultice, and the bland, commanding power of the nurse.

"I'm very ill," he thought. "I'm worse. I'm much worse. This everlasting breathing business is hell. When in God's name will the dawn come? When shall I see the first glimpse through the curtains? When will she put the light out and draw aside the curtains and draw up the blinds and let me *breathe*?"

What a silly idea that he would breathe more easily when that was done! He wanted to kick up a devil of a row and worry the nurse by a relieving display of naughtiness, but he dared not; she might superiorly reproach him and make him feel a humiliated fool... He was in the Ministry; he was entering the Ministry; the fellow at the door, the porter, whom he had put into a new uniform, was receiving him with the most ridciulous, character-harming deference, – harming both the porter's character and his own. By means more recondite than the Marconi-waves word was flying through the Ministry that the great man, the autocrat, had arrived, whose word was law, whose smile made, whose frown unmade... Of course he was not in fact an autocrat, but within the Ministry the illusion of his autocracy was universal and complete, sometimes deceiving even himself. To-day the autocrat had not been there; to-morrow he would not be there. The Ministry had lost its tonic, was slackened. The authority of Timmerson was naught, and Mayden, in order to give his full value, needed a master. He, Sam, yearned to squeeze the last drop of efficiency out of his personnel. Nobody could do it as well as he could do it – had been doing it. He desired efficiency for the sake of the country. He was filled with passionate love for Britain, the greatest of all countries. The papers containing the news of his illness were at that very moment radiating throughout the country in trains...

What was he wasting his tired thought upon? All that was nothing. At that very moment Delphine lay in the arms of another, of the ranker-officer, or officer-ranker – which was it? For the life of him, in the midst of his frightful breathing, he could not be sure which it was. Where had that "terrible scene," of which Gwen had spoken, taken place? It must have ended with a kiss, a kiss made voluptuous by their recriminations. His confused imaginary pictures of the pair together, quarrelling and embracing, expiating hatred in hot passion, were in the highest degree agonizing. Why had she left her portrait behind? No doubt an ingenious act of cruelty disguising itself as kindness. Immediately after the scene with Gwen in the office she had come up and lied to him with deliberation, lied with tenderness and the show of love in her voice. What skill and practice in deceit did not that denote! Yes, the young to the young, and the old to the old: that was what it was and must be. How could she love such as him? She could only pity, fondle, tolerate her old, fat Sam – for what he could do for her, for what she got out of him.

He seemed to wake up: which would indicate that he had been asleep. But had he been asleep? He simply could not decide what state of consciousness he was in. He impatiently pushed back the rich magenta counterpane. The nurse quietly shifted her book-marker, closed the book, put it down, turned to look at the clock, rose and came towards him. Damnable deliberation! He shut his eyes, determined not to be bothered with her… She was bending over him. He felt her nearness.

"You aren't really asleep, you know," she said softly. "It's time for you to have your teeny-weeny dose of brandy."

He opened his eyes, victimized. She looked odd in her spectacles. To Delphine he was an old man; but to the nurse he was a little child. And he did not know which was the more degrading. "Teeny-weeny!" Odious! No! The nurse did *not* understand him. If she had understood him she would not have used such utterly exasperating language. However, his lips accepted the brandy, which seemed to have but little savour.

68

Geoffrey's Visit

He saw a kind of glow in the doorway that gave on the landing. He had not observed the door open. All was dim and vague. The figures and the sensations in his delirium or dream of jealousy had been thin, phantasmal – figures on a tapestry seen through gauze, and the sensations proper to such figures. Real enough, but so faint. The glow in the doorway, he perceived, came from a gorgeous dressing-gown, and Geoffrey was wearing the dressing-gown. Yes, it was Geoffrey, smilingly watchful over him. A wonderful dressing-gown. It must have cost lots of money: which pleased him, showing as it did that Jeff understood money, was not afraid of money. Being compulsorily in khaki, Jeff could not spend much on clothes, but he could display, and was displaying, a taste and a large extravagance in his less formal raiment. Strange that the sight of this dressing-gown caused him to admire Geoffrey more and more! The lad, with his air of authority, was quickly becoming for him the ideal of a serious millionaire's son. He, Sam, had always somehow been afraid of money; he had never quite been able to escape from the scale of Eccles.

Geoffrey grandly entered the room and stood at the foot of the bed, nodding to the nurse, who appeared not to resent the incursion in the least. She vanished silently with the empty brandy glass into the next room.

"You up!" Sam murmured, after a few moments. "It's very late, isn't it?"

"Oh, no!" Geoffrey answered easily. "When somebody's *ill* there's no late and there's no early. It's like on a ship, the machine has to keep going all the time. Night and day are only names." He laughed.

This notion appealed to Sam, made the scheme of his illness seem more natural. He at once thought of the house as a voyaging ship. The lad had ideas – ideas which lifted up existence. The lad stood benevolent, his hands in the pockets of his dressing-gown and pulling the sides together.

"Pyjamas as fine?" said Sam, feebly grim.

The lad nodded, but did not offer to exhibit the pyjamas.

"Little girl all right?" Sam affected an easy interest.

"Yes, I think so. Anyhow old Thorping tells me she's asleep. She'll look after her."

How strong, firm and assured was the lad's tone! What a contrast to his, Sam's, quavering, querulous, uncertain voice!

"Who's up?"

"Oh! I don't know. Several of 'em, I think." Geoffrey took his hands from his pockets, and leaned a little over the foot of the bed. "I say," he added, lower, confidentially. "She's told me. I thought I'd better make her."

"Told you? What?"

"She's told me." Geoffrey repeated with significance.

As he comprehended that his secret was now his son's, Sam ought to have blushed, to have felt awkward and ashamed. But no! He was aware simply of relief. The necessity for concealment and duplicity was over. Everything seemed natural. And why not? Sam was a man; Jeff was a man. And the bond between them was tightened. They understood one another. Sam admitted that his feelings had been too imitatively conventional. Jeff had taught him a lesson. "I thought I'd better make her." Queer phrase, demonstrating the lad's complete belief in his own authority and powers! So "several of 'em" were up! The ship's crew, navigating! And Jeff was apparently the captain – not the nurse and not "old Thorping." The lad had all of them under his thumb. It was wonderful, comforting, reassuring, delicious. With a lad like Jeff in charge any invalid was bound to come through. Sam said 'no word, gave no sign.

"Don't you worry," Geoffrey went on placidly. "She'll be found. I shall have a word with Mayden when he comes. Mayden's the goods."

"What do you know about Mayden?" Sam demanded sharply.

"Oh! I know Mayden."

So they had been hobnobbing, unknown to the great man! Well, the great man didn't mind. On the contrary he was rather tickled. Odd! Odd! But he felt better. He felt that virtue had passed into him.

"I had quite a lively evening," said Jeff, in the way of conversation. "*Quite* a lively evening, what with one thing and another."

"Oh?"

"Yes. Newspaper fellows."

"Have *they* been there?"

"Have they been here! I tell you they're thick on the ground. The Anchor Hotel 's full of them. Emmy hadn't been able to go to bed when last I heard."

"Emmy?"

"The daughter at the Post Office. Telephone going till two o'clock. However, she seemed to like it. I spoke to her over the 'phone."

Sam took the greatest delight in the tidings about the pressmen, a delight without alloy. Everything else might be all wrong, but the advent of the pressmen proved that he was still the great Raingo and a front-page item. He, breathing precariously in the fear of death itself, he with the affairs of his heart in a state of disaster if not catastrophe – he ought to have been above all thoughts of publicity. But he was not.

"You didn't snub them?"

"I did not."

The nurse re-entered, bearing two more virginal pillows which she had gathered from somewhere in the dead of night.

"Ta-ta," said Geoffrey casually, and he gave another curt nod to the nurse and went. Eccles!

"Yes! You'll sleep again now," said the nurse encouragingly, when she had arranged the patient once more.

"I may," Sam agreed.

He dimly saw the door closing as Geoffrey carefully pulled it to from the outside. The lad must have stood waiting behind it for at least a minute, waiting perhaps to assure himself that Sam really was settling down. Silence. Not a sound in the vast, mysterious ship. The nurse resumed her easy chair and her book. She coughed faintly. She opened the book with a certain eagerness. For her Sam was after all only one in a procession of patients.

69

Day

He was now half asleep, now half awake; at any given moment he could not be sure which. But he yielded himself more easily and comfortably to the hallucinations produced by the drug and his malady. He saw Delphine the mistress of his house, and clung almost luxuriously to this dream. He could not understand why it had not occurred to him to dream the soothing dream earlier in the night.

There she was, physically splendid, adoring, and spiritually sympathetic, efficient in the direction of the great organism of the household. Her mere presence was curative. Her movements were balm to the eyes, her glances heavenly. Everybody worshipped her, turned to her for guidance and inspiration. While she deflected, by some magic, all the worship to himself. In his weakness he was the fundamental power. She was selfless, between the Raingo on the bed and the embryo Raingo within her. (For he imagined her fecund.) She liked him to be fretful, capricious, childish. He could not irritate her, ruffle her benevolent, passionate calm. At intervals she would sit down, because of the being within her. Unnecessary to urge her to sit down. She knew when she ought to rest. But he had a feeling that she took repose not for the sake of the welfare of the unborn, and certainly not for her own sake, but in order that he, Sam, her adored, should have no reason to worry. She was loving him into recovery.

Of course she had volition. She knew how to assert herself, to impose herself, especially towards Gwen, but the authority which she exerted was only an emanation of his own authority. All knew this; she made everybody understand it – even Geoffrey, to whom her attitude was quite special, because by some means he had been responsible for putting her where she was.

Sam dreamed this dream again and again, with enchanting variations. His breathings were a net, and the dreams passed to and fro across the swaying net like iridescent water. It was confusing but delicious...

She had done right to leave him. And if she had practised duplicity upon him she had done so simply to save his feelings. His thoughts of her had lacked breadth and philosophy. Who was he, gross, ageing, ungraceful, unattractive, to monopolize her youth and beauty and faculty for love? She had given and vowed herself to him. Yes, but under strong temptation, too strong. He should be the last person to blame her for escaping from the consequences of her yielding. He was unfit for her, in the deepest sense unworthy of her. Was he a gaoler, a turnkey? Had he not sufficient greatness of mind to deliver her, with generosity and without rancour, to her rightful felicity and fate? Could he not suffer and smile? In abandoning him she had obeyed an instinct which it would have been a shame to disobey, an instinct which properly should override every consideration foreign to itself. In obeying she was sinless. Renunciation was his secret role. Think of the nurse's devotion to a creature whom a few hours earlier she had never even seen! In renunciation there could be ecstasy...

What was that steely shaft lying on the floor near the window? There were two strange, steely shafts – like swords or rapiers. The curtains of the windows were semi-transparent screens, and he could see the figures of his delirium and his dream moving mysterious tapestries behind them. Some change had happened in the world while he was not looking. For he was convinced that he had not slept. The reading-lamp of the nurse was unnaturally dim. Had Wrenkin forgotten, in the multiplicity of his duties, to make the electric current? But Wrenkin never forgot anything; Wrenkin was the right hand of God himself. He looked at the magenta coverlet; here and there it had a bluish tinge. He saw it in two lights, the light from the lamp and another. He saw himself in a mirror, which he had not noticed during the night, half sitting up, a terrible throbbing figure. And the mirror was full of bluish reflections.

He understood. It was the longed-for, impossible dawn that had happened unobserved. The steely shafts on the floor grew brighter and brighter, but shorter and shorter; and the lamp dimmer and dimmer. The nurse was not reading; the book lay on her white lap; she was dozing. "Nurse! Nurse!" he wanted to cry. He wanted to be fully delivered from the endless thraldom of the night. He was very ill. He was the cynosure of all England. And she slept! No! Let her sleep. Renunciation. He could abide. Even now he did not surely know whether he was awake.

The next time he beheld the universe of the room everything was altered. The curtains were withdrawn, the blinds up, the lamp extinguished. The naturalness, the ordinariness, the sanity of day reigned in the room. His brain was excruciatingly clear. He was a pneumonia patient and no more than that;

and the nurse stood erect and alert by the bedside, smiling at him. Her face was bright from soap and water. Her eyes glittered with fatigue. On the table by the bed was a basin and soap and a towel.

"Good morning," said the nurse, no longer wearing her spectacles. "Sir Arthur Tappitt is here. We must get ready for him. We must have you nice and tidy for him. He and Dr. Heddle are having breakfast downstairs. He telephoned early that breakfast must be prepared for him."

"But – but – what time is it?" Sam stammered, bewildered.

"Nearly half-past eight."

Sam pulled himself together. His dreams were so distant that he could not remember any of them. Not half-past eight, and the formidable Canadian-born had driven nearly seventy miles – to an invalid of national importance! The fellow must have started at six o'clock at the latest, and driven like hell along the empty morning roads! Yes, he thought of himself, flattered, as an invalid of national importance.

70

The Arch-magician

It immediately appeared that the importance of the patient, however great, was lower than the importance of Sir Arthur Tappitt. The patient and the room had to be made impeccably presentable for Sir Arthur, and with the utmost celerity – lest the arch-magician might be kept waiting for even one second. What mattered was no longer the sensitiveness of the patient, nor yet his condition, but the respect due to the august presence of Sir Arthur.

Before the nurse had quite finished arranging the patient for the ordeal, a housemaid timidly entered, and she was followed by no less a dignitary than Miss Thorping herself, who superintended the light dusting of the chamber and personally wielded the vacuum-sweeper on the carpet. Not a word was spoken till, at the close of the operations, Miss Thorping murmured:

"I think that will do, nurse."

The nurse agreed. Simultaneously the stir of men was heard on the landing.

"Quick!" Miss Thorping whispered, affrighted, to the housemaid, and these two vanished with their tools through the secondary door, like sinners fleeing in scared silence from wrath.

Sir Arthur and Dr. Heddle appeared. Sir Arthur was looking at his watch.

"Good morning, nurse," said Dr. Heddle.

"Good morning, doctor."

Sir Arthur ignored the nurse, except that he casually included her, with the patient, as one of the objects in the room over which his glowing eye comprehensively ranged. Beneath a heroic simulation of impassive calm the nurse was much flustered, in an agreeable way, by the arrival of the mighty.

Sir Arthur went straight to the bed, and took the patient's offered hand.

"We had a glimpse of each other one night at No. 10, Lord Raingo," he began, in a deep, low, nasal, vibrating, soothing tone.

Sam nodded.

"You must have started very early," he replied, rather inconsequently, with a quiver of apprehensiveness in his tone.

"I left at six."

"It was very good of you."

"Not at all. I always get up at half-past five, unless I'm kept out of bed after midnight. Besides, you're no ordinary ' life,' you know. Not a mere prince. The country needs men like you, and I regard it as an honour to be called in to help you. My old friend Heddle couldn't have pleased me better than by sending for me."

Sam looked interrogatively into the arch-magician's eyes – the eyes of a savage – and the arch-magician firmly returned the gaze. Sam seemed to be saying:

"What's the meaning of all this palaver?"

And Sir Arthur seemed to be half humorously retorting:

"What's that got to do with you, you sick man?"

From that moment Sam ceased for a time to be anything but a case. The excessive personality of Sir Arthur ruthlessly dominated the case, the bed, the room, and the other people in the room. His immense head, with the scanty, ruffled, evenly distributed hair, and no chin to speak of, hung poised above Sam's body like a hawk preparing its swift, downward stroke. Sam was hypnotized, he was intimidated and fearful, as though the arch-magician could bestow life or death.

"What sort of a night?" Sam heard Dr. Heddle ask the nurse; and the nurse's nervous reply: "Excellent, doctor. Slept nearly all the time."

"Excellent, was it?" thought Sam resentfully. "That's the sort of a night you call excellent, is it?" And he remembered all the horrors of the night.

Dr. Heddle glanced at the chart, which the nurse had brought up to the hour. The examination began. Sam was not questioned. Indeed the affair seemed to be conducted without the slightest reference to himself as an individual; he was merely a body. Sir Arthur might have been saying: "He doesn't know anything about it, anyway, and it would be a waste of time to consult him."

When, after a protracted period, the two doctors went into the next room to talk with free professional detachment about the case, both Sam and the nurse felt like children suddenly released from the presence of a superhuman schoolmaster. They exchanged a rather sheepish, self-conscious smile, admitting as it were that the overpowering emanations of the silent arch-magician's individual force had nearly been too much for them. The atmosphere of the room seemed to be physically lightened. Mere contact with Sir Arthur had almost robbed Sam of his thinking faculty. Indeed he could not think. He did not want to think. He did not care what doctors decided or what happened. The arch-magician had imposed himself terribly, if perhaps unconsciously: but Sam said to his soul that in an average state of health he could have withstood forty such arch-magicians and rendered back just as much hypnotism as they gave. Only he was a sick man, a man taken at a disadvantage, and he must be resigned; he must wait for another day. His first reaction was to attend, with an exaggerated anxiety, to his breathing. He was a very sick man, and everyone must and should know that he was a very sick man. His second reaction was against the nurse, whose verdict about the excellence of his "night" he still resented. After all she was only the nurse, and he was Lord Raingo of Eccles, the greatest invalid in the country.

"Do sit down a bit, nurse," he enjoined her somewhat testily, for to see her standing fatigued him – or he persuaded himself that it did.

"No, thanks," said she negligently, ignoring his wish. "I've been sitting all night."

He gave up the effort to destroy the equality between himself and the nurse which the arch-magician's immense superiority over both of them had established.

"Well, if she won't, she won't," he thought. "I've done my best for her. Let her go to the devil." And he began to mutter quite inarticulately to himself." Is this delirium? "he thought." It isn't, but she may as well think it is." He actually wanted to be delirious... Someone else was standing by the bed, not the nurse. Or, if it was the nurse, why was she wearing trousers and a gold watch-chain, and why was she scratching her scalp under the sparse, short hair? He heard a deep, masterful, soothing voice and gave a little start; and then he adjusted his relation to mundane phenomena, and admitted to himself that the gold watch-chain was hung upon the person of the arch-magician. The little, fierce man must have tiptoed into the room. No! Of course he had not tiptoed.

The next moment everything became clear, almost unnaturally clear. Sir Arthur was on the left hand, and Heddle on the right. Heddle was diffidently trying, not with complete success, to show by his demeanour that he had been Sir Arthur's senior and superior in their hospital days and that even now he was not less than Sir Arthur's equal. The nurse had withdrawn far behind. There she was, pale as a corpse, safe from professional observation, yawning. He, Sam, could see her yawning, and she knew it; but Sam was naught to her. Sam, indeed, during the hundredth part of a second felt sorry for her, and resentful on her behalf against these slave-drivers of doctors. A spasm of compassion, come and gone! He ignored the doctors and gazed with affected absorption at his favourite field of vision, the ceiling. Then, as it were against his will, he shot a glance at Sir Arthur, now his enemy; a wistful glance, appealing for mercy, or at any rate a respite.

He thought, with a terrible sinking:

"The moment has arrived. I shall know my fate. He cannot hide it from me."

And he made his breathing pathetic. He was acting a part nearly all the time, or thought he was.

Said the deep, confident voice:

"I can congratulate you on one thing – " (Ah! Only one thing! Bad!) – "You've got the best type of the disease, not Nature's latest fashion, which we call broncho-pneumonia. We never know where we are with broncho-pneumonia – " (Then you ought to, with all your professional swagger!) – "because as fast as it improves in one part it grows worse in another. Lobar pneumonia – that's your kind – is simpler. It starts quickly and it leads steadily up to a crisis. No caprices about it."

"How long before the crisis?" Sam muttered gloomily, though he was rather uplifted.

"Say a week more. Eight days. Nine days. Now, of course, I'm not going to talk to you as I would to an ordinary patient" – (You say that to every patient, you comedian!) – "I tell you at once there's no specific for pneumonia. Oxygen and energy are what is required. Especially energy. Vitality! Determination! Don't waste energy on anything else. Everything will naturally be done to increase your vitality, or rather to conserve it, but you yourself are the chief agent" – (I seem to have heard all this before. Is it to tell me this that you've been careering about the country at six o'clock in the morning?) – "Don't worry. Worry saps energy."

"But surely I've got something to worry about," Sam protested, with pained querulousness.

"Yes, you have" – (What flattering candour in the positive tone of the reply!) – "All I mean is, don't worry about anything except your illness, and only in reason about that."

"Well," said Sam. "I must do something. Nothing is worse for me than being bored. It's boredom that saps my energy."

"Oh, quite! Quite! And about avoiding boredom we must trust to your common sense" – (You needn't be so patronizing!) – "Dr. Heddle's treatment will be continued. It couldn't be better."

Sam had not taken his eyes off the ceiling. He had an absolutely baseless grudge against the great consultant; he had forgotten all gratitude to the arch-magician for being so extraordinarily active so early. The fellow was a comedian and was doing a stunt, for effect, for advertisement. He might be a great man, probably was, but for all his Canadian nasality and free deportment, he was what Sam called a snob. Nevertheless Sam was afraid of the power of his individuality and the disturbing vibration of his voice. And he knew, too, that he was being unjust to Sir Arthur. But he liked being unjust. The fellow was strong enough to bear without damage a lot of injustice. And Sam could not take his eyes off the ceiling... And now he was estimating his chances, seriously. He had to confess that the fellow had talked no nonsense, had not been jolly, hearty, nor desolatingly buoyant; had not prophesied smooth things.

Bad! The outlook was bad! And it was bad as much by what the fellow had not said as by what he had said. No word about his weak heart! No word about the possibility of pleurisy following the pneumonia! And comedians or not, fashionable practitioners did not rush careering around the country at daybreak without good cause – even for the most fashionable patients. Heddle must have telephoned to London a very grave view of the case. Heddle was a simpleton, but certainly not a fool. (He often said this to himself.)

He had a vision of the frightful precipice; he was on the very edge of it, and infinitely far down below, just discernible in the faintly lit darkness, ran the broad, smooth, ruthless, river. Vision as brief as his spasm of pity for the nurse! But he had had it. He had been out naked and lonely in the freezing spaces between two worlds. "I'm up against it this time," he thought. He was afraid, in a sense in which he had never been afraid before. Nothing and nobody mattered, not even Delphine, save this fear. Earth at its very worst seemed heaven itself, so warm, cosy, friendly, familiar, understandable. "Yes, I am very ill. I'm only just beginning to realize how ill I am."

The arch-magician was saying:

"Oh, yes, of course, there must be a bulletin issued. The question is: can it be a signed bulletin?"

"I see," said the simpleton, thrilled at the prospect of signing a bulletin in conjunction with the illustrious Sir Arthur Tappitt about an illustrious patient.

"With royal patients I always sign my bulletins. But one isn't supposed to sign any others. Still, there have been exceptions. And this case may be called exceptional. I'll tell you what. We'll draw up the bulletin, and I'll take it with me, and I'll telephone to the Palace and ask for permission for us to sign it. They're generally rather good-natured there...in their own odd way."

Heddle, who felt that he was at last moving in the great word, assented eagerly.

Sam thought, bitterly resentful:

"Have they got the slighest notion what it is to be ill? With their talk about signing or not signing bulletins! Here I'm all alone and naked and dying – dying – and I don't know what to do, and I *am* all alone, and it's the most appalling, sickening, horrible thing that can ever happen to anybody. It's not like anything else that ever was. Nobody could imagine it. And I'm all *alone*. And they're scheming to sign my bulletin!"

Still, in another part of his consciousness, Sam was just as interested as the doctors in the important signature question, and just as anxious as they were that the bulletin should be signed. He had another heavingly dizzy glimpse of the precipice and the dark river. Then he was talking, but whether to himself or to the doctors he did not feel quite sure.

"Please have a word with my son before you go. Please speak to Geoffrey. Please – "

"Yes, yes," he heard distantly. "Yes, yes. You know he had breakfast with us. He's waiting downstairs!"

An indefinite sort of conclusion to the visit. Sam attended to his respiration once more, still staring at the ceiling. Then, cautiously, he glanced about him. The room was empty. No. There was a nurse; but nor Nurse Kewley. A stoutish, short creature. Mysterious changes!

71

The Newspapers

"There';s someone to see you," said Geoffrey softly, coming in through the principal door, which was now being kept always open.

The windows were wide open, and the room was full of summer air and scents. The windows framed clear blue sky, and green, semi-transparent, slowly stirring leaves with glimpses of dark branches, and a dove unsteadily but constantly cooed somewhere out of sight.

And Sam, whom the arrival of any visitor instantly rendered conscious of his supreme importance as a man desperately ill, half lay, half sat, flushed and anxious, on his rich bed. For a moment he had the silly, beautiful notion that by some act of divination Geoffrey or Mayden or somebody had found Delphine, and brought her. His watchful and suspicious eyes noticed that Geoffrey made an infinitesimal sign to the nurse, who at once disappeared into the next room. They had come to some agreement, then, these two! He understood that Jeff possessed his own faculty of quickly getting on terms with everyone. But he himself had not got on terms with the day-nurse who had succeeded Nurse Kewley. Nurse Kewley had become an old friend, whose faults, though tiresome, one always condoned. The successor was a stranger, and Sam was nourishing against her one of his sick prejudices. Also he had had with her what seemed to him a tremendous duel about his false teeth, which duel he had won; the teeth remained in the place which they had been designed to fill, and Sam could look the world in the face. Herein was the last vestige of his physical pride – call it vanity.

"What's that woman's name?" he demanded rapidly, between intakes of breath.

"Dashed if I know."

"Dashed if I do either."

"She seems pretty good."

"Yes," Sam agreed negligently, thinking: "After all, I needn't be childish about the creature."

"How did you sleep – in your *room*?" he asked, with a faint note of quizzicalness in his voice, as if teasing the lad's perverse partiality for the open air at night.

"Topping. Four and a half hours of the best."

Mayden came limping in, his hands full of newspapers.

"I found I'd dropped most of 'em on the stairs," he began informally. "Well, chief, how are you?"

Sam could not remember that Mayden had ever called him "chief" before. What did the change signify? The man's voice was low and very pleasant, even enheartening. Nothing in his demeanour showed that he felt himself to be in the presence of a sick person, but everything showed that he knew Sam to be in need of sympathy and encouragement.

"Good acting," thought the actor in Sam appreciatively. "And not too good."

If it had been too good it would have been offensive. The spectacle of the two healthy men in their khaki, one youngish and the other very young, shamed the invalid; but at the same time it inspired him to the determined energy which might save him; it completed the restoration of his sanity and mental poise. And now Sam must do a bit more acting.

"I say, how are your hotels getting along?" he asked, as Mayden, having deposited the papers on the bed, took his hand. He had forgotten for weeks that his pet Mayden, fetcher and carrier, factotum and soother, was, after all, a great hotel-manager – and destined perhaps to be the greatest in the country.

"I hear they're doing as well as can be expected, thanks," Mayden smiled, accepting Sam's sheer bravado, as a perfectly natural inquiry. "And you?"

"Oh, I'm better since I had my oxygen," Sam answered.

Already oxygen was "his" oxygen. "My temperature's gone down." And he honestly did feel better. It seemed to him that, faced by the two lads, he was breathing with comparative ease. "How's the Ministry, my boy?"

"Ah well, you mustn't expect too much, sir. It's about in the same state as my hotels – that's what I should say."

More tact – the finest tact. If he'd said that everything at the Ministry was quite all right, he would have implied that Sam's absence could make no difference to its efficiency. Sam, however, had in reality ceased to be interested in the Ministry. He did not care what happened to it. He did not care a pin if his once-cherished new projects for it came to nothing. He felt no more reponsibility for it; and this dying away of the sense of responsibility was a delicious relief. In the depth of his mind was the insistent thought: "Delphine.

Delphine." And at a still profounder depth the still more insistent thought: "Am I done in? Or not?" His breathing grew more difficult again.

"Sir Ernest sent all sorts of messages to you," said Mayden. "He is writing." Then he added, after a brief hesitation. "He hasn't been so happy since the weeks before you became Minister."

With a gesture Mayden imitated Timmerson's fussy manoeuvring of his ample cuffs. Sam gave a responsive though somewhat mechanical smile, not because he was amused, but because he did not want Mayden to think that he resented this freedom at the expense of a superior. The fact was that he had never before known Mayden to permit himself any satiric reference to Timmerson – a born subject for satire. What did the new freedom mean? Did it mean that Sam was regarded definitely as no more a minister, as kid permanently on the shelf, as marked in the minds of men for death? In Sam's brain every phenomenon somehow thus related itself to his illness.

He looked at Geoffrey, who was staring out of the back window. Not once, so far as Sam had observed, had the boy twitched his neck. And he had slept four and half hours of the best under a roof. The boy was surely recovered. The idea of succeeding to millions must have helped him, given him confidence – but not consciously of course, subconsciously.

"How's that little girl?" Sam asked, with an effort after natural jauntiness.

"Oh!" said Geoffrey, turning. "I forgot to tell you. She's not very well this morning. Stopping in bed. Heddle's had a look at her. He says it's nothing."

The nameless fat, little, thirtyish nurse came back again, and in a moment Geoffrey and Mayden were going.

"See you a bit later, dad," said Geoffrey; and they were both gone.

Nothing arranged; nothing discussed; nothing vouchsafed. It was still more evident to Sam that the nurse and Geoffrey had fixed up a bargain: if the nurse would vanish when Geoffrey arrived, Geoffrey would vanish when the nurse thought that the visit had lasted long enough. The patient's wishes were neither consulted nor considered. Sam affected to himself to resent all this; but in reality he was glad that on the present occasion it should be so, for he felt weary. He was relieved to be rid of the young men. He had much of the greatest importance to say to them and to hear from them; but he was weary, and, after all, his physical condition, his breathing, alone had importance. Delphine? No! He must rest.

It was after receiving food from the nurse that he suddenly, with a start, remembered that there were unopened newspapers in the room – newspapers for which, earlier, he had been almost passionately longing. He thought, disconcerted, that he must be in a very peculiar mental state to have so completely forgotten the day's newspapers. Mayden had laid them at the foot of the bed; they had slipped to the floor on the side opposite to that on which the nurse performed her numerous ministrations. A parley ensued. She wanted him not to attempt to read, but having in half a day learnt something about his temperament, she soon gave him his eyeglasses. She would not let him unfold or even hold the paper himself; she said that the physical strain of doing so would seriously impair his strength; and he admitted the force of the argument.

She did not sit on the edge of the bed – that would have been too unconventional in a vocation which could not decently survive without the strictest and oddest conventions – but she set a chair close by the bed and perched herself on a corner of it, and thus with spine uncomfortably contorted she held paper after paper before his face. And she too read, glancing at him now and then to see whether he was ready for her to shift the position of the page or to turn over. Their heads were close together, and when she looked at him her gaze, he thought, was touchingly ingenuous; she seemed to be basking in his glory, to be intimately sharing his lot; it was as if he and she alone in the world had this glory all to themselves.

Of course she faintly annoyed him by her ingenuous exclamations:

"Oh my! Well, I never! Well, I never did! My word! They *do* think well of you. What a horrid portrait! Oh, and here's a picture of the Hall. Do you know I could hardly believe it when they told me I was going to the great Lord Raingo. And *then* I didn't really know how great you were. You must mind what you're about, Sister said. It's a great honour, she said. Fancy those Germans saying that there never has been any mutiny at Brussels! As if anyone would believe them! My word, you do read quickly!"

He would have told her to be quiet, had he not been queerly moved by her *naivete* and still more by her extraordinary patience in unfolding and folding and holding and turning over – the everlasting, selfless patience of the trained nurse.

The newspapers were wonderful; they more than satisfied him. He was the principal front-page item in all the papers which gave their first page to news, and the principal item in all of them without exception. In some papers the heading of his illness streamed across the top of the entire page. In other it was a two-column title. Of course there were a few .that confined the title to a single column, but these in their antiquated conceit would have confined the head-line of the approaching end of the world to a single column. So that their affected calm about himself did not hurt him. There was not much real news of his illness; but such news as there was had been enlarged by verbiage, and supplemented by accounts of his career, descriptions of his house and habits, and even by technical articles on the disease of pneumonia. No trifle was too small to swell the volume of matter. And the provincial papers were quite as full of him as the London dailies. Taken in the mass, the press gave the illusion, if illusion it was, that the entire country was sympathetically agog concerning his condition, and that this illness of this towering figure constituted the greatest misfortune that could have happened to a sore-tried nation. It took precedence of war-news and robbed an advance in Belgium of the sharpest edge of public satisfaction.

Then there were the press-cuttings, numbering over two hundred, from the newspapers of the previous day, and having to do chiefly with the debate in the House of Lords – and in particular with Sam's revelation of the German mutiny in Brussels: leading articles, reports of the debate, parliamentary sketches, views of experts, paragraphs of gossip, and cabled quotations from organs of opinion throughout the world. It was astonishing how that simple item had uplifted the spirit of the Allies, and even coloured the exposition of the war-news, throwing into dramatic relief those parts of the official communiques which gave hopeful signs of a turn in the tide of the war. By three minutes of talk to hereditary legislators Sam had put half the earth into a good temper and created optimism on a gigantic scale. And the name of Raingo was everywhere in the columns. And by some natural confusion of thought credit was allotted to Lord Raingo for the mutiny itself. It was as if he had magically brought the mutiny about. His personal triumph was tremendous.

He had expected much, but more had been given to him. He had said to himself on the afternoon of the speech that he would have to pay for the indiscretion. But he knew now that he would never have to pay for it. He was grown into a demigod, and nobody, not the highest, not the head of the government, would dare to take him to task for what he had done in a moment of speaker's panic – the results were too splendid for any criticism, and jealousy itself was silenced.

And when he thought of all that, and of the apotheosis of the banquet, and of the pressmen wandering hungrily around Moze Hall in search of any scraps that might be called news, he could not but regard himself as the greatest exponent of the arts of publicity and propaganda ever born. He could surely think no less of himself. His ministerial career was a fairy-tale, a romance, an epic; it was scarcely credible.

And then his eye met the eye of the nurse, and he was naught but a frail, very sick man after all, fighting for breath, trying piteously to edge away from the precipice and the gloomy, mysterious river. The nurse it was who had dominion. Impossible, however, that he should be content for long to see himself thus. If he was sick, he was a sick Titan, and from his bed he dominated the country. His bed had majesty. The house was subdued to his bed. The house had been hushed and reorganized about his bed. The house had no life beyond himself. Fighting for breath, he was the source of its life. It functioned solely about his bed. And it functioned with eminent efficiency – he knew from the smoothness, silence, and exactitude with which he was being nursed. There was perfect co-ordination between the housekeeper's room, the kitchen, the doctor's house, and his bed. It might have been that invisible and impalpable wires ran from his bed along all the corridors and even out into the roads down to the village and even to Clacton. Yes, he was very ill, he was pathetic, he was humiliated and broken, but his illness was marvellous, and in its terror and grandeur it was the most marvellous thing that had ever happened to him.

72

The Clue

He had visits during the long remainder of the day. Dr. Heddle came, unruffled and ingenuous, and would not agree to Sam's plaintive assertion that he was worse.

"I won't say you're better," said he, "because you couldn't be, it's too early to hope for improvement; but everything is going normally, and you've no right to say you're worse."

Sam critically considered every word and saw nothing but prevarication in the pronouncement.

"You're a Jesuit, Heddle. Don't I know I'm worse?"

Dr. Heddle tossed his white head and smiled.

"I've had a telephone message to say that the bulletin, signed, will be in this afternoon's papers," he said with satisfaction. "The people at the Palace were most sympathetic, it seems."

"What does the bulletin say?" Sam was about to ask, but he forbore. It was too much trouble to ask. Why ask? What did it matter? He himself was a far better authority on his condition than any bulletin. He decided to scorn the bulletin.

Geoffrey strolled in, according to his casual fashion, with a nattering tale of telegraphic and telephonic inquiries, and of cards left. The Prime Minister had telegraphed; Miss Packer had telephoned. Sid Jenkin had announced that he might come down if the doctors would permit an interview; the newspaper men were still persistently active. Not a word about Gwen.

"How's Gwen?" Sam demanded, suddenly suspicious.

"She hasn't got up yet," Geoffrey replied, rather selfconsciously as it appeared to Sam.

"What's wrong with her?"

"Oh! Don't know. You know what girls are." Geoffrey left.

Sam was convinced that she was not ill at all, and that they were merely keeping her away from him lest her presence might unduly disturb him. But he kept his notions to himself. He was aware of a strange tendency in himself towards a new secretiveness. On every side they were trying to hoodwink him. Well, let them go on trying. He would live his own private life.

Later, Mayden entered. It was clear to Sam that an order had been given forbidding two persons to see him at once. Mayden had an air of purpose – unlike his usual casual demeanour.

"I'm thinking of going back to town now, sir," he said, in a low, careful voice, leaning a little over the bed. "Unless of course you'd like me to stay."

"No object in staying," Sam murmured, as if in disgust. "No object in your coming. I'm too ill." Then he softened, conscience-struck. "Glad to see you, my boy – always." A painful, forced smile, gone in a second.

Said Mayden, after glancing at the nurse, who was unstitching a cover away near the front windows:

"About those two brothers of Miss Leeder – tailors at Islington."

The sick man was shocked into real attention. "What?" "You know."

Sam remembered that Delphine had once mentioned to him the existence of two half-brothers of hers, who had very violently quarrelled with her as to the division of some trifling furniture. They were the children of the first marriage of Leeder senior; Delphine was the child of the second marriage, and Gwen of the third.

"Yes," he admitted, gloomy, ashamed, fearful. "Well. This afternoon I got on to a man I know very well, very discreet, and asked him to go up to Islington and inquire for me."

"But how did you know the address? I never knew it," Sam snapped.

"Miss Gwen gave it to me."

So all three of them, Mayden, Gwen and his own son, had been freely discussing his affair. And Gwen might be ill in bed, but the lads had been seeing her. Strictly, nothing had happened that ought to surprise him. Gwen knew the story; Geoffrey had forced the story out of Gwen, and had told his father that he should speak to Mayden, and Sam had not forbidden him to do so. They had all accepted the situation naturally and nicely. There had been no hypocritical modesty. They all knew that Delphine had disappeared and that Sam was terribly anxious to discover where she was. And Mayden was taking steps – rather original steps and worthy of his resourceful mind – to seek information. What could be more proper in the admitted circumstances? Yet Sam was once again most painfully humiliated. He felt himself to be "the old gentleman"; also he was dangerously ill and should have had thoughts beyond the loveliness of girls; and these three youngsters were conspiring together for the welfare of his illicit liaison! What would old Mrs Clyth have said? The thing was awful. It would not bear examination. Imagine it being related in the witness-box of a court of law! And the villain of the piece a public darling – *the* public darling!

"Well? And then?" Sam looked up at the ceiling, just as he had done while listening to the arch-magician after breakfast.

"I've just had the answer from my friend. He spun them a suitable yarn, of course. The brothers haven't seen anything of her, or heard anything; and they object to being bothered by any inquiries about her." Sam said nothing. "But you needn't worry yourself, I think," Mayden proceeded. "She'll turn up again all right. And she'll explain everything to you. They always do."

It was the last three words of this speech that deeply wounded Sam, and dashed his faith in the hitherto quite perfect Mayden. Clearly Mayden regarded the affair as an ordinary amour, sensual on one side and venal on the other, between an old roue and a young woman who knew how to exploit her qualities.

As no more than that! Sam, an old roue! Delphine, venal! It was outrageous. Sam's desperate breathing became the frightful respirations of the volcano within. An imperfect simile, but it appealed to him. He still said nothing, and shut his eyes, for a sign. Mayden left, without even saying definitely whether or not he should return to London, or whether, if he went, he should come back the next morning.

Nurse Kewley resumed duty, marvellously fresh, spruce and white. Sam gave her a friendly smile; it was all he could do to show his pleasure at her arrival. The two nurses had held a short colloquy in the next room. At first they had talked together inaudibly to Sam; then they had chattered more loudly, gossiping with little giggles in the light-hearted manner of schoolgirls or nuns. Then Sam had heard good nights. Nurse Kewley appeared, all brightness, drew the curtains, and switched on the electricity.

At nine o'clock Dr. Heddle paid his third visit of the day and took careful observations. He had brought a copy of *The Evening Standard*, containing on its first page, in leaded type, the bulletin, which he showed to his patient with modest, touching vanity. He had lost nearly all his deference. Sam could read the bulletin without eyeglasses. "Lord Raingo is suffering from an attack of lobar pneumonia, both lungs being affected. His lordship passed a good night, and his strength is maintained. The progress of the disease is normal. Arthur Tappitt. John Francis Heddle, Capt. R.A.M.C." Both lungs!... The "good night" still rankled in Sam's mind. If that was what they called a good night...

Dr. Heddle soon sent the nurse into the other room and followed her with a new, tiny parcel of drugs. The newspaper had dropped open on to the bed. Sam, alone in the chamber, idly picked up one loose sheet of the paper. By holding it at arm's length he could just decipher the ordinary type. He saw, at the foot of a column, "Mysterious affair at Brighton" above a paragraph of a few lines: "An inquest was held yesterday upon the body of a young, well-dressed, dark woman who had apparently thrown herself from the cliffs between Brighton and Rottingdean. Every mark of identification had been carefully removed from her clothes. She was scarcely disfigured, having fallen into four feet of water. The jury returned a verdict in accordance with the evidence."

No more. In time of peace the story would have made a front-page item of at least a column; but the war and Sam's illness had reduced it to nothing. Sam loosed the paper. He felt just as if a local anaesthetic had been applied to every organ in his body.

"That's it," he uttered with absolute conviction. "That's it. Why did she do it?"

In a few minutes he had no feelings. Neither the doctor nor the nurse noticed any change in his condition or appearance. The nurse put the sheets of the newspaper together and folded them, and put the newspaper tidily on a side-table with all the other newspapers.

What he felt was an intense, utterly desolating loneliness. He was the centre of a nation's interest; dozens of people at hand and in London were intimately anxious to succour him and to save him, to prove their solicitude by loving and skilful service, to assure him in continual devotion of the companionable friendliness of humanity. But he was alone, like a child or a dog that has been lost for hours and given up hope of ever being found again. He was as distressingly and intolerably alone as in his delirium, edging away from the precipice and the dark river. The nurses, the doctors, Wrenkin, Mayden, Mrs Blacklow, Swetnam: all the faithful and all far, far off, unimaginably distant! Jeff? Of course there was Jeff. He would perhaps have liked Jeff to come and hold his hand. But Jeff would not and could not have understood, and what use was there in having your hand held by one who did not understand? Everybody was the same in this; the inability to understand.

Nobody, not even the best, was any better for the relief of solitude than his relatives at Eccles and Chorlton-on-Medlock, an aged uncle and three cousins, implacably proud in their north-Midland way, who had years and years ago told him to go to hell with his riches because they had quite mistakenly supposed that he had meant to patronize them and come the heavy swell over them. A terrible family, with their wives and husbands and children, self-satisfied and critical as only certain provincials can be. He could guess the tone in which they would be saying to each other at that moment: "Ah! So *my lord* is ill, is he? Ah! His *lordship's* strength is maintained. What a blessing! *Lobar* pneumonia, eh? Plain pneumonia isn't good enough for his *lordship*" And yet they would be most damnably stuck-up to their friends about their connection with his lordship. What an odious joke if one of them one day inherited the title! Deplorable persons. He greatly disliked even to let them occupy his thoughts. To have any of them at his bedside was unthinkable. Well, not one of his friends, colleagues, or servitors, not his son, would be more effective than they to abolish his loneliness.

There he half sat, half lay, panting and burning, and there was the nurse, conscientiously living in the sole desire to be of help to him! There they were in the night, he and she, and the night should surely have drawn them together. But no! He was alone; and his glory was dashed down, and his illness was no longer majestic – naught now save a wretched physical woe.

He was all the more alone because after reading the paragraph as to the inquest he had instantly and absolutely decided to say nothing about it to anybody. If one of them around him happened to read the little paragraph and had the wit to put two and two together, so be it. But by no word would he start the train of horrible complications which would inevitably result from a disclosure: visits to Brighton, police inquisitive-ness, perhaps – for she would probably be under the ground by this time – an exhumation and a new burial. She was his secret. His grief for her was his own, a precious possession which he would guard jealously. She was dead and could not be revived. The idea of the nameless grave, the pauper's grave – she would be buried at the expense of the parish – did not offend him. All worrying about the formalities of funerals he regarded, and had always regarded, as morbid, barbaric, as a sign of low intelligence. In a funeral he would have decency, and no more. He abhorred ceremonial ostentation in the presence of death. Indeed a nameless grave was almost his ideal. The dead were dead, and if any part of them lived, to mourn and honour what was corrupted was an insult to that part. Let her rest. Let her corruption lie in peace.

But something was due to Gwen's feelings. Sooner or later Gwen would have to know; and he would have to tell her, if nobody else did – and if he was alive. But not now! Not now! Delphine was his. Delphine was drawing him away from earth. Not on high, towards any chimerical paradise. Not even towards the precipice and the river beneath. (How impressively strange that he should have imagined the precipice – after *her* precipice, and the river after her sea!) No! She was merely drawing him away, no whither. The conception which he had was not one of an ultimate arrival, but simply of a departure, an escaping from loosed bonds. He did not want to recover from his illness now. He did not want to help the doctors and the nurses, nor to give joy to the public. If he still fought for breath as desperately and tenaciously as ever, it was because he must, not because he would. The physical instinct to live overbore his spirit.

He was filled with an agonizing compassion for Delphine, and with remorse. He had been monstrously unjust to her. He had pictured her faithless in the arms of her soldier, and while he thus pictured her she was dead. He truly understood now why she had taken nothing with her from the flat, had destroyed all writings; and left only her portrait. For her journey she needed nothing. He imagined her journey; he spared himself no detail: the taking of the ticket, the sitting in the train – it was at night, she would be sure to go after dark; the constraint of the gaze of others, the giving up of the ticket, the leaving the station, the walk through darkened Kemp Town, the leaving behind of black streets and blinded houses, the open road ascending and then descending, the whiteness of the road in the dim, diffused light of the night, the night-wind, the night-odours, the low fences, the peering for the right spot – here, no, farther on, a little farther on! – the decision, the halt, the resolve… All by herself, all alone.

He saw now that she must have long played with the idea of suicide. Once she had stayed at Brighton, and he remembered how she had confessed to him that she had never passed particular spot on the Rottingdean road without a strong desire to throw herself off the edge of the cliff. He had replied, easily, with his Midland impassiveness, that most people experienced such desires and that nobody ever yielded to them. She had yielded.

What force of resolution to carry her to Brighton and to the savage spot with her resolve unimpaired! Why had she done the most desperate, terrible and brave of all human acts? She had been happy with Sam, surely? When they were together she would prove to him all the time, by her tenderness, her admiration, her acquiescences, her adoration, her passionate-ness, her watchfulness over his welfare, that she loved him despite his age and physical imperfections. If her demeanour did not mean love, not only sensual but affectionate and even spiritual, then demeanour had no significance whatever. And she must have known that he was completely devoted to her. The soft, bitter memory of a thousand caresses, tones, gestures, rose into his mind, – an overwhelming assurance that he could not possibly have been deceived as to her feelings. He had contented her, as well as any man could. They had never quarrelled, never had a scene since the great, disagreeable scene in which he had borne down her resistance. He had been generous to her beyond her desires, and would have been far more generous had she permitted. She could have had anything for the asking, and for less than the asking. He had offered her marriage.

Of course she had lived a solitary life; but she liked solitude; throughout the day she liked to dream in solitude of his arrival in the evening. That was her idiosyncrasy, and she had been ideally situated to indulge it…

A cruel act, this leaving the world and him in it. The cruellest of all acts towards himself. She must have been aware, or she ought to have been aware, if she possessed any imagination at all, that in committing it she was accomplishing the ruin of his existence. And yet, driven by some dreadful goad, she had committed it.

But just as he could not maintain resentment against her when he believed that she had deserted him for the soldier, so he could not maintain resentment now. What pained him now was the imagining of her misery. His thoughts of her were inspired by an immense, enveloping, compassionate kindness. She had taught him tenderness. He had not known what tenderness was, he had been afraid and ashamed of tenderness, until he came under her tutelage... She had taught him, not by a single precept, but by ever-continuing example, without a word. Tenderness was her supreme quality, and it was one of the greatest qualities, a quality which might well atone for the absence of any other.

As for her plunge, the occasion of it might be obscure, it might or might not be connected with her soldier – but the disposing cause of it was plain enough to him now: a war neurosis. She was yet another victim of the war. And how could he in decency accuse her of lack of imagination towards himself when he for his part had not had sufficient imagination to take her melancholia seriously? He had failed to appreciate that her melancholia was the symptom of some grave and disconcerting disease, a disease which was just as much a disease as his own pneumonia. In his heart he had smiled superiorly at her melancholia, as something avoidable and unintelligent. Yes, he had resented her melancholia; he had permitted it to lower her in his esteem. Spiritual pride! Her tenderness had a deeper, a more comprehending wisdom than all his brains... He thought all these thoughts over and over countless times.

He moved his head to look at the clock. Nearly half-past one. He must have slept, though he could have been quite sure that he had not slept. Nurse Kewley's lamp was burning behind the screen. She had altered its position from the previous night, so that he could see only the radiance and not the lamp itself. The long curtains of the front windows swished slightly as the wind from across the estuary curved them inwards, let them drop straight, and curved them inwards again. The stirring air was warm. There was sufficient light to show the features of the room. The doors stood open. He could just hear the very slow, soothing tick of a large clock which Geoffrey had that afternoon fixed on the landing. No other sound in the still house; but someone somewhere would be sitting up, ready to answer the nurse's call, for everything was organized.

The scene and the moment frightened Sam, somehow filled him with awe. He was weary, stricken, hopeless. He felt that he had nothing to live for, and nothing to die for. As he came more fully to his senses, he realized that he was worse, much worse. He was very hot, very thirsty. The pain in his side was more acute. His breathing was more difficult. The sensation of disorder and corruption was frightfully distressing. He wanted help, moral rather than physical.

"I am *ill*," he thought. "Nobody understands how ill I am. I cannot go on like this. I cannot."

His cough had earlier been strangely easier; but now he coughed and coughed, and the effort seemed to lacerate his throat. Not a sign from the nurse. His glance went in fretful inquiry to the screen. He saw her feet sticking out a little from behind the screen, flat heels uppermost and the toes of her shabby shoes bent into the carpet; also a few inches of her stockings, horizontal. She was kneeling; she was praying. For an instant he forgot his woe in a sort of intimidated shock. She was communing with the skies. She had her secret life, and he had overseen it, he was spying on it. She possessed what he could never possess, faith; she was engaged on that which he could never engage in. Could she be praying for him? Did she include prayer in her solemn duties? Had Delphine prayed before she threw herself from the cliff? The hidden, tremendous tides that flow beneath the surface phenomena of being seemed to be on the point of revealing themselves to him; they were all about him; they were moving him.

"Nurse!" he cried faintly, desperately.

The feet moved. The nurse came to him, smiling and helpful.

"I'm here," she said, low, with such solacing sweetness, such freshness, from her intercourse with heaven, that she might have been the Mother of God.

73
The Change

Five nights later, and about a couple of hours later in the night, the patient noticed, amid his delirium, his dreaming and his ceaseless preoccupation with the heavy task of getting enough air into his body, that he had began to perspire.

"This is the end," he thought, for his state had gradually grown worse, and he might have despairingly exclaimed with far intenser feeling than before: "I cannot go on like this. I cannot."

The perspiration reminded him of the disturbing night-sweats which he had experienced just previous to his illness, and he interpreted it, as he had rightly interpreted those, as a herald of calamity.

Nurse Kewley, summoned from her book, gently opened the jacket of his pyjamas and inserted the clinical thermometer under his armpit.

"It's lower," she said, after peering long under the lamp at the slim instrument, and, turning to him: "I do believe you're better."

There was quite a new tone in her voice. Always she was cheerful and consoling – save now and then about six a.m. when fatigue and the prospect of an interminable further two hours of duty might harden her voice and even make her a little impatient of his demands – but now she seemed to be praising him for an action righteous and unexpected.

"Oh?" he murmured, pretending to be indifferent and gloomy.

"Yes. It's a lot lower. I do believe you've got round the corner."

"Is perspiring a sign of that?"

"Why, of *course*!" she cried, almost shrilly. "Didn't you know?"

He had not known.

He said to himself that he must therefore sweat more and more. In an hour his woollen pyjamas were heavy and sodden with moisture; they might have been thoroughly soaked in water.

"Where the deuce can it all come from?" he remarked, grimly arch (arch in spite of himself – his body was speaking, not his soul).

"It comes from *you*!" the nurse answered gleefully, as she prepared fresh clothes for him.

The dawn had arrived, unperceived by either of them in the happy commotion. She drew aside the curtains. It was raining, but the rain had no significance and could work no reaction against the optimism of the room. The perspiration continued increasingly. Sam eagerly drank every glass that was offered to him. When at last the day-nurse came on duty, Nurse Kewley would not go; she could not bring herself to leave the thrilling scene; and the two nurses mingled their joyous exclamations like children watching a show. The patient's temperature did not cease to fall; it behaved as a barometer falling for a tremendous change of weather. The good tidings spread through the house. Geoffrey appeared in the illustrious dressing-gown, and actually chaffed his father. The tidings wandered down the roads and reached the village. The rain became ridiculous in the general gaiety. Miss Thorping, as a special favour due to her importance, was admitted to a momentary sight of the wonderful patient. The patient ate – and with relish; he could not help eating. His breathing was easier and less noisy; the phlegm was easier; the cough was easier; the pain in his side was much easier.

Dr. Heddle came half an hour earlier than usual. The doctor had no intention of accepting the gossip of nurses. He put on an incredulous, non-committal air, and proceeded to make his own examination, treating even the chart with suspicion.

But when he had read the thermometer he burst out startlingly:

"By God! It is a shade below normal!"

To cover this unseemly exhibition of excitement he spoke coldly, almost inimically, to the day-nurse; the night-nurse had gone ostensibly to her rest, but in reality to chat with Miss Thorping in the housekeeper's room.

As for Sam, he could hardly recognize himself, so extreme had been the change in six hours. He mumbled aloud, having acquired the habit of talking to himself:

"I always did say the most marvellous thing on earth is the recuperative power of the human body."

"Jeff," he said later. "Have the press-cuttings been coming?" For five days he had displayed no interest in his relations to the world outside.

"I should say they have, dad. It's no exaggeration to say they've been coming."

"Bring 'em along then."

"In a clothes-basket, eh?"

74

The Tonic

Sam soon, wearied of the green piles of press-cuttings. He wanted only to read the daily bulletins, but was too proud to say so, and in the disorder he could find nothing for himself. Such cuttings as he glanced at seemed to be rather monotonously alike in substance and tone; but the immense quantity of the whole, spreading all over the bed, gave him a satisfaction which reading could scarcely had deepened. Moreover the nurse issued a warning against overstrain.

Further, Sam was not really interested in any of the press-cuttings. He was merely pretending to himself to be interested in them. As his condition improved, so he became more and more preoccupied with the thought of Delphine. And he could think clearly now, perhaps for the first time in a week. "Why did she do it? Why did the poor little thing" – she so big and powerful! – "throw herself over that cliff?" The problem agonized him. It appeared to him to be far more terrible than ever before. The secret which he was keeping, and had determined to keep, was growing heavier than he could bear. Could he continue to keep it? Ought he to keep it? And did all or any of them know it? He looked covertly at the nurse. Did she know? Had it leaked out? Was it common property? Was everybody by concerted arrangement hiding it from him?…

He dropped asleep for an hour and a half – good, energizing sleep.

"How could I have slept?" he thought on waking.

Geoffrey entered. Did Geoffrey know? Surely he could not know, or it would have been impossible for him to be playful, chaffing, as he had been! Sam suddenly decided that he was bound to tell Gwen; it was obviously his duty to tell her; and he was just about to make his decision irrevocable by asking for Gwen when Geoffrey said:

"I say, dad. Here's Mr Sid Jenkin, come down specially from London to see you. What d'you think? Could you stand it?"

"Oh, of course," said Sam, without thought, "if he's come all that way. Bring him in." He was both startled and flattered.

"Not so fast," Geoffrey's raised hand seemed to say. "What do you think, nurse?" As if patients could be permitted to settle such important questions for themselves!

The nurse blushed and moved uneasily. She had authority and was afraid of the responsibility of authority. Mr Sid Jenkin, the leader of the Labour Party, the man who notoriously had risen from the coal-face to the War Cabinet! Who was she, from a little hospital at Clacton, to keep out or to let in so great a personage?

"I – I don't know what to say," she stammered.

"Well, you'd better know," Geoffrey grinned at her, jocosely threatening. "It's your job to know."

"Perhaps for a quarter of an hour."

She was dying to set eyes upon the legendary leader, and yet very fearful at the prospect. Sam was now a little excited at the same prospect. The nostalgia of politics asserting itself over every preoccupation!

Geoffrey and Sid Jenkin made their entry arm-in-arm, as thick as two thieves. There he was, the celebrity, dark, bulky, shabby, genial, at. ease, yet plainly conscious of his immense renown in the world!

"How do, Sam, lad?" he began, in a very quiet voice, and gently shook hands.

Then instantly he turned to the nurse and astonished and delighted her by shaking hands with her too.

"Now, nurse. You needn't be alarmed. It's Sid Jenkin here. And he's had more experience of sick-visiting than all the other members of the War Cabinet put together." He glanced at the Empire clock, and went on, still in a very quiet voice – not at all the voice that once had rung across Trafalgar Square and silenced hecklers in the Free Trade Hall at Manchester: "When that clock strikes the half-hour I shall go."

The nurse blushed again. He was a regular dear, and the image of his portraits in *The Daily Mirror.*

"Now I'll take a chair," he said, and sat down by the bedside. The nurse moved into the background. "You needn't go, nurse. This isn't one of my days for eating nurses."

As for Sam, he was back in London; but he felt self-conscious and could not think of anything to say.

"How's things?" he asked, after a second's delay.

"There's only one thing," Sid Jenkin replied, spreading his knees and moving his hands slowly along the shiny cloth of his trousers. "And that's you. You've 'eld the fort, no mistake. Nobody ever 'ad such a boom as you're 'aving. You've ended the war, Sam. Of course it's still going on, and we've got 'em on toast, we've got 'em stiff, 'but nobody takes any notice of victories these days. It's all Raingo, Raingo. I was at the Palace day afore yesterday, and first question 'Is Majesty asked was about you. I couldn't tell 'em enough. But you're a fraud, Sammy. Ye don't look a sick man – at least not sick enough."

"I'm better to-day," Sam said modestly. "I'm told I've turned the corner."

"Of course you're breathing's bad, but I've heard worse."

"Bad!" Sam expostulated. "You should have seen me yesterday. It's much better this morning, isn't it, nurse?"

"Oh much, my lord," the nurse agreed nervously. "It's getting better all the time."

"He isn't the same man to-day," said Geoffrey, leaning over the foot of the bed, his favourite position in the room.

"Well, all I can say is I chose my day well. I said to meself this morning, ' I've got a bit o' time off to-day. I'll run down and find out for meself 'ow the 'ero is.' I sent word I might come, didn't I? Mind ye, I didn't 'ardly 'ope to see you – not from all as was printed. But I said to meself,' They won't keep Sid Jenkin out if they can stretch a point.' Not as I should 'ave insisted. No! I've seen Tappitt every day. Your medico 'ere was telephoning to 'im every day, so I got the facts. I must say Tappitt was always optimistic. 'E's as big a circus as I am meself – ye know that – but 'e's the stuff, Arthur is, and ye did right to 'ave 'im. Oh yes, 'e's the stuff. Same 'ere. Now tell me a bit. And don't look so grim."

If Sam looked grim it was because his thoughts were still moving in a world more tragic than Sid Jenkin's amusing world. Sam was saying to himself again and again: "My life has been given back to me, but what can I do with it – now?" And he was saying also, with a grimness sardonic and desolate: "I may be very ill and very weak, but how tremendously alive I am compared to her!" He regarded the performing Sid with a certain mild disdain, which, however, was gradually transformed into a feeling of understanding and grateful affectionate-ness. For Sid was giving out vitality and geniality and good-humour. He might be a schemer and a bit of a charlatan, but he was well justified in describing himself as the "stuff." His interest in his fellows was genuine, and he had the great virtue of cheerfulness. Like everybody else, Sam yielded to Sid's diverting and eager personality.

"You'd be grim if you'd been through what I've been through," said Sam benevolently and yet a little superiorly – from the height of his experience of pain.

"Well, I've been through a thing or two myself," Sid Jenkin mildly retorted.

"I expect you have," Sam agreed with quick sympathy, and then gave some details of his illness. But he had not the common invalid's desire to talk at length about his physical woes, for his brain was full of another matter, and his remarks upon pneumonia were neither ready nor informing.

"Never you mind, lad," said Sid Jenkin. "I can see 'ow you are without you telling me. Of course ye 'aven't read the old man's anniversary review of the war? In the 'Ouse-day afore yesterday. Four columns. No, ye 'aven't. Worth-reading when ye feel perky enough. It'll give ye a rare laugh. 'E gave all the fat to the Navy. Made ye think the Army's only a bit of a side-show after all, and 'ardly worth mentioning. Just because 'e"s just been 'aving one of 'is shindies with the C.-in-Q What got 'im on the raw was Tommy Hogarth going against 'I'm in that business. They've nearly quarrelled, Tommy and Andy 'ave, and Andy's afraid Tommy 'll resign and go back to 'is old party. Nobody ever knows with Tommy. Great success Andy's speech, though. But that wasn't the funniest part of it. The funniest was 'is pessimism. 'E kept on saying we aren't out of the wood and false confidence was to ibe deprecated and all that! Good old word, ' deprecated,' ain't it? Wanted to show the beautiful public as 'e's a real statesman and not a gas-bag. Keeping his 'ead in a victory, and so on. Some men lose their bloomin' 'eads when everything's going like a house afire: but the greatest don't, and Andy 'asn't lost 'is because 'e's the greatest and is going down to 'istory as the Prime Minister who was as great in triumph as 'e was in disaster. Ye see the line of argument. 'E knows the dope they want, Andy does, no mistake. Fact is, 'e's really so cock-a-hoop 'e don't know what to do with 'imself. 'E's won the war, and yet to look at 'im 'e's as calm and collected as if 'e'd lost it. Well, 'e *'as* won it. I give 'im the war. He wanted it."

"Sid," said Sam, smiling. "You've got a low, mean, jealous mind."

"I 'aven't. I'm all for Andy, and 'e knows it and everybody knows it. But 'e's the biggest actor on any stage. 'E's a bigger actor than Sid Jenkin; and why shouldn't I 'ave my bit o' fun? I don't mean all as I said, but I do mean it all the same. So ye can make what ye like of it. And there's summat else. I came 'ere to give ye a bit of a lift. And how can I cheer ye up if I talk about Andy's speech like a Hansard report? Dozens o' doctors 'ave told me I'm the finest tonic their patients ever had, and worth a ton of Easton Syrup. And so I am. But I don't do it by catching the style of His Panjandrum the Earl of Ockleford, my boy. I do it by standing on me head and letting the coins drop out of me pockets. There's no deception an' I'll turn up me sleeves if ye like." He looked at the nurse; "Aren't I a good tonic, nurse?"

"Oh, sir!" murmured the nurse, utterly flabbergasted by these shocking revelations of the realities of political life.

"No," Sid Jenkin resumed, much pleased with himself, "I wouldn't deceive ye, Sam. It isn't about the C.-in-C. affair that Tommy and Andy 'ave got near to quarrelling. Word's coming up from the constituencies that the Government's in danger. Yes, my lad, the Government, and you, and me, we're all in danger."

"What! And the war won!" Sam interjected.

"And the war won and all! That's the grateful public, that is. It's all along of calling up these men of forty-six, seven, eight, nine, and fifty. Fathers of families, Mainstays of commerce. Little shopkeepers. Yes, and some of 'em grandfathers. Can you beat conscripted grandfathers? That's how they look at it up in the constituencies. What do ye want with grandfathers in the Army, they say, when the Boche is on the run? Every M.P. is getting ten thousand letters, about, by every post. It isn't succeeding, Andy's Man Power Act ain't! They want it altered, and if it isn't altered there'll be hell raised. And Andy won't give way. 'E never gives way. 'E'll stick it. And that's another reason why 'e was so pessimistic in 'is speech. 'E wanted to show us as we still need every man alive. Tommy Hogarth 'll back anything as 'e thinks 'll succeed, and nothin' that 'e thinks 'll fail, and that's why 'e's agin the Government now. Kettlefuls of fish! I'll tell ye another thing. Ye may expect a visit from your old Eccles friend Andy pretty soon: 'E might come this afternoon. That's one reason why I came this morning. I like to get in first – see how the land lies, like. Don't say I'm not frank with you." He glanced at the clock, rose, and took Sam's hand. "Au revoir. See ye in London in a month. I congratulate ye. Come on, Jeff."

As the clock struck the half-hour he left the room, nodding to the nurse as if to say: "Was that a performance or wasn't it, my girl?"

75

Gwen Gone

"Where's Gwen Leeder? I want to see her," Sam said, rather curtly, as soon as Geoffrey returned to the bedroom.

His tone straightened out the smile from the boy's face, and it presented a flow of comment upon the phenomenon of Sid Jenkin and any sinister expression of foreboding about the astonishing predicted visit of the Prime Minister. There was a little mischievous malice, as well as a little vanity, in Sam's -mood. He wanted to silence *naivete* by pretending that Sid Jenkin and the great Andrew Clyth were no more to him than tie common objects of daily existence; nor did he care to admit that Sid Jenkin had, as it were, baptized him again in the magic water of politics and, despite his sorrow and pre-occupation, awakened in him a thirst for the old life.

Geoffrey hesitated: "She isn't here. She's gone back to London," he said at length.

Their eyes met, and Sam's glance, like Geoffrey's, dropped self-consciously.

"De» they know? Have they found out all about it? Do they think they're hiding it from me? Or don't they know anything yet?" thought Sam. What a situation! How crushing was the weight of the secret in Sam's heart! He said aloud: "You'd better get her. Where is she?"

"I don't know. Probably at Orange Street."

"You do know where she is. You aren't telling me the truth. And you know Delphine is dead and buried," thought Sam. He said aloud: "Telephone them. And tell her to come to-day."

"Won't you be too tired, dad?" the boy suggested, intimidated. He looked at the nurse for help, but the nurse gave none; she too was intimidated.

"Well, if I am, I suppose she can stay here till to-morrow."

"Yes, of course. I'd better telephone to Mayden and get him to see to it."

"Why Mayden? The fellow's got quite enough to do at the Ministry without spending his time in meddling in my private affairs."

Sam began to breathe more loudly, as if to warn everybody that he could not be crossed without danger. He had a deep grudge against Mayden, because of Mayden's careless, unhappy phrase about Delphine. Forgotten were all Mayden's almost filial kindnesses to him. Forgotten was his high affectionate esteem for Mayden.

"Very well," said Geoffrey submissively, and left the room.

"I'm behaving in a disgusting way," thought Sam. "I ought to be able to do better than that." And when Geoffrey at length came back with the satisfactory news that Gwen would arrive in the afternoon, he said, smiling benevolently, all his demeanour asking pardon: "Thank ye, my boy. You've soon managed it for me. Thanks. You may be sure if I feel the least bit tired I'll tell you."

Geoffrey held an unopened telegram in his hand.

"What's that thing?"

"Oh, it's just come. I expect it's only one of the Central News telegrams." He opened it. "Yes, ' Central News learns French not yet crossed Vesle. All bridges broken. Enemy retreating region Rheims.'"

"Oh!" Sam exclaimed. "So they haven't crossed the Vesle after all," though he had known nothing about the Vesle. He had an instinct to pretend to look on the black side, and to imply that war-news was very unreliable. "A nice thing, that!" He quite ignored the statement about the bridges and the enemy retreating. He thought: "Why in Hades do I go on in this childish way?" He could not understand himself.

Geoffrey did not argue. Instead, he informed his father that on the previous evening the King's private secretary had telephoned for news.

"Urn!" Sam grunted.

"You've had lots of letters from your overseas friends," said Geoffrey lightly.

"And you've been opening 'em, have you?"

"Well, I thought I'd better." Geoffrey was a little dashed.

"Quite right, Jeff. Of course you had to open them," Sam relented, catching hold of himself just in time.

"I've kept 'em all together for you, and I've answered one or two of 'em. I wonder why all the Americans write ' too bad.' Still they were awfully decent. I think I'll clear out now. You might be able to sleep a bit."

"Here, why this hurry? Tell me – how are things going on generally? Anything from Swetnam?"

"Yes. He suggests coming down."

"Well, he needn't. Tell him to send Mrs Blacklow. I've had Swetnam down here before, and he's no good when he's off his own stool."

"Mrs Blacklow – is she the clerk? He said she's left."

"Left!" cried Sam. "Good God! She's in trouble, and all he can think of is to dismiss her!"

"He didn't say he'd dismissed her. He said she'd left."

"Well, you tell him from me to un-dismiss her, and quick I And send her down here. Listen here, Jeff," Sam continued, very gently. "She's going to have a baby and she's got to be looked after. See?"

"Suite."

"That's all right, then. And how are things round here?"

"Oh, fine! Only Wrenkin's a bit shaken – under his stony calm. He's received his railway ticket and notice to report at Colchester on Monday."

"Not for the Army?"

"Well, what else d'you think, dad?"

These last tidings upset Sam completely. He felt the futility of even trying any more to play the kindly, large-hearted philosopher. No sooner had he returned to life than the responsibilities and harassments of life seemed to crowd down upon him and suffocate him. As if the awful disaster of Delphine were not enough, there were piles of letters to be attended to, and the faithful ass Swetnam was acting the fool with Mrs Blacklow, and Gwen had vanished, and everybody was deceiving him for his own good – damn everybody! – and now Wrenkin was called up! He simply could not conceive the Moze estate without Wrenkin. Wrenkin alone held it together. Why, if Wrenkin went, even the hot-water supply would cease to be. Trouble of the worst kind all round!

"I won't have it!" he burst out. "I will not have it. Here the war's practically over. Germans retreating everywhere, and burning bridges behind 'em – I should say that was sign enough. And yet they go on calling up men of forty-six and over! It's monstrous. I tell you I won't have it. I rather think I've got more than enough influence to keep Wrenkin here, and I will too." He glared feebly.

"I expect you've got the influence all right, dad, but you can't use it for yourself."

"And why not?"

"Well, you can't. It wouldn't do. Wrenkin must stick it, and we must stick it; but I quite agree it's idiotic."

Sam no longer glared; he stared; the boy's tone made him pause.

"Look here, son, who the deuce do you think you're talking to?" But he smiled, pleased with Geoffrey, full of admiration for him. "All right. Do as you like." He realized that in the self-centredness of his malady he had been forgetting that a state of war meant hardships – even for invalids.

"I think his lordship should rest now," the nurse intervened, speaking to Geoffrey.

76

More News of Visitors

Sam woke up renewed from a longer continuous sleep than he had had for a week past. The clock showed three-thirty, and he remembered nothing since one o'clock, when he had eaten – and with appetite. In spite of calamities, visits, worries and grievances, he was marvellously, almost incredibly better. The rain had ceased, the room was full of warm afternoon light; and the green branches were gently waving beyond the window-panes. He felt more surely than ever that he was back again, well within the house of life. The sensation was sweet, and very disturbing too.

But even now, he gradually perceived, his mental state was not quite normal. For several seconds passed, possibly quite a number of seconds, before he realized that he was alone in the room, and that a regular droning sound which he heard was the low murmur of voices talking rapidly in the next room. The door between the two rooms was half open. He identified the voice of the day-nurse and Miss Thorping's voice – both excited.

"Skinner came running to me. 'Mrs Heddle's on the telephone at the Post Office,' he says, ' and I've asked her to hold the line,' he says. ' The Prime Minister's in the village,' he says. ' He's called at the doctor's,' he says. ' You'd best go and speak to her.' I said, ' But it's your place to answer the telephone, Mr Skinner.' ' Well,' he says, ' I fair can't do it. The Prime Minister's in the village and he's coming up here, and I must change my clothes and I'm all of a shake. I'm an old man, Miss Thorping,' he says. And so he is and ought to retire; I could run this place much better without the poor old dodderer. Mrs Heddle told me the Prime Minister had just gone off to Clacton – oh, in a very luxurious car, and there was a lady with him, and it was the lady who'd got ont and knocked at the doctor's door. It seems she was very nice and charming and beautifully dressed. Dr. Heddle was just going out to a confinement, but she saw him. She wanted to know whether it would be right for the Prime Minister to see his lordship. Dr. Heddle said yes, for a quarter of an hour or

"That's just what *I* said for Mr Sid Jenkin this morning," the nurse put in, pleased with herself.

"It shows how right you were, dear," said Miss Thorping. "Well, the doctor went out to speak to the Prime Minister in the car – only a minute, because the Prime Minister was in such a hurry to get to Clacton, and so was the doctor to go back to the confinement: but he ran back to Mrs Heddle – the doctor did, I mean – to tell her how nice and flattering the Prime Minister was: he'd heard all about the doctor from Sir Arthur, you see. It was Sir Arthur who had told the Prime Minister he'd better call at the doctor's first. But they all knew his lordship was better – I suppose it's all over the country by this time. Mrs Heddle tells me everything, you know. So he's coming, the Prime Minister is. I thought you'd like to know about it, Emily."

"Yes, indeed. It's most thoughtful of you, dear," said the nurse. "I sh'd think I should like to know indeed! I must tidy things up a bit, and his lordship too. How's my hair, dear?"

"Your hair's beautiful, dear. It always is."

"But fancy the Prime Minister! I don't know what I shall do. No, I don't. Mr Jenkin this morning – that was a bit of a knock for me. You see, dear, I'm so shy. People think nurses have no feelings. However, I'm getting used to it. It'll be the King next." A giggle. "Fancy the Prime Minister!"

"Shows how important his lordship is to the Government, doesn't it?" said Miss Thorping proudly.

"Doesn't it!" the nurse agreed, with equal pride.

"What I wanted to ask you, dear, was what about tea, what about offering them tea, in the hall or the small drawing-room-What do you think?"

"Well, they can but refuse it. But shan't you ask Mr Geoffrey?"

"Mr Raingo isn't in. He's gone out and nobody knows where he is. Thank goodness I've got plenty of cakes. Mr Raingo's that fond of cakes! Never touches a drop, but he loves cakes. Eats them in bed. Yes, Edith told me about cake crumbs in his bed of a morning. Then you think I'd better prepare tea? I thought so too, but I'm glad to have your advice – I daren't think how Skinner will serve it – if they decide to have it; I almost hope they'll say they've had tea at Clacton."

When the nurse returned into the bedroom Sam shut his eyes.

"My lord!"

He made no movement.

"My lord!" She had come nearer to the bed.

He slowly opened his eyes and stirred, lest if he carried his shamming further she would detect it and so have to blush for her indiscreet palavers with housekeepers under his very nose.

"I'm sorry to disturb you, but they've just telephoned to say that the Prime Minister and a lady will be calling soon to see you and the doctor says you can see them for a quarter of an hour, the same as I said to Mr Sid Jenkin, and I thought perhaps you'd like to be titivated up a little before they come."

He could see that she was tremendously excited, as, indeed, both she and the housekeeper must have been to carry on such a conversation as he had overheard almost in the doorway of the bedroom. Without doubt the entire household was tremendously excited. The entire village, the entire peninsula would be aware that Andy was in the district. He was a master of the tactics of showmanship, was Andy. The news of the great event would somehow travel faster than his car, and at every hamlet, and particularly in Clacton, the luxurious car with the beautiful lady in it would be acclaimed with lifted hats and cheers. Assuredly the nice and charming lady was Rosie Packer. A Prime Minister could not be expected to wander about the country without his confidential secretary.

Mrs Heddle would be passionately wondering who the lady could be; she would, of course, be convinced from the start by mysterious processes of intuition that the lady was not Andy's wife... Obviously Mrs- Heddle could not keep the supreme news to herself. She had had to rush out instantly to the Post Office and impart it. The Prime Minister had called at her house and her husband had spoken with the Prime Minister... Astonishing how those friendships between women, parts of the same organism, could ripen in a few days. So the nurse's name was Emily. He began to think of her as Emily. She was younger, she had more of the sap of life in her, than Miss Thorping. Miss Thorping was like a plant in a herbarium, yet perversely alive... He seemed to have learnt quite a lot about his household. Of course he had always known that Skinner was grossly incompetent, but he could never bring himself to dismiss the man, even on a pension; he could not humiliate the man. Strange he had not known that Jeff was a teetotaller. Jeff used not to be a teetotaller. Imagine the kid eating cakes in bed. Perhaps he did it to console himself for having to sleep on a bed at all.

Sam had a misgiving about Geoffrey's absence from the house. He suspected – absurdly, he did not deny – that Geoffrey had gone off in order to avoid the risk of meeting Andy. The lad was a queer fellow, and sometimes gave indications of intense likes and dislikes. Andy was certainly not among the likesss

Through the open main door Sam heard a scurry on the stairs and girls whispering. Excitement! And he himself was excited – perhaps as much as anybody in the house or out of it. He felt sure Andy wanted to estimate from his own observations what were the chances of him, Sam, getting back to work; and, if at all, how soon. Andy probably wanted him; his popularity would make him a most valuable support to any government, and if Andy's government was insecure... He was an important piece in the great game. He thrilled – yes, with pleasurable anticipation. He was stricken and ruined, and yet he thrilled with joy. There was room in his mind for the most diverse and mutually contradictory emotions.

"I don't need any titivating," he said, with affected negligence to the nurse. "If I could have a shave – "

"We must send to Clacton for a barber to-morrow, my lord."

"Not Clacton," said he. "Colchester."

77

Andy

Andy Clyth, in a pale tweed suit, came striding swiftly into the bedroom, yet with a cat's tread: tall, scraggy, authoritative, his big ears as it were cocked to catch the slightest indications of whatever might be useful to him. He bent lithely over the bed and masterfully took Sam's hand. He was in admirable health; his wavy, silver hair had the gloss of health. Sam might have fallen, but Andy, with ten times Sam's political anxieties and embarrassments, was still strongly running the war, still the greatest man in the world. No difficulties could upset him, nor trouble his sleep, save only an illness of his mother. He gave a tremendous impression of power.

But Sam, in defence, said to himself:

"Yes, Andy, but you don't know the terrible things that are in my heart; they are so terrible that they put me above you. You are a mask, and I know it. But I'm a mask and you don't know it, and that's why while I'm looking up at you I'm looking down on you. And I'm strong, too. I'm one of the minority of men past fifty who have come through double pneumonia – in spite of a weak heart. I've won."

"Sam!" breathed Andy, in his rich, softened voice. And there was the most marvellous sympathy in his tone and in his glance. In one word and one look he conveyed that he understood Sam's late ordeal as well as though he had been through it himself. His very soul seemed to pour itself out into Sam's.

"That's his special gift, that's his trick," thought Sam – vainly; the effect had been accomplished. "I'm too hard on him," thought Sam, and said aloud in a moved voice: "Awfully good of you to come all this way to see me, Andy."

"I was determined to see you," Andy replied enthusiastically, and the words were somehow charged with memories of Eccles made pure and romantic by time.

Then Miss Packer came in, and Skinner, in his relief over one duty done, vanished and shut the door which ought never to have been shut. The total blaze of glory was too dazzling for the nurse, who, unnoticed, slipped into the shadow of the other doorway, whence she could keep watch without being seen. Miss Packer was in her favourite modest blue, and as neat as if she had just been taken out of a drawer; the fact was that Miss Thorping, summoned by Skinner in a sudden crisis in the hall, had had the honour of removing Miss Packer's motor-coat and helping her to put herself in order. And Miss Packer bent her wondrous, mature complexion and her rich curves and her subtle perfume over the bed, and smiled and was gracious, and was silent in the presence of her master. She sat down, a little away from the bed, as was meet. Andy remained standing, towering.

"Lord Raingo looks wonderful, considering," said Andy to his confidential secretary, it being now his duty to bring her into the conversation and so reclaim her from lowliness.

"Wonderful!" Miss Packer agreed warmly, with a new, soft smile.

But her tone seemed a little to lack conviction, and Sam was thereby somewhat dashed. In the process of titivation for visitors the nurse had given him a hand-mirror, and his appearance had not impressed him as very pretty. How, indeed, could he look "wonderful" (even "considering "), especially by contrast with these two radiant, satisfied creatures, all of whose faculties and functions were obviously in excellent order and good use? And then there was his breathing, still loud and difficult, still continuously to some extent an anxiety. He knew that people coming up the stairs could not help but hear his breathing. He was safe, but seriously battered, and he did not want visitors to dwell on his looks.

"Now tell me," he said, with an air of eager interest to Andy, "how is your mother?"

"Ah!" said Andy, staccato, as if to say: "Now I've got something important to tell you about that subject." And he added to satisfy Sam's curiosity at once: "The dear old lady is in the most marvellous form again."

He glanced at his confidential secretary, and Miss Packer opened her bag and drew forth an envelope, which she held towards Andy.

"No," said Andy. "You're in charge of it. Better hand it to Lord Raingo yourself, hadn't you?"

"In this ingenious way, the way of an incomparable social expert," thought the evil-minded Sam, "he gives prestige and deference to Rosie Packer. But did the old lady confide the letter to Andy or to his confidential secretary?"

Miss Packer left her chair and handed him the letter.

"May I read it now?" Sam asked with engaging impatience.

Andy was delighted at his keenness.

"Do!" said he, and gazed in a sort of ecstasy at Sam as he opened the envelope, which contained a letter and a small package stitched up in cotton wool. Sam glanced at the letter and glanced at it again, affecting to read, but in fact scarcely comprehending its purport.

"D'you know what's in it?" he inquired of Andy.

"Do I know what's in it? Of course I don't know what's in it! The old lady can be the most secretive little thing you ever saw when she chooses. She simply said the letter was to be delivered into your hands or not at all. Do *you* know what's in it?" He glanced at Miss Packer.

Miss Packer signified complete ignorance.

Sam, contemplative and still smiling, replaced the letter and the package (which he had not disturbed) in the envelope, and without changing his posture twisted an arm backwards and inserted the envelope beneath his pillow.

"You'll tell Mrs Clyth how very grateful I am," he said. "Very grateful indeed! And I shall write to thank her as soon as I am able. Perhaps to-morrow. But I expect it'll have to be in pencil."

His lively demeanour contented Andy, who came to earth again and explained that that day he was fulfilling an old promise to inspect some of the coast defences on the Clacton peninsula.

"Very remarkable," he observed, and winked at the patient.

"And what are the latest loving-kindnesses in Whitehall?" Sam asked.

For some reason he felt impish. Perhaps this was to be counted a sign of returning vigour. Andy laughed, showing his formidable teeth, and he looked for an instant covertly at Miss Packer, as if to assure himself that he was about to produce the right effect.

"The latest is," said he, "that some of 'em have got the foreign name craze again. I hear they're going through the departments with a small tooth-comb, and anybody with a Hun name, or what sounds like a Hun name, or with a Boche greatgrandfather or third cousin twice removed, is being shifted. Bit late in the day, eh?"

"Why don't you stop it?"

"Because I haven't time. But I suppose I shall have to find a wee bit time soon."

At this point Miss Packer smiled a little "Oh!" having decided that the moment had arrived for her to say that she had seen the nurse.

"If that's the nurse, I must just speak to her," she said. Sam heard an affrighted, charmed gurgle from Emily, and then the quiet, steady hum of women's voices in the next room. A fine example of Miss Packer's tact.

Andy perched himself like a true pal on the edge of the bed.

"The fact is," he said, "I've more than I can do. I doubt if even you can realize the weight of the load on my shoulders." Weakness and languor came into his changeful voice." If I hadn't managed to take a day off to-day I don't know what I should have done. I've missed you, Sam. Yes, I've wanted your harsh, good old Lancashire nous more than once this last week or so. When d'ye think the doctors will let you come back?"

Sam fixed his gaze on the ceiling and answered dreamily:

"God knows. I've had a doing this time, Andy. Your coming's cheered me up and excited me. If you'd seen me this time yesterday you wouldn't have had much to say about me going back. You'd have thought it was a case of going out of the house feet foremost." He was very privately and quite amicably grinning.

"You've got extraordinary powers of recuperation, then."

"Well, I don't know."

A pause.

"We need you, Sam. We need you."

"I'd give anything to be back. But you mustn't count on it. And I don't see that it matters so much now. The war's over – from all I can hear."

"Well, it will be over. We're out of the wood, unless some blunderer over there goes and does something idiotic: which is always possible. There's a lot of friction – I don't mind telling you."

"How's Tommy Hogarth getting along?"

"Staunch. He's always staunch."

"You surprise me," said Sam. "Of course you know him a thousand times better than I do; but personally I'd never trust him with my last sixpence."

"You're unjust to him, old friend. Of course he's very bellicose – needs handling, but he's the ablest man I have."

"Perhaps I am unjust," Sam admitted, still dreamily. "Anyhow I'd be the last person to question his ability. But ability isn't everything."

"No, it isn't," Andy concurred thoughtfully.

"I gather that owing to my illness I've been rather unusually popular."

"It's not your illness that's made you popular. You've got the gift of popularity and you've proved it."

"I'm not so sure. Seems to me I'd better leave well alone. I tell you, you won't want any more propaganda now. And I shall never be the same man again."

"Nonsense, Sam."

"That's how I feel, at any rate."

A pause. Andy began to walk about.

"I'm thinking of enlarging the Cabinet – strictly between ourselves."

"The War Cabinet?"

"Yes."

"Well, well!" Sam murmured negligently.

"Seems to be a desire for it. And of course we have to keep our ears to the ground. There may be trouble ahead. My mother thinks so too."

Sam had it in mind to say:

"And what does your wife think?" Never once had Andy's wife been mentioned between them. "No trouble in my Ministry, I hope," he said casually, as he continued to peruse the ceiling.

Andy laughed easily at such an impossible notion.

"I'm afraid the nurse thinks we oughtn't to stay much longer, Prime Minister," said Rosie Packer, emerging so graciously from the other room.

"Not at all," Sam protested.

"Yes, we mustn't stay. The nurse is quite right. Well, Sam, ye're a braw lad, and a credit to the medical profession, and I shall run down and see ye again. I like this part of the world. It's very bracing for one thing."

"You'll have some tea downstairs before you go?"

But no, they would not. They had a rendezvous for tea at Chelmsford.

"By the way, how's that son of yours?" Andy asked as he shook hands.

"He's better," said Sam. "I think he's out this afternoon. If he'd known you were coming he'd have been in, I know. But you keep your movements so mighty quiet." Sam added the last words impishly. "Thanks again for coming."

Emily timidly appeared to conduct the visitors to the head of the stairs. Sam heard the car drive away.

"And so I'm offered a seat in the War Cabinet, because I'm so darned popular," he said to himself. "To back Andy against Tommy. Queer affair. And I forgot to tell him Sid Jenkin had been here. But did I forget?"

Strangely he was full of sympathy with Andy. He took him with all his faults and liked and admired him as the greatest fighter against the greatest odds in the war, and had a fellow-feeling for him.

Later, Geoffrey arrived, and in reply to a question said:

"Oh! I knew I shouldn't be able to stick the fellow, so I kept away."

"Have you ever spoken to him?"

"No. And I don't want to."

The tone was testy, and Sam deduced from its freedom that he himself really was believed to be getting better: which solaced him for Miss Rosie Packer's lack of conviction in praising his looks.

He gave a hint that he desired rest, and with a long sigh abandoned his mind utterly to sad thoughts of Delphine.

78

The Packet

Sleep soon claimed him. When he awoke more than three hours had passed, and the doctor and Geoffrey, as well as the nurse, were in the room. Night was just beginning to fall. In the intervals of somewhat excited talking about the visit of the Prime Minister and his confidential secretary Dr. Heddle made another examination of the distinguished patient whom great statesmen travelled scores of miles to see for a quarter of an hour, and delivered the verdict that the visits had apparently done no harm and that all was well. The doctor then went off to write the daily bulletin which for nearly a week he had prepared alone but had not signed because Sir Arthur was not able to sign it. He would have given much, very much, to sign the bulletins alone. Etiquette, however, mysteriously forbade – or Sir Arthur forbade. To-night's bulletin would certainly be the chief sensation in the next morning's papers, and Heddle, to whom heaven had not denied caution, knew that in the composition of it he must write very warily.

Geoffrey was restlessly in and out of the bedroom. He seemed to be nervous and self-conscious, and once or twice Sam noticed the twitching of the neck – phenomenon now become extremely rare. Sam judged that the youth had not yet quite recovered from the incursion of the fiercely-hated Prime Minister. Sam waited until the doctor should be clear away, and then asked:

"When's that girl due?"

"Who? Gwen?"

"Yes."

"I shall be going to the station in a minute or two to meet her."

"Well, bring her up here as soon as she comes."

"She'd better have something to eat first."

"Then as soon as she's had something to eat."

"Hadn't you better wait till to-morrow morning? She's bound to be tired."

Sam grew fretful.

"Tired be damned. She's young and strong. It isn't a two hour journey. Look at the P.M., far more than double her age; he can motor here and back to London in the day and he's as fresh as paint, and motoring's far more tiring than a train journey."

"Well, I think it would be too tiring for you too. You've had three visitors to-day already." There was authority and some determination in the lad's tone.

"Nonsense!" Sam felt that he was getting truculent, but he could not help it. He understood now the reason of Geoffrey's nervous constraint – the lad had decided in his absurd domineering self-sufficiency that it would be bad for his father to see Gwen that night; the lad was taking a great deal upon himself.

"I'm sure the doctor wouldn't like it."

"Have you asked the doctor?"

"No."

"Well, why didn't you? He must have been here for at least half an hour." This remark, as Sam knew, was reprehensibly disingenuous, considering that with the cunning of an invalid he had expressly forborne to say one word to Geoffrey about Gwen until the doctor had gone, lest the doctor should be consulted and lay a veto on the interview. "Of course he wouldn't object. Didn't you hear him say I was going on splendidly? Anyhow I must see the girl to-night, and the sooner the better. I hope that's clear, Jeff." On the last word he put a little stress of affection, which softened his truculence in the nick of time.

"Very well," said the boy gloomily, and left.

Sam was now alone, for the improvement in his condition had slackened discipline and the day-nurse had slipped away before the arrival of the night-nurse. As soon as Geoffrey had gone Sam's love for him surged over his ill-humour and shamed it to destruction. He most sensitively regretted the scene. He wanted always to be close, close, to the boy; he wanted nothing ever to come between them; he was beginning consciously to regard the boy as his sole link with existence, his sole refuge against unnameable despair. Still (he thought with his queer, callous humour), truculence in an invalid was a sure sign of physical improvement.

And Jeff did not know him yet, had not comprehended that his old father was not a man to be dictated to. Had he, Sam, not issued an order that Gwen was to come, and was she not coming as a matter of course, and was he to be told at the last moment that he must wait a day before seeing her? His truculence was richly justified. But Jeff would comprehend in due time: Jeff had intelligence. The fact was that Sam had been slowly screwing himself up to the ordeal of the interview with Gwen. He dreaded it, but duty forced him to accomplish it, and to postpone it would have been more than he could bear. Gwen had to be told of her sister's death. He was convinced beyond any doubt that she did not know of it, because if she had known Geoffrey would have known, and obviously from his consistent light demeanour Geoffrey did not know. Only Sam knew in the wide world.

Nurse Kewley entered, white and blue, fresh, eager as a young girl.

"I saw him," said she at once. "Miss Thorping wakened me, and I looked over the banisters and saw him as he was crossing the hall. And then I looked out of the window and saw them drive off. So the lady's his secretary! His *secretary*! Wouldn't *I* like to be his secretary!"

"I really must try to be nice with' people," thought Sam, and indulged her with some intimate details about Andy's daily life. He could see that the Prime Minister's visit had raised him in his nurse's estimation.

"Oh! Your pillows! Your pillows! I wouldn't like to say Emily's been neglecting you. I suppose you've been restless."

She set to work to arrange the architecture of the pillows.

"What's this?" she asked, drawing forth old Mrs Clyth's packet.

"Give it to me," said Sam, shocked. He had entirely forgotten it!

As soon as the pillows were finished, he opened the envelope and read the letter with careful concentration. A handwriting firm and clear – astonishingly so for Mrs Clyth's age. "Dear Sam. Please excuse an old woman addressing you in this way, but I have never thought of you as anything else but Sam – and never shall. I want to thank you for all the help you've been to my dear son. I send you the enclosed precious object because of its wonderful power. It belonged to my mother, and was blessed by the Holy Father Pius Ninth. It has saved my life several times, as I *know*. I have recovered when every doctor was sure that I could not recover. It was under my pillow. Please put it under yours and trust in the Divine power. I pray for you. Truly yours, Eileen Clyth." With hands rendered clumsy by sudden emotion, Sam undid the cotton-wool and saw a Virgin and Child crudely portrayed in a mosaic of coloured stones and framed in tinsel gold. It had no style, and he took it to be the work of some pious amateur craftsman in the recesses of provincial Ireland. The *naivete,* the faith, and the amazing unselfishness of the bestowal made Sam cry. "Of course I'm very weak still," he thought, crying. He wrapped up the miniature and put it under his pillows. The whole world seemed to be a better world.

79

The Reasons

Sam was still in the exalted mood engendered by the strange sight of the gift from old Mrs Clyth when Geoffrey returned. Rather more than an hour had elapsed.

"She's coming up now," said Geoffrey. "She wouldn't eat – at least scarcely anything." He was clearly very nervous indeed.

"What's up with the boy?" thought Sam benevolently. All his resentment against the young upstart had melted away.

"You'd better leave us alone together," he said, not as a command but as a suggestion, though he was absolutely determined to have Gwen to himself for the ordeal awaiting him. Geoffrey gave a movement of surprise, which was also relief.

"Yes, of course, dad," he agreed, indicating by his tone that he too bore no ill-will on account of the duel in which he had been worsted.

Sam jerked his head in the direction of the other room, where Nurse Kewley was, and Geoffrey nodded an understanding that the nurse must not intrude either. Sam heard a light step on the stairs, and he saw Geoffrey, in the doorway, give a heavenly, gentle smile towards the landing and stairs. The boy's reassuring, affectionate smile at the approaching, not yet visible, girl remained in Sam's memory. Geoffrey then went out.

"It's all right. He doesn't want me to be there," Sam heard Geoffrey's murmuring whisper. Immediately afterwards the other door, between the two rooms, was softly closed.

Gwen appeared, from the landing. Sam shook at the sudden sight of her. She was transformed in everything except her unalterable beauty. The bright, lovely coiffure was plainly the effective and enhancing work of an expert. The frock, severe in line and without any ornamentation, must have come from a first-rate fashionable dressmaker, and the shoes matched it in style. Her beauty had at last apparel worthy of its splendour, and she could carry the attire worthily. All trace of the girl's modest origin had vanished from her carriage; she had no class save the class of her beauty.

But what had so shaken Sam was that she was in mourning. In a flash he comprehended that she had nothing to learn from him about Delphine. Nor had Geoffrey anything to learn from him. Geoffrey, in the belief that Sam was entirely ignorant of Delphine's death, had been playing a part for his father's benefit – and with what skill and assurance! The boy's extreme nervousness had been due to the fact that he was expecting the moment when he and Gwen between them would have to break to Sam the news of the suicide, which Geoffrey had been keeping back until some improvement in the invalid's health would permit him safely to hear it. By insisting on Gwen's attendance, Sam had hastened the disclosure. And Geoffrey's relief had followed from Sam's suggestion that he ought to see Gwen without Geoffrey. In his intense perturbation Sam knew not whether he was glad or sorry that things had so fallen out.

Gwen slowly shut the door. Then she stood at the foot of the bed, leaning against it in the manner of Geoffrey.

"This is a dreadful moment," thought Sam, as he saw the anguish in her face – too young and ingenuous for such pain.

"So you know, my dear," he said.

She nodded, and added, as if astounded: "Has Mr Geoffrey just told you?"

"No. Geoffrey hasn't told me at all. Geoffrey doesn't know yet that I know." He related his story.

"But why didn't you tell anyone?" she asked innocently and yet reproachfully, more astonished still.

He said:

"I couldn't somehow bear to talk about it. But of course I knew I should have to tell *you*, my dear. That's why I sent for you to-day – to tell you. I didn't know you knew. I didn't know anyone knew – except me. I simply wasn't equal to talking about it. And Geoffrey never gave a sign."

"He didn't want you to be upset before you could stand it. He did act for the best, sir." She seemed to be somewhat impatiently imploring justification of Geoffrey's secrecy.

"Tell me…tell me. You've been down there…the funeral …you've seen her…she wasn't disfigured, it said."

Gwen shook her head, and began a tumbled recital of events, all of which had been elaborately hidden from Sam. It was Captain Mayden who had seen the paragraph in the papers and divined the identity of the suicide, and telephoned to Geoffrey. It was Captain Mayden who had met Gwen at

Liverpool Street (on the morning when Geoffrey had told his father that she was indisposed and in bed) and taken her to Brighton. And Captain Mayden had managed the police and the coroner in the most wonderful way and arranged for a proper funeral – for the body of Delphine had not been removed from the mortuary. It became apparent to Sam that between the diplomacy of Mayden and Gwen's appealing youth and beauty the official passion for formalities had contrived to discipline itself. Only Gwen and Mayden had attended the funeral. Geoffrey had conferred with them in London, but he could not leave his father for more than a few hours together and so had not been able to reach Brighton. It was Captain Mayden who had found out the landlord of the maisonette in Orange Street and been referred to the landlord's solicitor and discovered that this solicitor had made a will for Delphine by which she left all her possessions to Gwen. And this was the man who in an incautious, hasty phrase had slighted Delphine, the man against whom Sam was bearing a grudge, and of whom he had angrily said that the fellow had enough to do at the Ministry without meddling in his private affairs! Sam was contrite; he repentantly placed the overthrown image of Mayden on its pedestal in his esteem.

"Come here to me, my dear," said Sam, as he pictured the funeral.

Gwen moved towards him, and he clasped her soft, weak hand. At the pressure she wept a little.

"Why did she do it? What do you think? Was it anything I'd said – or done? It couldn't have been."

Gwen broke into sobs; then collected herself.

"Captain Mayden looked at the casualty lists every day for a week past – I asked him to – Harry Point's name was there. Killed he was… That was it."

"Then it was Harry Point she was fond of!"

"No, no!" Gwen cried. "No, she wasn't. I told you before. But she must have thought she'd killed him – I mean made him want to be killed. You know how girls do think. It must have driven her out of her mind." She gave a gesture of indignant despair, and added wildly, out of control: "I never,, told you one thing. She said to me once that you ought to get married, but she couldn't face being Lady Raingo, and you'd never marry anyone else as long as she was alive. Yes, she did – she told me that!" The universal grievance of all women against all men was in Gwen's tone; and it was as though she had said to Sam: "You and Harry Point have killed my poor, adored sister between you."

"My dear!" Sam was a little alarmed at the prospect of hysterics, and wondered whether he would be able to soothe her if she gave way completely.

Her voice rose:

"And what good does it do me, all these smart frocks and things Captain Mayden made me have at Jay's because Geoffrey said I was to?"

She drew her hand from Sam's clasp, and then after mastering with difficulty an impulse towards another outburst, she sank limp, face downwards, across the bed; and Sam had the weight of her body on his calves and could feel the thumping of her heart. Sam could scarcely think of himself; for the unconscious egotism of her youth absolutely ignored for the moment both his grief and his malady. He had a new light on Gwen's personality. She was not a bit like Delphine. She was different from his conception of her – more complex, more dangerous, more baffling. Delphine was the exception to the great rule that all women who charm and challenge are half angels and half devils. Gwen was no exception. With sudden, impish, brutal cynicism he said to himself: "If Jeff takes this on he'll be in for some lively times." Surely a strange saying, and strangely inept in the circumstances!... First she had called him "Mr Geoffrey," but later only "Geoffrey."...Yes, he wanted them to fall in love with each other; he felt sure that they were already falling in love with each other; he wanted them to marry – no fashionable, luxurious, money-swallowing bride for Jeff! And he was quite willing for Jeff to go through "lively times." A certain wise malice in this willingness! The experience would be good for Jeff! Just as a woman had to be "made" by a man, so a man had to be "made" by a woman, and the woman would do her part, however young and callow she might be. Trust her.

She had practically accused him, Sam, of causing the death of her beloved, self-sacrificing sister! Could you imagine it? Could you possibly have foreseen such a charge? No! They were all alike – save Delphine.

Gwen weighed down on him in utter abandonment. But for the beating of her heart she might have been dead – with her arms (shining pale through the thin stuff) stretched straight out, and her fingers hanging over the other edge of the bed. She stirred, sighed, stood up, smiled sadly at him.

"I'm sorry," she said. "Please forgive me, sir. I'm so unhappy and worn out – I don't hardly know what I'm saying. And I was so taken aback when you told me you'd known for days. It was just that that was the last touch. It knocked me over. I know everything must be terrible for you. I'm not really so selfish that I can't see *that*. Say you forgive me, sir."

"My dear!" Sam took her hand again and patted it.

Her child-like glance profoundly touched him. She was marvellous; an angel pure, impossible to believe that there was any devil in her. That she should ask forgiveness was monstrous and exquisite; it was he who should ask forgiveness. A creature so tender, helpless, and divinely foolish could not do wrong whatever she did.

He smiled inwardly at her grief. She thought it would be eternal, but he knew that it would pass from her and that soon she would grow cheerful again, perhaps gay, hopeful, expectant of miracles from life; and these desolating moments would be as though they had never been. But not thus must she be comforted; to tell her that she would not grieve for ever and ever would amount to an outrage upon her mourning woe. He must cherish her and shield her.

As for himself, he did not care what happened to himself. He was on the way to recovery, and he did not care. Another visit from Andy: a seat in the War Cabinet! No! No feeling of exultation! He was indifferent. Desire had failed. One question alone agitated him: Why did she do it? Gwen's answers to the question were infantile. It was inconceivable that Delphine should have killed herself in order to leave him free to marry as he ought. The notion was silly. And scarcely less inconceivable that she had killed herself from remorse. She had killed herself because she loved this Harry Point, and he was gone. Such was the true answer, and it excruciatingly agonized him. He could not bear the thought that she had loved Harry Point: she had loved himself. He could not be mistaken. She could not have deceived him. Then why? – Yes, she had deceived him. They were all actresses, even the kindest of them. She was in the grave, stretched moveless in everlasting repose. Never would he know the truth… How clever of her, how business-like, to make a will in Gwen's favour – but not a word about it to himself! That showed how secretive she could be… Proof after proof that she had never fully revealed herself to him, never trusted him.

His ear caught a kind of muffled thud – thud. Gwen heard it too, and started. Guns, far off! Gwen clutched his arm.

"The Germans are landing," said she, in a fever. "Delphine was always afraid of you living so near to the coast!"

Geoffrey came into the bedroom, and then the nurse. Geoffrey affected the most perfect nonchalance, but the nurse made no attempt to hide excitement.

"It's Zeppelins," said Geoffrey. "Our planes are fighting 'em at sea, about twenty miles off the coast. Post Office has just telephoned. I thought I'd better tell you in case you might get alarmed."

The thuds continued. Nurse Kewley went to a window, and in defiance of military regulations drew aside the curtain and lifted the blind.

"I think I can see flashes," she exclaimed. "Yes, I saw one."

Geoffrey went to the window.

"By Jove! There *are* flashes! It must be a regular stand-up scrap. Well, I'm dashed!"

To Sam it seemed that the conflict in his heart was being fought out, rendered majestic and epical, up there in the skies. He glanced at the young girl.

"Jeff!" he called very sharply.

Geoffrey turned. Sam pointed to Gwen. Geoffrey rushed forward and she fainted in his arms, under his alarmed and tender gaze.

"I'm afraid there are too many people in this room," said the nurse, whose indifferent attitude towards Gwen's swoon hurt Geoffrey's feelings. When she had got the young pair out she used the thermometer upon her patient. "A little up," she said, disquietingly, and added: "But not as high as this time last night."

80

Temperature

In the morning, after quite a good night undiversified by delirium or dreams, Sam was carefully examined by Dr. Heddle, and at the end of the examination the doctor rather surprisingly said, in a casual way, that Sir Arthur Tappitt would come down to see him either that day or the next. In reply to Sam's question the doctor explained that Sir Arthur had telephoned his intention to come and that naturally Sir Arthur was anxious to see for himself the great improvement in the patient's condition; after all, it was Sir Arthur who was in supreme charge of the case. Sam felt a little disturbed. He recalled the insincerity of Miss Packer's "wonderful" applied to his looks. He recalled, too, a certain peculiarity in the tone of Nurse Kewley's "A little up" apropos of his temperature on the previous night.

"Nothing wrong, is there?" he asked the doctor, and before the doctor could answer: "I didn't overdo it yesterday?"

"Oh! I don't think so. I hear you saw people for about an hour in all, with naps in between. That oughtn't to harm a healthy invalid like you."

Something strange in the doctor's tone also! But then the doctor's tone was generally a bit strange, as though whatever he said might imply anything or nothing. Sam was beginning to understand the excellent doctor, and he had arrived at the conclusion that what the simpleton lacked was emotional quality. His voice was placid, too evenly kind, too mild, too imperturbable, to be quite satisfactory. He would probably leave a deathbed as calmly and good-naturedly as he would leave the bed of a man rescued from death. Still, something strange in the doctor's tone!

Further, the household, so far as Sam could judge from the bedroom, seemed to be less uplifted than it ought to have been, and had been on the previous day, considering that he was on that celebrated road "the highway to recovery."

Then Geoffrey, of whom he was seeing less than usual, had lost all his sprightliness. But of course he had lost all his sprightliness, for he no longer had a part to play with his father! It was his duty now to respect and share his father's grief in the death of Delphine.

"I'm absurdly suspicious," said Sam to himself.

He wanted to see Wrenkin, but Geoffrey told him that Wrenkin had bicycled over to Harwich.

"What for?" the suspicious Sam demanded.

"To wangle some more coke from the Gas Company," Geoffrey convincingly replied.

"Yes, I *am* suspicious," said Sam to himself again.

He wanted to see Gwen, but Geoffrey told him that Gwen was in bed.

"Or in London?" Sam grimly inquired.

"In bed. Positively."

Nurse Emily, with an air of candour, proved to be uncommunicative. When she gave him the hand-mirror after his toilette, and the appalling spectacle of his beard made him ask about the promised barber, she said that she really didn't know, but she supposed the man would be coming over soon – if not to-day then to-morrow. Vague!

"I've wasted a lot, haven't I?" he asked, noticing for the first time, with a shock, the hollowness of his cheeks.

"Oh! You'll soon pick that up – when you get started," she said, and turned away. Why?

He ate fairly well, but not too well. He put his hand to his side, and immediately asked himself: "Now why did I put my hand to my side?" And he drew it away as though he had done something wrong, something dangerous. Had the old pain in his side returned? Well, it had never quite gone. It was naught – a mere malaise. "My breathing's louder," he said, "Is it?" answered the nurse. "Surely not." No conviction in her voice.

He had the old sensation of being netted in a conspiracy of being a "case," and the only person in the house not entitled to know in exact, reliable detail how the case was proceeding.

However, he was permitted to look at his newspapers and press-cuttings unaided: which was to the good. The headlines about his improved condition pleased him... He seemed to hear the exhalation of a sigh of relief from the whole country. He thought the actual bulletin rather bald and guarded; but of course doctors had to be careful. The newspapers with large circulations read into the bulletin everything that was not there. He glanced at the accounts of the Zeppelins v. aeroplanes encounter.

"I see they brought down one of those Zeppelins," he remarked to the nurse.

(Nobody had told him.)

"Oh, yes," the nurse answered, with exaggerated brightness, naively neglecting to hide her relief that he had found a topic which she could discuss frankly. "Several people round about here say they distinctly saw it fall."

"They would say that – twenty miles off!" Sam remarked, grimly sardonic.

But he soon tired of the papers. Even the uniform excellence of the war-news bored him. As for the press-cuttings, they were too numerous to be studied with any care. The deep undercurrent of his emotional life absorbed all his interest save the lightest and most superficial.

In the late afternoon he was sure that the pain in his side, like his breathing, was appreciably worse, but he said nothing to Nurse Emily on the point, lest she might confirm his idea, or, more annoyingly, put him off with detestable duplicity. At six o'clock not a word had been said about Sir Arthur's coming.

"Isn't that fellow Tappitt coming then?" he exclaimed suddenly.

"Seems now as if he wouldn't be coming till to-morrow," said the nurse quietly.

The reply was at any rate reassuring, for he guessed that his two doctors had been telephoning to each other like the devil, and the nurse to Heddle also; so that if he had really been worse Tappitt would have come.

Doctor Heddle came earlier than usual and took his temperature and sounded him and listened to his arcana and variously examined him all afresh. No information given to the patient.

"What is my temperature?" he asked, crossly impatient.

"Well," said Dr. Heddle. "I've known worse."

"Damn it all!" Sam broke out. "Can't I know my own temperature?" He felt savage, despite weakness.

"One hundred and two," answered the doctor, cornered, intimidated, beaten.

But Sam too was intimidated. One hundred would not have frightened him; but one hundred and two! And perhaps worse to come.

The undercurrent of his emotional life surged upward to the surface. She was dead. He had known for days that she was dead; but till Gwen's circumstantial evidence there had always been a glimmer of doubt. His sure instinct just might have misled him. Now she was incurably buried. The chapter was finished. Sorrow had shut him in with his memories of her, and made them terrible. And his cheeks were hollow, and his temperature was one hundred and two, and the night lay before him. He took his memories of her and crushed them laceratingly to his breast – closer, closer. The torture was exquisite, but he wanted nothing else; he was determined to be indifferent to his temperature. A sardonic smile crossed his face.

"What's the joke?" asked the doctor, deferential as he had not been for days.

Sam did not reply. Invalids were privileged not to reply to idle questions. He had recalled that he might be in the supreme War Cabinet if he chose.

81

Operation

"Now you and I have got to have a chat," said Sam, physically feeble, but with resolution rising through the weakness of his voice.

He was much worse, after a torturing, exhausting night. Though the pain in his side was somewhat less acute, his cough was harder, his breathing louder and more difficult. He felt that his body was full of horrible poisons. He hated his bed; he hated the everlasting posture which was neither sitting up nor lying down; he hated his white, invalid's hands; he hated the sunshine, and the thought of the summer fields. He was jealous of the fine health of the other people in the room, and ashamed of his inferiority to them.

"Yes," said Sir Arthur benevolently, and drew a chair up close to the head of the bed.

"Is my case serious?"

Sir Arthur paused an instant, gazing full at Sam, sounding his mind as he had just been sounding his body. His glance was stern, but it was also magnanimous.

"Yes," said he. "Your case is serious. If it wasn't, do you suppose I should be here?" His deep, vibrating, calming, nasal voice, sympathetic and yet somehow insolent, seemed to be saying: "Be good enough to remember who I am, and the tremendous competition for my services. I can understand egotism, for I'm an egotist myself; but we must keep the sense of proportion."

"Is it more serious than it was before, – I only ask because you haven't been to see me since your first visit, and now this morning you're here again, all of a sudden."

"I see I can hide nothing from you," quietly boomed Sir Arthur, with a faint, teasingly benevolent smile. "I want you for just one minute to look at this thing from my point of view. I have to ration myself. I don't like it, but I have to do it. That doesn't mean I've been neglecting you. I've had two or three telephone conversations with Heddle every day about you. I trust Heddle. I've known him a very long time, and you may take it from me he's a good all-round man, and full of sense. There was no need for me to come earlier. If I'd come I couldn't have done anything that Heddle didn't do. You ask me if your case is more serious than it was. No, I don't think it is. You've come through one crisis safely and there's every chance you'll come through another. I'll tell you what's happened to you. Mind you, I wouldn't gossip with every patient like this" – (That's your catch-phrase.) – "There's some fluid in your pleural cavity."

"Is that why you stuck that stiletto thing into me?"

"The syringe? Yes. It means pressure on the lungs, and pressure on the lungs means more work for the heart. Now that heart of yours has done pretty well up to now; it's shown pluck, and I expect it will keep on doing pretty well, and we shall give it all the help we can. I've got rather a high opinion of the moral qualities of your heart."

"How shall you help it?"

"By drawing off the fluid in the cavity."

"Water, is it?"

"Water, yes. But poison too, and we don't want any poison in you. It means just a tiny operation – making a little orifice for draining. Nothing. And nothing to do with the disease itself. Purely a sort of engineer's job."

"Then it's pleurisy I've got, eh?"

"Yes – if you want labels."

"And what about pericarditis?" asked Sam, who was busy recalling old fragments of hearsay concerning pneumonia. "What's that?"

"The pericardium is the cavity that the heart lies in. It's a sack. If it's affected too, then people who like labels would be justified in saying that you had pericarditis."

"And have I?"

"Not yet."

"That means I shall have it."

"Not necessarily."

"And when shall you do the operation?"

"*I* shan't do the operation. *I* never do anything but talk. Sir Tremlett Wynes will operate. He's our best man. Heddle is telephoning to him now." Sam noticed for the first time that Heddle was not in the room. "I thought from Heddle's report that we might have to have an operation, so I warned Wynes last night. He promised to put off everything and come. He ought to be here before lunch. You'll be back safe in bed again inside half an hour."

It all seemed to Sam to be in the natural order of things. He thought he ought to feel alarmed – an operation was no joke, at best – but he felt no alarm. In bravado he asked for his press-cuttings. Sir Arthur assented. "I can see something in this fellow," thought Sam. "Last time I didn't so much care for him. But he's got points… He must be a regular devil if you happen to get across him."

"Jeff," he said later, when the arch-magician, having given certain detailed instructions about the immediate future, had gone off to make a little time-killing excursion with Dr. Heddle, and incidentally to cancel all his London engagements by telephone: "Where's Gwen to-day? Is she better?"

"She's all right, dad."

"Well, bring her up."

"D'you think you – "

"I only thought I'd like to have a look at her. I don't want to talk to her. In fact I'm not equal to much talking. Only a minute or two." He was plaintive, appealing.

Nurse Emily, already in collaboration with Miss Thorping, preoccupied by the arrangements for the operation, offered no objection.

"I'll bring her," Geoffrey agreed, quickly and cheerfully – and produced Gwen at once; he must have known just where she was at that moment.

She was wearing the same dress as on the previous night; looked even better by day. She blushed and smiled. She had a most sensitive faculty for blushing.

Sam thought:

"Does she blush like that before customers in a shop? No. Impossible. She isn't one girl, but two. I expect they all are. Well, I wanted to see her, and I am seeing her." He had pleasure in the exquisite sight of her; but he was again humiliated." What kind of an object must I seem to her?" he wondered. His odious beard! No talk of a barber now!

"I've got to have a little operation," he said, taking her hand. She gently squeezed his hand, thrilling him.

"Yes, I know," she said. "What a shame!"

Tears came into her eyes. She glanced at Geoffrey, as if for support, and with a glance Geoffrey gave it to her; whereupon her expression changed to one of relief and assuagement. Sam had been waiting to see some sign of instinctive, unavowed intimacy between them; he saw it. She now had to remind herself that she was bereaved and unhappy, otherwise she might have forgotten her woe.

Sam thought again, as he had thought at their previous meeting:

"Time will cure her sorrow, though she doesn't know it and would hate to think it."

And then suddenly he had another thought:

"And what about my sorrow? I should hate to think that time would cure my sorrow. But wouldn't it? Look at yourself objectively, my boy. Wouldn't it? No! I'm too old. Time would only deaden it, could not kill it."

Gwen left her hand in his because she was too shy to withdraw it. Its pressure on his had slackened. He squeezed her hand; hers responded. Magic! Magic currents flowing and receding!

A thought blazed in his dark brain and lit its chambers like a fire:

"What a miserable coward I am, giving way! I must fight. I shall fight. I will be healthy and strong again as the others are. I can get better and I will. In a few weeks I shall be shaving myself every morning, just as usual. And I shall go to the Ministry and it will be in the papers that I am in the War Cabinet, and they will all listen to me, and I shall be a bit impish with them, and I shall be always sad inside, but nobody will guess, and it doesn't matter. What's happiness, after all? Work's the only thing – not being beaten."

He said aloud, almost gaily:

"But I shall come through their tuppenny operation. You'll see if I don't!"

The young pair looked at one another, exchanging admiration of Sam, and were much cheered.

"I can drop her hand now," thought Sam. And he dropped it. "Delphine is in her heart and in her mind too," he thought, as, followed by Geoffrey, she went out of the room.

Time flew along with disconcerting rapidity. Sir Arthur and Heddle returned. They said that Sir Tremlett Wynes had arrived. It was incredible, miraculous. They superintended the placing of a long table in front of one of the windows. Wrenkin it was who had charge of the actual carriage of the table. He seemed to catch sight of Sam by accident. "Afternoon, m'lord," he grunted, but Sam knew that he was terribly moved. A strange nurse entered and was addressed as "Sister." She was from London and had a presence, and Nurse Emily in front of her sank to the status of a kitchen-maid. Sundry leather cases were brought up. Then a man came in all dressed in white.

"This is Sir Tremlett Wynes, Lord Raingo," said Sir Arthur.

And there followed immediately yet another man – the anaethetist, also from London. Four experts about Sam's bed Their bodies darkened Sam and the bed as they consulted. Sam could not see what was going on at the table by the window, but he could faintly hear the Sister talking to Nurse Emily. He smelt the fumes of a spirit-lamp. Geoffrey stood nervously near the door. Sam felt himself to be the most important person in the room and the least. He was extremely self-conscious. The room seemed to be full of people.

"This is getting awful," thought Sam. His courage and resolution began to ebb.

"Now, Lord Raingo," said the great surgeon, who had cancelled everything in order to come. "This is really a very slight business. I needn't – "

Sam stopped him with a hand humorously raised:

"No, you needn't. I'm perfectly all right. I've had chloroform before – at a dentist's."

"But this will be ether," said Sir Tremlett, also with a touch of humour.

Delays! Endless delays! "This *is* awful!" thought Sam. They were doing strange things to him, the nurses were! Sam gazed fixedly at the ceiling, but out of the tail of his eye he saw Dr. Heddle give a sign to Geoffrey, who vanished, and with him Sam's last crutch of support. He was lifted and carried, with astonishing ease and smoothness, from the bed to the table, and deposited on his side, face to the light, which rather dazzled him.

"It's perfectly all right," he repeated, foolishly as it seemed to him. But he was sick with fear. The War Cabinet was a fantastic mirage. He thought: "By God! It isn't a minute since I was first told of the operation, and now it's here! In another minute I shall be unconscious, and there'll be blood... Curse this beggar in white. It's simply appalling." He was afraid he would faint before they could drug him. He had no heart and no stomach. And there was such a singing in his ears that he lost the familiar sounds of his own breathing. He had a glimpse of the precipice.

82

The Virgin's Fall

The next morning. The engineering operation had been entirely successful, and to Sam it seemed a long way back in the past. Ill as he was, he could smile at it and so reduce it to its proper proportions as a mechanical trifle. The foremost surgeon-in London, the foremost anesthetist in London, had gone, and the Sister with them, as well as the apparatus. The table had been removed. The affair, seen in perspective, had a magical quality, showing the extraordinary power of money. And yet money had never been mentioned, either to Sam or to Geoffrey, or by the chief actors to one another; because everybody concerned knew by faith that here the available supply of money was limitless. Sam thought that not till then had he really appreciated the value of money. Poor Adela had never helped him to appreciate it. In their joint life money had been like a djinn imprisoned in a bottle, and neither of them had known the word of release.

Now he had a childish idea that money, having accomplished so much, ought to be set to accomplish more: rid him of his pain, of his pervading discomfort, overthrow the fear of death and ten thousand causeless worries. He wanted to expel from his system the narcotic which after the operation had given him heavy sleep. But for that money was powerless. He wanted to stop the pain at the seat of the operation, – pain which had just been acutely intensified by the withdrawal and replacing of a rubber tube that was the chief article in the engineering gadget designed to ease the strain on his loyal heart. But here again money was powerless. He knew that he was ill, but by no means so ill as during certain wakeful intervals in the night. He knew that he looked ill, with his eyes half shut and his mouth 'half open, and his pale, spiritual hands restless among the sheets and on the counterpane. And he knew that he was considered to be more seriously ill, by the increased wearisome complexity of his existence as an invalid. Every minute, as it appeared to him, something had to be done, to be undone, or to be administered, to be inspected, to be checked, to be encouraged. His heart was an engine on a reliability trial, and no attention was too minute or too laborious for it. It was like a living thing, not like an engine.

"You're doing quite well," said Sir Arthur. And Sam noticed the nuance, for he had learnt to weigh every word uttered about himself. "Quite well" was good; but "very well" would have been better. Sir Arthur had seen to the dressing himself, Dr. Heddle having not yet arrived. Sir Arthur had become a woman. His voice and hands had a surpassing tenderness.

"I think I'm entitled to good marks," Sam replied, in the way of playfulness. Unfortunately, miscalculating his strength of mind, he added: "You're too good to me, Tappitt," and his voice broke, and he dropped a few foolish tears. In addition to being a woman, Sir Arthur was now for Sam the grandest man in the world. His tenderness was really more than Sam could bear to think of.

Weakness, of course, on Sam's part! It was a lapse. Sam had to recover from it, and did recover from it – by laughing through his silly tears, by a bold glance at Sir Arthur that explained: "Those drops of water have nothing to do with *me*, and the muscles in my throat haven't anything to do with me either." Such was the bravura display of a man who had determined that naught should stop him from getting perfectly well, and looking a healthy, active man in the face as an equal, and returning in triumph to his Ministry, and accepting with all self-reliance a formal invitation to join the War Cabinet. Sir Arthur knew nothing of the sorrow in his soul, and should never know, and no one should ever know: even the dearest and most intimate should only guess darkly. The sorrow in his soul was his most precious secret possession, and jealously he would guard it.

Sam said steadily:

"You staying on here, Tappitt?" A difficult respiration. "Have they been looking after you properly?"

"Your son is as good a host as you could be yourself. I shall run up to town this morning; but I shall be back again this afternoon."

What energy! Sam wanted to say: "It's awfully good of you," but he had the sense not to take a second risk, with those untrustworthy eyes and that traitorous throat.

Sir Arthur, watchful, made a diversion. He fetched the newspaper and read out the bulletin, names and all. An impressive contribution to the news of the morning – and three signatures to it, two of them august! Very pleasing!

Sam was slipping down in the bed.

"Afraid you're not very comfortable," said Sir Arthur. He glanced round for the nurse, who happened to be out of the room for a moment, and then he began himself to arrange the pillows, handling them with originality and skill and lifting the wasted Sam with easy strength. He might have spent a lifetime in fixing pillows.

"How's that?" he inquired, rather satisfied with his own performance.

"Fine!" said Sam, and sighed. "Much better."

There was a faint noise of some object falling on the floor. Sam knew instantly what it was. Sir Arthur stooped and saw the miniature of the Virgin, and close by it a wad of cottonwool from which it had escaped in falling. (The nurses had not seen the miniature outside its envelope, and had been told to leave the mysterious package where they found it.) Sir Arthur was about to exclaim in wonder, but he had the wit to perceive that he had accidentally come upon a secret. He, who had long since decided that nothing in human nature could surprise him, was now so astonished anew by this vagary of a hard-headed millionaire that he had to collect himself. He did collect himself. Without a word he picked up the sacred charm, wrapped it in its wool, and reinsinuated it very gently under the lowest pillow. Sam kept silent. He was extremely depressed by the incident. He could not understand his own depression. The Virgin had fallen on the floor. Well, what of it? Still, Sam could not reassure himself. He wanted to explain to Sir Arthur the Virgin of the miniature, and to make it clear that he, Sam, was not really superstitious. But he could not begin to do so. Shortly afterwards Sir Arthur departed for London, having spoken to Dr. Heddle first in the hall.

83

The Mother

"Dad," said Geoffrey, leaning over the foot of the bed while his father was taking some food – apparently with firm determination to sustain himself and his deserving heart, "can you stand a bit of business?"

Sam, flattered by the bright, confident tone, answered in the sense which he saw was expected from him:

"Do I look as if I couldn't?"

But he did look as if he couldn't, and he was in considerable distress, mental as well as physical. His pluck felt the strain upon it.

"It's only this. I'm managing your affairs for you. I supposed *you* manage them on your head. They aren't so easy for me, but I suppose I can face 'em, especially if I have a free hand. How would it be if you signed a power of attorney giving me full power to act for you? Then I shouldn't have to worry you at all; and I shouldn't feel – you know – as if you were looking over my shoulder all the time. Makes me sort of nervous. I'd take all the blame, if any – I say if any – afterwards, when you've recovered."

Sam was a little shocked. He paused, saying to himself:

"I must be careful. I must try to appear in a good light to the lad."

But despite the lad's tactful phrasing of the suggestion he obscurely resented it. He felt somehow as if the skies were closing in on him, as though this was the beginning of the end, and the first sequel of the insult to an offended Virgin. It was absurd, but so it was. His private business affairs were now to be removed from his control. "Steady! Steady!" he said to himself. "The lad hasn't the slightest idea what he's putting me through. Well, perhaps he has."

"As you like," he replied agreeably, but not too agreeably. A consent over-eager might have been mistaken for weakness, and it was necessary that he should seem strong, impartial, full of right reason.

"Good! I'll have the thing sent along this afternoon and you can sign it." ,

Sam glanced round at the clock.

"What are you talking about?" he demanded, indulgently superior. "How can you get a long document like that here by this afternoon? It's past twelve o'clock now."

"And why can't I? I'll telephone to Colchester. It stinks of lawyers, Colchester does. And tell 'em to send a clerk over with it in a car by five. A power of attorney must be a common form. They'll only have to copy it out. Do 'em good to give 'em a bit of a shake-up."

Sam held with pride a chip of the old block. Why indeed shouldn't a Colchester solicitor have a bit of a shake-up? On the other hand, why all this hurry? Steady! Steady! No morbid suspiciousness. The lad merely thinks that if it is to be done it may as well be done instantly. Nothing more. Why shouldn't he make the lawyers feel his weight?

"Hi!" cried Sam, as Geoffrey was leaving the room. The' lad halted and turned, with his porcupine hair and permanently wondering eyes. "Anybody seen anything of any jewels at Orange Street?" he asked, with strange inconsequence. He made his weak voice as matter-of-fact and casual as possible. "There was a very fine jade necklace."

Geoffrey replied in a similar tone:

"Oh, yes. They're all right. Gwen brought them down here with her. She didn't want to leave them in an empty house, you see."

"But – " Sam stopped, rather bewildered and uncertain. He too vividly recalled the evening when he had clasped the jade necklace round Delphine's magnificent neck. Dead! Dead! The necklace had an extraordinary painful sentimental value for him. He had given it to Delphine, but yet in some mysterious way it had remained his.

"They're Gwen's, you see – under the will. Everything's hers."

"Quite!" Sam concurred judicially.

But he had had another shock. He had meant to bestow the necklace on Gwen. And it was hers already; he had nothing whatever to do with it! The skies were still lowering on him. A dreadful sensation. But he had some fight left in him. Geoffrey was about to issue an imperious order, proving the power of wealth and of the autocratic spirit. He himself had issued such an order a day or two earlier – he could not remember exactly when – and seemingly it had been ignored.

"Hi!" he cried again, more sharply, and Geoffrey halted a second time. A sick man was entitled to halt his son forty times if he chose. "Didn't I tell you Mrs Blacklow was to come and see me? Had you forgotten?"

"That's all right," said Geoffrey. "She's here. Wrenkin met her at the station."

"Then why wasn't I told?" Pettishly.

"My dear fellow!" Geoffrey exclaimed with the most charming, sweetly chiding smile…

But fancy him addressing his father as "my dear fellow"! The insolence! No! Steady! Steady! It was delicious. And it was original. The lad had real originality. "My dear fellow" transformed Sam into Geoffrey's brother, friend, pal. It equalized them, in a manner flattering to Sam. Also it tended to show that Geoffrey did not consider him to be so very gravely ill. Geoffrey would never call a doomed man "my dear fellow." No ordinary lad, this lad! . Geoffrey continued:

"She'll be up here to see you soon. She's not very well at the moment. The state she's in, you know – they have to be handled with care. Jolting about in Great Eastern trains isn't much use to 'em. Wrenkin had to drive slowly up from the station. Old Thorping's looking after her."

Sam was ashamed. When autocratically demanding her immediate presence at Moze Hall he had momentarily forgotten her condition. A lamentable lapse, due, no doubt, to his naughty desire to rap Swetnam over the knuckles. All wrong! He made no remark. He had to examine himself…

There she was, Mrs Blacklow, standing near the door. For an instant he took her for an apparition, then realized that he must have been dozing. Geoffrey had probably conducted her to her threshold and left her. Like him! Always discreet! There she was, tall, attendant, submissive, patient. She wore dark grey, with a thin, figure-concealing mantle over the dress, and a rather attractive hat; and she was not wearing the eternal shabby gloves; her hands were thin and pale as his own, and her face was thin and pale, with a queer shininess of the skin; gleaming eyes.

Sam gave her a faint smile of welcoming recognition, and held out his left hand, because a chair happened to be placed to the left of the bed. She advanced and took his hand.

"Good morning, my lord."

He motioned her to sit down. Yes, she was big. Swetnam could not possibly have retained her in the office. And yet why not? Why these ridiculous conventions about maternity, as if maternity was a sin? And was she not getting ready to do her share in repairing the damage of the war? Swetnam the uxorious, the family man, should have been the last… Why must she conceal her figure? She at any rate – Sam knew – was not ashamed of her state. Force of convention; she had to pretend to be ashamed of it. Perhaps Swetnam was right. In Swetnam's place would Sam have acted differently?

"Glad to see ye, Mrs Blacklow," he began feebly. "But I'm a very ill man. A very ill man."

He wanted her to flatter his appearance. The nurse peeped in through the other doorway and vanished again.

"I hear you're making a splendid fight, my lord," said Mrs Blacklow.

"So that's what they say, is it? But shall I win – that's the point?"

"Of course you will, my lord. They all say so."

He regretted her last four words. He would have preferred her to prophesy a victory for him out of the mystic knowledge of instinct, as she had done before, at their interview in his room at the Ministry. His recollection of what she had said then was so clear that in his brain he could hear her very tones saying it: "I feel it'll be all right in the end, my lord." It had been all right, gloriously all right. He wondered whether that prophecy applied only to the Afflock vendetta, or whether he would be justified in applying it more largely to his career as a whole. He wanted her to reassure him against the omen of the insult to the Virgin. Infantile desire!

"And what did Mr Swetnam tell you to tell me, eh?" he asked in a voice carefully prosaic.

But just then a spasm of pain took him and he coughed several times, so that afterwards his breathing was more agitated and noisy. The nurse peeped in again, anxious, and Sam sternly controlled his organs. Mrs Blacklow placidly waited. "He only gave me a big envelope full of things, my lord, and Mr Raingo has taken it."

Well, of course! (Sam reflected.) What else could Swetnam do? After he'd once dismissed her, he couldn't confide the business of the office to her. The fellow had to maintain his prestige like anybody else. "And Mr Raingo has taken it." Naturally Mr Raingo would take it. "Um!"

"Oh, my lord, I can't help telling you how glad I was when Mr Swetnam telegraphed for me and told me you wanted to see me and I must come down, and as I was coming I might as well bring the envelope with me. I was afraid I mightn't be seeing you again."

"I'm afraid the journey upset you a bit," said Sam, touched and exalted. "Fact is, I didn't think – "

"Oh, that was nothing, my lord. It's quite gone already. I wouldn't have missed coming for anything in the world."

"And how's Gerald getting along? Or is it Rose now? You can take him into the parks all day and every day now, can't you?"

She blushed, partly with soft pleasure at his recalling those two alternative names, and partly because he had found her out in her uncertainty concerning sex.

"To tell you the truth, my lord, sometimes I think it Gerald, and sometimes Rose. It's funny how you're sure one day, and the next day it's all altered. But it's a happy child. I know it's a happy child. And that's all owing to you, my lord. I don't mean so much the money – you've been so nice and kind. I couldn't have believed there was anybody so good. It isn't as if you'd known me before… And you remembering their names like that." Suddenly she stood up, and her mantle was thrown back. "Yes, even their names – both of them."

Sam was uncomfortable, disconcerted, and pleased. He wondered what she was going to do next. But she only cried for a moment, smiled, and sat down again. Sam could not speak. "This is going to be too much for me," he thought. Yes, she was big with her happy child. He imagined the adored Delphine like that. The secret vision of Delphine carrying his happy child in her glorious body electrified and desolated him. Dead! Dead! Stretched out in the dark in everlasting stillness. No man could bear it. His eyes, fixed on the ceiling, showed emotion, which Mrs Blacklow, with the instinctive egotism of the mother, attributed to herself and her condition. They were silent.

"And you – are you all right? Happy?" he asked quietly.

"Oh, yes, my lord. I'm just waiting. It's very long, but I like it. I've made all the arrangements, so there's nothing else for me to do but to make things for the little one and go for walks and think. You see, I'm never lonely. Can't be. And as I'm married people aren't annoying."

Sam saw that she was utterly absorbed in her immediate prospect. She had no thought for the further future. She had not imagined, would not imagine, the ultimate meeting with her husband. She was not a wife, not a sinner. She was a mother, and could be only that. Delphine would have been the same. Why did Delphine throw herself over? She could not have loved the soldier. Did not Gwen swear it? Impossible that she could have loved anyone but himself. Melancholia, that was it: melancholia, a definite disease. Yet supposing that she had loved that soldier – Harry Point, was that his name?...

"And money?" he asked. "How are you for money? Enough?"

"Oh, my lord!" she exclaimed deprecatingly, as though she had millions at command.

He had given her a couple of hundred pounds and then another fifty, because two hundred and fifty seemed to him to be a rounder figure than two hundred.

Now he was dying with desire to bring the conversation to himself, so that she might pronounce words of hope, of assurance, and nullify the wrong to the Virgin. But she said nothing, and he dared not broach the topic, lest she might unwittingly condemn him to death by a single innocent phrase.

The nurse coming in to close the interview, frightened the visitor by her curtness.

"I do hope you'll soon be better," said Mrs Blacklow, holding his hand, and she wept as if she was a criminal in the sight of the nurse. Not much comfort in such words – "I do hope." Not much comfort in her facile tears! Why couldn't she have smiled and predicted with certainty his recovery, and spoken of seeing him again and showing him the child? The nurse had ended more than the interview.

As soon as she was gone he sent for Geoffrey.

"Jeff," he said, "I want ten thousand pounds to be settled on that Mrs Blacklow. She may be in serious difficulties in a few months if she isn't looked after. See to it at once – with your confounded power of attorney." He sighed, "I'm rather tired." He slipped down in the bed, thinking of Mrs Blacklow's praise of him.

84

Answer to Prayer

That night, after Sir Arthur had finally left him, at a quarter to twelve, Sam felt what Eccles would have called "very low." The presence of the great, large-headed Canadian arch-magician, with his benevolent and sagacious nasal booming, seemed to act on Sam throughout the long evening like continual doses of a powerfully tonic drug – he dared not even in the innermost privacy of his mind admit "lowness" while Sir Arthur was by his side – but as soon as the doses were stopped he was a tippler deprived of whisky or a habitual cocaine-taker deprived of cocaine. His spirits sank; his brain clouded. He was burning with heat, especially in the cheeks, each of which showed a central spot of red. He could not keep still because the bed was on fire as well as himself. He tried to feel his pulse but he could not find it; to measure his respirations by the clock, but he could not count them. He dozed, he dreamed, he had nightmares, and yet he seemed never to lose waking consciousness.

"Well, you must keep it up," Sir Arthur had said in quitting him. A nice thing to say to a man! As if he wasn't keeping it up! He was thinking about nothing but his illness; he was completely absorbed in the fate of his body.

And many phenomena had a disturbing effect on his will to conquer. Not only the insult to the Virgin and the failure to prophesy by the seer in Mrs Blacklow; but matters more subtle. Geoffrey's demeanour to him had altered during the day; it had grown less playful and more grave. "The boy-is beginning to realize at last what I have lost in Delphine," Sam had said to himself, "and wishes to show his sympathy."

But now, alone with Nurse Kewley, he would attribute the change to a conviction in Geoffrey that the patient's chances were dwindling – were gone. Again he had the suspicion that in signing the power of attorney he had been renouncing the mortal right to live. And worst of all was his night-interpretation of his directions to Geoffrey concerning the settlement on Mrs Blacklow. Why had he been so precipitate in that affair? Obviously his haste was unwittingly due to a subconscious foreknowledge of doom, for if he was to survive he could have seen to the settlement himself, and there could be no hurry about it. Sam had now invested the subconscious with an importance exceeding that of the conscious. Indeed, values were shifting like prices on the Stock Exchange in a financial crisis.

"I keep slipping down in bed," he exclaimed weakly and pettishly. "I do wish these pillows could be arranged better." "It's only because you're tired," the nurse answered sweetly, manoeuvring the pillows afresh. Sam thought, but did not say: "You mean by that I'm losing strength." "I'm in pain," he said. "It's this awful tube. And I'm sure my breathing's worse. And my cough hurts me."

The nurse gently wiped his lips, upon which a sort of brown crust was continually forming.

"And what's this confounded bubbling business in my throat? It feels like a ball balanced on the top of a fountain – always going up and down."

The nurse smiled kindly at such an odd comparison. "Everything seems worse at night," she said firmly. "You know that by your own experience by this time. If you ask me, I dare say you aren't quite so bad as you think you are." He was grateful for this trifle of solace.

"Yes," he said. "You're quite right about nights being worse."

After a few moments she said surprisingly: "Shall you mind if I say my prayers? I always like to say my prayers."

Strange creatures were women! As if she hadn't said her prayers every night! Several times he had seen her on her knees, and she must have known that he had seen her. Then why ask permission now? You could never understand women. He gave the permission, wearily.

The next instant she startled him by dropping down, not in her own screened corner, but at the chair by the side of his bed. His first thought of her at prayer had moved him; on later occasions he had been indifferent; he was now resentful, in addition to being frightened. The woman had taken this method of indicating to him that he ought to prepare for death by invoking the mercy of God. He well knew that Geoffrey would neither dare to suggest such a course to him, nor dream of suggesting it; not would the doctors; and there was nobody else. He had never at any time said a word about religion to Geoffrey. He had absolutely no dogmatic religious beliefs, and he did not think that Geoffrey had any. He never went to chapel or church! Adela used now and then to go, but the sole effect on her of a service was apparently to move her to speak disparagingly of parsons and their wives. Convinced that he could not possibly form any satisfactory idea of the nature of God, he had long since definitely and without regret given up the attempt. He was afraid of death, or more correctly he hated the notion of dying; but he was not afraid of what experience, if any, might be awaiting him after death; and in any case the theory that those experiences might be rendered more palatable by dint of spiritual exercises on his death-bed was revolting to his individual variety of common sense. The theory that the adventures, in and out of his bed, of the miniature of the Madonna could influence his earthly fate was equally revolting to his common sense; here, however, his common sense had to humble itself before the strong domination of atavistic instincts. He admitted that he was absurdly inconsistent, but he could not help being inconsistent; everybody had to be absurd in his own way, and nobody could escape being absurd.

Hence he did not object to the nurse being absurd in her own way; he could not deny that perhaps her way was better than his. At least she showed a courage that was unusual; for there were various persons in and around Moze Hall – Miss Thorping, for instance, and possibly Doctor Heddle – who were absurd in Nurse Kewley's way, but who would let him go to everlasting damnation rather than defy convention by boldly warning him. And the nurse had delicacy too. Nothing could have been more delicate than her manner of thus alluding to the awful dangers which beset him. He resented the allusion; but she must have foreseen that he would resent it, and she had braved his resentment.

He followed in his mind the chain of events. She had feared that he was losing ground. By a tone, by the lifting of the eyebrows, she had communicated her fear to Dr. Heddle. By a tone, by the lifting of the eyebrows, Dr. Heddle had confirmed her fear. Sir Arthur, of course, shared it, for Heddle would never confirm the nurse in an opinion opposed to that of the great man. The doctors had given a hint to Geoffrey, Geoffrey to Gwen and Miss Thorping, Miss Thorping to the rest of the household, the household to the village, the village to the peninsula. Everybody had learnt the professional view of Lord Raingo's case. The nurses had discussed it together. Only the newspapers could be trusted not to print a word of it at present.

And Nurse Kewley, seeing that no one else did anything in regard to the patient, had decided that she was bound to do something herself, and she had chosen this method of prayer close by his side. She was praying for him, for the welfare of his soul. His resentment against her faded out as he beheld the long lines of her uniform, and her shabby shoes, and her hands pressed hard against her eyes. Not a sound anywhere save his breathing and the ticking of the clock. No motion of the curtains. His resentment slowly vanished; but not his fright. She had shown him the dreadful precipice and the mysterious river deep below. (Delphine's precipice it was, too.) He ran back from the precipice, but somehow it came after him. Then there was no precipice and no river. There was nothing. And this nothingness was more formidable and terror-striking than the precipice and the river. He wanted knowledge; he would have been content with hope, with any mere theory, however absurd, that he could hold to, that would destroy the nothingness. But there was still nothing. He understood then that what made death sublime and affrighting was ignorance, and that so it would always be. The whole room, which, nevertheless did not exist, was full of sinister magic. The minutes were appalling. They changed him. He never forgot them. He brought them to an end with a blow of his feverish hand on the sheet. Resolution came to his aid.

"I'm not dead," he cried in his heart. "And what's more, I'm not going to be dead."

All sinister magic was dissipated. The room existed once more.

"I'm better," said he, with a vigour in which was a certain pathos, when the nurse rose from her mystic intercourse. Her eyes shone. "She'll think it's an answer to prayer. Supposing it is?" he said to himself.

They were very near to each other in the night, he and Nurse Kewley, though they spoke little. Yes, he somehow felt that no patient of hers had ever been so near to her as himself.

In the morning, as early as seven o'clock, the arch-magician, fully dressed and intensely alive, came in as quietly as a mouse, bringing with him the tonic of his presence, and all the actuality of day. While under examination Sam said:

"There seems to be a lot of people round about here that think I'm a goner."

"Why do you say that?" Sir Arthur asked.

"I don't know. I feel it. Only I want to tell you I'm not a goner, and don't let there be any mistake."

The arch-magician most unusually glanced at the nurse, smiling, and she blushed and smiled.

"If you keep on in that strain," said Sir Arthur, "you'll give me quite an appetite for breakfast. You feel better? Well, I can tell you you're much better than you were last night."

A dubious saying.

"You going to London again to-day?"

"Not if I can help it," said Sir Arthur. "I may have to, but I hope not. If I stay here they'll think you're worse, but you won't mind that, will you, if it gives me a bit of a holiday?" "You're the cleverest fellow ever born," thought Sam, sardonic, "with your damned tact. But I am better. And you can think what you like."

85

The Pretence

Geoffrey came in, in the middle of the morning, with his hands full of newspapers and press-cuttings. Sam had sent for his son, whom he had already seen for a few moments twice that day. He had now resolved on a course of action which should firmly demonstrate that he was better.

The early pow-wow between the doctors had taken place, and they had gone out together. Dr. Heddle having his bicycle, the arch-magician had said lightly that in younger days he was a great cyclist before the Lord, and he had borrowed Wrenkin's machine, which was as shabby as Wrenkin himself.

"Are those two' off the place?" Sam asked. Nurse Emily had discreetly retired to the next room, and Sam was glad. He would have said anything in front of Nurse Kewley, who had a spirituality which comprehended; but Nurse Emily, though kindly enough, was a commoner, plump little thing without real understanding.

"Yes. They've run over to Clacton ages ago. Tappitt was tickled to death at his own condescension in riding the gardener's jigger; and I bet you they call at the hospital, so that Tappitt can have the pleasure of turning it upside down by the enormous flattery of his advent. A red-letter day in the history of the establishment. See?"

Sam, pleased at this evidence of harsh insight on the part of the boy, said:

"You're fairly grim."

"I take after you, guv'nor."

The boy was more cheerful to-day; which seemed to Sam rather a good sign.

"Where's Mrs Blacklow?" asked Sam, who was curiously hesitant about coming to his point.

"Oh! She's gone. Went back last night," Geoffrey answered casually.

They came, Sam saw them for a tiny space, and they departed, and not a word said! Something tragic, pitiful to Sam, in these silent, swift vanishings.

"And Gwen?"

"She's here. But she's making a great fuss – wants to go back to London to look for a job:"

"Job be damned!"

"Yes. That's what I said. She didn't like it."

"Oh! Didn't she?"

"No. Made quite a good imitation of a scene. You'd think butter wouldn't melt in her mouth, but she's got a bit of a devil in her."

Sam was delighted to hear of a scene between the pair; it proved that their intimacy was deepening.

"And is she going?"

"Not if I know it!" said Geoffrey, with easy assurance. "You bought her some nice clothes." "Well, I thought you'd prefer her to look decent. They're down to your account. I had to put it on to you or she wouldn't have had 'em."

"Um!… And Wrenkin?" Sam still could not come to his point. "When's he got to go?"

"I think it's the day after to-morrow. I've engaged old Hall, you know, the ostler that used to be at the ' Anchor.' B.C. something, or early A.D. Anyhow, he's at least a hundred and one, but I expect I can screw some sense into him. All the same you'd better look sharp and get better, dad. I shall have to report myself again to Head-Quarters in three weeks."

"Oh! They won't send you very far just yet," said Sam confidently.

He had reasons unknown to Geoffrey for this assertion, reasons which would have made Geoffrey angry had he been aware of them. The fact was that the unprincipled Sam had employed powerful influence immediately after Geoffrey's previous medical examination, and had obtained a promise that the boy should be seconded to his own Ministry if health permitted. It was all very wrong and inexcusable, but Sam considered that the lad had "done his bit," and he had the weakness and the elastic conscience of fathers. A discreditable episode.

"Look here, Jeff," said he. "I don't want to waste my strength any longer on miscellaneous newspapers and press-cuttings – I'm sick of press-cuttings. I'm getting better and I ought to begin to keep abreast of things again, so that when I go back I shan't be hopelessly out of date. The sooner I start, the easier it ought to be for me, oughtn't it?"

"Quite," Geoffrey agreed laconically.

"I must have all the ' secret' documents from the Ministry, and especially the War Cabinet minutes. And Hansard. Like that I shall soon know where I am."

"Quite."

"You can help me."

"Yes." No expression in Geoffrey's voice, save one of amiable detachment. Neither discouragement nor encouragement.

The sick man's wasted, hairy face had a wistful look. Geoffrey glanced away from it, would not confront those burning, apprehensive eyes.

"When can I have them?"

"If I telephone now they could be down here some time this afternoon. Shall I?"

"Jeff," said Sam, putting out a hand of appeal. "Aren't they here already? Haven't you been receiving them every day, and not saying anything about 'em?"

"Well, until to-day you haven't been in much of a state for keeping level with things at the Ministry, have you, dad? Yes, they *are* here. And don't say I haven't been straight with you now. I'll fetch them."

"Wait a second," Sam murmured. "Shut that door." He indicated the door between the two rooms.

When he had done so, Geoffrey perched himself familiarly on the side of the bed, the right foot on the floor and the left knee on the coverlet.

"Your tunic's in a sad state." Sam was still hesitating to come to his point.

"It's only an old one."

"You say you're being straight with me. Then tell me I How am I? Really. Tell me the truth. I know I'm better,, but I want to hear what the doctors think."

Sam tried to look steely, but could not be sure that he was succeeding. Sheer nervousness made him cough, and the cough hurt him, and the wound between his ribs was very painful after the morning's dressing. Nevertheless he held himself firmly together, and tried to look steely. Silence, except for the laborious, rapid breathing: *Ah-ah. Ah-ah..*

"I'll ask you another," said Geoffrey at length. "Supposing it was *I* who was ill, and I asked *you* what the doctors thought – what would *you say?* Should you tell me the truth whatever it was? Straight now!"

Sam said nothing. Geoffrey continued:

"And if I did tell you, and it wasn't favourable, you'd be upset. And if it was favourable you wouldn't believe me – you'd think I was lying, just to keep your spirits up. So what's the good? You are an ill man, but you are a man, and you can't help seeing my argument."

Sam was indeed impressed by his son's argument. He liked the phrase: "You are an ill man, but you're a man." It appealed to him. The lad was wonderful.

"Tell me," he insisted obstinately, touching Geoffrey's knee with a nervous, timid gesture.

"Very well, I will. Tappitt thinks if you keep on doing as well as you are doing you'll pull through. He's hopeful. We all are. But you don't believe me."

"Yes, I do," Sam protested. "Why shouldn't I? It's what I think myself." But in his heart he was saying: "The lad isn't a very convincing liar." Still, he would not be cast down.

Soon, with Geoffrey's aid, he was reading his documents, which were handed to him one by one. Now and then Geoffrey commented. "Yes, yes, I know," Sam would mutter impatiently. His spectacles annoyed him by slipping down his nose at intervals. Never before had they slipped down. When the nurse interrupted to accomplish one of the hundred ministrations which his body, and particularly his heart, required, he made little resentful movements and noises as though he was utterly absorbed in work and had not a moment to spare from it. He frowned in concentration, read through the same document twice, said: "Well, anyhow, *that's* clear enough," said, "Give me a pencil," and scrawled crosses in margins. The nurse watched him with surprise and admiration. Presently she left the room.

Sam thought:

"Ah, she cannot keep it to herself. She's gone to tell Miss Thorping that his lordship is working once more."

He liked to think of himself being referred to throughout the house as "his lordship." Yes, he had always enjoyed the ceremonial fruits of his peerage. He even regretted that the nurses so seldom addressed him as "my lord." They usually didn't call him anything; they just talked to hire, acquainted intimately as they were with the vanity of human pomps. He had been sardonic (to himself) about Mrs Blacklow employing the "my lord" while imparting to him matters which in their sublimity far transcended the greatest of earthly distinctions; but he would have been disappointed if she had ceased to use it.

He had a vision of the entire household thrilled and exalted by the news that his lordship was working. In the twinkling of an eye the village would know it, the journalists, the country, the world! "It is understood that yesterday morning the distinguished patient was able to deal for a few hours with official work." Relief everywhere! Smiles everywhere!

It happened to him, however, sometimes, to read a document without comprehending it. Yet he would lay down the paper pretending that he had grasped its contents. His mind would wander. He would see the shadowy figures in the Ministry: the watch-dog, the too deferential hall-porter, the railway director, whom he had sacked in a glorious storm of contumely and just vituperation. Once, when Geoffrey had to go to a table to deposit documents and bring others, Sam picked up one or two press-cuttings which had been carelessly dropped on the bed, and read them with the naive satisfaction of a child. A sad lapse for a minister destined to a seat in the War Cabinet.

"Aha!" said a deep voice. It was the arch-magician returned somewhat heated from his triumphant cycling excursion to Clacton. He still had steel trouser-clips round his ankles. Doubtless Geoffrey would say that he had retained them on purpose to advertise his activities, and make an effect. Sam pretended to be so occupied that he had not noticed the grand entry. He looked at Sir Arthur under his spectacles as if Sir Arthur had drawn him momentarily out of a passion of toil.

"All right, isn't it, Sir Arthur, this working a bit?" Geoffrey asked.

"Certainly! Certainly! If he feels like it. And doesn't overdo it."

Sam detected the insincerity in the benevolent tones as infallibly as though he had been the reader of all hearts. He could almost see Sir Arthur winking at Geoffrey, almost hear him whispering: "Doesn't matter much what he does now. Let him follow his fancy." So morbid and sensitive was his imagination!

Yet by another act of imagination he ignored all that, and went on pretending to work, and treated the important doctor as perfectly non-existent. Then he grew tired of the sham, and continued it hopelessly – with the dogged, feeble, pathetic hopelessness of a boat's crew pounding and sweating in the wake of winners who are passing the post. And then he pushed all the papers away with a disillusioned sigh. The pretence was at an end. He did not care, now, who knew it had been a pretence. Let them all think what they chose.

The nurse brought him food. He took a spoonful, then pushed the basin away as he had pushed the papers away, and some of the contents were spilt on the bed. He groaned, and slid weakly down the incline of pillows toward the interior of the bed, and became an emaciated, unshaven, panting sick man with fright and despair in his eyes.

And the look on the three watching faces changed; but Sam's eyes did not see the change. His woe was too self-centred even to picture in his mind the change that would so quickly occur in the mood of the household, the village, the Anglo-Saxon -world.

86

The Photograph

Geoffrey came into the bedroom with some of the contents of the afternoon post, not at all expecting that his father would be prepared to discuss them, but the sick man had shown in the two days gone by that he liked to have the refusal of his mail. He was now apparently unconscious.

"It might be as well to rouse him," said Sir Arthur, who was sitting by the bed and who had just arrived back from a visit to London.

Sam was very ill. His face was thinner and greyer, and even in unconsciousness had an expression of intense anxiety. His hands, which lay on the coverlet, were thinner and whiter. It was astonishing that he could sleep through the incessant laborious panting of his respiration. It was astonishing that his heart had not already surrendered to the tremendous odds of the battle for breath.

"Say, my friend," Sir Arthur spoke loudly and firmly in the patient's ear, and lifted him a little higher on the pillows.

Sam half opened his eyes, sighed, and murmured something quite inarticulate.

"You must take some food – a drink."

"Eh, eh?... Oh, yes." With his eyes still half opened Sara glanced uneasily and wearily round from one person to another. "That's not Jeff, is it?"

"Yes, dad. It's Jeff. And here's Sir Arthur," said Geoffrey, speaking very clearly, as though to a child who was in process of being wakened.

Sam replied, but nobody could make out a word, and the three watchers looked at one another in surmise. Nurse Emily gently wiped his lips and teeth, which were crusted with brown, and he sipped at a glass which she offered him.

"Ah, you!... Ah, yes!" he muttered, more distinctly. "Yes. I see." And sighed again. He seemed to be saying, negligently and without interest: "I'm fully abreast of the situation, so don't think otherwise, any of you."

The watchers waited in silence.

"In a minute. In a minute," said Sam, meaning that in a minute he would do anything they wanted. "Jeff, I must write a letter. I'll write it in pencil."

"Yes, dad. I'll get you some paper," Geoffrey agreed, insincerely humouring the whim of one who was no more capable of writing a letter than of making a speech to a public-assembly.

"Yes. It's old Mrs Clyth I want to write to. She wrote to me."

"I should leave it for a bit, dad," Geoffrey suggested.

"Yes, perhaps you're right, lad. Leave it. A bit. No hurry. Do any time."

Worn out by the extreme labour of speech, he was very docile – in contrast with a certain pettish obstinacy which he had displayed at intervals on the previous day and in the night, He gazed at the ceiling, just as if he had been alone in the sunlit room. He wished to reflect. He was not interested in the progress of the malady. What he obscurely desired was to review his life, in a philosophical spirit. He had reviewed it days ago – seemed months ago – and everything in his life had held together logically then. He had blamed himself then for taking risks which ought not to have been taken. But the aspect of his life was not so simple to him now.. Why should he blame himself? Circumstances had compelled him to take the risks and to defy the commands of common sense. The point was – what was the point r He had once grasped the point, but it was eluding him. Yes. The point was: If he had to live his recent life over again, would he have taken the same risks again? Yes, he would. He would, he would. That was the point. He was glad he had got the point clear, at last. He was not to blame. Life was to blame, and he couldn't help that. He did not understand God and he did not understand life either, and he wasn't going to bother. He was tired and bored, and it was not his job to answer conundrums. A nice thing!

"Anyhow she thinks well of me. She praised me. She *did* praise me," he murmured. He was dwelling with satisfaction on what Mrs Blacklow had said: "I wouldn't have believed there was anybody so good." That sentence had continually comforted him. He murmured again: "Anyhow, I've done something." His mind flitted back again to old Mrs Clyth's magic gift; and he thought: "It's still there under the pillows. There must be *something* in it. The old lady's so good." For a space he saw himself slowly getting better and was feebly triumphant.

And there was another ground for triumph, a very important ground. What was it? He could not instantly recall it. Yes, of course he could recall it – his brain was all right. Invitation to join the War Cabinet. Food for thought for those relatives of his!

Through the open principal doorway he saw someone coming along the landing from the head of the stairs. It was Gwen. Yes, he could not be mistaken: it was Gwen. Nobody else in the room could see her, because all had their backs to the door as they watched him.

She was still wearing the smart, new, black frock, probably because she had no other mourning. In her hand she held a large, thin packet. Her beautiful face was palest ivory; not a spot of rose in it anywhere, save the lips and the blue eyes. She crept forward, as it were timid and uncertain, and yet with resolution. Sam wanted to warn the others that they were about to be startled, but he could not decide to do so. She was within the doorway. No sound. Sam could clearly see the look on her face. A look of defiant determination, as if she was announcing:

"I have as much right in this room as anybody. I'm Delphine's half-sister, and if she'd lifted a finger I might have been his sister-in-law now."

The nurse, catching sight of her, gave a jump. The men turned their heads, and with masculine superiority maintained a perfect calm.

"May I come in?" Gwen asked, falsely submissive.

Her white face was drawn and twitching; she was trying, and failing, to keep her lips still; they moved nervously as though she would burst into hysterical sobs. Geoffrey was obviously perturbed and at a loss what to do. She approached the bed, until she was standing between the nurse and Sam. Then her features surprisingly broke into an angelic smile.

"It's yours," she said to Sam, with the softest, tenderest smile. "And so I wrote and asked Captain Mayden to get it and post it to me and it's just come." And she ledged a large photograph of Delphine against the foot of the bed.

The chocolate-tinted mount was a foot long.

The new photograph – head and shoulders only – which Delphine had left behind her, was a dramatic portrait full of high lights and dark shadows of black hair! Delphine was in evening dress, and the jade necklace hung round her majestic neck. A life-like portrait, but a thrilling intensification of life! What lips! What a shoulder rising out of the dress! Sam gazed at it transfixed. It was she, in all her living, dreaming, passionate effulgence. (But she lay stretched out under the coffin-lid in everlasting rest – the apotheosis of her genius for contemplative quietude.) Melancholy in her eyes!

Sam's mind was now more normal, restored to the use of its functions. Why had she thrown herself over? Why had she done it? She could not have been happy. The happy do not kill themselves. But who could have made her happy? The young soldier? Did she so love the young soldier?... No! Sam could not bear, the thought of such a love, which implied such a perfidy – moral, not physical – to himself. She did it because she must. She had in her the fatal seed of death. She was appointed to unhappiness for herself, and to spread un-happiness round her like a contagion. Yet with her he had been at moments marvellously happy – too happy to recall his irrecoverable bliss without the direst pain. Yes, they had been united – she, in her magnificent beauty, and he – he the wasted, unshaven, broken, wrecked, panting, poor old thing on the bed.

Yes, she had loved him. Yes, her honest arms had folded him in love. But all the time the seed of death was within her. She must have known it, and it was this mystic knowledge which had inspired and maintained her dark and exquisite gloom.

Young Geoffrey was distressed, apprehensive and angry: the nurse bewildered; Sir Arthur watchful, perceiving as he did the plain signs of hysteria in Gwen's lovely face.

"She had to do it!" Gwen cried out at last, with a fierce, resentful stare at the defenceless man propped on his crumpled pillows. Her tone and glance were in the strangest contrast to the heavenly smile which a moment earlier she had given him. They savagely implicated him in the suicide. She might have been saying again: "Between you, you drove her to it, you and Harry. You particularly. She wanted to leave you free." The senseless idea seemed to be fixed in her brain. "I've nobody now. I'm all alone," she cried out. "And no one knows what she was to me, and I couldn't tell anyone. And nobody would believe me if I did!"

Sir Arthur made a movement towards her. She proudly straightened herself, and her blue eyes gleamed at him warningly, and he drew back.

"Gwen! Gwen!" Geoffrey, beaten, appealed to her, like a child to a child.

Her features changed, softened. She seized Sam's hand.

"I'm so sorry. I know I'm wrong. But I couldn't help it. It comes over me. It did before. Perhaps you know what she was to me. Nobody else does. Geoffrey doesn't." The last words were a little defiant. She melted again. "I'm so sorry, I *do* love you. And *she* did."

Geoffrey took her by the arm. She resisted, yielded. She gave Geoffrey a long glance: her head fell on his shoulder, shamelessly.

After Geoffrey had led her from the room, the arch-magician benevolently coughed, twice; then he picked up the photograph to remove it.

"Leave it!" said Sam shortly; and it was his lordship who issued the command.

87

LIGHTING

Passing through the hall on his way upstairs, Geoffrey heard the crunching of a motor-car on the gravel, and saw through a window, the curtains of which had been carelessly left undrawn, the hooded lights of the vehicle. The front door was ajar. He looked out for a moment. Sir Arthur's chauffeur was arranging two leather cases in the space next to the driving seat. A warm night; no moon, but many stars; the fields slid mildly and vaguely down towards Mozewater.

"What the deuce is all this?" he thought. He had an impulse to question the chauffeur, but he checked it. What could he ask? As the effective master of the house he ought to know at least as much as the chauffeur about the movements and intentions of automobiles in his grounds. Besides, nothing mattered. He shut the front door. On the hall table lay a green packet of press-cuttings. Idly he picked it up, then dropped it. Some negligence of the old idiot Skinner. The 'packet must have come an hour earlier with other packets by the evening special private courier from London, and Skinner had overlooked it in carrying the mail to the study.

Lights were burning everywhere, – in the hall, in the dining-room, the doors of which were open, in the inner hall, in the drawing-room, on the stairs, in the passages. During periods of crisis discipline slackens, and servants can indulge their deep instinct for lavishness in electric illumination.

"They must go round and turn 'em on on purpose," said Geoffrey to himself.

On the stairs he met Sir Arthur in a thick overcoat.

"I'm going now, Mr Raingo," said the arch-magician with the deference due to a young man of character who would soon be a peer of the realm and the possessor of millions of money. "This youth will be a figure in the world," thought Sir Arthur. "He will use his millions. He will keep state. He will not be content with a house like his father's."

"Oh!" murmured Geoffrey, non-committal. This was the first word to reach him of Sir Arthur's departure.

"Yes," the great man boomed quietly. "I can be of no further use here. And I've so much urgent work waiting for me in town – I mean really urgent." He held out his masterful hand.

"Of course! Of course!" Geoffrey agreed.

They separated, with only a formal word of thanks from the lad. Geoffrey was too disturbed to accompany Sir Arthur to the front door. Nor was it a night for ceremonial.

"Rat!" he muttered as he ran up the stairs. He was extremely unjust. But had Sir Arthur overheard the epithet he would have sardonically forgiven it, for he had the lowest opinion of the humanity of patients and their relatives.

Geoffrey went into the room next to the sick-room. Gwen was seated there, and Miss Thorping and Nurse Emily. Nurse Emily would not go to bed. No one would go to bed. In a corner stood old Skinner, dirtier than ever. Geoffrey wanted to say to him: "Skinner, why haven't you cleared the dining-room table?" But he had not the heart to pester the inefficient old man. Moreover, it was Miss Thorping's job, not Geoffrey's, to worry about dining-room tables. Gwen looked at him with soft, wet eyes; her body seemed to move towards Geoffrey; he gave her a tonic masculine glance of encouragement, and for an instant a sad smile lit her appealing white face. Miss Thorping and Nurse Emily stood up respectfully in the presence of the master.

A few telegrams were scattered on a table. He had left them there hours earlier. They were addressed: "Hon. Geoffrey Raingo," and contained messages of sympathy and hope. (The bulletin printed that morning had finished with the words, "continues to be grave." In dozens of newspaper offices obituaries, special memoirs and anecdotal sketches were being prepared.) One telegram was signed "Sid Jenkin," another "Ockleford," another and longer one, "Mayden." Nothing from Andrew Clyth, who was' doubtless too busy searching for a supporter in the War Cabinet to compose telegrams about useless dying men, or even to instruct Miss Rosie Packer to do so. Andy's telegram would come later, and it would be threnodical.

Geoffrey passed into the sick-room. The clock showed a little after ten. By it, on the mantelpiece, stood up the photograph of Delphine, dimly shining in the subdued light. Dr. Heddle, chin in hand, sat contemplative in his eternal monotonous khaki by the bed. Nurse Kewley stood opposite to him like a statue. Dr. Heddle looked at Geoffrey but said naught. The statue moved slightly away. Something curiously small lay on the bed, on its back. It was panting heavily. Its eyes were closed and its mouth opened. It had a straggling short beard and short whiskers.

"Is he unconscious?" Geoffrey whispered, advancing on cautious, silent feet. ..

The doctor nodded. Geoffrey stood still, thinking of Gwen's tragic face. The clock ticked. The curtains shifted – now concave, now convex. The big clock on the landing insisted on being heard. Geoffrey's ear caught a faint sob. It was Gwen's message to him that she was suffering and without help. He ignored it. Then there were incomprehensible shuffling sounds on the stairs. Silence. More shuffling sounds. Old Skinner entered, creeping, and offered to Geoffrey the packet of press-cuttings on a salver.

"Must have forgotten it, sir," he quavered sheepishly.

"Good God!" thought Geoffrey, savage in his heart. "Is it possible that any man can be such a stupendous ass as to bring me press-cuttings now?" He controlled himself, and said, sternly quiet: "Put it in the study."

And old Skinner bore off the bundle of journalistic tattlings.

"Good God!" Geoffrey repeated to himself. "It struck him all of a sudden. He'd forgotten something. His conscience awoke."

The organism on the bed continued to pant. Gwen gave a louder and more desperate signal: Geoffrey ignored it. An hour or more passed.

Sam stirred and fidgeted. His white hands, with their long finger-nails, moved on the edge of the sheet. Nurse Kewley wiped away the continually forming rust from his lips and teeth. He seemed to be aware of the operation, first to chafe against it, then to appreciate it. The lips moved. His ebbing vital energy turned and flowed, mastering for a while the poison which now deeply infected the whole of his body. This was the last ineffectual fight. Geoffrey looked at the doctor, who nodded as if in confirmation of something that Geoffrey's glance had said.

Gwen slipped into the room and stood close by Geoffrey, touching him; then she laid her light hand on his wrist and then she clasped his hand. The young man could no longer ignore her. He had resented her appeal, but now he was content that she had insisted on having his support: he put a faint pressure on her hand, and she appeared to him to be infinitely pathetic, fragile and touching. Nurse Emily walked as by right boldly in and joined her colleague. Miss Thorping stationed herself in the doorway and Skinner stood near her, also in the doorway. Other figures of servants, drawn forward by the sinister and irresistible attraction of approaching death, were congregating on the landing, near the main doorway. All the life of the house was gathered around the toxin-ridden organism on the Empire bed. The house, peopled everywhere with Geoffrey's rich and tasteful furniture, stretched out enormous under its dozens of electric lights. The whole suite of rooms comprising the ground floor were seen as one glittering vista by two cats who were dallying tantalizingly with one another in the solitude. The stairs had grown higher, the passages longer, in the night. One girl, apart from the rest, sat on the top stair, crying; it was Edith. Minutes went by.

Then there was a creeping step on the stairs. Edith started, and pressed herself against the wall to make way. The next moment Miss Thorping heard a noise behind her, and saw a man in khaki peeping over her shoulder into the sick-room. Miss Thorping was outraged. She detested Wrenkin, who always had difficulties with every woman on the place. What right had an outdoor employee to invade the private apartments unannounced and uninvited? He was taking a great deal on himself. Wrenkin, however, was no more an outdoor employee. He was a soldier, and being a person of weight and famous in the vicinity, he had got leave from Colchester – not to visit Us wife and two boys from whom Andy Clyth's hasty measure of recruiting had snatched him, but to look for the last time on his former master. There he was, clean-shaven, his hair close-cropped, neat, spruce, and cleansed as never before. A sight to startle the entire neighbourhood.

He glared gloomily and challengingly around, according to his custom. And Miss Thorping had to accept the situation. Wrenkin saw his master, to whom he was devoted with an acid passion. He deemed it his duty to pay these respects and he was paying them. But he still was not content. Just as Miss Thorping's sense of propriety had been outraged, so was Wrenkin's sense of efficiency outraged.

"Lights is going down. Hall hasn't made enough current and they're wasting it everywhere," he muttered, scarcely audible, to deaf Skinner, who did not catch what he said. Geoffrey heard the muttering and looked round. Miss Thorping had accepted her situation, but Wrenkin could not accept his. He simply would not bear it, and was driven to depart.

Sam opened his eyes wide and gave a sigh amid his panting. He was semi-conscious. He clearly perceived that Dr. Heddle and both nurses had moved a little towards him. He was rather mystified to see two nurses. "Why two nurses at once?" was the dim question in his mind. He saw Geoffrey and Gwen. The room seemed to him to be full of people. But he felt very lonely. Not pain and ceaseless labouring were his affliction, but a terrible, desolating loneliness. It did not occur to him that he was dying. The idea of death troubled him not in the least. He thought that somehow it was a darker night than usual.

And it was. The electric lights were indeed gradually losing their .brilliance. Everybody noticed it, but nobody spoke or moved. Everybody thought how fitting, how impressive, how supernatural it was, that as Lord Raingo lay dying the lights of the house should fade. Everybody except Wrenkin. The lights suddenly went up – not much, but a little. Wrenkin had turned off every light on the ground floor. Time passed. Then the thudding beat of the dynamo in the engine-house by the garage came into the room through the opened windows. Wrenkin, making the situation tolerable for himself! The lights slowly resumed their proper brilliance.

Sam saw that the night was not dark after all. To the onlookers his bubbling throat was creating a great, frightening noise. His respirations became more and more deliberate. Each one threatened to be the last. The onlookers could scarcely breathe in the tension. But Sam was sitting in the easy chair in Delphine's little silk-hung drawing-room. He was leaning back in the chair. And Delphine, telephone in hand, sank into his lap, and pressed herself against him. He could feel the heavenly weight of her form, smell the scent of her hair. Enchanted moments… She had vanished. He was all alone again in the awful void. He murmured appealingly in the final confusion of his mind: "Adela!"

His jaw fell.

Arnold Bennett

Clayhanger

In this, the first volume of an ambitious series intending to trace the parallel lives of a man and woman from youth to marriage and from marriage to old age, Bennett introduces the character of Edwin Clayhanger. A sober portrait of a boy growing up under a tyrannical father contrasts with young Edwin's glimpses of the mysterious and tantalizing Hilda Lessways. As the lives of these two characters unfold before us, Bennett uses autobiographical detail to beautifully depict the constraints and spiritual adventures of young life in the Potteries.

Hilda Lessways

In the second volume of the Clayhanger series, events in *Clayhanger* are retold from the perspective of Hilda Lessways, who is embarking on a relationship with Cannon, a charismatic entrepreneur, whose success has taken him from the Five Towns to Brighton. As Hilda's fascination with the young Clayhanger grows, one of Bennett's most living heroines must face up to her conflicting emotions, and the reality of her hopes and tragedies.

These Twain

In *Clayhanger* and *Hilda Lessways*, Bennett followed the development of a relationship from two very different perspectives. He now draws these perspectives together in a gripping novel which sees the two young protagonists embarking upon married life. One might expect a fairy tale romance, but both Edwin and Hilda are extremely strong-willed, and this clash of personalities makes for a marriage that often hovers on the brink of failure.

This volume of the Clayhanger series contains some of Bennett's very finest work, depicting superb scenes from provincial life and painting a powerful picture of the conflict of wills in an inharmonious marriage.

ARNOLD BENNETT

THE ROLL CALL

The final volume of the Clayhanger series sees Hilda's son, George Cannon (who quickly changes his name from Clayhanger), as an architect, in many ways representing the ambitions held by his stepfather Edwin Clayhanger. However, he possesses an arrogance endowed by family wealth and Bennett examines the difficulty of bringing up children without spoiling them with some aplomb. It is a riveting tale which sees George eventually in the army and a fitting finale to one of the finest series in English literature.

A MAN FROM THE NORTH

Fleeing a drab and dead-end existence, Richard Larch moves south from Bursley to London, intent on pursuing a career as a writer. He is also looking for companionship and love, but finds his high hopes dashed when life in the capital is fraught with difficulties, and the glittering career proves to be more elusive than anticipated.

Melancholic and starkly realistic, *A Man from the North* is Arnold Bennett's first novel.

THE OLD WIVES' TALE

Arnold Bennett's masterpiece, *The Old Wives' Tale*, chronicles the lives of sisters Constance and Sophia Baines, daughters of a Bursley draper. Constance, a conventional and sombre young woman, marries the shop's chief assistant, while the spirited and adventurous Sophia elopes to Paris with Gerald Scales, an irresistible but unprincipled cad. This is the utterly compelling story of their lives and loves, their triumphs and despair from early teens to old age, told with Arnold Bennett's characteristic insight and truthfulness.

How to Live on 24 Hours a Day

'You have to live on...twenty-four hours of daily time. Out of it you have to spin health, pleasure, money, content, respect, and the evolution of your immortal soul'.

This timeless classic is one of the first 'self-help' books ever written and was a best-seller in both England and America. It remains as useful today as when it was written, and offers fresh and practical advice on how to make the most of 'the daily miracle' of life.

'Mr Bennett writes with his usual crispness, point and humour' – *Times of London*